Drift

Amanda Bentley

Copyright © 2022 by Amanda Bentley

All rights reserved.

No portion of this book may be reproduced in any form without written permission from the publisher or author, except as permitted by U.S. copyright law.

This book is a work of fiction. Names, characters, businesses, events, and incidents are either products of the author's imagination or used in a fictitious manner. Any resemblance to actual events or persons is purely coincidental.

Cover Designer: Emily Wittig Designs

Drift

ISBN (Ebook): 979-8-9868923-1-3

ISBN (Paperback): 979-8-9868923-2-0

Amanda Bentley Books LLC

amandabentleybooks@gmail.com

Contents

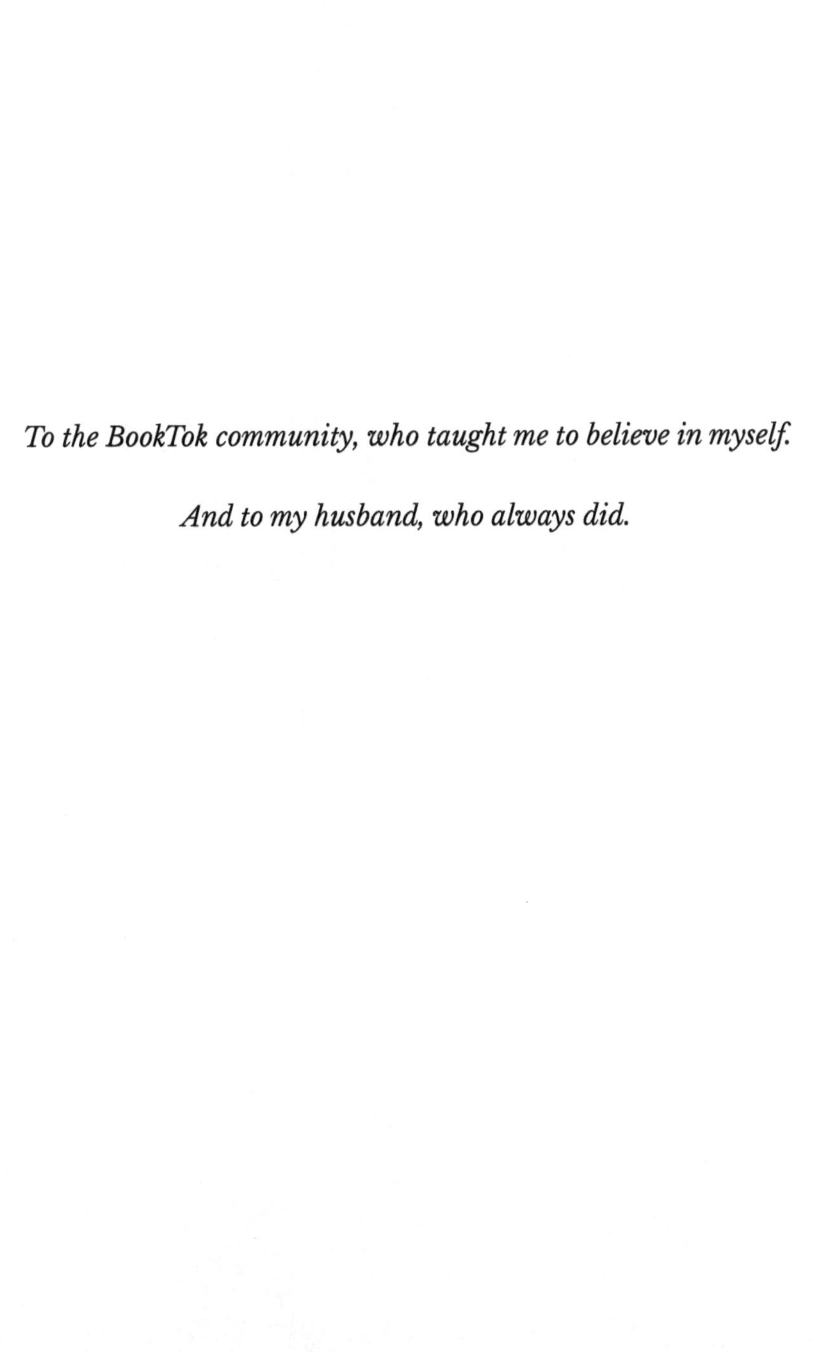

To the BookTok community, who taught me to believe in myself.

And to my husband, who always did.

Playlist

Listen on Spotify!

1. "Have You Ever Seen The Rain" by Creedence Clearwater Revival
2. "I Still Haven't Found What I'm Looking For" by U2
3. "Start of Something New" by Troy, Gabriella Montez, Disney
4. "Everything Has Changed" by Taylor Swift, Ed Sheeran
5. "Coastline" by Nuncc
6. "No Shade" by Brooke Eden
7. "Don't Stop Believin'" by Journey

8. "Buttons" by The Pussycat Dolls
9. "Take on the World" by You Me At Six
10. "A Thousand Years" by Christina Perri
11. "Perfect" by Ed Sheeran
12. "Hurricane" by Bridgit Mendler
13. "Gravity" by John Mayer
14. "Dandelions – slowed + reverb" by Ruth B., slater
15. "Wonder" by Shawn Mendes
16. "Fallin' For You" Colbie Caillat
17. "Ever Fallen in Love (With Someone You Shouldn't've)" by Buzzcocks
18. "Indestructible" by Disturbed
19. "Sometimes Love Just Ain't Enough" by Patty Smyth, Don Henley
20. "Say Something" by A Great Big World, Christina Aguilera
21. "Back To December" by Taylor Swift
22. "Moral of the Story" by Ashe
23. "Numb Little Bug" by Em Beihold
24. "Barbie Girl" by Aqua
25. "Falling" by Harry Styles
26. "Die For You" by The Weeknd

27. "I Can Tell" by 504 Boyz
28. "Realize" by Colbie Caillat
29. "She Will Be Loved" by Maroon 5
30. "Until I Found You" by Stephen Sanchez
31. "Love Of My Life" by Harry Styles
32. "Us (Acoustic)" by Hannah Ellis

Content Warnings

- The Holiday Hookup is the first novella in the Festive Fun Series, which follows Kate and Lorenzo's story on holidays throughout the year.
- This is a romantic suspense series with darker themes than your average contemporary romance.
- If you are looking for a light and fluffy holiday read, this isn't it.
- The series features mature themes and content that may not be suitable for all audiences.
- For content warnings, please check the author's profile links @amandabentleybooks

Chapter One

Marlie

"Oh, it rained!" she said, walking through the front door.

I was never one to like stating the obvious. And my mother looooves stating the obvious. I think it's her way of coping with the world—talk about superficialities so the real stuff doesn't come up.

"Yeah," I reply, sounding sulky. Okay, not just sounding sulky; feeling sulky.

She looks over at me and sees me brooding but doesn't comment. Of course she doesn't. I grasp the door knob, ready to shut the front door.

She turns to her silver Mercedes coupe and shouts, "See ya!" with a wave while pressing unlock on the key fob. The *beep beep* cues the tension in my body to release. I fight my eye roll as she holds a button down on the fob and the engine roars to life.

I watch as the rain splatters on her perfectly manicured toes, the crimson color blurring while she picks up her pace to the driver's side. When she gets in the car, I wave goodbye as I close the door.

I lean my back against the shut door and close my eyes, inhaling the biggest breath I've taken since she arrived two hours earlier. Before I can exhale, I hear the door knob rattle behind me. My eyes pop open in alert, and I move as the door opens, letting the damp air touch my skin.

“Hey, babe,” Zander says as he shakes his head, water droplets splattering on my arms and face. I wrinkle my nose in response, and his eyes meet mine. “Sorry, babe,” he says, catching my expression.

“It’s fine,” I say. I move aside to let him walk in. He kicks his shoes off while standing on the door mat. “How was your day?” I add, deciding not to bring up Mother or the time we spent together.

“Fine enough. My mom says hello,” he responds, and plants a kiss on my cheek before walking off to the kitchen. “We didn’t eat. I’m starving!”

“I have leftovers on the counter if you want to throw them in the microwave,” I offer, thinking of the Styrofoam container with half of my veggie burger in it. I left it out while Mother overstayed her welcome, which wasn’t welcome to begin with. I shudder at the recollection. “My mom just left.
”

“Thanks, babe,” Zander says. I can hear the few condiment bottles rattle as he yanks the refrigerator door open, followed by the sound of the Styrofoam being squeezed under his tight grip. “I love the food from Laroom’s.”

Laroom’s. Mother's favorite restaurant. The only place we eat when we plan a lunch date.

It’s not like anything that happened today was out of the ordinary, or in any way surprising. The predictability doesn’t amend the way I feel. Any time spent with my mother is a crappy experience.

Zander appears in the entryway of the kitchen with a soda water in one hand and the burger in the other. “How did it go?” he asks as he chews, the question muffled.

I shrug, moving to the living room. He follows suit and sits on the other end of the loveseat. I lean back against the firm couch pillow, and I watch him take another bite. He doesn’t seem to have a care in the world.

"Shitty, like always," I mumble. I recall Mother staring at my unkempt hair and I shudder. I can always tell when she's judging me. I suppose I judge her as well, with her pin straight, freshly ironed hair, and a pile of makeup on her face. Her *feigned* face, void of any real emotion.

"Babe?" I hear Zander say. It sounds distant, pulling me from my thoughts. "Are you listening?"

"Sorry, what did you say?" I ask.

"I said, at least you put effort into seeing her. She's your mother, after all," Zander says encouragingly.

"Yeah..." I reply, my voice flat. I lean my head back on the cushion and let out a sigh. "Whatever, I want to forget about it. How are your parents doing?"

Zander goes into a report about his mom's health problems and his dad's new promotion. My thoughts drift back to my crappy afternoon, and I feel angry. If Zander didn't go to his parents house every Saturday afternoon, I wouldn't feel obligated to see my mother. Zander is highly supportive of my keeping up a relationship with her. As he finishes talking about his dad's new promotion, I sigh and stand up.

"I'm going to shower and get ready for bed. We work in the morning," I state, stretching my arms above my head before I walk towards the stairs.

"Thanks for the burger, babe. I feel much better!" Zander exclaims, rubbing his stomach. He stretches his legs in front of him, completely unbothered by my abrupt departure. "I'll see you in the morning, I'm going to play Call of Duty with the guys tonight."

I don't even respond as I walk up the stairs into the narrow hallway above. Straight ahead is the room I share with my boyfriend. I turn to the door on the left, where a hot shower awaits me at the turn of a knob. I close the door behind me and look in the mirror.

Chocolate brown eyes stare back at me, taking in my exhausted expression. You would think, by the looks of me, that I had partaken in a marathon at the break of dawn. Emotional turmoil will do that to you, I guess. I remove my yellow polk-a-dot sundress and underwear, and I turn the shower knob to my perfect spot—three quarters of the way hot. After testing the temperature, I enter the shower and close my eyes as the water washes over my hair and face, beads quickly trickling down my back.

Water has always soothed me in a way that nothing else can. I let the building steam clear my thoughts, and I feel my shoulders relax. It's not fair, the effect she has on me. Two minutes is all it takes for her to look at me and make a nasty comment. Mother's voice in the back of my mind causes me to shudder, despite the hot water raining down on me.

"You really should wear some makeup, honey, your eyes are so plain."

"Are you leaving in that outfit?"

"You should find a better job, one that pays more."

The words cause my fists to clench in anger. I open my eyes and grab the shampoo bottle, flipping the lid with more hostility than the bottle deserves. As I lather the sweet jasmine scented substance into my hair, I force myself to stop thinking of my mother and her bullshit. That's why I left her house in the first place—so I wouldn't have to suffer from her dialogue all the time.

"Shoot him, you idiot! Shoot!" I hear Zander shouting below me. I roll my eyes as I put conditioner in my hair and step out of the water to let it sit for a minute. I've never liked video games; I can't understand the appeal. But Zander loves them, and he made that clear on our first date.

"I don't do much. I work, play video games, and watch TV. Always have, always will."

He's always so sure of himself.

Rather than getting annoyed at the sounds coming from below, I direct my thoughts to tomorrow. I return to work after our holiday break, and I cannot wait to see my coworkers. I never dreamed of working in the corporate world, but the opportunity to be a processor in the mailing center arrived in the form of an internet search, and I took it. It didn't pay anywhere near as much as my mother thought it should, but it sufficed.

Zander works in the IT building on the other side of the picturesque campus. We met at the in-house cafeteria where breakfast and lunch are served. I was walking towards the cashier to pay and tripped over my own feet, dropping my food. He rushed over from the chip stand and helped me clean up. When we stood up, he handed me my book and our eyes met.

It was a very typical encounter. He said hi to me every day for a week after, and then asked me out. I said yes. Simple.

After rinsing out the conditioner, I step out of the shower and wrap myself in a towel, thinking about the upcoming meeting after work ends tomorrow. Zander and I normally ride together, but this meeting is going to run longer than the normal 8-5 business day. I feel myself getting a little excited; I can zone out and listen to the music I love on the way to work!

I put on my pajamas and lay down, shooting off a text to Zander to remind him that we're riding separately in the morning. I close my eyes and "I Still Haven't Found What I'm Looking For" by U2 plays in my mind as I drift to sleep.

I couldn't get the song out of my head, so I hum along quietly to "I Still Haven't Found What I'm Looking For" as I make a left turn, the giant green letters of SYMBIOSIS planted on the entryway of the parking lot coming into view. The company is the main source for electricity in our town of Winter Haven, Florida, and I'm one of the 2,000 worker bees who keeps it running.

I park Blueberry—my shiny, blue Toyota Yaris—in a vacant spot towards the back of the massive lot. I exit my car and holster my laptop backpack onto my left shoulder as I watch Zander pull up next to me in his old, gray pickup truck.

He gets out and pops a kiss on my lips. "Missed you on the drive to work," he says as we make the trek up to the building entrance, joining the pack of sheep in the electrical herd.

I scan my badge and respond robotically, "Ditto." He smiles at me, and I smile back, waving as I turn right and he walks straight to the elevators.

When I reach the mailing center, I place my bag on the floor next to my chair and plug my laptop into the docking station. I look around the open warehouse as I wait for the computer to load. There are two bins full of thin envelopes, surely payments mailed in by our older clients who refuse to get with the times. Most people forward their documents via email to a general inbox. It's our job to review any incoming documents and note the appropriate file or get it to the right person for handling.

"Yo, yo, yo!" I hear from behind me. I swivel around in my chair to see my favorite coworker, Eli.

"Eli!!!" I exclaim, rising from my seat to let him envelop me in a bear hug. "How are you?"

"Anotha day, anotha dolla," he responds as he releases me. He tosses his bag by his computer chair next to mine and takes a seat. He swiftly types on his keyboard to log into the laptop he just docked.

"You know we were supposed to turn those off over the long weekend, right?" I say exasperatedly.

"Whoops," he responds with a lopsided grin. "Let's go grab some coffee while we wait for your dino to boot up."

That's one of my favorite things about Eli—he's untroubled. He brings out a much lighter side of me with his optimism. Zander has a calmness about him and he comes across as carefree, but it's not like he doesn't worry about things. Eli is legitimately carefree.

"Yes, please," I say, standing up as he starts walking towards the swinging doors. We walk the short distance to the cafeteria and get in line as Eli tells me about the epic party he went to the day after Christmas. As most of his stories go, he drank too much and hooked up with some random woman.

"So, what did Zander get you for Christmas?" He nudges me in the ribs with his elbow as I reach for our colada. I grab little cups so we can share.

"He got us a set of matching necklaces," I respond shyly, reaching for the new chain hanging on my neck. It's thin and white gold, a Z pendant hanging delicately.

"WOW!!! Talk about serious," Eli states, holding the swinging door to the mailing center open for me as I walk through. He extends his hand toward the pendant and holds it lightly on his index finger. "So, he has an M?"

I nod my head and tug the chain so Eli releases the Z, the white gold glistening in the fluorescent lighting as I tuck it safely into my shirt.

"Did he like the wallet you got him?" Eli asks me.

"He said he loved it, but it can't possibly compete with the necklaces," I reply despondently.

"I'm sure he loved it, Marlie," Eli states encouragingly. I give him a meek smile in response.

We turn to our computers and start our day. We work in silence, catching up on the emails received over the long holiday weekend. Five minutes before noon, I receive an instant message from Zander.

Lunch in 5?

I send my replying yes with a pizza emoticon. Zander sends a smiley face.

Lunch passes by too quickly, and the afternoon is filled with a lot of scanned documents and email replies. When Eli gets up from his desk at 5 pm, I curse under my breath. Days like these cause my head to ache.

"Let's go, chica, before we're late for the meeting!" Eli says exasperatedly. An outsider might see our exchange and think Eli needs to be on time. Really, he knows I have a tendency to push myself with work and he reminds me to chill out often.

I rush to shove my phone in my bag and meet Eli at the door. We make the walk to the conference room at the end of the hall, facing the lake. Eli holds the room door open and I enter, taking a seat furthest away.

I stare across the room through the windows facing the lake. I watch the sun shimmer over the water and the trees swaying with the gentle breeze as our coworkers enter and take their seats. Finally, our manager, Matt, enters and takes a seat at the head of the conference table, the lakeview behind him.

"Hi, Team!" Matt exclaims, smiling brightly. His pearly white teeth glisten brighter than the opaque, white lighting of the conference room. "I hope everyone had a great holiday break!"

Everyone mumbles their agreement. One of the temporary employees, I think his name is Stan, unabashedly yawns.

"I realize everyone is tired and wants to go home, so I'll make this quick. HR is on our back for getting everyone involved with the Employee Incentive Program. For those who don't know, or don't remember, this is where you choose an extracurricular class that may help with your social skills, technical skills, what have you," Matt explains. "I realize this could have been sent to you in an email, but I wanted to express the importance of programs such as these. There is no cost to you, and it looks great on your resumé. The classes aren't boring. They're meant to be engaging and fun!"

No one in the room seems convinced, no matter how much Matt smiles and bounces from one leg to the other. "I believe there are three classes to choose from," he continues boldly. "There is a web developer course, an improvisational acting course, and a writing course."

Everyone in the room sits a little straighter. Eli and I take a quick side glance at each other, eyebrows raised.

"See, I told you they're meant to be fun!" Matt encourages, picking up on the energy shift in the room. "HR wants this to be a form of escape, while also building skills to help you with your jobs. That being said, you should try to focus on choosing a class that will help with your current or aspiring position within the company. The courses run for 10 weeks and the costs are covered by the company."

As Matt rambles on about logging into the portal to sign up, Eli whispers to me, "You owe me a drink every time he says 'with that being said'."

I stifle a laugh.

"You have until Friday to select your courses. With that being said"—Eli elbows me in the ribs and I cough to hide my laughter—"go enjoy your evenings!" Matt beams at us as if we've been told we have the week off. Everyone slowly exits the room, and I pick up my bag as Eli pushes in his chair.

"You'll take the acting course with me, right?" Eli says with a grin. I watch him and smile back with a nod. How can I tell him no? Plus, the alternatives suck.

The week passes in a blur. I hit the send button for my reply to the last email on Friday. I hear the familiar *swoosh* as the email leaves my outbox to its recipient, the clock in the lower right hand corner changing to 5:00 pm.

"Dale, chica," Eli says enthusiastically, practically exploding from his chair.

I close my laptop and unplug it from the docking station connected to the office monitors. I feel a little more energized today than I normally would. Not only because it's Friday, but because we have our first improv class today.

"Come on, come on, show some excitement!" Eli begs me, giving my shoulders a little shake. "We're going to love this, I just know it. I think it's exactly what you need!"

"Okay, okay!" I can't help but grin at Eli as I grab my now packed bag and rise from my seat. His energy is infectious, another thing to love.

"That's the spirit!" Eli practically shouts. The new girl in the corner of the room whips her head towards us, her bright eyes wide in shock.

I follow Eli, who may as well be sprinting, out of our office and to the parking lot. We decided to ride together for our first day, so he got a ride to the office this morning. Since it's Friday, we were able to wear our casual jeans and tees that we'll wear to class. The email we received after signing up said to wear neutral and comfortable clothing.

Exactly what you need...

Eli's words echo in my mind, and I feel an inkling of hope that he's right.

Chapter Two

Chain

BEEEEEEEP.

I lay down on my horn impatiently, unwilling to wait for this jackass driver in front of me to get off his phone and get on with his left hand turn. This is exactly why I can't stand a guy who drives a Prius. I realize that might make me a dick, but I don't really give a shit. They somehow always have their heads shoved up their asses.

Prius jackass finally gets a move on, and I follow a bit too closely behind while the light turns yellow. I glance at the clock as I switch lanes and zoom past, leaving him behind.

Two minutes until the class starts. I'm rarely ever late, and I don't want to set that precedent now, but pressing matters at work made it so I couldn't leave early. I had to skip the gym this morning, too, which always screws up my mood.

Although, you have been skipping the gym more often than usual lately.

I bumpily turn right into the parking lot, as indicated by my GPS. My eyes roam for an empty spot.

Damn it. My quick analysis confirms there are no more spots left. I make another right out of the parking lot exit and pull down the residential street. I park in an empty parallel spot in front of a quaint, rose colored home with one window to the left of the door.

I grab a mint from the stash I keep in the car and remove my key when I hear my phone ping. I hop out of my white Chevy Silverado and let the door shut behind me as I remove my phone from my pocket.

Ashley: I guess I'll see you when you get home...

Ashley's text has me rolling my eyes as I move quickly towards the building. I don't have the capacity to deal with her shit right now. I stare at the two-story brick building before opening the door. A black sign with a brilliant, violet font reads SPARKLE COMEDY. I'm instantly met with a narrow staircase that has steep steps. I take them two at a time, glancing at the clock on my phone.

6:32. *Fuck, I'm late.*

I reach the landing and turn left, coming to a halt. A group of people, likely my classmates, are standing right outside of the door in front of me. They send quick glances my way. I walk to the right of the small circle of eight and pull out my phone. *Awkward silence it is then.*

I've never been one to shy away from new encounters. It's part of what makes me a successful lawyer. Allowing others their shy time, I swipe on the message from Ashley and start typing on my iPhone.

Me: Sounds good.

I type and delete 'love you', debating whether to include those words. I know she's pissed. Again. We've talked about this so many times. She wants to spend more time with me. I get her point, we only hang out once a week. Between her busy schedule and my own, timing is already tight.

But honestly, once a week feels like too much. I don't want to hear another long-winded story about her coworkers' drama, or her friend's ex-boyfriend problems. Sure, it gets me a good lay that night, but it's pretty boring otherwise. This improv class will help me towards my comedy writing. At least, that's the hope. I wanted to take stand-up comedy but there weren't any nearby classes available. This was the next best thing and I figured, why not?

I explained this all to her. Leave it to Ashley to hyper focus on her own feelings. I hit the send button, deciding to leave the 'love you' out. She doesn't need anymore ammunition.

I hear the door click open below, then feet landing on the steps. I look up from my phone and turn my head towards the staircase.

I watch a breathless guy and girl halt at the top step, taking in the group standing in front of the door.

"Welp, looks like we ran up here for nothing, chica," the guy says to the girl.

She bumps his arm with her shoulder, letting out a sigh of relief. She's wearing jeans and a black and white striped tee that has a loose fit. Still, I notice the way it hugs her breasts and alludes to her holdable hips. The guy has on a similar outfit—jeans and a loose, white, V-neck tee.

I take in the outfits of the others, five girls and three guys. Everyone seems to be in jeans or leggings and a comfortable shirt.

Glancing down at my own attire, I realize I may have missed the memo. I have my blue and yellow striped tie neatly done and in place. The dress slacks and white, long sleeved dress shirt I sport are expected of me at the firm I work for, Dwight Brothers, P.A. And while it would make sense that the two men who own the firm would be related, they just happen to have the same last name.

I look around and see another hallway down to the right. I quickly make my way through the hall in search of a bathroom. Finding it, I enter and tug at my tie, loosening the knot and removing it from my collar. I stuff it into my right pocket. I glance in the small mirror above the sink.

I ruffle my hair a bit to make it look less.... Corporate. Quite frankly, I didn't think about the attire for tonight. And while I'm used to wearing them, they've never really grown on me.

I wear them because I have to. Just like I took the job because I had to. I went to school for law because I had to.

A good job, a secure job, they meant everything. That was one thing Ashley and I could agree on, at least. The importance of societal role and success.

I take one last look in the mirror and exit the bathroom, satisfied with my make-shift casual appearance. I walk back down the hall to find it empty. I fasten my pace and quietly open the door.

"...level 1, where we will go over the basics of improvisation and learn to get comfortable on stage!" The person standing front and center on the stage booms over the small theater. He's tall and thin, almost frail looking, with salt and pepper hair and a beard. *He must be the teacher.*

There are approximately 50 chairs split in two with a walkway between them, facing a small stage. My classmates take up the first and second rows.

I make my way down the aisle and sit in the empty third row to the right, ducking my head to remain out of sight.

"We're going to start today off by getting on the stage and getting to know each other."

He claps his hands together and grins, seemingly waiting for us to jump for joy.

When no one moves, he claps his hands together twice and shouts, "Up, everyone!"

I remain seated as my classmates begin to rise from their chairs and shuffle towards the stage. I grab the armchairs and haul myself up, the last one on stage.

I stand next to a girl with long, blonde hair. I can feel the anxiety emanating off of her. Her shoulders are caved in and her blue eyes are wide. She's the epitome of a deer in headlights.

"Everyone grab a partner. Quick, quick!" the teacher quips.

I make eye contact with anxious blondie and quickly look away. I am *not* going to be stuck holding someone's hand. I learned at a young age to never wear your emotions for the world to see, and that includes by proxy.

I begin walking up to a guy with a beard but he gets approached by another dude. I make a sharp left and walk straight into a brunette girl. She lets out a startled yelp and falls backward. I hold out my hand to her, but she scrambles up on her own.

"You, tall guy in the fancy clothes!" The teacher shouts at me from behind. "You're the odd man out, get with these two," he points towards a guy with naturally tan skin standing next to a girl who's whispering something in his ear. *The two who ran up the stairs after I arrived.*

I walk over to where they stand on the stage and exchange a head nod with the guy. *At least somebody here doesn't have a problem with nerves.* He nudges the girl, who turns her head to look at me.

Our eyes meet.

Pools of chocolate with swirls of caramel stare at me. My heartbeat fastens and it feels like the floor is falling out from under me.

I'm vaguely aware of a low voice speaking, though it sounds distant.

"Yoooo," the voice comes closer and I realize it's the guy standing next to her. I tear my gaze from her and look back at the guy.

"I'm Eli, this is Marlie," he says. As I come back to my senses, I can hear that everyone around us is now speaking.

Fuck, so much for not being the awkward guy.

"Do you talk, or...?" Eli trails off.

I blink hard and mentally shake off whatever the fuck just happened.

"Long day, bro, sorry," I laugh and reach my hand out. "Chain."

Eli shakes my hand as he smirks. "Chain, huh?"

I look over at Marlie, who quickly averts her eyes. I slip on my mask of indifference.

"Marlie, Eli"—I nod at each of them, but Marlie avoids my gaze—"nice to meet you."

The teacher calls out and the class silences, diverting my attention. "We are going to hit the ground running by getting to know each other in a quite physical manner. Sit on the floor with your partner and close your eyes."

We scramble to the ground quickly and I close my eyes as instructed. My brain goes into overdrive.

What just happened when I stared at that woman? Why did it feel like time stopped? Like I wasn't even aware of the fact that I couldn't pull away?

The teacher's voice pulls me from my thoughts. "I want you to touch each other's faces with as little judgment and thought as you can manage," he says.

I peek my eyes open just enough to look around at what everyone else thinks of this. Is he serious? I'm just supposed to reach out and grope these strangers?? I could see my thoughts mirrored on the faces of others.

I close my eyes and chocolate eyes flash at my eyelids. Somehow, they don't strike me as a strangers.

"It's meant to feel weird and awkward—embrace it!" the teacher exclaimed. "You will soon realize that improvisational acting requires a vulnerability most are unwilling to allow."

Vulnerability?! This was not what I anticipated this class would entail. I thought we'd crack a few laughs, learn how to be angry or happy, and call it a night. I spend most of my waking moments escaping the feelings I don't want to deal with.

I feel a rough hand on my cheek and freeze. The fingers squeeze a bit, and I let out a breath. Okay, I'm here. I need to try. I reach my hand out and start swatting the air, reaching for a face.

Instead, my hand makes contact with hair, sending an instant tingle through my fingertips. I pat down, confirming the hair goes past the shoulder. *Marlie.* I move my hand forward and graze her jaw, and my heart starts racing. My fingers find her lips and I feel them part on a sharp intake of breath. Maybe I'm freaking her out. My hand moves up to her nose, and I feel myself wanting to explore her. This should feel awkward, but somehow, it feels right. I use my index finger to trace the shape of her eyebrow, warming me.

What is going on, Chain?! Get it together.

I let my hand drop and it feels as though my fingers were suddenly dunked in ice. I reach out with my other hand, finding rougher skin. This must be Eli; no weird heart racing here. I pat his cheek when the teacher shouts, "Open your eyes!"

My eyes flutter open and I look at Eli, a smirk on his lips. "Nice face, dude," he says jokingly.

"How did that feel?" Jon pauses, looking around at us on the stage. "That's what I want you to focus on for today's class. The way things make you feel. Allow yourself to be vulnerable. With yourselves and with your classmates."

It's at this moment I realize I don't know his name. "What's your name?" I ask him aloud.

"Jonathan Romero Delacruz," he says, turning to me. "But please, call me Jon. And you would have known that answer had you arrived on time, Mr. Matthews."

What a fucking hypocrite. He wasn't even here on time!

A few classmates laugh. Marlie isn't one of them.

Chapter Three

Marlie

"Hey babe, how'd it—" Zander's voice is cut off by my lips crashing on his. I kick off my shoes as he returns my rushed kisses, inserting his tongue into my desperate mouth. I straddle him over his chair and he tosses his controller to the side, letting it clatter onto the floor.

I love Zander. I know I do. He's safe, and light-hearted, and everything I've ever wanted. I need his kisses to remind me that I'm happy; that I'm okay.

I don't need to keep thinking about Chain, like I did the whole way home. I don't need to think about his dark hair and how it would feel to run my fingers through it. I don't need to think about his bright green eyes on mine and how they mesmerized me.

Zander pulls away long enough to give me a look over. I bite my lower lip and run my hands down his bare chest, something I know he can't resist. His pecs tighten at my touch and he groans. His lips land on mine as I run my hands down his stomach. My heart rate accelerates, the heat rising in my cheeks.

Zander runs kisses down my neck, biting at the soft spot between my shoulder and neck, something he knows I can't resist.

We are well rehearsed; practiced. He knows me as well as I know him.

But those green eyes. It felt like they pierced into my very soul, lighting me up from the inside. How was that possible? I don't know Chain from Adam. What kind of name is that anyway, Chain?

I moan as Zander bites me again, eliciting the response he was looking for. Satisfied, he peppers my neck with kisses as I unbutton my jeans. Zander tugs down on his cargo shorts, his boxers giving way to the large bulge in the center.

I start rubbing distractedly and Zander pulls back from my neck, his eyes fluttering closed and his head tipping back.

"Yeah, babe, just like that," he moans. I continue my strokes, begging my own core to respond.

I move my hand to his waist and pull him close. He moves his hands around to my ass and scoops me up while holding me to him.

We continue our hurried kisses as he carries me to the stairs, our tongues clashing forcefully. I drop down to hurry into our room, where he turns me and tosses me on the bed before landing directly over me. We tear our clothes off and roam each other's bodies, my hand finding his dick.

His girth has always been the best part. I angle my mouth and start sucking the head of his length. He places his hand on my head to gently guide me. Zander knows I don't like a hand forcing my movements, controlling the way I give pleasure.

After a few sucks and licks to the base and back, I withdraw my mouth and look up at him. He doesn't tower over me, seeing as 5'9" isn't too far from 5'5". His length isn't enormous but I've found that it proves the whole big dick thing wrong, and he knows exactly how to get me off.

He moves his hand to my pussy, lightly padding my clit with his index finger as he makes his way down to my entrance. He pushes the first finger in, then the second.

I'm sure he can feel I'm only slightly wet. He proceeds with his fingering anyway. Nothing to get the engine started like forcing the key in the ignition.

Zander gives me a light push on the shoulder, urging me to lie back. I concede and close my eyes to focus on the feeling of his fingers. He moves his head between my legs and runs his tongue over my clit.

My body loses tension, and I start to feel the high of the oncoming orgasm. He knows exactly what I like, and takes pleasure in getting me there.

His fingers reach in deep and hook up towards my G-spot, and I give him an applauding moan. He picks up the pace with his tongue, increasing the pressure.

I take flight, allowing him to remove me from my thoughts. I moan and he starts to thrust his lower body into the bed. He's into this, and that adds to my pleasure.

"I'm going to come if you don't stop," I warn with a whisper, the flick of his tongue keeping me satisfied.

He moves his free hand above my clit and presses down on my abdomen. "Come for me Marlie, I want to feel you shake," he pleads.

His hips are moving more and I allow myself to come undone. I groan his name as he holds his fingers deep inside of me, my walls pulsing over them. My legs shake from the sensitivity.

I feel the wetness gush out of me. I sigh, sated with the high of my orgasm.

He removes his head first, then his fingers. He lifts up and his cock is rock hard, the vein throbbing with need.

He moves forward and leans over me, entering me slowly. Once fully immersed, he begins to thrust quickly, his orgasm close.

I feel him getting there right before he pulls out and throws his hand over his dick in one swift move. He jacks and the cum shoots over my belly. He goes limp, releasing his dick and holding himself up on the bed over me.

"That was so good, babe," he tells me with a quick kiss on my lips. He hops off the bed and puts his hand under his dick to catch any cum that might spill. He tosses me a shirt from his hamper before he stalks over to the bathroom and I close my eyes.

I'm buzzing from my orgasm, but my thoughts slowly trickle back in.

Chain.

His voice floats through my mind, and I pop my eyes back open just as Zander returns. I wipe my own wetness off first, then his cum. I hand him the shirt and he tosses it into his hamper.

"Did you enjoy that?" Zander asks me, looking over inquisitively. I brave my usual grin onto my face.

"Oh, yeah." I sit up and give him a kiss. "Let's go to sleep."

I get up to get my underwear back on and he grabs his cargo shorts and boxers.

"I'm actually going to finish my last round with the guys, then I'll be up," he informs me as he redresses.

"Okay." I rarely even feel the disappointment of him playing anymore. But today, it really stings.

Sensing my dejection, he hands me the remote and tells me to pick whatever I want and that he'll join me soon.

I watch him leave and turn on the TV. Waiting for Netflix to load, I crawl onto the left side of the bed. My side. I get comfortable and settle, letting my eyelids close for a moment.

Green eyes appear, and I drift to sleep.

Chapter Four

Chain

"You were supposed to commit more time to me!" Ashley's wailing forces its way into my slumber. Groggy, I open my eyes to find her standing next to me at the edge of the bed, a pillow in her grips.

I found her sound asleep when I arrived from class, and I wasn't disappointed in the slightest. Although now I'm slightly regretting not waking her up.

"Did you seriously wake me up with a *fucking* pillow?!" I shout, snatching it from her and tossing it on the bed. I turn over and glance at the alarm clock on the bedside table. "5 am?! It's 5 am, Ashley!"

I close my eyes and she slaps my arm, effectively ripping away any hope I have of sleep. I look up at her and see tears well in her eyes. *Fuck.*

"I'm sorry, love, I didn't mean it," I concede, the pet name she forces me to use burning like acid on my tongue.

"I feel further from you than I ever have, Chain, and I just want something. Not a lot, but something." She wipes at the lone tear rolling down her cheek and I cringe.

Fuck, this is serious.

It takes a lot for Ashley to cry. And it's true, she doesn't ask for much. If you asked me a week ago, I'd have told you she's just as content with the dynamics of our relationship as I am.

That tear tells me how very wrong I was.

"I know we need to hang out more," I tell her as I struggle to get myself out of bed.

"I don't even need more time, I just need more of you in our time," she says. "Lately, our one night a week has felt more lonely than our nights apart."

"Let's carve out more time." I try to do what I do best, problem solve.

"What time, Chain?! What time? I'm busy, you're busy. And then you sign up for an *improv* class a day before it starts, on our only scheduled day together?" she half shouts.

Okay, so I may have only told her about the class the day before it started. Afraid of her reaction, I delayed telling her. By a month.

"Jack told me about it and I decided to go for it." Another lie. I found it while looking for stand-up comedy classes. It was a childhood dream and lately, it's felt like something was missing. I needed something new and exciting.

"You could have talked to me about it." Her eyes bore into mine. She's not backing down from this.

I look down, a weak move. I know it is. But what else am I supposed to do? I fucked up, and she knows it. I know it.

Ashley is not my soul mate, and I'm fine with that. I'm not looking for true love; I'm hard pressed to believe it even exists. Brown eyes spark in my mind and I snap my attention back to Ashley.

I need to remember who the fuck I am—Chain Matthews.

"Ashley, you're right. I should have. But I didn't. So let's just move towards a solution." I keep my eyes trained on her bright blue ones.

"How long is this class?"

"Two and a half hours and then I'm all yours." I give her my best smile.

"I meant how long does it run, don't play coy with me." Nope, not backing down.

"It's 10 weeks. One down, 9 to go."

She huffs. She's accepting this, good.

"I don't want us to drift further apart," she confesses.

"I know, love, me neither, so let's resolve this. I want to see you more, I swear." Another lie; it comes out effortlessly. "Let's go get breakfast. 5 am is the perfect time for breakfast," I joke, trying to lighten her mood.

It doesn't work. "I've got a coffee date with Lauren." Oh, god no. Lauren's the one with the ex-boyfriend and I already know what I'll be hearing about later.

Ashley is an accountant for her father's firm, so naturally she makes excellent money. Her work keeps her behind the scenes. While some lawyers can stay behind the scenes, I'm not one of them. I live and thrive in the courtroom.

"Fine, how about later today? I've got a meeting I can push 'til tomorrow," I try.

"I'll be home around 10. I'll see how I feel."

"Come on, love, forgive me, puh-lease," I purr. I grab her wrist and tug. "We can cuddle, put on your favorite show, maybe have some sex."

She pulls out of my grip. "I'll let you know. I'm going to get ready for my exercise class and go straight from there to the coffee shop."

"I love you," I say. One of the best weapons in my arsenal.

She walks out of the room. At the threshold, she turns back and says begrudgingly, "Love you."

She's going to say yes, I know she is.

I typically spend my Saturdays going to a movie with my mom and then working. Ashley and I have always enjoyed our alone time and it's one of the things that allows for the type of relationship we have.

My offering to spend my Saturday with her is a rarity, and she knows it. That's why I offered it to her.

We probably won't have sex. While my dick is not delighted about that, it doesn't bother me the way it used to. I should want her more but I've grown accustomed to being turned down often by her. We have sex because I push for it, and she gives in because it gives her something to discuss with her friends.

I lay back down, ready for sleep to take me. I should take my own ass to the gym but I can't find the motivation. The moment my eyelids shut, brown eyes peer at me.

Chapter Five

Marlie

Zander and I decided to use part of our Saturday to go to the mall and spend a gift card we got from my mom for Christmas. I don't love the mall, and luckily, neither does Zander. But we have nothing better to do because our best friends, who we usually spend every Saturday with, are busy today. I pull out my phone to text Stella.

Me: I hate you for this.

Stella: I hate Jason for this. He makes plans and doesn't tell me until the last minute. I wanted to hear all about your improv class! Maybe we can meet up tonight.

Stella: The guys can play games and we can hang.

Me: Fine. Just know that I'm going to the mall because of you.

"Thanks for driving, babe. I'll get gas tomorrow," Zander says as I drop my phone into the cupholder and throw the car into reverse. I give him a small smile in response.

We drive to the mall in silence except for his music playing in the background. I pull into a spot towards the back, the lot already full of cars. I look at the dash and realize it's already 11:30 am.

"I didn't realize how late we woke up," I say to Zander as we head into the mall.

"Late? I could have used a few more hours," Zander scoffs. I don't reply. He stays up late gaming and would gladly sleep the day away. I don't sleep in as late as he does, but since I have nothing better to do, I sleep more than I probably would.

He sips his coffee and we navigate directly to the clothing store we have the gift card for. It's to some small boutique I've never heard of, no doubt filled with clothing I wouldn't ever shop for myself.

We peruse the boutique and Zander finds some nice work shirts. I gladly let him use the money; there's nothing for me here. We exit the shop a half-hour later and head back to the car when I hear a familiar voice coming from ahead.

"...we're here right now, why can't that be enough?" I locate the source of the gravelly voice, landing on—

Chain.

His voice rings in my ear and I drop the bags I'm holding. I do not want to run into him right now. At a mall. With Zander.

"What the fuck, babe?" Zander says, grabbing the bags.

"I actually need a new pair of shoes, come on." I link our hands, intent on pulling us in a new direction, but it's too late. Chain looks over, and his eyes meet mine as if drawn by magnets.

Thump-Thump. Thump-Thump.

My heartbeat is in my ears and my hands start to perspire.

"Hey, Marlie," Chain calls out and I come to a halt. Zander looks over as Chain walks towards us with a woman following close behind. She's a pretty, blue-eyed blonde with perfectly set curls on either side of her face. A stark comparison to my mostly straight, auburn hair that I only brushed halfheartedly.

She catches up to him and links his arm with hers, giving us a very, very small smile, which is notably unfriendly.

"I, um, h-h-hi," I force out. Oh my god, I'm making a fool of myself. I pray to whatever god is out there that Zander doesn't notice. "This is Zander!" I practically scream. I make more of a fool out of myself by using the hand that is clasped with his rather than my free one.

"What's up, man? I'm Zander," he says, oblivious to my panic.

"Chain. This is Ashley," he says, but his eyes haven't left mine. *Why haven't they left mine?*

I collect myself and turn to Ashley. "Hi, I'm Marlie. I just met Chain at yesterday's class."

"Yes, he just said your name. Nice to meet you." Her expression opposes her words. Her eyes sweep over me and they narrow ever-so-slightly.

"Well, we were just leaving," I say, dying to end this exchange immediately. My heart won't stop pitter-pattering.

"I thought you said you needed shoes?" Zander says.

"I've changed my mind," I say quickly.

Zander shrugs and gives Chain a look like, *women.* Chain gives Zander an unamused look before speaking.

"It was good to see you, Marlie."

"Yeah, you too," I reply. "Next week, right?" I chuckle awkwardly and for some reason I feel like he sees right through me, aware of my anxiety.

"Yep, 9 more weeks," he replies smoothly. Ashley grips his arm tighter and wheels him away.

"Nice to meet you!" Zander says.

"Yeah," Chain says as they walk away. Ashley says nothing.

"Seems like a cool guy. I don't know why but I imagined improv people to be a little more..." Zander begins as I pull out of the parking lot.

"What, nerdy? Coming from you that's a stretch," I say haughtily, immediately on the defense.

"Woah, I was going to say shy, but I see how you feel about me," he retorts.

Shit. I reel it back in. "Sorry, I didn't finish my coffee. You're not nerdy, I just meant that gaming is certainly seen as a nerdy hobby," I tell him.

"No worries, babe, I wasn't insulted," he takes a sip of my coffee and hands me the cup. "Here, finish it. I just mean that I'd expect more insecurity or shyness? But that guy was definitely sure of himself."

"Yeah," I say with an awkward chuckle to portray a sense of dismissal.

Sure of himself, he was. He had a beautiful woman on his arm and didn't seem the least bit flustered to run into me.

I can't figure out why *I* was so flustered, though, which sends my brain into overdrive. Feeling flustered means I feel something for Chain. But I don't know Chain. How can I feel something for someone I don't know?

My phone pings and I glance at the screen.

Stella iMessage

I pick it up and swipe to read her message.

Stella: Plans got canceled! Still wanna hang?

Me: YES.

Stella: Uh-oh, period instead of exclamation point? What's wrong?

Stella has been my best friend for seven years. It doesn't seem like much in quantity, but we clicked instantly and have a natural way of knowing each other. It's no surprise to me that she can pick up on my emotions from a simple change in punctuation.

"Stella and Jace are coming over!" Stella is the only person who actually calls Jace by his full name, Jason. "Their plans got canceled, I guess."

"Sweet, are we gaming?" Zander asks as I pull into a free spot on the street of our condo complex.

"I guess we'll see when they get here," I say. But we won't see. We'll all chat for an hour or two and they'll load up the Xbox while Stella and I figure out what we want to do. As we walk back into the house, I conclude I don't feel anything for Chain. He just has that effect on people. Like Zander said, he's sure of himself.

Me: All good, I was driving. Just got home, come over!!!

Nothing is wrong. Everything is perfectly fine.

Chapter Six

Marlie

Zander blows me a kiss as we part ways to our respective buildings. I catch it and pocket it with a smile. I settle into my desk and get my laptop up and running. It's 8:01 am when I send a text to Eli.

Me: Where are you?

He reads the message but doesn't respond. I hear the mail room door open and glance back to find Eli walking in lazily while pocketing his phone. The door shuts behind him slowly.

"Hey, chica. I woke up late," he says, tossing his bag by his chair.

"Hungover?"

"Yep," he says with a groan. He pulls out his laptop and lays his head on the desk while it powers on.

"I can get the colada for us," I say, getting up. He perks up at the mention of coffee.

"I'll come. The sooner it's in my veins, the better," he insists.

I wait for him to log in and then we walk.

"So class was pretty great, huh?" he says groggily, rubbing his eye with a closed fist.

"I don't know, Eli," I say hesitantly.

"That's the most alive I've ever seen you! You told a hilarious story and everyone was laughing. You can't tell me you didn't enjoy it."

"I just... I don't see how this is supposed to help me in the long run. What does this have to do with work?"

Jon had given each of us 3 minutes on stage to do absolutely anything we wanted. A brunette woman, I think her name was Liv, sang a beautiful rendition of "Part of Your World" from *The Little Mermaid*. One guy, Damon, laid down and closed his eyes for a pseudo-nap.

I chose to tell a funny story I'd heard at work that day from a co-worker.

"What's wrong with enjoying something for the pure fun of it?" Eli asks as we enter the dining hall. He stops walking and turns to me. "Is this about Chain?"

I stop dead in my tracks and stare at him. "What do you mean?"

"You heard me, chica," he replies with a knowing smirk that I want to slap right off his face.

I glance around to check who's nearby; I don't need Zander or any of his coworkers hearing this.

"What about him? He's a classmate," I deny with a small stomp for emphasis.

"Sure. He's a classmate. All our classmates couldn't stop staring at you."

Eli's sarcastic response has me averting my eyes. I had noticed Chain shooting furtive looks at me throughout the class, but I played them off. He was just interested in checking out his new peers. As was I.

"I just don't want this to become another thing I have to do. I've got enough on my plate." It was partly true. I have to work at a place I don't care about. I have to deal with a mother I don't like. I mean, I have free time, but I prefer spending it escaping the things I don't want to do.

"Then find a way to have fun with it! Come on, you've got spunk. I know it, you know it."

"I guess."

"Chain knows it."

"Eli!" I stalk off towards the cafeteria.

He catches up within seconds. "I saw your eyes light up, Marlie, don't deny it. It's only natural, the guy's attractive. I'm sure a lot of women react that way."

See? Chain is just that guy. He has that effect on everyone, it's not just me.

"Well, he has a girlfriend," I counter.

"Oh, looking him up, I see?" he smirks again and I shove his shoulder.

"No! I saw him at the mall on Saturday, asswipe!" I can't help the laughter that escapes me. "Stop being so dumb."

"There's that spunk!" Eli says with a grin. He stops to order the colada and grabs a few cups.

"He really had a girl with him? Wow," Eli muses while we wait. "Well, I'm just saying, the guy obviously has swag and you seemed to know it."

"Sure, he's attractive. But I have a boyfriend. I'm happy. I don't have a thing for Chain." The barista hands us our colada over the counter and I grab it.

"Okay," Eli says. We make the walk back to our desks in silence. My mind is reeling. Where does Eli get off?

"Hey, I didn't mean to piss you off," Eli says as he pours the colada into the little cups. He hands me one and shoots one back. "I want you to be happy, that's all."

"I am."

"Okay." He grabs the other cups and passes them out to our coworkers.

I log back into my computer and go through my emails.

I love Zander. We're saving money for a house, we get along, we have great sex. That's love, right? What more can I want?

The week passes quickly. I head out of the office at 5 pm Friday, Eli walking at my side as we head to the main entrance. Zander waits for us outside of the sliding doors.

"Sup, Zander?" Eli says to him and they fist bump.

"Hey, Eli," Zander says as he walks in stride next to me. "Hey, babe."

"Hey, you," I reply affectionately, forcing the love I have for this man to ooze out of me.

"Catch you later, Marlie. Have a nice weekend Zander," Eli calls out as he breaks off towards his car.

"Bye!" Zander replies, and he unlocks his truck as I circle around to the passenger side.

"I'm so glad it's the weekend," I let out as Zander reverses.

"I just remembered you've got that improv class now," he says. I stow my bag below my feet and settle in.

"Yeah, should be fun," I reply. "I wish you would have taken it with me."

When I signed up for work, I tried to convince Zander to join me. His position with the company is niche and secure, so they don't push these extracurriculars on him.

"I know, but you know that's not my thing," he tells me. "I've got my thing."

"I know, you game. But would it kill you to try something new?"

"Probably."

He chuckles and I don't respond.

"I'm ready for you to get home already, I can tell you that," he side-eyes me with a dark look in his eye. I giggle and reach for his thigh.

"Oh, yeah? I bet you are," I tease him with my hand, running it up his thigh close to his dick.

I get excited when it starts to harden. As he pulls the car out of the campus and onto the street, I decide this is exactly what I need. A fun car quickie to keep my thoughts off anything, or *anyone*, else.

I run my hand up and down his thigh, starting at his knee and edging closer to his dick each time. As I place my hand over the bulge in his pants, he thrusts his hips up.

I unbuckle my seatbelt, and he turns his head sharply in my direction before quickly returning his eyes back to the road. He knows where this is going and unbuckles his seatbelt.

I make quick work of unbuttoning his pants, then lowering the zipper. He lifts his hips and I pull his pants and boxers down, releasing his fully erect cock. I abandon the clothes, leaving them bunched around his knees.

I fist his length from top to bottom and lower my mouth over his head. He lets out a groan and my stomach flips in response. I flick my tongue over his shaft and he lets out another groan.

Flick, flick, flick, move my head up and down. I run my tongue up and down his cock while simultaneously sucking.

Zander places his hand on my head and follows my movements. I feel my own body responding, wetness gushing onto my panties and tingles at my fingertips.

I continue my pattern of flicks and licks, and Zander tenses, confirming he's close.

I ask him if he likes that, which is muffled due to his dick. I don't need an answer, I know he does.

Through clenched teeth, he answers anyway. “Fuck yeah, don’t stop.”

He knows I won’t.

I pull into the last available spot in the lot and exit my car, locking the manual doors to Blueberry.

I rush inside and take the flight up. I use the bathroom and walk into class, where classmates are already seated and talking in the front left row.

I take a seat in the front right row, closest to the aisle. The blonde girl in the seat across from me turns and waves.

“Hey! Marlie, right?”

“Yeah, hi, Jessica!” I say brightly. I decided to take Eli’s advice and have fun. Today, I brought the spunk.

“Where’s your boyfriend?” She looks around as if she expects him to be hiding behind a chair or in the sound booth.

“Oh, I’m not with Chain,” I tell her swiftly.

“Oh, no, not Chain. Eli. Didn’t you come in with him last time?” she replies. “Sorry, I just assumed you knew each other.”

“Ohhh, Eli!" My cheeks turn cherry red as I realize my mistake. "No, we’re coworkers. We were encouraged to take this class at work.”

“Wow, pretty cool job! Where do you work?” she asks. I fill her in briefly on my position at Symbiosis, but my thoughts are reeling.

Chain. You said Chain. Why would anyone think you were with Chain???

As if on cue, Eli drops into the seat next to me and jokes, “Are you seriously talking about work, Marlie?”

"It's my fault, I asked her how you knew each other," says Jessica.

"She thought we were dating," I inform Eli.

We both burst into laughter. "Hah, no not us."

Eli and I have always had this silent understanding that while we have a great friendship, there's no sexual attraction. It's one of the reasons we get along so easily.

"Hello, hello, day 2 is upon us!" Jon exclaims dramatically as he saunters up the aisle. He hops on stage and turns toward us, clipboard in hand.

He makes a show of counting us out and says, "Missing 6. I don't mention on the first day that it's very common for at least one student to drop the course."

Eli and I exchange a curious glance and refocus on Jon. "No matter, no matter, we shall await—ahhh!"

I turn my head towards the door, which is behind the left side of seats, tucked behind a half wall dividing the entry from the chairs.

Finn enters with his head down, followed closely by Liv. They take the seats behind Eli and I. Finn mumbles an apology.

"Don't apologize. Never apologize for being you!" Jon says. "You paid for the class, after all. It makes no difference to me whether you are here or not."

I hear the door open again and turn around, and I feel an expectancy bloom in my chest. I squash it just as quickly, not allowing myself to hope for Chain to walk through the door.

"Hello, Gaby! Happy to see you've returned," Jon shouts. Gaby gives him a wave and takes a seat in the left second row.

"Let me run through my roster here, let's see," Jon looks down briefly and looks back up. "So we're missing Bill, Lorraine, and Chain."

Damn, he's good.

"I'm right here, sir," a voice booms and my heart soars. *Chain.* I keep my eyes focused on Jon. "There was a chick behind me, but I don't remember her name."

Did he seriously call her a chick? I shoot my heart and send it back to my chest.

And stay in there.

"Welcome back, Chain. You must be referring to Lorraine."

A brush at my head tells me Chain is moving in behind me.

Great.

"Sorry I'm late, Jon!" Lorraine enters and rushes over to a seat next to Gaby.

"Lorraine, lovely to see you," Jon says while marking on his clipboard. "Let's get into it, folks!"

He pairs us off into two person scenes where we get a word from our 'audience' and use it as inspiration. The class flies by. I laugh a lot at the scenes I watch, more than I expected to. I went up three different times with Damon, Lorraine, and Jessica.

Class ends with a dramatic parting from Jon, and I exit the room with Eli after Jessica and Finn.

We walk down the stairs and after exiting the building, Finn turns to us.

"You guys down for a drink?" he asks. I turn to Eli and let him answer with his resounding yes. Eli never turns down a drink.

"You're coming, right, chica?"

"What do I have to lose?" I say with a shrug. "I brought the spunk today."

Chapter Seven

Chain

I walk into Envigoration, a bar down the street from Sparkle Comedy. Liv asked me if I was coming before I turned to my car, and I figured why not. On the short walk over, Liv informs me that most people, but all locals, call the place Vigs.

The space is small and intimate, an obvious relaxed vibe about it. Lo-fi beats play in the background. The bar is to the immediate right, stretching down to about half the length of the room. There's an area beyond the bar with tables and chairs. The area in front of the bar has small cocktail tables, a few occupied by patrons drinking. In the back left corner is a small, black, L-shaped couch, where our classmates have gathered.

I follow Liv as she heads over to join them. The couch is occupied by Eli, Jessica, Finn, and Damon. Gaby and Toni have pulled up chairs and sit around the small coffee table in the middle.

I try to ignore the small drop in my stomach when I realize Marlie isn't here.

I grab two chairs from a nearby table and drag them next to Gaby, making my presence known with the loud scrape of the chairs. He looks up and leaps out of his chair. "Hey, Chain!"

"Hey Gaby, what's up?" I settle into my chair and Liv takes the other one. I turn to everyone else with a head nod. Eli reaches out his fist. I lean over and bump it before settling back in my seat. It's then that I realize the seat next to him is empty.

"Hi, Chain," Toni says. After today's class, I've learned everyone's names.

"Hey," I say distractedly, my eyes glancing around the faces again before settling on the empty spot.

Eli pats the spot and says, "For Marlie."

So, he's perceptive. And not afraid to call me out. I give him a glance before turning, placing an impassive look on my face.

"I'm going to get a drink, anyone want anything?"

"I'll come with you! I need a rum and diet coke," a female voice comes from my left, but not *hers*. Lorraine drops her bag by the table and Marlie plops down next to Eli.

I stand up and head towards the bar, not allowing my gaze to linger on Marlie. Lorraine is close on my heels.

We order our drinks from the bartender and wait in silence. With my old-fashioned in hand, and a rum and diet in hers, we return to the group and I take my seat. Lorraine looks around and I place my drink on the table.

"I'll grab you a seat," I say, heading towards the vacant chairs.

Luckily, the bar is empty enough that there are no people sitting at the tables. Lorraine looks at me and smiles, her pearly white teeth gleaming at me in the low light. I grab a chair and pull it up next to Toni, effectively extinguishing any indication she may have that I'm interested.

Lorraine resembles Ashley a bit, with her long, blonde hair. It would be fun to play with, and her small waist would compliment my large hands. But I don't think further of it. While I may have a lot of faults, a fucking cheater is not one of them.

I don't share, and I won't be shared.

I take a sip from my drink, feeling the warmth in my chest as the others exchange pleasantries around me.

“What do you do, Chain?” Finn asks me.

“I’m a Civil Litigation Lawyer,” I state easily. I’m used to being asked about my career.

“Big job, how’d you end up in an improv class?” he asks curiously.

“I—” my phone vibrates in my pocket and I pull it out. I see Ashley’s photo pop up with a heart emoji next to her name; her doing, of course.

Fuck, I didn’t text her.

“Excuse me.” I get up and swipe as I head to the front of the bar.

“Where are you?!” she screams into the phone before I get a chance to speak.

“Hey, love,” I say calmly. She responds with a manic laugh.

“‘Hey, love?’ Really, Chain?” she scoffs.

“Some of the class decided to grab a drink after class. I’m going to head home soon.”

“God, Chain, you’re just—”

“I know, I should have texted you. I’ve been caught up talking with people and it slipped my mind.”

“Just—” she pauses and I wait in silence, refusing to give her any ammo for more rounds. “I’ll see you when you get home.”

She disconnects the call. I pull the phone away from my ear and stare at the screen. It goes black, and I return to my seat wondering why I deal with it.

“All good, man?” Eli asks me as soon as my ass hits the seat.

The fuck is up with this guy?

“It was my girl, had to answer,” I reply lightly, playing it off.

"You guys good?" Caught off guard, my eyes make their way to Marlie of their own volition. She's staring at me with those big, round orbs, and I can't pull away.

"We, uh," *God, they're so beautiful.* "Not really, she's pissed at me."

WHAT. THE. FUCK.

My admission breaks the spell, and my eyes dart to Eli. I am suddenly aware that everyone has stopped talking to stare at me. When the hell did that happen?

Eli and I face off silently. This feels like a test, somehow.

"We fight a lot," I blurt. I'm more stunned by my confession than the group of people listening to me.

Chain. What. Are. You. Doing?!

I know Eli's speaking but I don't hear him. I just admitted that I fought with Ashley. I just admitted to having problems. I just gave them a fault, willingly, with no strategic thought for its use.

Gaby nudges me. I look at him, then back at Eli. "What was that?"

"Damn, sorry bro," Eli tells me. But his eyes show a hint of cunning. I'm trained to recognize that look anywhere.

"I fight with my boyfriend all the time, too," Jessica exclaims. I'm thankful for her confession, albeit awkward.

"Guys are jerks," says Toni.

"I just want us to go back to how it was when we first started," Jessica confesses with a small voice. Damon pats her knee awkwardly as tears pool in her eyes.

Oh, lord. Here we go with the waterworks.

I welcome them for the simple reason that the attention is off me and I can gather myself. I glance back at Eli, who's sizing me up. I school my features, deadpanning.

"I'll fix it, it's all good," I give a lopsided grin and turn towards Finn. "You were about to tell me what you do," I state rather than ask, not giving him an out.

Finn explains his work as a software engineer and I sip my drink, leaning back in my seat.

Externally, I feign intrigue to whatever the fuck Finn is saying. Internally, I'm fuming. Who the fuck does Eli think he is?

I'm no stranger to conflict. There's a reason I ended up working as a litigator. I'm dressed up and reserved now, a polished version of my true self. I dealt with my dick of a father growing up, Frank. He was both verbally and physically abusive.

That is, until I joined the high school wrestling team. Working out five days a week and learning strategic moves made it so I could defend myself and my mother, Valerie.

My father never would have allowed me to join. Luckily, I learned from a young age to work smarter, not harder. I didn't say shit to him or my mom. The day I clocked him right in his jaw was my first step towards freedom. I still feel the same satisfaction I did that day, when his expression turned into a mixture of shock, anger, and admiration.

I don't know what the fuck that confession was after Eli's question, but it won't happen again. I've worked too damn hard to protect myself and be who I need to be. And if Marlie causes me to fuck that up, she can't be good for me.

Chapter Eight

Marlie

"Fine, you guys don't have to come, but we're going for drinks," Stella tells Jace as he plops down next to Zander on the couch. Controllers in hand, the Xbox loading on the 75" TV screen.

"Have fun, honey," he tells her. Zander calls me over with his finger, and I oblige him, popping a kiss on his lips.

"I'll have her home by 10, Jace," I joke, looking over at Zander's best friend. This is another perfect dynamic of our relationship. Stella is my best friend, and Jace is his.

"Please, don't. I'd like to get a few rounds in," he jokes, staring at the TV. He maneuvers the controller and I can tell we've already lost them.

Stella rolls her eyes. "Shut up, Jason." I giggle. "Come on, let's get you dressed and out of here," she tells me. We head upstairs and to my room. I open my closet and pull out my favorite tee.

"No, no, no, I wanna dress you up tonight." Stella gives me the puppy eyes she knows I can't say no to.

"Ugh, fine. But it needs to be comfortable." I eye her coffee colored linen shorts and simple gray tank top, reminding myself that she pulls off comfort and style effortlessly. She sifts through my clothes, landing on a peach crop top with a daisy flower in the middle.

She tosses it to me and I catch it while she hastily opens my drawers, looking for bottoms. I pull out my phone and connect it to my speakers, playing "No Shade" by Brooke Eden.

"Here," she calls as she tosses my favorite high-waisted, ripped jean shorts to me. I don't look up in time and they fall to the floor. "Look sharp, babe. We're going out and I need you to be with it."

"Give me my wedges," I tell her with a laugh. She grabs them and closes the closet, turning to me. The shoes have matching peach straps with beige heels. I dress quickly and pocket my phone, moving to leave the room.

"Makeup!" Stella rummages through the small bag I have on my dresser, pulling out black eyeliner, mascara, and lipstick.

"I'll do it in the car." I grab the makeup from her and shove it into my back pocket.

"I'm so excited!" she squeals. She gives my shoulders a light squeeze and we zoom down the stairs.

"Bye, guys!" I say, opening the front door.

"Love you!" they shout at the same time, without looking up from their game.

Stella drives us to our favorite bar, The Meeting Place. We pull into the lot, which is more packed than usual. We exchange curious looks and head inside.

"Ladies, how you doin'?" Luke's voice booms over to us. We grin and take seats at the end of the patio bar, overlooking the water. He heads over to us immediately, earning him annoyed looks from the other customers waiting to order.

"Luke, you don't usually work this early on Saturdays!" Stella gushes.

"They needed an extra hand today," he replies as he grabs two glasses. "It's always nice to see you pretty ladies. The usual?"

I nod and he gets to work preparing my mango mojito. He shakes and pours, adding the mint leaves.

"Thanks, Lukey," I say with a smile. Stella looks at me approvingly.

"An outfit always sets the mood," she says with a sparkle in her eye. Stella's energy is so infectious, I feel my thoughts lightening as I take a sip of my drink.

Luke finishes making her gin and tonic and moves on to other bargoers. Stella squeezes the lime and discards the rind on a napkin.

"Let's stay at the bar," I say. Normally we'd find a more secluded table, but I feel like breaking routine tonight.

"Let's," she agrees. She takes a swig of her drink and sets it down, turning to me. "So how's the improv class going?"

Emerald eyes flash through my mind, and I bat them away with my lashes.

"It's going great, we went out for drinks after class last night." I ponder sharing with her about Chain, because we typically tell each other everything, but I decide against it.

"Sweet! So you're making friends?"

"We'll see, but the potential is there for sure. Everyone seems really great." *Especially Chain, but we're not talking about him.*

"Ohhh, I love this song!" Stella says as "Don't Stop Believin'" by Journey starts to play.

"I dare you to point out one person in this bar who doesn't." I tap my foot to the beat, ready for the room to burst into song the moment the lyrics begin.

She looks around as I bring my mojito to my lips. The sweet mango mixes with the lime and I revel in the warmth I start to feel on my cheeks.

I close my eyes with an inhale and the room explodes with the start of the song. My eyes fly open when I hear a voice that is *not* Journey. I turn and find that karaoke is set up towards the back of the room. A guy is belting the song into the mic with a seltzer can in his other hand.

So that's why it's busier tonight.

"There's one!" Stella proclaims, tapping me on the arm. I follow her gaze and land on—

Chain.

Leaning back in a booth seat that lines the entire back wall, arms extended over either side of him, he looks completely cool and collected. There's a guy next to him, and two on the opposite side of the table in chairs. Half-full drinks and empty cups litter the table, indicating they've been here a while.

"He's hot, right?" My head whips back to Stella and I feel my jaw has gone slack, mouth slightly ajar.

Shutting my mouth, I clear my throat. "Uh, yeah, he's all right."

He's hot as fuck.

I take a gulp of my drink to wash down the nerves but it's a fruitless attempt. I steal another glance at Chain and I can't peel my eyes away.

His face is angled towards the karaoke singer, giving way to his strong jaw line and slight stubble. His dark eyebrows are full and thick, exuding his natural self-confidence. His broad shoulders are on display due to his extended arms. His defined chest is evident in the black, button down shirt he has over a fitted, white tee. His hair is my favorite, though. It's a brown so dark, you'd think it was black. The front has this sexy volume to it, flowing into the wavy locks that narrow and end at his neck.

"You can't stop staring!" Stella giggles, putting her drink down. I force my eyes away from Chain and land on Stella's grayish-blue ones.

Do I tell her he's in my class? Why don't I want to be honest with her? I never hide things from Stella. She's my best friend.

"He's obviously good looking, so what?" I say dismissively. "He's in my improv class."

"Whaaaat?" She's really interested now. She looks over at him and I watch her take him in, scrutinizing.

"So, do we have anything left to do before your wedding?" I say, trying to steer this conversation in another direction. She tears her gaze from Chain to me. I watch her battle between pushing the Chain discussion further or allowing me to divert.

"I think we're about done. I need to finish the favors but I'll do it with my mom," she says, picking up her drink and taking a sip.

Chain conversation over.

"I can't wait, only 3 weeks and you're a married woman!" I'm the maid of honor in her small wedding. They're getting married at Jace's grandparents' farm. Since Zander is also the best man, we took a couple of days off work to help with the setup.

"I know! I never thought this day would come." She has the biggest smile on her face. It's always been her dream to get married, start a family, and live 'happily ever after'. "Hey, won't you miss your improv class?"

Damn, I hadn't even thought of that. "Totally worth it," I tell her. "I'll let them know next week."

"So, this guy is in your class?? I can't... wow." She looks back over at Chain.

Okay, conversation not over.

"What, you expected nerds?" I scoff, remembering the conversation with Zander.

"Not nerds, but not... that." She flicks her hand in Chain's direction.

"I'm not a nerd!" I assert.

"No, of course not, but you've got some quirk," she replies offhandedly.

"Whatever, I'm just ready to enjoy some time off, get your wedding together, and party." Jace's grandparents' retired farm is on 5 acres. I want to sip my coffee and swing on the front porch, listening to the birds chirp while staring at the luscious greenery.

"Meee, too." A look of peace overcomes her, mirroring my own. "So, are you going to say hi?"

She's relentless!

"No. I hardly know the guy!"

"Hmm." She swirls the stirrer around in her drink, seemingly absentminded. But I know her, and it's anything but.

Choosing to ignore it, I distract her with more talk about the preparations for the week before the wedding. We finish our drinks and wave Luke over to order another round. He serves us and I feel the need to pee. The bathrooms are on the other side of the bar, requiring me to walk directly past Chain's line of sight.

Fuck that. Wait for him to leave and then haul ass to the bathroom.

Of their own accord, my eyes make their way over to his table. He's turned in our direction, listening attentively to the guy next to him. He's so focused, I gather that it's not a lighthearted conversation. I wonder if it's about his girlfriend.

NO, you don't.

I shatter my thoughts and prepare to turn back to Stella, when Chain's gaze moves slowly from his companion to me.

Frozen. I'm frozen and I'm helpless. I watch the comprehension slowly dawn on him that I'm someone he knows. And then his eyes lock with mine. I thaw, the freeze overtaken by the warmth in my belly. The small fire crackles, like energy lighting me up and spreading through my veins.

Chain breaks the contact, and I feel my heart racing in my chest. I turn to Stella and find her watching me.

Fuck, did she notice?? Fuck, fuck, fuck.

I say nothing. She says nothing.

I reach for my replenished drink and take a sip, holding her gaze. I hadn't even noticed Luke replaced it. I try to collect myself but my body is tingling. I place my drink down as she picks hers up and takes a sip, a strange little standoff as we battle who will speak first.

"You know what? Yeah, let's go say hi," I say to her in a snap decision. Chain is nothing to me and I need to make that clear.

"Okay!" She leaps off her bar stool, grabbing her drink with the napkin stuck on it from the perspiration.

I grab my drink and wave to Luke. Stella waits patiently for me to lead us to the table where Chain and his friends are. I look in the direction of his table and see that he's refocused on the guy next to him.

Oh my god, why did I suggest doing this? Why?!

I lift my chin and put some pep in my step, portraying the confidence that I completely lack. As we approach his table, he looks at Stella. Then his eyes roam to me. I come to a halt behind his two friends and place my hand on the back of one of their chairs.

"Hey, Chain," I say brightly. I plaster a dazzling smile on my face and glance around at his friends. "Are we just going to keep running into each other?"

Because seriously, what are the damn chances?

"Hello, Marlie," he replies with a light smirk, his expression otherwise unreadable. "It seems so."

"This is Stella, my best friend," I introduce.

"Stella, a pleasure. I'm here with some of my associates—Donald, Trey, and Gregory."

"Please, call me Greg." The guy next to Chain stands up and takes a step toward us. Stella reaches her hand in an offering to shake his, but Greg takes her fingers in his hand and, without breaking eye contact, lowers his mouth to them, placing a gentle kiss.

"Well, now I'm jealous," I pout jokingly and reach my free hand out. The effects of the mojito are *obviously* taking over.

Greg locks his amber eyes with mine and makes a show of kissing my hand. I give him an impressive grin, dropping my hand to my side when he's finished. Chain shifts in his seat but I refuse to look at him and crack the fragile strength I've summoned.

"Always showin' us up, man," Trey says. He gives us a smile and picks up an empty glass before noticing and switching it out for a filled one.

Trey has dark skin, with dark eyes to match, and exudes power. In contrast, Donald keeps his blue eyes trained on the karaoke area. The "Don't Stop Believin'" guy is no longer singing and background music plays.

"Nice to meet you, Donald," I offer. He gives us a quick glance and head nod, then turns back.

"You'll have to excuse Donald, he's, ah, *working*," Greg informs us.

I follow Donald's line of sight to the man in charge of the karaoke set up. Turning back, I ask, "What, you're suing him?"

"Attorney-Client Privilege," Donald returns his gaze to us. "How do you know what I do, anyway?"

"Chain," I reply hesitantly. I look to Chain, who has his gaze fixed on his hand gripping his drink on the table.

"Where did you all meet?" Trey asks with a quirked brow.

"They met doing improv," Stella takes over, reading my silence. "I'm meeting him now."

Chain looks over at her.

Is he purposely avoiding me?

Stop being paranoid.

"Well, we just wanted to say hello. We'll head back." I remove my hand from the chair, taking a step back. Stella is rooted in place.

"Stay, I insist." Greg charmingly pats the seat next to him on the booth. Stella takes it instantly, and I'm left standing awkwardly, the small distance I took from the chair feeling like I'm in a different country. Chain stands up and walks away with his gaze centered in front of him.

What's his deal? He's just going to leave us with his people?

I move to take his seat and land lightly next to Greg. I look at Stella, who takes a large swig of her gin and tonic.

"Who's ready for another?!" She cries out. I laugh, because this is *so* Stella—ready to party and let loose. To an outsider, her behavior might scream promiscuity. But any man tries to talk to her, and she's the first one to not only turn him down, but bring him down to size for even trying.

She's not afraid to be who she is. She knows her place in this world, and she thrives in it.

"Let's go." Trey smiles and stands up.

"Need another, babe?" Stella asks me. I give her a nod, anger beginning to bubble in my chest.

Where does Chain get off? I do the right thing, I say hello, and this is how he treats us?

I seethe silently and polish off the last third of my drink swiftly, slamming the glass back down on the table.

I look up to see Chain eyeing me with a quirked brow, sliding a chair up between me and Trey's empty seat.

So that's why he left.

"You all right?" Chain asks me. I blink. He takes a seat in the chair as I move to stand up.

"Sorry, I'm in your seat."

"Stay." It's not a question. I lower back down and look away. "You didn't answer me."

My eyes snap back to him and the cauldron of anger in me boils. The second drink is making its way to my head and I'm losing the fucks I normally cling to.

"I'm fine," I answer with a bite in my tone. "And you?"

The music changes abruptly, and the sound of "Buttons" by Pussycat Dolls distracts me. I watch as a woman stumbles her way up to the karaoke table and takes the mic from the guy.

She is going to butcher this song.

I watch as she drunkenly starts to sing, holding the mic far away from her mouth so we're not complete victims to the next 3 minutes of probable torture.

"Excellent," Chain responds. I return my attention to him and he leans back. "Ashley and I made up; we're better than ever."

I feel like a bucket of ice was plunged into that bubbling cauldron. Donald and Greg turn their attention to Chain, too.

"Didn't know you were having problems, man," Greg says sympathetically. *So Mr. Charmer's got a heart.*

"She's a hot piece of ass," Donald comments. *Donald does not.*

Chain doesn't answer them. "That's great," I say. Chain doesn't respond, taking a final swig from his glass.

"How's your boyfriend? Randy, was it?" His green eyes land on mine and I hold his stare. His eyes are curious, the electric green around his pupil stemming out.

Answer him. "Zander," I correct. "He's great, home with Jace."

"Jace?"

"Sorry, Stella's fiancé."

Trey returns to his chair between Donald and Chain.

"What?" Stella asks, handing me my drink as she takes her seat next to Greg.

"Stella has a fiancé," Donald declares.

Greg and Trey whip their heads to Stella. She takes in their shocked expressions and sighs.

"I know, I don't act it, right? Why can't a taken woman do as she pleases without there being an assumption made about it?"

"It's not that, love, we just don't mess with another man's woman," Greg explains. I notice a faint accent and conclude it must be British.

"Now, *that* is a rule I can abide by," Stella says, ending the topic and putting down her new, golden drink. *Crap, she switched to Happy Honey.* "Who wants to dance?!"

She stands up and picks up her drink again, taking a swill from her glass before placing it back down and swaying her hips to the song. She doesn't seem to notice the glares coming from the table next to her or the off-key vocals pelting out the lyrics.

Backing her up, I rise and look at Chain, waiting for him to move so I can get around his chair. He slowly stands and pushes the chair into the table. He backs up, leaning on the table next to us so I can squeeze between him and the chair. As I walk past him, my arm brushes his upper body. The shock from the tingles it sends through me causes me to stumble.

Chain's hand shoots out and holds onto my elbow, steadying me. I look up at him and our eyes meet. He has a slight tilt to his lips. The sight of it fuels the sparks to reignite in my belly. They launch at my ribs, a small inferno that no one can see.

I jerk my elbow out of his grip and continue to move out. Stella reaches my side and I turn back to the table. "It was nice to meet you all. I'll see you Friday, Chain."

I reach over Trey's shoulder and try to reclaim my drink. I look at Greg and he passes it to me in silent understanding.

This is goodbye.

Chapter Nine

Chain

"Today, we are going to do an interesting exercise—one of my favorites," Jon says. He's at the front and center of the stage, watching us. "We are going to cycle partners so everyone gets a chance with each other. I want you to find one thing about your partner that you like. Once you have that thing, hold it in your mind's eye and tell them in as much detail as possible."

The class is silent with rapt attention.

"It is normal for our minds to criticize and pick apart a scene, as well as ourselves," he continues. "The focus of the exercise is to look for the good and express it."

We get on stage and I make my way around the class, giving compliments on appearance, humor, or something I saw one of them do in a scene. I mean, we don't know each other that well. How much can I say?

I'm making strategic moves to put off pairing with Marlie. I can feel it in the way I avoid her gaze and purposely don't move in her direction. As if putting it off will make it so I don't have to partner with her.

Why is this woman, beautiful as she is, having this effect on me? I'm not one to back down from an interaction. I have no problem with socializing, nearly fearless communicating with people. So why don't I want to approach her?

I finish telling Eli that I admire his ability to be honest, if not bordering on blunt. He tells me he thinks I'm a catch, which isn't surprising. I've been told my entire life that I'm good-looking, and I play into the part.

That's the thing about appearances though. You can be easily fooled by what you see. Human beings tend to trust what they think they know. Judging a book by its cover and all that.

But I'm not sure Ashley would say I'm a catch if you asked her, seeing as she's been upset with me more often than not lately. Taking this class took away the one night we always had together. I made the decision to take the class knowing full well. But it's only 10 weeks, and I rationalized it that way when I signed up.

I look around the members on stage and confirm I only have Marlie left. I hesitate, feet rooted in place as I watch her speaking with Liv.

What power does she have over me? None. She's another improv student in my class, and I need to begin treating her as such. I'm chalking this up to sexual tension, and I won't be intimidated by it any longer.

I need to face her head on. She's a friend, pure and simple. With my decision, my feet move as she turns her head in my direction.

I feel that energy buzzing, increasing with each step I take in her direction. She looks up and waves at me, and I smile.

See? Nothing to note here. We're friends.

"How are you, Marlie?" I ask her, taking the space that Liv vacated moments before.

"Never better," she responds.

"Good." There's a pregnant pause, so I add, "Shall I go first, or you?"

"You go," she says. She tucks a strand of hair behind her ear and her round eyes beg me to make them flutter shut. She bites her lower lip as I stare at her, causing me to imagine myself stepping between her legs, forcing her to take me in.

Quit it.

I focus on the intensity of her eyes, the hints of caramel rippling through layers of chocolate brown.

"Your eyes." My mouth betrays me before I can stop it. "They're not just brown. It's like they have..."

"Honey in them? I know," she says casually, as if she's been told a thousand times. Her nonchalance goads me to continue.

"Not honey, caramel. They're chocolate with swirls of caramel in them."

As if they heard me, I watch the caramel react, flowing further into the depths of her irises. Her mouth opens a nearly imperceptible amount before she clamps it shut.

"That's..." she clears her throat. "No one's described them that way before."

I hold back a smirk. *Maybe I'm not a catch, but I'm a damn good flirt.* "It's an honor to be your first."

"I admire your confidence," she tells me. I free my smirk, allowing myself to sink into the comfort of her words.

"I know," I tell her proudly. I've crafted this persona in order to never be taken for granted. To never be seen as *weaker*.

"Not in an obvious way, though. You don't feel superior to others. You're just sure of yourself and your abilities."

"So I'm not arrogant is what you're saying."

She laughs. "Right. You're confident in a natural way. You don't hold it over people's heads."

"As far as you know." She's wrong there. I use it, effectively, in my career and to some extent, my personal life.

"I bet you try, but deep down, you seem like a good person," she says earnestly.

"What if I'm just a good actor?"

"Well, you're a lawyer. I didn't say I think you're honest or pure."

I feel a flash of irritation at her judgment.

"I am a lawyer, and a damn good one. But I don't use dishonest means to achieve what I want."

"That's not what I meant, I—"

"Back to your seats, please!" Jon calls out from the aisle, tearing her attention from me to him.

"We'll finish this later," I mumble, moving back to my chair. I refuse to let her think of me in that way. When the class is seated, Jon gets onto the stage.

"Now, how did that feel? Was it difficult? Did you have trouble identifying a positive thing to say? Did you feel nervous to explain it to your partner?"

When no one answers, Jon sighs dramatically. "If you don't provide feedback, this will be a *very* boring few weeks, indeed."

This guy's drama is starting to piss me off. Can't he just say what he wants from us? He can't expect us to know what the fuck we're doing.

Deep breaths, Chain.

As much as I hate Frank, I unfortunately have a temper just like him. The difference is, I refuse to let it rule me.

"Chain told me he likes my honesty, so..." Eli starts. "I'm feeling like I don't know what I signed up for anymore."

"An astute observation, Eli," Jon says cheerfully. "Improv is not for the faint of heart. You will face your fears, face your feelings, and face your own inner workings. We do not leap and prance on stage for the world to ogle at. We act within the moment presented to us, and that requires a vulnerability voyaged by few."

There's that word again—*vulnerability*. Jon is really beginning to irk me with his pompous act.

"I realize it's only week 3, but I assure you that come week 10—" He pauses for what I can only assume is dramatic effect. I roll my eyes. "You will know each other in a way you could not have expected."

I order my whiskey, neat, at Vigs and wait, leaning my waist on the bar and propping my foot on a barstool. I have my back turned from the couch area where the class sits.

I texted Ashley on the walk over, letting her know I'd be home late, which may have been a mistake. She called me, half asleep, telling me to do whatever I want. She said she doesn't care anymore, which we both know is a lie.

She likely would have woken up when I got home, but there's no guarantee she would have checked the time. I could have snuck in, laid down, and she wouldn't have been the wiser.

The bartender passes me my drink and I walk over to the group as they chat animatedly. I locate Marlie on the edge of the couch next to Eli, talking across him to Lorraine. I wanted to pick up our conversation from earlier and ensure that she knows I'm not a snake.

Although, why it's important to prove myself to her, I refuse to think further about. Since there isn't a spot next to her, I move towards the only open seat between a couple of the guys.

"I'm telling you, they're going to win," Damon tells Finn.

"You willin' to put money on that?" Finn sneers.

"Hello, gentlemen," I say, sitting and taking a sip from my drink.

"Chiefs or Buccs?" Damon demands, whipping his head toward me.

"I don't care much for sports," I reply, crossing my ankle over my knee and lowering my drink. Damon looks defeated. "But Chiefs are definitely gonna take it."

"See!" Finn exclaims. I smirk, taking another sip of my drink. I lean back as the burn makes its way from my throat to my chest, settling in and bringing me ease.

Ashley will get over it by the weekend, and we'll be fine. I know I need to make more of an effort with her. She expects little from me, satisfied with the standard of living we've created. But I can't even seem to give her that lately.

The worst part is, it's not just her I'm not making an effort for. I've slacked on the gym, skipping it altogether most days. That's never good for my esteem or my mind. I'm not sure what's gotten into me lately. I've relied on physical exertion to keep me calm and focused for over 10 years.

It started as a means to fight Frank off in order to defend my mother and I. But it evolved into more. I found that it not only kept me safe, it made me feel strong and in control.

Putting it to the back of my mind, I glance in Marlie's direction. She listens raptly to Eli and Lorraine deep in discussion, of what I'm not sure. I watch as she slowly lifts her hand to the necklace she wears. She reaches her index finger and thumb into the start of her shirt, pulling out a pendant and toying it idly.

Deciding that I need to speak with her, I interrupt. "Lorraine, do you mind switching seats? I'd like to speak with Marlie."

"Oh, um," she glances between me and Marlie before saying, "Sure."

I stand and move decisively to her chair. Lorraine gets up, and I scoot the chair back before taking my place in it.

"What are you drinking?" I eye Marlie's glass with clear liquid and lack of garnish.

"Tequila."

"Straight?"

"That's the best way."

Interesting. I wouldn't have pegged her for a straight up type of woman. She continues toying with the pendant. My jaw ticks when I notice what it is—a Z.

I take a sip of my whiskey, then another. I watch her raise her drink to her luscious lips, sipping the tequila fully. She doesn't flinch, either. What I wouldn't give to be that tequila, to make sure she *does* flinch...

"So, what did you want to talk to me about?"

I clear my throat. "I wanted to pick our conversation back up."

"Oh, I really didn't mean anything by it, Chain." She dismisses me with a wave of her hand after she places her drink down on the table.

"I want to be clear that I don't engage in any sort of foul play or deceit in my work." That need to defend myself won't go away. I don't want her to have a false perception of me.

"Of course not," she says.

"I take justice very seriously." In the dim lighting, I can just make out the colors in her eyes blending together with an amused twinkle.

"I'm sure you do. You bring the scales of justice to an even keel. "

"Damn, right," I murmur. I polish off my whiskey and stand up.

"I could use another round," she tells me, standing up with me. I hadn't noticed her height in comparison to mine until now. She's just shy of a head shorter than my 6'1".

"Anyone else need a drink?" I offer. Eli looks over from his conversation with Gaby and shoots his drink back.

"Sure." He stands.

"I got it, what's your order?" I ask him.

Eli glances at Marlie before settling back into his seat. "Jameson on the rocks."

I give him a nod and turn towards the bar. I'm halfway there when I feel her presence behind me. I don't bother to turn around as I lean across the bar to order.

"I'll take a Jameson on the rocks, your best whiskey, neat, and a teq—"

"A Mojito, actually," Marlie tells the bartender, who nods without looking up. I give her a curious look.

"Gotta drive."

It irritates me that the bartender hasn't looked at us, but I let the anger simmer without reacting to it. While getting into wrestling and being fit was a saving grace, it was also a demise. I got into a lot of fights due to my misplaced anger in high school. By the time I got to college, I knew I didn't want to continue on that way. I started seeing a counselor on campus, who taught me some techniques.

I pull out a tin of mints from my pocket, throwing a couple into my mouth. I hold the tin out to Marlie, and she takes one. The bartender still doesn't look up. I drum my fingers over the bar top as I pocket the tin.

Marlie shifts beside me, and I focus on the conversation I want to have with her. The bartender moves to the bottles that are displayed beautifully behind him on tiered shelves with led lighting, giving me more room to think.

"I don't mean to harp on about this. I just don't want you to have this false notion that I'm a shark that only cares for money. I got into this career because I give a damn, and want to see the right thing done."

She watches me for a long moment. The bartender places our drinks next to my elbow and I dig in my other pocket, pulling out my wallet and slapping four twenty dollar bills down.

"You're doing it for the scales of justice."

"Exactly." *She's getting it.*

"Thank you, you didn't have to do that," she says with a nod towards the cash lying next to our drinks.

"Anytime." As we grab our drinks, I add, "It doesn't hurt to be confident in my field, though."

We smile at each other and I feel that zap of electricity again, the air between us supercharged. Luckily, she breaks the connection by turning back towards the group. I'm not sure if I would have been able to. I hand Eli his drink when we get back, returning to the seat near Marlie.

"Thanks, man." He takes it with a head nod, sipping the drink before placing it down on the table. He claps his hands and says, "So guys, I was thinking we should exchange numbers. It might be nice to have a group chat going for our class."

Everyone nods and murmurs their agreement. Jessica takes all of our numbers and creates a group chat called 'Improv Class'. Super original. She instructs us to send our name so everyone can save it. I see Marlie's name float across my screen and feel a small wave of excitement. Ignoring it, I set to work saving everyone's numbers while the chatter begins around me again.

I lean back in my chair once I finish and my gaze roams over to Marlie, as it often seems to. She's laughing at Eli as he speaks animatedly, her bright smile drawing me in like a moth to a flame. My heart flutters and I find myself wanting to be the cause of that smile. *Jeez, that's sappy.*

I continue watching her, entranced by her movements and mannerisms. She's resumed fiddling with the pendant on her neck, the metal reflecting brightly in the low lights.

I refuse to wonder why I feel a pang of jealousy in my chest.

Chapter Ten

Chain

"I'm not quitting this class, Ashley. I paid for it and I will see it through!" I shout into the car.

"So what, five more weeks of this? What does it matter to you, anyway? Since when do you act?" she shouts back.

"Six more weeks after tonight," I correct through gritted teeth. But her questions get me thinking.

What does it matter to me? I wanted to do stand up. This is about the furthest thing from it. Improv is off the cuff, and albeit funny, it doesn't allow for instigated laughter. There's no telling where a scene will go; that much I've learned from the three classes we've had so far.

"Even worse!"

"I'll see you tonight." I click the disconnect button and grip the steering wheel.

I didn't have an answer for her. It's true I've had fun the last three classes, but was this an effective use of my time? Was this helping me towards future goals that I have for the firm and my passions?

As a kid, I dreamed of having an audience at my fingertips. I craved their laughter, validating that I can bring light into this world. That I wasn't just a ball of anger and trauma, caused by my father. I desired the power of their undivided attention, willingly allowing me to have an effect on them.

I could achieve that through improv, couldn't I? There's still a willing audience, I'm just not in control of the effect it will have. Jon said improv is about allowing the scene to unfold and take its natural course. Our job, as the improviser, is to learn to play with it.

As I grew up, the need for financial security got the better of me, compelling me to focus on college and law school. I always thought if I had money, I wouldn't need my father or anyone else. I secured my place in the firm, which in turn secured my place in the world.

My phone pings and I glance at the screen.

Ashley iMessage

I take my phone and pocket it, ignoring the message, and pull into the parking lot a few minutes early for class. I use the bathroom before taking a seat at the front left of the theater.

Lorraine, Damon, and Toni are already here. I wave to them and pull out my phone to keep myself busy so I don't have to make small talk. I scroll through emails, organizing them into folders by priority to deal with Monday or sooner, if it's a pressing matter. Students file in and take seats around me.

"Hey, Chain," Liv says as she takes the seat next to me. I put my phone away and give her a smile in response.

"Hey, Liv, hope you're well," I say to her. *Cut the email talk.*

"Thanks, you too," she replies and settles into her seat.

Jon's voice ends our exchange. "Everyone out of their seats and up on stage!"

We collectively do as he asks. I take a place at the back of the stage and face the empty audience when I feel the energy shift around me. Attributing it to all the movement, I don't pay it any mind.

But then I see *her*, and the energy pulses within me. She's walking up the aisle with Eli, dropping her bag onto the seat

I'd claimed and joining the rest of us on stage. When her eyes meet mine, the energy morphs into a hum in my chest and *goddamn* does it feel good.

I nod my head at her and she turns, taking a place in the forming circle. I immediately miss the feel of her warm, caramel-laced eyes on mine.

"I confirmed that Bill is no longer a part of our journey through this course," Jon starts off dramatically. He instructs us to warm up with a few games, then sends us back to our seats. I move to the opposite front row, letting Marlie take over my previously claimed spot. Eli sits next to me and we exchange a fist bump that he initiates.

I feel someone watching me but when I turn my head I find that it's Liv, not Marlie, giving me an inquisitive look. I shrug and return my attention to Jon, trying to keep my focus on the class and not *her.*

Marlie. She's just Marlie.

Jon informs us that we'll be working on more duet scenes and exploring emotions within them. We'll ask for a relationship dynamic from the audience, in this case our class, and focus on the feelings that emerge naturally from it.

"Are there any questions before we begin?" Jon concludes, standing up and moving his chair off stage behind one of the wings, leaving two lone black chairs at our disposal.

"It's not a question, but I won't be here next week," Marlie says.

I feel as though a rock drops in my stomach. I clench my abs, ignoring it. *Why should it matter if she's not here? Where the hell is she going, anyway?*

"Thank you for letting us know. I hope whatever takes priority is important," Jon tells her passively, taking his usual seat in the fifth row behind me. I huff involuntarily, earning me a chuckle from Eli. *Didn't take long for Jon to piss me off today. Like this class is the most important shit in our lives.*

"I'm the maid of honor at my best friend's wedding," she says. *Stella.*

The guys had a field day over her after they went to dance. But my eyes kept trailing back to Marlie. I watched as Stella swayed her hips and Marlie side-stepped. It seemed like she was holding back, letting Stella have all the fun while only partaking as an onlooker. It was evident in the way her eyes darted around her surroundings, taking it all in but not letting it overtake her.

It's utterly confusing why I can't seem to take my eyes off her yet know hardly anything about her. But that's honestly not even the hardest part to swallow. It's how desperately I *want* to know her. It's not just physical, although she's definitely sexy as hell.

"Wonderful!" Jon claps his hands jovially, yanking me from my thoughts. *So he's human, after all.* "Anyone else? No? Let us begin, then, shall we?"

He calls up Jessica and Toni. Jessica asks us for a type of relationship, stuttering with nerves. *She really needs to get a grip.*

Various students begin to call out, Liv being the loudest with her suggestion: coworkers.

When their scene is over, Jon reads off his clipboard, "Marlie and Chain."

I stand up and make my way onto the stage as my stomach does a little flip. Marlie follows, staying towards the front to ask for a relationship. The shouts from the class begin, and Marlie points to Damon. Everyone falls silent, and Damon repeats what he said.

"One-night stand," he says.

"That's not a relationship," Marlie retorts.

"Ahhh, we're at an interesting crossroads here, folks!" Jon leaps out of his seat dramatically. He begins pacing the aisle, tapping his pen to his chin.

"Imagine, if you will, you are opening a show for a live audience. The crowd has applauded you in welcome and settled to watch you. You ask for a suggestion, as Marlie just did. She pointed out an audience member, and they provided the answer Damon did. One-night stand."

Jon stops pacing, facing Marlie and I. His eyes bore into Marlie and he asks, "Tell me, Marlie, is there a relationship when a one-night stand occurs?"

The fuck is his problem? Anger trickles into my veins, my fists clenching in response. His condescending bullshit has been pissing me off and I can't help the protectiveness I feel over Marlie.

"Yes."

"What could it be?"

"Lovers."

"What else?"

"Umm..."

"Enemies, long lost friends, or abso-fucking-lutely nothing," I interject. The anger made its way to my tongue, letting my thoughts loose. "I'm not sure what your point is, *Jon.*"

Jon focuses on me. My eyes slit daringly in question.

"We cannot dismiss what an audience member has provided simply because we're not willing to explore a dynamic," he replies, his eyes unwavering.

"We can do whatever the fuck what we want, it's our show."

What are you doing? Chill the fuck out. He's not your dad and she's not your girlfriend.

I seem to have no effect on him, which doesn't help to reel in my anger. I refuse to back down from this. The anger reaches boiling point.

Jon continues, "It may be your show, but without an audience, you have nothing."

What, does he think I need an audience? That I need anything?

"Be that as it may, you are the teacher here. It's your job to explain that to us. Don't—"

"It's fine, Chain," Marlie cuts in.

I look over and find myself standing right next to her. I hadn't even noticed I moved. I'm letting my anger get the best of me and I need to calm the fuck down. I take a deep breath and my eyes dart between her and Jon.

"I prefer to teach from a place that promotes internal thought, Chain," Jon states, ignorant of the tension in me, in the room. "I could have explained it, but as you saw, Marlie was perfectly capable of coming up with the answers on her own."

I look around at the class and everyone's eyes are on us. I need to get it together. I take a step back with a breath.

"One-night stand. Let's go, Marlie." I grab a chair with more roughness than I intend and slam it on the stage before sitting in it, my front to its back.

Marlie watches Jon return to his seat as if she's unsure, then turns her gaze to me as she remains rooted in place.

"I told you I wasn't going to do this." I start the scene, fueling it with the cooling anger in my blood.

"I—I—I—" she stutters. Her hesitation is so believable, I don't think she's acting.

"You what?" I stand up from my chair and take a menacing step towards her. "You thought this meant something?"

Her mouth is agape, her eyes wide.

"Aww, did you catch feelings?" I taunt. Her eyes reveal a sting of pain. *Wait, did I actually just hurt her?*

"You thought this was real, did you?" Another step, shrinking the space between us. I reach out and stroke her cheek with my thumb.

"I just—"

"You thought wrong." My hand drops. The energy in that small space between us is buzzing. I'm convinced if I reach my hand out again, I'll be hit with electric shocks so severe I could become a live source to power the city.

Marlie glances down and I leap at the chance. I grab her chin and force her to meet my penetrating gaze, finding that most of the swirling caramel I've grown accustomed to seeing is gone.

"Don't come back here again," I say. I see the hurt flash across her eyes again. *This is a scene. She's acting.*

Suddenly, she forcefully rips her chin out of my grip and turns, walking to the end of the stage. She turns back and her anger meets my own.

"You can be damn sure I won't," she says. "I was only here to return your watch."

She mimes pulling the watch out of her pocket and tosses it to me. I catch the air that is the watch swiftly and look down at my palm.

"You left it in my car."

"BRAVO!" My head snaps in Jon's direction when his exclamation rips me out of the scene.

"That is precisely what this is all about," Jon adds as the class breaks into applause. When the cheers settle, he goes on. "No one laughed. No one joked. But ohhh, did we feel that."

I look back to Marlie and smirk, but she doesn't reciprocate. My face falls, but then I decide not to think further into it. I don't know what the fuck just happened, but I'm done with her having an inkling of power over me.

Chapter Eleven

Marlie

I bolt out of class the moment Jon dismisses us, but Eli catches me on the flight down the stairs.

"Wait up, chica!" he says. Against my better judgment, I stand off to the side to wait for him after I exit the building.

"You good?" he asks, taking in my expression. I haven't been able to shake off the scene I had with Chain. It felt so real, so... damning.

I don't know what I did to deserve his anger, but I *know* it was directed at me.

"Today was a lot, I'm just tired," I say dismissively. Eli keeps pace with me as I rush towards my car.

"You were amazing," he tells me. "*Amazing.*"

I dismiss his comment with a wave as I reach my car. "I'll see you at work Monday."

He watches me intently for a moment before absorbing me in a hug. "For sure, you've got a short week! Lucky."

I unlock my door and sit in the driver's seat, tossing my bag next to me. I close my eyes, lean back against the headrest, and inhale the biggest breath I've taken all day.

I hear Eli's engine roar to life next to me and exhale, opening my eyes. Putting my keys in the ignition, I start my own car and wave to Eli. As I move to shift my car into reverse, a knock at the window causes me to jump.

I place my hand over my heart when I see Chain's wide frame. I roll down the window, my heart pounding a mile a minute.

"You scared the *shit* out of me, Chain," I confess.

"Sorry, I didn't mean to scare you."

What about onstage?

"No problem, what's up?" I manage to say, fighting the thoughts whirring in my brain. The momentary scare distracted me from the scene we had. With his looming presence in my window, it returns full force.

Why did you jump in when Jon was questioning me? What was with all the anger in that scene? Why did it feel like we weren't just acting?

"I just wanted to make sure you understood that I was acting up there," he says earnestly, as if reading my thoughts. When I don't reply, he says, "*We* were acting."

"I know," I mumble. *Why does it feel like we weren't, then?*

"Good. Have a nice night, send my regards to your boyfriend," he says. He lingers a moment, and I examine him. His eyes are so green, and yet I can hardly see their brightness in the nightfall. His stance is domineering, his hand on the door frame above my window, demanding that I give him my attention.

"Say hi to Ashley," I reply and shift my car into reverse. I roll the window up, forcing myself to focus on the road. I don't give him another glance as I back out, turn, and exit the lot.

On the drive home, I process the events that transpired, the words from our scene replaying in my mind.

You thought wrong.

Chain hasn't been privy to my thoughts, yet the statement felt so personal. Is this all in my head, then? Could I have imagined the defense he took up for me? And the anger he felt when we were doing our scene?

He's a lawyer. It's his job to defend and protect people. I should know—my ex wanted to study law. I don't know if he ever did, seeing as we broke up before finishing undergrad.

Chain was angry because I cut him off and Jon wasn't intimidated by him. Attorneys get their kicks from dominating people, and I, for one, am not going to be prey to that again.

Chain doesn't deserve to occupy space in my head, rent free. As I park my car and walk into the condo I share with Zander, I decide to formally evict Chain and any future thoughts of him that might be waiting to steal any more from me.

Thursday morning, after rolling our packed bags to the car, I call Stella as Zander loads up the truck.

"We're heading out now, I'm waiting on *Jason* to finish getting his crap together," she answers. She doesn't miss a beat, this girl.

"We're putting our bags in the truck and we're going to stop for coffee," I reply, a smile on my face.

Stella bitches a lot about Jace. It's another facade, because I know she adores him as much as he adores her. They call each other out on their shit, and I love them for it.

"See you soon. I'm gonna light the fire under his ass," she says, the sound of her yelling, "Jason!" in the background before she clicks.

I keep my phone in my hand as Zander puts the last bag into the backseat of his truck. As much as I love my little Blueberry, she doesn't do well on the highway.

I open my music collection and sift through, landing on the perfect song to start our trip. We get into the car and I connect the aux cable. We both have older cars, and

Zander loves his as much as I love mine. They're familiar, comfortable, and serve their purpose.

"Let's go!" Zander exclaims, and I hit play on "Take on the World" by You Me At Six.

When we first started dating, we'd return home and lay on his bed to cuddle. We were listening to my music station, and this song started playing. He turned to me suddenly and said, "This is our song."

After the song plays for a minute, I look over at Zander and smile. "It's our song," I tell him.

He reaches for my hand and squeezes, linking them between us on the console. "I know."

My mood slowly went from excited to agitated. For some reason, the monotony in our relationship is all I've thought about on our two and a half hour drive to Archer, Florida. Have we always been this... boring?

We switched to Zander's playlist halfway through the drive and hardly spoke a word to each other. "It's only fair," I'd told him, pulling out the aux cord.

Pulling up to the open gates of the farm, I shake off the negative energy. There's a breeze that has the tree leaves swaying gently, welcoming a sense of peace to overtake me.

We pull into the driveway and see Jace's red Mazda RX parked behind his grandpa's old, single cab Ford F-150. The gray paint is peeling off the doors and hood, but the engine still operates as if it rolled off the lot yesterday. Zander parks his truck behind Jace's car and I open the door, stretching my legs in the open space.

"We made it!" Zander says, hopping out of the truck and slamming the door. I place my feet on the ground and a black labrador rushes from around the truck, licking my feet excitedly in greeting.

"Aw, hi, Lucy," I say to her. She looks up at the mention of her name and leaps her front paws onto my thighs. I rub behind her ears and give her kisses as she licks my face.

We've stayed at the farm with Jace and Stella once before, when she graduated college with her degree in teaching. She works with kindergartners, and she loves it. Her family and Jace's family threw her a party. Being her best friend meant I absolutely had to be there.

"Ayyy," Jace says from the front porch. It's divided in two by the entry door Stella walks out of. They meet us at the truck as Zander pulls out our bags.

"Lucy, down!" Stella says and Lucy leaps off, running laps around the truck.

I give Stella and Jace a hug before helping Zander bring the bags inside. I walk past the dining room to our left and into the kitchen, where Grandma Brookes is cooking.

"Marlie! Oh, how are you, dear?" she shouts, putting the spatula on the holder and rushing over to me. She takes me into her warm embrace, then clasps my shoulders as she gives me a once over.

"I'm good, so excited to be here," I gush. She tells me I look great then moves to hug Zander, who's walked up behind me.

"Come on, babe, I'll help you put your bags in the room," Stella tells me. She grabs the bags from Zander while he catches up with Grandma and Jace. Stella leads me across the living room and to the left, opening the bedroom door at the end of the small hallway.

"I can't believe we're here. It's officially happening," I say brightly to Stella, grinning.

"I know, right?! Now let's get to work."

"I can't believe how much we were able to get done today," Jace says, cracking his can of beer open and taking three massive gulps.

"Jeez, Jace, how can you drink like that?" I comment.

"Impressive," Zander adds, opening his own beer and taking an average sized gulp. It's only a matter of time before they get into a shotgun competition.

"I can't chug to save my life," I say with a giggle. Stella takes a sip of her beer through her own laugh.

This is exactly the moment I've been looking forward to for months. Sharing drinks with my best friends, inhaling the cool air, and taking a load off.

We're gathered at the white, plastic table on the front porch. Zander and I sit in separate plastic chairs opposite Stella and Jace. The other side of the porch has a built-in swing, which I intend to use while drinking my coffee in the morning with Zander.

I brought monopoly with us and it lays, unopened, between us on the table. We've got a cooler full of beer, and three citronella candles lit atop the railings. They provide a comforting, flickering light.

I sip my beer calmly, feeling better than I have in months. It's taken just one day being on the farm to know that I've been in a slump. Life has become routine, but this weekend I plan to break right out of it.

"Okay, so tomorrow night we're staying at the TripleLeaf Hotel?" I ask.

"Yep, my mom paid and we've got separate rooms. Can't let him sleep with the bride before the wedding night," Stella says with a wink.

"I'll have you all to myself," Zander jokes with Jace.

"Fuck yeah, we're going to party it up!" he replies with a shit eating grin.

"You better be back here on time for the reveal, or I'll kill you." Stella punches Jace lightly on the shoulder, and he grabs her fist, kissing it.

"You know I will, baby," he says.

"I can't believe this is it. Saturday, you guys will be married," I say thoughtfully. "You've been together five years, it makes sense."

"You've been there for it all, bestie," Stella says. I've heard about all their fights, their joys, and everything in between.

"Oh my god, are you going to start having babies?" I wrinkle my nose involuntarily. *I'm not ready for any of that yet.*

"They better, we need a third player," Zander jokes.

"I can't start having kids until you do, Marlie," Stella says. "Our kids are going to be best friends."

"Pfft, then you've got a while to go," I respond. I take a large swig of my beer and place it on the table, wiping the back of my hand across my lips to keep them dry. The sun has completely set and night is settling in, chilling the air.

"What, you don't want kids?" Zander looks over at me.

"Maybe, I don't know," I say dismissively. "Definitely not now, or anytime soon."

"Oh," Zander says dejectedly. There's an awkward silence where we each alternate between drinking our beers and placing them on the table.

"I can't wait to have kids," Jason says in an attempt to break the tension.

"I definitely want to have kids," Zander says, turning to face me fully. "You really don't know?"

Haven't we talked about this before? I try but find I can't think back to a time where we've discussed children. We've talked repeatedly about saving for a house and have put away a large amount of money. We've always included each other in our plans for the future. But somehow, it seems we've never talked about starting a family.

"I, uh, guess I haven't given it much thought," I mumble through my surprise. I'd even talked about kids with my college ex, who made it very clear he was never interested. That was *before* he cheated on me. Maybe it was a red flag. But then again, I'm not even sure I want them myself.

Bringing my thoughts to the present, I go on. "I don't even know if I want to get married, let alone start a family."

No one speaks. The silence is heavy, bulldozing the peace I felt mere moments ago. I peek at Stella, who is fiddling with the pull-tab on her can. Jace downs the rest of his beer, then stands up and grabs a fresh one from the cooler.

"That's not a big deal, right?" I say nervously to Zander. "We've never discussed getting married."

"I mean, I definitely see myself getting married," Zander responds. He won't look at me. He's staring at the majestic oak tree with Spanish moss draped throughout.

"Hey." I reach for his arm and rub it soothingly. "I haven't given it much thought, I'm just saying I'm not in a place where I'm ready."

"Will you ever be?" He moves his arm lightly, my hand dropping to the arm of his chair. I stare at him.

"Uh—"

"Marlie's probably just feeling jealous of us," Jace jokes.

Zander and I whip our heads to him. I give him a somber look and turn back to Zander.

"I'm not sure why this matters so much. If we love each other and want to be together, isn't that enough?"

"People who love each other get married," Zander presses.

"I don't agree with that," I snap. "People get married for all kinds of reasons. And there are plenty of other couples who love each other and never get married."

The cold air hovers over my bare arm, the heat radiating on my skin preventing it from penetrating. I can't remember the last time Zander and I have argued about anything. We bicker from time to time over who needs to do the dishes, or that kind of thing. But the real stuff?

I focus my thoughts on figuring out when the last time we fought was. Anything to avoid the tension that hangs over us like a dark cloud.

"That's it!" I exclaim, remembering.

"What's it, Marlie?" Zander says to me harshly.

"I couldn't remember the last time we fought," I say with ill-timed fervor.

"We're not fighting," he retorts. "And I'm not sure how previous fights have anything to do with this."

"This feels like a fight," I tell him. I sink into the memory from last summer, thinking it better to leave it unsaid. We went on a trip with his parents and his mom had made a passing comment about my hair. I hadn't washed it in days and she called me unkempt. I stayed quiet, because it was my first trip with his family. But Zander did, too. That night, I had it out with him.

The fight itself didn't last very long, but I was really hurt. I felt completely judged and unwanted, and then my own boyfriend didn't even back me up. He explained that he's always had an issue standing up to his mother, and told me to just ignore her because she judges everybody.

My feelings eventually dissipated and I let it go. It was the last night of our trip, so we left the next morning and I haven't had to suffer through any other outings with his family. I've only been to their house a few times for dinner since.

"Maybe you guys just need to figure out how you feel about it?" Jace offers.

"Yeah, remember Jason didn't want to get married for a while there," Stella pipes up.

"I didn't not want to get married, I just didn't want to at that time," Jace amends. They exchange a frustrated look before turning back to us.

"Whatever, the point is that obviously Marlie just needs to think about how she feels about marriage," Stella says.

"Just like she had to think about being exclusive with me, right?" Zander accuses.

"What the fuck?" I'm completely thrown. "That bothered you?"

"Of course it did! Who wouldn't be bothered by that?" he blows out.

I think back to that night when we listened to You Me At Six.

"This is our song."

Zander turns to me and kisses me slowly, his tongue gently brushing on my lower lip, waiting for permission. I grant it, my tongue meeting his. They mingle slowly, savoring every twirl.

I pull away, opening my eyes. "Why?"

"Because. I want to take on the world together."

I smile and he pulls back, looking at me intensely. "Please, be my girlfriend. I love what we have."

"Me too," I say breathlessly. He's so sweet and kind.

"Yeah?" His eyes brighten, and it's the cutest thing.

"Yeah!" I giggle and kiss him, exploding within.

"She was crushed by her ex, you have no idea what that was like." Stella defending me catapults me back to the present.

I look over at her, then back to Zander.

"No, he's right," I say. "I have a problem with commitment, I guess."

"In major part because of that dickhead!" Stella argues.

"I know, but that's not on Zander," I say. Jack was my first true love, and he destroyed my heart. I wasn't innocent before college, but Jack was the first guy I really fell for. He took advantage of my naivety and trust, cheating on me at parties while I was working.

When I got suspicious, he made me feel crazy and I believed his lies. When Stella and I finally figured it out, I confronted him. The breakup was messy, and he denied the cheating. To this day, he's only admitted to it happening once. I felt humiliated and stupid. I believed that I was crazy, betraying myself in the process. I lost trust in not only him, but everyone. How many of his friends kept silent, knowing what he was doing?

"I get it, but I'm not that guy, Marlie," Zander says.

"I'm not still torn up about that." It's partially true. I did a lot of work on myself and made peace with what happened. I learned to trust myself and others, and it's mostly restored. But there are some things the heart won't forget, and being shattered into pieces and ripped out by someone who was your everything is one of them.

"When you're with the right person, everything falls into place," Jace says.

The right person...

That idea was torn from me in tandem with my heart. Am I willing to open myself up and let it back in?

Chapter Twelve

Marlie

My coffee is on the front porch railing, likely ice cold from the frost in the air. And my neglect.

I've been swinging, alone, for 45 minutes. Zander still hasn't left the room. We all had a few more beers and started a game of monopoly, the pieces left hopefully on the board atop the table.

When Zander and I returned to the room, we busied ourselves preparing for bed and taking turns using the bathroom. The only sound was that of our looming emotions, waiting to explode. Every avoidance of eye contact, every sidestepping of our bodies, was tectonic plates pulling apart in the volcano that was threatening to erupt.

We finally laid down in bed on our respective sides which we replicated from our normal sides at home: me on the left, him on the right. I laid still, my arms pressed anxiously to my sides and my wide eyes glued to the ceiling. I hadn't looked at him, but I could feel him mirroring my position.

The pressure was building and I feared we couldn't avoid the explosion that was ready to destroy.

I could no longer ignore the chasm in my chest that had fissured. The river of my emotions steamed with the heat of our discussion, eager to escape and preventing me from stitching it closed.

Zander wants to get married. I think I always knew that deep down, but my persistent hold over the hole where my feelings hide allowed me to ignore it. I realized, laying motionless in a foreign bed, that maybe I've never thought about marriage because I didn't want to know what that meant.

I didn't want to face the trust issues I buried deep within. I didn't want to face the potential that Zander may not want me if he knew I wasn't willing to get married, or start a family.

But do I really want him?

What? Of course I want Zander. I just don't know if I want the traditional life. The simple story of man meets woman, falls in love, marries her, and has babies. It's a lot of pressure, and it doesn't equate to love. I know that much to be true. But do I really not want to get married?

As if he'd read my thoughts, Zander shattered the palpable silence. "Is it that you don't believe in marriage?"

I took my time formulating a response. I tried to respond with my brain, but the troubled waters in the newly opened chasm crashed against the walls, demanding my attention.

"Kind of," I said feebly.

"Kind of?"

I let out a breath I didn't know I was holding. "I believe in marriage for others, I just don't know if it's right for me."

"Could it be?" He turned his face to mine but I kept my eyes fixed up, roaming between kernels of popcorn on the acoustic ceiling.

Could it? I don't consider myself against marriage. I see benefits to both sides, but I haven't decided which side of the coin I land on.

"I'm really not sure," I told him. I'd finally turned and returned his stare. "I will think about it, I promise. It's not fair to you and I don't want to put you through this."

"I love you, Marlie," he said, but he didn't have to. I saw it in the way his brown eyes moved ever so slightly, bouncing between my eyes. “It’s not like this is a deal breaker for me. I’ll be happy any way I can have you.”

The effect of his words took over as I felt his love emanating on to me, but a part of me felt off. Why is he so willing to sacrifice his own beliefs? And if he’ll be happy any way he can have me, why were we talking about this at all?

Zander has never given me a reason not to trust him. He’s been so good to me. We rarely fight. He loves me, and I love him, too.

Right? The crashing waves unsettled me, shaking the foundation I’ve stood on for so long with him.

“I love you, too,” I told him. He gave me a light kiss and rolled over, facing the wall with his back to me. I resumed my examination of the ceiling textures.

I thought I wouldn’t sleep well that night. I didn’t know I wouldn’t sleep at all.

Try as I did to keep the chasm shut, it had opened. The waters made themselves known and they showed no signs of relenting.

I reach for my now iced coffee on the porch railing and take a gulp. I swing gently, urging the wind to sweep away the lingering emotions from last night. The caffeine isn’t nearly as effective as I need it to be, only insulating the frigid feelings of my ever-present distance from Zander.

I hear the screen door open and turn, finding Stella in a bulky jacket with a mug of steaming coffee in tow. I turn back to the oak tree on the front lawn, avoiding her scrutiny. I scoot over so she can take the seat next to me as she mumbles good morning.

When I don’t respond, she rubs her eyes and looks over at me. “You didn’t make up, did you?”

I shake my head, staring down at my cold coffee. I have gloves on, so the chill from the mug can’t merge with my already frozen heart.

"Wanna talk about it?" she asks softly.

"I wouldn't know where to start," I reply just as quietly. "I mean we kind of made up, but I don't feel any better." She takes a sip of her warm coffee, offering the mug to me when she notices the lack of steam in mine. I place my cup back on the railing and take hers.

"Are you happy with Zander?"

Her question cuts through the red tape surrounding my denial. *Happy?* I've never thought I *wasn't* happy with Zander. The events of last night rattled the secure foundation I stood on, and I couldn't think straight with the residual tremors. My emotions were reduced to tumbling rubble that I need to sort through, but I can't seem to summon the strength to do so.

Looking away, I slowly reply. "I love Zander. We're building towards a future, we get along. Things are great."

Stella stays oh-so-silent, and it speaks volumes, but she doesn't want to push. I'm about to beg her to say something, anything, but the door opening interrupts us.

Zander stands in the center of the doorframe looking rested but uncertain, like he's been taken over by the same lingering presence of thoughts from last night.

"Hi," he whispers softly. Electricity hums down my arms to my fingertips. I faintly return my own hi.

He begins the walk down the short steps off the porch and nods his head to the left. Reading the signal, Stella pats my leg and I stand up to follow him. Stella doesn't say a word, and I'm so grateful to her for it.

We walk away from the house and the oak tree. There's a large space with a smaller spruce tree that hosts a bench swing Jace's grandpa made for the grandkids. Zander turns and takes a seat on it.

I move to stand next to the swing when he reaches out and takes my hands in his tenderly. The action causes my eyes to water, and I watch as he begins to trace gentle circles over the backs of my gloves.

"I want to apologize," he begins. His words cause my eyes to shoot up to his. *He's* sorry?!

Seeing the lone tear that trickles its way down my cheek, he drops one of my hands to catch it on my jaw. I start to move my head back down, feeling ashamed.

Why should he be the one that's sorry?

He prevents me from doing so by dragging his hand from my jaw to my chin and lifting it with a slight nudge.

"Don't." He fixes his eyes on me. The tears begin to fall freely, gushing from the open chasm and leaving me dry. I start to sob, and he moves his hand around while standing up, bringing my head to his shoulders.

"I shouldn't have pushed it," he whispers into my ear. "It's not a big deal, it really isn't. It just took me by surprise."

I sob harder. A sob so hard, you don't even know why you're crying anymore. I pull back but he holds my head down. This angers me, and I rip my head and hand out of his grip before taking a step back.

"You don't get to be the one who apologizes," I tell him.

"What? What are you talking about?" It takes me a moment to recognize the emotions behind his eyes. He looks confused and... hurt. It's foreign to me. This is the first time I really lose my grip around him.

"I'm the one telling you I may never want to get married! That I may not even *believe* in getting married! And *you're* apologizing?!" I shout. He gawks at me. I've never shouted at him like this. I've never revealed this much emotion. I keep it tucked away, refusing to ever show weakness again.

After a few seconds, he recovers. "Marlie, you owe me nothing." He sits back down on the swing and takes my hands in his again, pulling me closer.

"If I don't want to get married, what happens to us?" The tears have slowed, the anger causing them to dissipate.

He laughs, but the humor doesn't reach his eyes. "We do what we've been doing. We keep saving money, we'll buy our house, and figure out what's next."

His affirmation pacifies me. I look into his brown eyes, a brown so different than my own. The nearly ebony shades somehow glow in the light of the rising sun. The temperature is warming as well, and I suddenly feel the need to remove my jacket.

I move to pull my hands away but Zander holds them firmly in his grip. I'm not used to him taking charge like this, and he hurries his words before I can resist him.

"I just want you. That's it," he says, his voice cracking with the raw need for me. I let him keep my hands in his. I force a smile, unsure of why I don't feel relieved.

"I want you to be happy," I tell him. *Can you be happy with what I'm willing to give you?*

"I am happy. I have you, that's all I need."

"What if it's not enough?"

"You'll always be enough."

I try to let his words settle into my heart. It's the words any woman would want to hear from their man. *Why don't I feel better, then?*

Unaware of how long I've been silent, Zander pulls me from my thoughts. "Aren't you happy with me?"

I see the hope that had filled his eyes moments ago waver. *No, don't leave.*

"I love you, Zander," I tell him, more tears slipping from my eyes.

"I love you, Marlie." He leans forward and I meet his lips for a soft, feather light kiss.

When I start to pull back, his hand rushes forward and pushes the back of my head, forcing our lips to stay connected. He thrusts his tongue in my mouth, hurried and rushed. I feel his need for me to meet this kiss with passion, with equal fervor. To show him that we're okay, to prove that we love each other.

Before I can try, Jace shouts at us. "Lovebirds, get in the damn house! Breakfast and go time!"

Zander tears his lips from mine. "Coming!" he shouts to Jace, then moves his gaze back to me.

"I'm going to think about this marriage stuff and give you a proper answer," I tell him seriously.

"Babe, don't worry about it. I'm happy either way." He smiles at me, and I finally feel a bit better. I smile back, and we take off towards the house to get started for the day.

Chapter Thirteen

Marlie

"IT'S HAPPENING!" I shout. Zander, Stella, and Jace laugh, and I lean back in my seat, grinning widely.

We set up just about everything for the wedding tomorrow. The hired companies dropped off the bench seats for the ceremony, and the tent, tables, and chairs for the reception. The entire wedding is going to be held outdoors.

Stella and I sifted through all the decorations we previously crafted or purchased while Jason and Zander set up all the fixtures. Close family members arrived throughout the day and assisted, which led to us finishing earlier than we anticipated. We rehearsed the ceremony twice, which was done efficiently due to the minimal amount of people involved.

When the DJ played the piano tribute of their song, "A Thousand Years" by Chrishtina Perri, my eyes glistened with the emotion of watching Stella walk out of the barn and up the aisle we created between the bench seats. I can't think of a couple who is more perfect for each other than Stella and Jace.

I feel loads better, and I had today's work to thank for it. Helping set up for the celebration of their love reminded me of my love for Zander, and before I knew it yesterday's argument had drifted away. The chasm's waters left me in peace.

Jace blasts the radio as we drive along the interstate to the TripleLeaf Hotel. We belt out the lyrics until he lowers the volume when we pull into the hotel parking lot, earning himself obnoxious boo's from the rest of us. We grab our overnight bags from the trunk and he locks the doors with his fob.

We enter the lobby, which has an open layout leading to the front desk. Behind it is a long bar that loops into a half oval, overlooking the pool. To the left is an opening to a patio area, adorned with patio furniture and games. Strung lights line the bar and across the patio, the amber bulbs twinkling at us.

Jace and Stella check in while Zander and I wait on a couch in the lobby with all of our bags. We pull our phones out and catch up on notifications we were too busy to check while we were preparing today.

Jace and Stella interrupt my Instagram scrolling, confirming we're all checked in. We head to the elevators and up to the 5th floor, where our rooms are located. Zander and Jace's room comes before ours, so we stop at their door to say goodbye.

"I'll see you tomorrow," Zander says to me. He holds me in a loving stare that I return with a smile.

"Can't wait. I'll miss you tonight," I tell him.

"Me, too."

"I love you."

He presses a kiss to my lips before giving me a warm hug. "I love you too, babe."

Stella and Jace finish their goodbye at the same time.

"You better not be late!" She shouts to Jace as we leave. "I'm holding you responsible, Zander."

"We'll be there! Can't promise how many pieces we'll be in though," he says with a smirk before they rush into their room and slam the door shut.

We laugh as we make our way to our room. Stella scans the key card and we enter, each claiming a bed by placing our bags atop.

In an effort to keep the wedding small, Stella and Jace decided not to have groomsmen and bridesmaids. We left our dresses at the farm, where we would be getting dressed after getting our hair done in the morning.

So tonight, we were free to do whatever we wanted. I glance at the alarm clock centered on the night stand between our queen-sized beds: 7:25 pm.

I look over to Stella, who is unzipping her bag. "What do you want to do tonight, my queen?" I feign a royal bow with a pompous look.

She pulls out a bottle of champagne from her bag in answer, waving it around and leaping onto the bed.

"Party!" she yells exuberantly.

"Stop shaking the bottle or we won't be able to open it!" I say between laughs as I leap onto the bed and join her.

She ignores me as we start jumping, untwisting the cage around the cork before popping it off. Champagne sprays all over the bed, the nightstand, her bag, and me.

"You asshole!" I shout at her, laughing. I grab the bottle and throw some of the bubbling liquid right on her shirt.

"Ahhh!" she shouts and tackles me. We land on the pillows and laugh as she rolls off of me. The champagne spills onto the bed before I can right the bottle.

"Well, I guess no champagne, then." I place the nearly empty bottle on the table and stand up.

"Pffft, please." She reaches for her bag and pulls out an identical one. "You really think I would have wasted the only bottle I bought?"

"You, my friend, are a genius," I tell her, grinning from ear to ear.

"Duh, that's why you love me."

"There are many reasons I love you."

"I'm listening."

I laugh and take off my now wet shirt, tossing it at her. "Guess you're sleeping on my bed tonight," I say as I glance at the soaked bed comforter.

"I'm sure they have extra sheets, but if not then get ready to cuddle up, bestie." She tosses my dirty shirt by the dresser and follows suit with her own.

She pops the top off the new, unshaken bottle of champagne and the bubbles fizz.

"To me!" She declares, taking a large swig of the elixir before passing it to me.

"To you!" I shout in agreement and match her swig.

I pull out my pajamas from my bag and change while Stella does the same. She walks over to the curtains, pulling them back to reveal the sliding glass door leading to a balcony. She opens the door and steps out.

I follow her lead with the champagne in tow, snagging two glasses from the coffee machine area. Stella leans over the coffee-colored railing and I take a seat in one of the two chairs.

The view is nothing special, revealing the end of the pool deck and plain trees beyond it. To the right is the parking lot, and to the left is a continuation of hotel buildings. We knew we'd get to the hotel late and leave early for all the preparations, so we didn't bother going all out.

Stella takes her seat and I pour us full glasses of champagne. We sip silently as we ruminate. As the calm settles, my thoughts find their way to this morning's conversation with Zander.

As if by telepathy, Stella asks, "So what happened with Zander?"

She's trying to hide her curiosity, but I could tell she put off asking me all day. There were various moments when she'd pause what she was doing, look over at me with her mouth ajar, then snap it shut and return to her task. I didn't press her to tell me what was on her mind because I was happy to leave it alone.

And after the great feeling of today, I don't want to squander it by discussing this marriage thing again. *Especially* on her wedding night.

"He apologized and we made up," I tell her shortly. "He says he wants to be with me no matter what, and I promised to think about the marriage thing."

Sensing my lack of desire to discuss this, she replies, "I'm glad."

We return to our companionable silence, but I can't escape the thoughts of my earlier conversation with Zander.

How am I supposed to figure out how I feel about marriage? The promise I made is weighing on me. The burden has me reaching for my drink, taking three large gulps to bring the desired effect I suddenly crave.

After a few minutes, the alcohol begins to make its way to my brain and I feel vaguely lighter.

"A toast." I raise my glass to Stella. She lifts her glass to meet mine, leaving a small space between them. "To your dreams coming true."

"A-fucking-men!" We clink glasses and drink. I focus on the fizz in my throat as the liquid makes its way to my belly where it can work its magic. I take a few more glugs and polish off my drink. I reach for the bottle and pour more.

"I really hope you brought more of this," I tell her jovially.

"I gotchu, girl, don't worry," she replies, watching as I fill my glass and top hers off. I place the empty bottle beside my chair on the balcony floor, noticing that my chair wobbles to the right with my movement. As I sit back up, the chair wobbles back.

"How do you feel about me and Jace getting married?" she asks me.

"I've told you, like, a million times how happy I am for you guys!"

"I know, I know!" She beams at me. "But you don't see that for yourself?"

I should have known it was a trap. I should have known she wouldn't just let this go.

Sighing, I take another gulp of my drink. My thoughts are beginning to slow. *Thanks, champagne!*

"I don't know, Stella. I'm not against the idea of marriage, I just don't know if I want it for myself."

It's a hard thing to explain to a person who loves the idea of marriage so much. I just never felt like it was the end all, be all. If it feels right, great. If not, it doesn't prove anything. Love can be shared with or without a document confirming a lifelong commitment.

A therapist might say I'm scorned from my parents' relationship, and maybe they're right. I don't personally feel like that's it, though. I honestly think marriage doesn't prove anything other than getting married. Which is great, if you want it, but it's not a need for me.

"I get it," Stella says. I pin her with a disbelieving look. "I do! Look, I get why someone may not ever want that, even if it's just because they're not with the right person."

"Are you saying I'm not with the right person?" I sound more defensive than I intend to.

"No, Marlie," she says with forced patience. "I'm just saying, maybe some people don't want to get married because they haven't found the one."

"And what about me? What's my reason?" The alcohol has loosened my tongue and I speak before I think.

"I think Jack may have fucked you up more than you care to admit," she says after taking a large gulp of her drink, placing the cup on the table between us.

"Not this again," I say argumentatively. *What has gotten into me?* The thought crosses my mind but it's quickly drowned out by my need for answers. I try to take another gulp of my drink and only get my tongue wet before realizing the glass is empty.

"I'm not coming at you, babe. You asked me what I thought," Stella says patiently.

"I'm gonna grab the other bottle," I tell her, standing up. I locate it in her bag before returning outside. I sit down and the chair wobbles again.

"Stupid chair," I mutter, messing with the bottle to try and get it open.

"Give it to me." Stella holds her hand out and I pass it to her, closing my eyes. The world goes dark and I revel in the quietude.

I hear the pop from the bottle and open my eyes, grabbing my glass and holding it out for Stella to pour. She places the bottle down on the table without filling her own glass.

"You're done?" I ask her incredulously. *Okay, the alcohol has definitely taken over.*

"I can't get wasted before my wedding, I'll look like shit in the morning. But have at it," she says encouragingly.

She doesn't have to say it twice. We move into conversation about the last minute preparations and I continue taking large drinks of the champagne.

I'm on my third glass of the new bottle when Stella gushes, "Tomorrow, I'll be Mrs. Brooke's and I'll live happily ever after!"

The amount of alcohol I've consumed prevents me from hearing the humor in her tone.

"What, and if I don't get married I'm doomed to misery for the rest of my life?" I slur the words.

"What? Don't be ridiculous, Marlie," Stella says with a flippant wave of her hand. "That's not what I meant."

"No, I'll tell you what's ridiculous." I stand up and stumble before righting myself. "TripleLeaf needs to fix these FUCKING chairs!"

Stella laughs before telling me to chill out.

"Oh, I'm chill, trust me," I say sardonically. "My heart feels like a damn icicle!"

"Your heart is gold," Stella insists like the best friend she is.

"It's not. This heart of mine is steel," I say while thumping my chest. "Hearts are stupid," I conclude idiotically, unable to think clearly through the haze in my head.

"Let's go to bed," Stella puts her glass down and grabs my hand, leading me inside.

"No, no, no," I tell her while being dragged limply. "It's your wedding night! Oh my god, I'm such an asshole, I'm ruining it. I know! Let's go to the bar downstairs!"

"I didn't want to stay up late, anyway," she says.

"This is the worst party ever."

"The real party is tomorrow. Don't worry about it, babe, seriously."

"One drink downstairs, come on!"

Stella eyes me with an arched brow before grinning. "Fine, but we're going in our PJs."

"Woohoo!"

I'm acting a fool and I don't give a damn. It's my best friend's wedding eve, and I want it to be memorable. We walk downstairs, barefoot and all, and order our usual drinks from the bar.

"No Happy Honey's, tonight," I tell her as she clinks her glass of gin and tonic to my mojito.

"No, ma'am!"

I polish off two mojitos by the time she finishes her gin and tonic. I stay pointedly drunk and we reminisce on college days and fun times.

"Don't you remember when we were at that Rocky Horror party for Arden's birthday?" I laugh as I remind her of one of our favorite parties.

"How could I forget? Jack left you there, *again*, and we got so wasted."

Her comment wipes the smirk right off my face. "Maybe you're right."

"What?"

"Maybe he did fuck me up more than I care to admit."

"No one could blame you, babe. You were in love and he shattered your heart. How could it not?"

I stare at the pool, the soft ripples of water from the jets entrancing me. "Do you think I could get married one day?"

"Aaaaand I'm calling it. It's time for bed. No waterworks on the night before my wedding night!"

"On wedding eve! I'm making it a thing, if it's the last thing I do!" I shout, pointing my finger at no one. I close out our tab and follow Stella back to the elevators and to our room.

I collapse on the center of her bed, uncaring of the spilled champagne that remains on the comforter. "Take my bed, the bride deserves only"—*hiccup*—"the best!" I pump my pointer finger in the air before letting it flop back down on the bed beside my head.

I close my eyes and pass out.

Chapter Fourteen

Chain

I drove out of the parking lot after class feeling a bit down. Class wasn't as exciting as it normally is, though I can't place why. Feeling the need for some excitement, I was hoping some of the classmates would want to get drinks. Most people had a reason to be up early and declined, so me and the willing others decided to call it.

On a whim, I decided to call Ashley. She picks up and answers groggily.

"Get dressed, we're going out," I tell her.

"It's 9:30, Chain. I'm already in bed."

"Come on, how often do we just do something?" When she doesn't answer I say, "It'll be fun."

More silence. I bide my time, letting her decide what I already know will happen. "I'll get dressed."

Ashley gets in the car wearing a black dress that's as basic as it sounds, with red heels and lipstick to match.

"Hello, beautiful," I tell her smoothly. We're going on our first date in months and I'm determined to make it a great one.

"Where are we going?" she asks as she shuts the door and I drive away from the front of our building. I pull a mint from the tin on the dash and pop it in my mouth.

"La Corte della Pioggia."

"Oh, I love their wine selection!" She perks up at the mention of my favorite restaurant, serving traditional French cuisine with waterfront tables.

"As do I," I reply, reaching for her hand and resting them linked on the console.

We get to the restaurant and are walked by the hostess to a private table towards the back of the open patio. We peruse the menu and order our drinks and meals when the server arrives.

"So, tell me something." I sip the water that was waiting for us at the table.

"What do you want to know?" She takes a sip of her own water while looking out at the lake.

"Anything." I continue to watch her as she takes in the view until her blue eyes meet mine. They're crystal clear, even in the minimal lighting provided by the night sky.

"Well, Lauren had an interesting story to tell today." She dives into a long winded explanation of Lauren's reuniting with her ex, or I suppose now, boyfriend.

"... and she just took him back! I honestly can't believe it."

"I can, that bitch lives for the drama." I grab the wine that was placed on our table during her tale, and I take a healthy gulp. The bitterness of the red tonic shocks my senses, and I feel my shoulders relax.

"Jeez, Chain! Watch your mouth. That's my friend you're talking about."

"It's a manner of speaking," I tell her dismissively, admiring the lake.

"Well, we'll see how it plays out," she replies tersely.

"Anything new happening at work?"

"Same old. You wouldn't believe what Rick did this time. He—"

"Rick?" I interrupt.

"The firm's new partner. Keep up, Chain." I turn to her and keep my thoughts to myself. *I don't give a shit about your work problems.*

She rants about the issues, but for the life of me I can't keep focus on whatever the hell she's saying. I continue my watch of the lake and take in a deep breath, focusing on the calm ripples from the delicate breeze. I nod and "oh, really?" at the appropriate gaps in her speech.

She concludes her story as the waiter brings our food. We eat in silence, enjoying the taste of the cuisine and polishing off our wines.

"Would you like to see the dessert menu?" the server asks while he clears our dishes.

"No, but I'll take a bottle of the same wine to go."

When the server walks away, Ashley gives me a puzzled look.

"You said you like the wine."

"Oh. That's nice of you," she says in a flat tone, unimpressed.

The server brings the bill and bottle of wine. I glance and tuck enough cash to cover the meal and tip into the binder.

Standing up, I hold my hand out to Ashley. She takes it with a radiating smile that doesn't reach her eyes. I recognize it well, having seen it at parties for our firms where I traipse her on my arm. She lives for appearances and I don't mind, because I use it to my advantage just the same.

We've perfected our show, and we perform it skillfully.

I excuse myself from Ashley as we walk towards the front of the restaurant so I can use the bathroom. When I reach the narrow hallway, I notice a small table between the doors with a small, brass scale on it. I've never noticed it before.

Thinking of my conversation with Marlie, I snap a picture of it to send to her. As I use the bathroom, I find her name in my contacts and prepare the message to send. Seeing her name on my screen sends me back to our moment at the bar.

I'm sure you do. You bring the scales of justice to an even keel.

The way her eyes glimmered flashes through my mind and I glance back down at my phone. It dawns on me at that moment why class felt boring today.

A small nagging voice in the back of my head whispers to me. *This isn't right.* My stomach does this weird flipping thing, and that's when it occurs to me...

Am I getting feelings for this woman?

Deciding against sending the photo, I delete the pending message and tuck my phone back into my pocket. I wash my hands and meet Ashley at the front of the restaurant.

"Have a drink with me," I say, holding our apartment door open for her. I head directly into the kitchen off the entryway while she walks towards the bedroom. I search for the corkscrew opener and bring down two wine glasses, placing them on the counter while I open the bottle.

"I'm tired," Ashley says from the doorway to the room. She's already changed into her pajamas, the hot pink satin reflecting brightly from the kitchen light I turned on.

"Come on, one drink."

"Fine, one drink," she says.

I grab the glasses and bottle, moving towards the couch and placing them on our coffee table. I sit in the middle and Ashley lands to the left. I pour our drinks, set them down, then tell Alexa to play a dinner playlist.

As a soft melody begins to play, I grab her around the waist and scoot her closer to me, placing my hand on her thigh. She reaches for her glass and takes a sip, moaning.

"God, that wine really is fabulous," she says.

"You're fabulous," I tell her and lean forward to kiss her. When she moves her head away and takes another sip, I ignore it. I take my own glass and chug it in one go.

"Well, that's one way to enjoy it," Ashley says bitterly.

"I'm ready for a second glass. I'll enjoy that one properly." I pour and sit back, placing my hand on her thigh and running a slow trail with my fingertips.

"I'm not in the mood, Chain," she says.

"Not in the mood for what?" I reply coyly.

"Sex."

I remove my hand and take a large drink from my glass. "Okay. What are you in the mood for?"

"I promised you this drink, then I'm going to bed."

I get up and open the curtains to the balcony, allowing the moonlight to enter the room. I return to my seat and put my arm around her shoulders.

"I just want to feel close to you." It was true to a degree. I didn't want us to be completely isolated from each other. The extra rigidness of the past few weeks was eating at me, especially after today's class.

"Then maybe you shouldn't have signed up for an improv class on our *only* night together." The ice in her tone sends a stab of guilt into my chest.

"Is that what this has been about?"

"I'm just saying."

"If this was still bothering you, why didn't you say something?"

"As if you'd care."

"I do care. You're not giving me a chance to care if I don't know."

"Of course it's bothering me, Chain. We're both so busy, we work late, you work weekends, we have families to keep up with."

"Once this class is over, we'll have Friday nights again."

"I just don't understand why you had to sign up for it at all. Am I not enough for you?"

Her question reverberates in my mind. She was. She used to be. I mean, she still is... right?

"Of course, baby." I finally say. Her eyes narrow at me at the use of baby, rather than love, but I press on. "I signed up because I thought it would be something that could further my comedic interests and—"

"Not this again! Are you seriously still considering that?"

"What's your problem?" I chug the rest of my wine and refill my cup.

"My problem? I expect us to start getting serious soon, Chain. I'm 28! You just turned 29. Did you really expect to just keep things the same?"

I frown. "Serious, how?"

"For starters, I'd like to buy this apartment. Then maybe a wedding, start a family! Something, Chain."

"I—I—" I clamp my mouth shut. I'm not a man who stutters. I take a big gulp of my drink and start again. "I'm not sure where this is coming from."

"Coming from?! God, you can be so *obtuse* when you want to be. And damn it, turn this music off!" She's started shouting. I yell at Alexa to turn the music off and return my attention to Ashley.

The sudden head movements mixed with the alcohol have my mind reeling, and the buzz takes effect.

"Better?" I ask.

"Much."

"We can talk about a future, if that's what you want."

"Is that what *you* want, Chain?"

I'm tipsy and I feel my self-restraint loosening. "Right now, I want you."

"Huh?"

I give her a wink and she slams her glass on the table, the wine sloshing violently.

Normally, I'd want to soothe her by this point and settle the anger that's bursting at her seams. But the alcohol took the front seat and I don't have the desire to fight what it wants me to do, so I remain silent.

"I'm done here, good night." She storms into the room and I chug the rest of the wine in my glass before setting it down next to the half full one she left behind.

This woman is talking about marriage and kids?! I guess I shouldn't be surprised. She's obsessed with looking up fucking weddings and loves to show me all the rings her friends get. Man, I really have been obtuse. *Fuck, I'm not dealing with this shit right now.*

I stare out of the window at the full moon. I tell Alexa to turn the music back on and lower the volume. The third glass of wine is creeping through my system and I allow myself to get lost in the brain fog taking over.

I sit back on the couch and before I know it, I fall asleep.

I wake up to sunlight shining directly on me through the window. It takes me a moment to realize I'm laying on the couch in yesterday's clothes. I rub my eyes and stand up, stretching. I turn to head to the bathroom and jump back in surprise.

"Shit, I didn't see you there," I grumble to Ashley, who's standing in the kitchen, staring at me.

"I want to talk to you." She doesn't move. The way she's ogling at me with wide eyes and her arms folded across her chest gives me an eerie feeling.

"Well, let me use the bathroom first." I take my time brushing my teeth and return to the couch, landing with a dull thud.

"Come sit," I tell Ashley, patting the spot next to me. I can feel the tension rolling off of her and I just want to go back to our normal routine.

"I think we should consider couples counseling."

I gape openly at her. *She's lost her fucking mind.*

"Couples counseling?" I finally repeat.

"We're at a difficult point in our relationship and I think it would be helpful."

I'm rendered utterly speechless, which is not common for me. I'm out of my element, not knowing where to begin.

I feel my phone vibrate and I hold up my finger to her, pulling it from my pocket and glancing at the screen.

Marlie iMessage

Chapter Fifteen

Marlie

"I'm telling you, she was determined to get drunk." Stella's whispers stirs me from my sleep. My head pounds and I don't open my eyes, refusing to let the blinding light in.

"I don't know, I hope not," she says in a hushed voice.

What is she talking about? I stay silent so as not to alert her that I'm awake and listening.

"Yeah, I know. That would suck. But I want what's best for her." There's a long silence after her statement. *She must be talking to Jace.*

"Yeah," she says. She sounds worried; maybe even sad?

"Okay. I love you, too."

Deciding it's a good time to let her know I'm up, I shift on the bed. The movement causes my head to throb.

"Well, good morning, sunshine!" Stella shouts purposefully.

"Urgh," I reply, the pounding in my head making it difficult to speak. I hear her footsteps and then she shouts in my ear.

"Rise and shine!" She rips the blanket off me, sending a waft of spoiled champagne in my direction.

"Not without ibuprofen and a gallon of water," I whine, wrinkling my nose.

"Done and done!" I hear a cup land on the nightstand and raise my thudding head.

"You're the best," I mumble before reaching for the water and pills. I pop them in my mouth and down the water.

"Let's go, we're getting our hair done in half an hour!" She runs over to the bathroom and I hear her turn on the shower.

I get out of bed and follow her in with my bag of toiletries, fixing myself up. The mint in the toothpaste heightens my senses as I brush my teeth, and I begin to replay last night's events.

"Thanks for sending my drunk ass to bed," I tell her after spitting out the toothpaste.

"No problem, bestie," she shouts, pulling the shower curtain to reveal her face and soapy hair. "And don't start feeling bad, I wanted to go to bed early. It worked out perfectly!"

I finish brushing the tangles out of my hair. "Come on, let's go grab some food downstairs," I say as my stomach grumbles.

"Yes, I'm starving!" She closes the curtain and I exit the bathroom, getting our bags together so we can leave.

Once we're both ready, we head down to the hotel lobby's small snack area. We each grab a water bottle from the fridge and turn to the area filled with containers of cereal. The rack is against a small table in the middle that holds small baskets of fruit. In the center is a large, decorative scale.

Why there's a scale in the middle of a TripleLeaf Hotel, I have no idea, but it causes me to think of Chain immediately.

I take justice very seriously.

I smile at the memory and pull my phone out, snapping a photo of the scale before opening my messages and entering Chain's name. When his name pops up, I select it as Stella peers over my shoulder.

"I'm sending this to Chain, we were just talking about justice and I think he would really like it." I press send.

"Oh, cool," Stella says carefully.

"What?"

"I didn't say anything." She reaches out and grabs a container of Frosted Flakes. I grab Cheerios and we head to the counter.

"It was too perfect not to send," I tell her, though I'm not sure if I'm trying to convince her or myself.

"I get it," she says, pulling out her card to pay. I beat her to it and swipe before she gets the chance.

"He's just a friend," I continue.

"I know." She picks up our cereal and we each hold onto our bottles. "Come on."

Jace's Grandma waits for us in Grandpa's truck, since Jace and Zander left with the car we came in.

"Did you say I have a heart of gold last night?" I giggle as she gets in the car.

"You do," she says simply, shutting the passenger door.

I open the back door and slide into the truck. Once we start driving, the open chasm makes itself known to me after 24 hours of avoidance. The water ripples against the walls, sending a quake of dismay to my abdomen.

Does a person with a heart of gold feel so unsure?

We're dressed and waiting in the room at the farm opposite of where Zander and I slept when we stayed here. Stella peers through the window blinds nervously, watching as guests begin to arrive. I glance at my phone for the millionth time, but there are still no new notifications.

Stop. It doesn't matter if he texts you back.

"Two minutes 'til the first look," I tell her, walking up to peer out of the window with her. She's absolutely stunning in an off-white illusion wedding dress, her large breasts just peeking out of the V-neck line. The straps are thin with embellishments that travel down the length of the dress, ending at the small train that's currently buttoned up behind her. Her sparkling silver heels match her eyeshadow, and her hair is styled with a flower crown and a side braid.

Her fresh bouquet of sunflowers and baby's breath waits on the bed next to my bouquet of white hydrangeas and a single sunflower at the border. My seafoam dress is a strapless sweetheart cut with lace that reaches the floor. My hair is half up with soft curls and I wear light makeup.

"I'm ready," she declares, turning from the window and shutting the blinds tight. She adjusts her dress and grabs her bouquet as I reach for mine. She gives me a tight lipped smile and I hold the bedroom door open for her as we escape through the front door and off to the tree where Zander and I talked yesterday morning.

Jace and Stella wanted a private first look. This area is tucked away behind the side of the house, hiding us from view of the arriving guests. I wait with an anxious Stella by the tree, holding her hand to comfort her. We stare at the front of the house where we'll see Jace and Zander emerge.

They appear minutes later, Jace walking leisurely with Zander a few steps behind him. Jace is in a gray suit and white undershirt with a sunflower boutonniere pinned to the pocket. I turn to check on Stella, whose eyes are brimming with tears.

I release her hand and take a few steps back, allowing them their moment. Jace's eyes are filled with tears and they break out in wide smiles as they walk towards each other.

I move my gaze to Zander and feel a lump surge in my throat. I find him studying my appearance, a look of admiration in his dark eyes. His tanned skin contrasts the white dress shirt he wears under a seafoam vest with a matching boutonniere. I give him a small smile, which he returns ten-fold.

Stella takes the remaining steps, closing the distance between her and Jace. He takes her into a loving embrace before stepping back and roaming his eyes over her again.

"You look so beautiful." His words were simple but his inflection said so much more.

"Even more so with you by my side." The truth in her statement is evident in the way she's absolutely glowing. She's a shining beam of light, her eyes twinkling with the reflection of the mid-day sun.

I can't wait to have this moment one day.

The thought surprised me, but I could feel the truth of it in my core. The chasm's waters settled in approval.

The ceremony passed by in a weeping blur. We're now waiting for Stella and Jace to appear in the reception tent so we can all eat. I, for one, am starving. It's open seating, and Zander and I make rounds, saying hello to familiar friends and family members of both Jace and Stella that we've met in the past.

Stella and Jace come in and have their first dance, followed by the opening of the buffet table. We join the line and sit at a table after getting our food. When everyone finishes eating, the DJ makes an announcement before changing the music.

"It's time to get the wedding party out on the dance floor to start the night off right!" he says enthusiastically. Zander and I exchange a look before making our way to the dance floor centered in the tent. I may not have the best moves, but I love to dance. Zander doesn't dance at all.

Stella and Jace meet us there, and the DJ starts playing "Perfect" by Ed Sheeran. Zander stands in front of me cluelessly, so I place one of his hands on my hip and take his other hand in my own. I start swaying my shoulders and he mimics, our feet lifting in turn while remaining in place.

Stella and Jace swing and dance lavishly all around us, and I watch in admiration. We're out of the way, allowing them to show off for all their guests.

"You look... fucking amazing," Zander whispers to me.

"Perfect?" I joke. Zander chuckles. "You do, too." His hair is styled in a way that allows his smile to shine and he's giving me his best one.

"Your eyes look so nice under the lights in here." He inhales deeply. "They're the best brown eyes I've ever seen, including my own."

They're chocolate with swirls of caramel in them...

Chain's words echo in my mind and I still.

Shaking my head and resuming the small movements, I give him a short laugh for his feeble attempt at a joke. He doesn't seem to notice I ever stopped moving, flattered by my laughter.

We gently sway and I place my head on his chest to avoid his gaze. *I need to stop thinking about Chain. Why does that keep happening?*

I ignore the butterflies building in my stomach and make a snap decision. I pull my head back and look Zander directly in the eye.

"I definitely want to get married."

Chapter Sixteen

Chain

I reach for the bucket of popcorn, taking a handful and placing it in an empty cup. Valerie and I settled into our movie theater routine, sodas in our cup holders and feet propped up on the bar in front of us.

"Honey, your father says you haven't called him back," she tells me, unscrewing the lid to her soda bottle.

Why does she have to bring up Frank?

"And?" I reply, tossing a single popcorn into my mouth and chewing slowly.

"He's your *father*, Chain." As if that means anything to me.

"And he's *your* husband."

"That's right, he is," she says with pride evident in her tone.

I roll my eyes and glance at my watch, then back up at the screen. The previews should begin any minute now.

Staring at the screen as if my focus will trigger the reels to spin, I ignore her.

"Why can't you let it go?" she says softly. The theater is nearly empty, save for a couple near the front and two girls in the back. Otherwise, I wouldn't entertain this conversation.

"I've let it go, Valerie. That doesn't mean I have to buddy up with the man."

"It would mean so much to him." *It really wouldn't.*

"I see him on holidays and that's enough."

"Chain—"

Music erupts from the speakers, causing her to whip her head to the screen. We have an unyielding agreement to remain silent during movies. We paid good money to be here, damn it, and we are going to enjoy it.

Plus, I only have so much to discuss with Valerie. And she's completely delusional about Frank. Just *thinking* his name feels like acid on my tongue. We don't agree on most topics, but movies were a satisfying middle ground for us both.

The trailers play and then the movie starts. It was her turn to pick the movie, so I have no idea what I'm in for.

The opening credits start with a scene of a child, around 5 years old, playing catch outside with a man who seems to be his father. The kid drops the ball and rushes to grab it, then looks at his apparent father apprehensively.

"That's the third ball you've dropped," the man says.

"I'm sowry," the child whispers.

"Do baseball players say they're sorry? Or do they catch the damn ball?!"

It's as if a scene from my own personal hell was plucked from my mind and placed in front of me. I looked nothing like the boy on the screen, but I knew the expression he wore better than he did.

I look over to Valerie, whose hand is suspended midair, holding a single piece of popcorn. *What was she fucking thinking taking me to a movie like this?!*

My dad was an abusive asshole, and not only in a physical manner. It was subtle, psychological. He made me feel like I was an idiot, like I wasn't good enough. Half the reason I became an attorney was to prove myself to a man I cared very little for.

Valerie moves her hand, getting the popcorn into her mouth before turning to me. She raises her eyebrows and gives a small grin, showing how excited she is. She's also proving her innocence, because I don't see a lick of cunning in her eyes. In fact, she's downright ignorant to how this affects me.

We turn back to watch the movie. The man turns out to be the stepfather, but that doesn't make me feel any better. The movie plays out and luckily the story was about the kid growing up to be a baseball player. He goes pro and succeeds, living a life of glory and owing it to his stepfather.

What a very different experience he had. Maybe that's because the stepdad never hit him. He never made him feel like he was powerless and as worthless as the dirt on the ground he walks on.

We exit the theater, throwing our trash away on the way out. I wait for Valerie to use the bathroom and follow her out of the building to the parking lot.

"What did you think? Wasn't that excellent?" she asks jovially. Her smile fades as I pin her with a ruthless, unforgiving stare.

"That opening scene is *exactly* why I don't call him back."

"Fuck, yeah," I moan as I fully thrust my hips forward. I take my time, slowly pulling my cock all the way out before immersing myself back into her smooth walls as she grips me.

After my third thrust, Ashley whispers in my ear, "I want you to cum for me."

I start to quicken my pace, understanding the meaning in her words.

I focus on the sensation and the tightening of my balls rather than her half-assed attempts at sounding into this.

At this point, I just need the release. The fact that she's not into it should bother me like it used to, but it doesn't.

When my breathing starts to get heavier, Ashley pulls back a bit to look at my face. Her ass is on the bed and I have my arm around her shoulders, hoisting her up.

I tuck my face between her shoulder and neck and provide another moan. "I'm getting close," I tell her.

"Don't stop."

Taking the green light, I blow my load into the condom while grunting. I feel the orgasm wash over my body before it makes its way to my head. Finishing, I pull out of her and step off the bed.

I walk to the adjoining bathroom and pull the condom off, tying a knot and tossing it into the trash can by the sink. I wash my hands and look into the mirror.

I see Ashley walk up behind me, tying on her robe. I look back at my reflection when she reaches me and rubs my shoulder.

"That was nice," she says.

"Mmhmm," I say, but it lacks the proper conviction. She doesn't seem to notice, because she gives me a small smile and slides her hand down my arm before releasing me.

I follow her out of the bathroom to put my clothes back on. She leaves me to it, walking out to the living room.

Fucking Ashley is mostly just that—fucking. I don't even bother to ask if she wants to come—I know the answer. Her telling me not to stop is code for "don't wait for me". The first time I tried to explore my—*interests*—she looked at me like I'd grown an extra head. So I stifled that part of me and don't allow myself to miss it.

But fuck, how much I miss it.

Back in my white tank top and gym shorts, I join her in the living room. I take a seat on the couch and she stops her phone scrolling, locking the screen and placing the phone next to her thigh.

"Did you want to do something?" I ask her, a bit perplexed. Normally by this time on a Saturday night, I review work emails while she scrolls mindlessly before she goes to bed. Then, I might go out with the guys or take care of some work. Or both.

"No, no, it's late," she says. I stay silent and examine her closely.

Her blonde hair is perfectly curled and her eyes are shockingly blue. It's as if she's unreachable, too put together. She taps her French manicured finger on her crossed knee.

"Did you give any more thought to couples counseling?" she asks quietly.

And there it is.

"Jeez, Ashley, I haven't even had 24 hours," I snap. "I just got home half an hour ago."

I got back from the movies with Valerie to find Ashley waiting for me in the kitchen. The dishes were done, her hair was styled, and she had on a nice, blue dress with a belt around the waist to accentuate her curves.

She sauntered up to me and started kissing my neck, my jaw, and then my mouth, before pulling me by the hand into the bedroom.

I jumped at the opportunity, my dick roaring up with the need to cum. I didn't think it through in the slightest, but now I could feel the disgust rising up in me.

"Is that what this was? Is that why you seduced me into fucking you, so I would be open to your insanity?!" My voice raises several decibels by the end of my sentence.

Reel it in, Chain.

"*Seduced* you?" She's standing at the end of the couch. *When did she get up?* "Is that what you call our making love?"

"Making love?" I scoff. "We haven't made love in over a year, at least."

She looks as if I've slapped her.

Seriously?? That pathetic excuse for sex is what you considered to be making love?

"We're coming up on 3 years together, and you expect me to just—"

"I don't expect you to do anything!" I cut her off. "Just like you shouldn't expect me to do anything. Couples counseling, Ashley?"

"I've had several friends tell me—"

"Oh, so now you're gossiping about us to your friends?"

"Would you just listen?!" She yells so loudly that I'm certain the neighbors are choking on their food or shooting out of their chairs. I stare at her to let her know she has my attention.

"Friends have gone to counseling, and they said it worked wonders. Why wouldn't it help us?"

"This isn't about us. This is about you trying to uphold a status."

Her blue eyes crystallize in front of me. I watch them glaze over and freeze like shards of ice over a pond of water in winter.

I've pushed it too far, but I don't give a damn. I'm not getting dragged to counseling to watch her put on a show for someone else.

"Just think about it." She walks away, leaving me on the couch.

Show's over—for now.

Chapter Seventeen

Marlie

We left first thing Sunday morning after packing and saying goodbye to everyone. We've just pulled back into a parking spot and are rolling our bags up the walkway to the condo when Zander asks what I want to do today.

"I'm pretty hungry," I tell him. We left so quickly that we only grabbed bananas on our way out of Jace's grandparents house.

"Me too. Let's unpack and get some lunch."

A couple hours later, bags unpacked and bellies full, we lay on our bed with the TV playing a rerun episode of The Office. My mind begins to unwind, relaxing in the comfort of our bed and watching a show I've seen a thousand times.

It's the episode where Michael 'helps' resolve conflicts amongst the staff. It's also the episode where Pam finds out Jim put in a complaint about her planning her wedding on company time. She's offended because she assumes it's personal. But really, it's because he doesn't want to hear about her future with Roy.

I've always thought Pam was purposely ignorant of Jim's feelings for her so she didn't have to deal with her own feelings. How could she not know he was in love with her?

My thoughts drift to work tomorrow, what I might have to catch up on after being out. Thinking about Eli and getting to gush about the wedding, which I've told him so much about, gets me excited. I'll have to ask him about what I missed from improv on Friday.

Chain.

Shit. Guilt surges through me and I glance at Zander, who's smirking at a scene between Dwight and Jim. He's watching without a care in the world, calm and relaxed. The guilt gnaws at me, unsettling the calm I felt just moments before.

He never responded to the photo I sent him. Remorse mixes in with the guilt, the concoction churning and unnerving me.

I shouldn't have sent that photo. What was I thinking?

Trying to get a grip of the emotions flooding me, I give myself a mental shake.

It was just a photo. A photo based on a conversation we had. It's not a big deal. He was probably busy. Or maybe I got his number wrong.

I couldn't have gotten his number wrong. The logical part of my brain reminds me that Jessica sent all the numbers to us in the WhatsApp chat and he responded with a thumbs up.

He was probably busy. Maybe he was with Ashley.

A new emotion creeps in with a bitter taste. My jaw tightens. Before I can identify it, Zander speaks to me.

"You wanna go to the little park?"

Every once in a while, we go to the playground at the back of the complex to see the ducks or get a breath of fresh air.

That's exactly what I need: a breath of fresh air. I sit up and look at Zander. He's not watching the show anymore. His eyes are on me, the darkness alight with the prospect of something. He's got a lazy smile on, his hair ruffled by the pillow. I love that look. I crawl over and straddle him, slowly grinding myself on his hardening dick.

"Sure," I purr to him. I start to kiss him slowly, my hand grazing his chest and traveling downwards. When I reach for his shorts and put my fingers into the band, he suddenly removes his tongue from my mouth. The lack of warmth from his kiss shocks my nerves.

A twinge of rejection hits me and it must reflect on my face, because Zander says, "I want to go before it gets dark."

"Oh," I reply, disoriented. "Okay."

In the nearly two years of our relationship, he's never rejected me. It's a strange feeling, particularly when I could really use the distraction right now. He nudges me with his hips and I feel the stiffness in his dick.

There's no denying he was into it. He must really want to see the sun, then.

I roll off of him and he stands from the bed. I follow suit and he clasps his hand in mine. We make our way out of the condo and around the building to the park. We start to walk, the coolness from the neatly trimmed grass tickling my bare feet. Zander tightens his grip on my hand.

That's weird. He usually lets go by now.

I look ahead and spot a brunette girl who looks to be in her teens. She's lying on her stomach, a picnic blanket beneath her. She has a book poised in one hand, the other prepared to turn the page.

Zander comes to an abrupt halt and wheels us the opposite way. He guides me onward, pulling us closer to a small pond behind the playground.

"Why did you want to see the sun so badly?" I ask him.

"It's just a nice day out."

There's a family of ducks ahead. I point at them and Zander stops walking again.

"Try to get close to them, I'll take a picture," he says, digging his hand into his pocket.

"Um, okay," I tell him. I take deliberate and steady steps, intent on not scaring the ducks. When one of the adult ducks jerks its head at me, I stop, deciding this is as close as I'll be able to get.

I turn back to Zander with a smile for the photo, but I don't see him at eye level. He's down on one knee with something in his hands.

He's holding a black, circular box in his palm, his other hand holding the lid open. I'm about a few feet away, but I can see a ring centered inside.

No, no, no. No, no, no. NO.

My heart is racing. I feel it in my chest, my neck, my arms. I hear it thrumming in my ears. The smile I was wearing is gone, my jaw slack with shock. I lift a hand to my mouth, feeling the sweat on my lips.

"Marlie, I love you and want to spend the rest of my life with you. Will you marry me?" he says. The setting sun shines light on his obsidian eyes, revealing the tender love he holds for me.

My eyes are as wide as tennis balls. They have to be. With my hand still covering my mouth, I slowly begin to nod my head.

Zander gives me a beaming smile, ear to ear, his eyes crinkling. "Yes?"

He wants to hear me say it. I lower my hand, still nodding like an idiot.

"Yes." My voice sounds shaky and not my own.

He shoots up and rushes forward, throwing his arms around me and pulling me into a tight embrace. I wind my arms around his waist and lay my head on his chest. The warmth and joy emanating from him slows my racing heart, but only by a fraction.

The longer we hold each other, the more I want to cry. *Fuck*, I'm starting to cry. Feeling my chest heave with a sob, he pulls back but keeps his hands on my arms, the soft velvet box rubbing against one of my triceps.

"What is it, Marlie?" His eyes dart between each of mine, searching.

"I-I-I'm just," I try to speak through the sobs. I wipe the tears from my eyes, forcing them to stop flowing. That's when I feel the chasm's water roar. It crashes viciously against the walls as if a severe storm was upon them.

"Hey," he says gently. He waits until I hold his gaze to continue. "We don't have to do this if you don't want to."

"It's not that." *It's exactly that.* The tears have slowed and my thinking is clearing. "I wasn't expecting this at all."

"Well, it wouldn't have been much of an engagement if you knew," he jokes, wiping the tears from my cheek.

I laugh, sounding nasally from the snot plugging my nose. He removes his hands from me to show me the ring. It's a thin, white gold solitaire ring with a round, shiny diamond placed simply in the middle.

Wow, a ring. An engagement ring. Holy shit, am I getting married?! I said yes. No, no, no.

"Do you like it?" Zander asks hesitantly. I give him a slight nod. My eyes are so wide, they're burning.

Zander uses his free hand to gently remove the ring from the box. He closes it with a resolute snap and tucks it into his pocket.

No, no, no.

He holds the ring between his thumb and forefinger, waiting. I try to reach out my left hand but it won't cooperate.

"Your hand?" I've never been so grateful for his obliviousness. My left hand finally rises and he lifts his palm out so my fingers are resting on his. My hand betrays me, trembling with the significance of this act. Zander pulls his hand away slowly, allowing all my fingers to drop off except the only one that matters right now.

Oh my god, I can't do this. Why is my heart racing like this? Why is this happening?

He brings the band to my ring finger and slips it on. I feel it passing my knuckle and landing at the base. He turns it so the diamond is perfectly centered.

"It's beautiful," I whisper. I don't want my voice to betray the thoughts I'm having. The thoughts I *shouldn't* be having.

This is every woman's *dream.* Every happily ever after, every imagined wedding, starts with this moment right here.

Does anyone ever freak out like this?

Zander beams at me. He looks absolutely blissful. His teeth are on full display and his eyes are shining. *He* couldn't be happier.

And I... can't process what is happening. How did we even get here?!

Zander tugs me forward by *that* finger and leans in for a kiss. Our first kiss as an engaged couple.

An. Engaged. Couple.

His lips touch mine and I let my eyes flutter shut. He deepens the kiss, the tip of his tongue slowly roving over my bottom lip. I can hardly focus and when he pries my mouth open, my tongue is delayed in meeting his for our usual dance.

Why am I freaking out like this? Do all women freak out when they get engaged? I've never seen this in the movies. No one talks about this.

All I've ever heard is that it's the best moment of your life when a man drops to one knee and claims you as his own.

I'm broken. That's what it is. I'm broken and Zander is crazy to even ask me to marry him.

How long has he been thinking about this? When did he get this ring?

Then it hits me. I pull back abruptly from our kiss. I watch his eyes open as he recovers from the sudden space.

"When did you get this ring?" I ask him.

"I got it a few months ago. Remember that night I said I was hanging out with my sister for quality time? That's what we were doing."

"Who knows?"

"About the engagement? No one."

"Who knew you had the ring?"

"My family, Jace, Stella, and your mother. Of course I asked for her permission first, if that's what you're worried about."

"No, no," I trail off, my mind reeling. I feel more in control with my questioning; more focused. Like piecing together how this came to pass would somehow erase the unease I feel.

"I wanted to do this on our trip in a few weeks, but..." he starts.

"But, what?" I urge him to go on, needing to hear this explanation.

"I don't know. After the wedding and our talk, I just... I didn't want to wait anymore. I wanted you to be my fiancée."

Fiancée.

"So I decided to just go for it. Actually, no one knows I did this now. Everyone is expecting it to happen on our trip to the cabin."

He's had the ring for months??

I remember him going out with his sister. They aren't super close but I never thought twice about it. He claimed she wanted to spend some quality time with him, that she missed him.

But why did he change his mind about doing it on the trip? And then it hits me—the words I uttered at Stella and Jace's wedding. *I want to get married.*

"Why did you decide to ask me now? Why didn't you wait for us to be up in the cabins?" I ask harshly.

"I already told you. The wedding got me all excited, and I just couldn't wait."

Did I cause this with my stupid declaration? Did he think I meant I wanted this *now*?

"I'm really sorry, I know our trip would have been more romantic," he says, misreading the intentions of my question.

I don't bother to correct him. How do I explain that I only meant I saw marriage as an attainable thing? That I made the choice between marriage or no marriage. It was only our conversation that night—

Wait.

"That's why you were so upset that night," I say, the realization hitting me like a ton of bricks.

"Yeah..."

"God, this makes *so* much sense now!" I exclaim. All the anxiety and fear is drowning in the excitement of the puzzle pieces coming together.

But anxiety and fear are skilled swimmers. They swim with the current and resurface, the excitement fizzling out. Stella and Jace knew. I was at their wedding, making claims about not ever wanting to marry, and they knew.

It's irrational, but I start to get angry. I feel like a fool. A trapped fool.

"I knew I wanted to marry you and you were saying you didn't know if you felt the same way," Zander says. The joy he was exuding earlier is gone, replaced by a look of distress. "It was breaking my heart, Marlie."

I was breaking his heart? What if he knew I was panicking right now?

"But I meant what I said. I'll take you anyway I can, and if that means no marriage, then no marriage," he continues. "I love you. I always have and I always will."

My eyes shoot to his. I can see the absolute truth of his words reflected in his irises.

"That's why I bought the ring. I am sure of my feelings for you, and I wanted you to know it. Not just in words, but in action."

"Zander, I—"

"You don't need to explain yourself. I saw the look in your eyes when you said you wanted to get married. I could see how hopeful and excited you looked."

Hopeful? Excited? Those seem like foreign emotions, certainly not belonging to someone who is shaking as much as I am, whose heart is racing with the fear of what this all means.

In attempt to push the fears back into the recesses of my mind, I try to move the conversation forward. "Well, should we start telling people?"

Zander smiles and takes my left hand, clasping it in his. The feeling of the ring between our fingers is strange. It will take some getting used to. "Let's get back inside. We can start texting people."

I allow him to guide me, returning the way we came. I see the same girl immersed in her book, completely ignorant to what just happened to us. To me. I'm reminded of his abrupt turning away from her, and that clicks, too. He wanted privacy.

How could I have been so blind to this? How did I not know this was coming?

We walk up the stairs in the condo and Zander pulls his phone out of his pocket. When my hand drops, I'm acutely aware of the added weight on it.

Chapter Eighteen

Marlie

She knows, she knows. Oh my god, she knows.

The guilt that has consumed me is clouding my judgment. Stella holds my hand, staring at the new piece of jewelry that has changed everything.

Honestly, who gave a ring so much power? I want to strangle them.

We're in front of Stella and Jace's house, leaning against Zander's truck. We decided we wanted to surprise our best friends in person, so I texted Stella and asked her what they were up to. When she told me they were just at the house, I texted her that we were coming by to show them something.

Zander drove and I spent the entire 15 minute ride trying to remain calm and collect my thoughts. Rather than reining them in, the drive caused them to go haywire. Zander asked me multiple times if I was sure about this. Each time, I gave him my best attempt at a smile and told him yes, even though my brain kept shouting no.

That stupid, stupid, chasm was roaring, the walls trembling violently. It was all I could do to keep a joyful expression on my face when all I wanted to do was Google how I was feeling.

No one ever talked to me about this. The possibility of complete and utter anxiety after getting engaged. I couldn't talk to Stella or she'd tell Jace and it would get back to

Zander. Plus, how would she feel knowing that I may be doubting this? Doubting us?

"Marlie!" Stella shouts, snapping her fingers in my face. She dropped my hand and I hadn't even noticed.

Fuck, get it together, Marlie.

"Sorry! I'm still so surprised." *Surprised, in complete panic—same difference.*

"I bet! He really got you, huh?" Jace jokes, giving Zander a light punch in the arm. Stella is watching me, and I can see her analyzing mind computing behind her gray orbs. I try to keep my expression composed, but my damn eyes are always a dead giveaway to her.

"So you decided to propose early, Zander? What happened to the cabin?" I let out a sigh of relief at Stella's attention on Zander instead of me.

Maybe she doesn't know about the waging war going on in the battlefield of my brain.

Everything is going to be fine, it's just engagement anxiety.

Why am I the only person ever to experience it, then?

Take calm breaths. You love Zander.

"Yeah, I was too excited," Zander replies, all smiles.

"I'm so happy for you guys," Jace says, looking at me, then Zander.

"Thanks, man," Zander replies, his shit eating grin still glued to his face.

Jace looks at me expectantly. I clear my throat and add, "Yeah, thanks, Jace. Looks like we're up next!"

I give a small giggle and Stella does, too. We give them a hug, get back into our car, and head home. I take conscious, deep breaths, but it does nothing to soothe the trembling or the persistent thoughts.

Back in our bed, I can't take it anymore. I turn over to Zander, deciding impulsively that what I need is a good lay.

"Aren't you supposed to have the best sex of your life when you get engaged?" I say seductively, running my hand over his chest and giving his shirt a tug.

I scoot closer to him and he puts his arm around my shoulder as I lean onto his chest. "I think you're referring to the wedding night."

The wedding night. Oh, god. This plan is backfiring.

Refusing to let that word deter me, I continue on. "Sure, but if we don't do it now, do we even love each other?"

Once the words are out I realize that my fears are slipping through the cracks. If we don't have sex after this momentous evening—the dream so many can't wait for—it will prove we shouldn't be doing this.

We have to have sex. We have to, now. I feel the energy shift in my body, my pulse rising and traveling downward. I feel my clit throb and push my hips on Zander's leg, letting him know just where I stand.

"We don't have to force it, babe," Zander tells me. He's drawing lazy circles with his thumb on my shoulder.

"I want to," I tell him. I move my hand from his chest down to his abdomen. I slip under his shirt and start trailing along his stomach, my hand traveling just a little lower each time.

He gives me a heated look, his eyelids lowering. He bites his bottom lip when I reach the top of his pants.

Delighted with his acceptance, I unbutton his pants with one hand while wiggling free of his hold. I lower the zipper and reach my hands into his boxers, feeling the smooth skin as I make a new trail along his hard dick.

He groans and thrusts his hips forward, urging me on. I pump my fist and he gives me another pleasurable groan. I feel my clit throb again, my pussy slicking with desire.

Zander swiftly frees a breast from the dress, cupping it then tugging on my nipple before pinching, hard.

I gasp in surprise, not expecting the sudden pain. He does it again and I inhale sharply.

"I want to own you tonight, babe," he says. I meet his hooded gaze, his eyes glazed over with need. I run my tongue over my lower lip and he lurches forward, catching my tongue in his mouth and sucking.

I moan and our tongues clash together. He leaves my breast out in a rush to free the other one as I continue fisting his cock. I keep the motions short, slowly lengthening them so that I'm pumping his entire length to the rhythm of my heart beat.

His mouth is on my freshly freed nipple, licking slowly around the areola before flicking at the bud. I lean my head back and my hand slows down. He thrusts his hips forward and back, fucking my hand. He bites my nipple which elicits a whimper from me.

I feel his lips tilt up and he bites me. Again, and again, and again. I try to pull away but he holds me to him with his hand on my back, and I start to writhe under his touch.

My hand is only gripping his dick, his hips jackhammering into me. He's going to be close if I don't stop him.

"Fuck me," I purr.

He moves his head and I remove my hand from his now bulging cock. The vein is thrumming, telling me just how much he likes this. He bites my other nipple and I cry out from the shock of it. He takes his free hand and shoves me into the bed, his other hand remaining on my lower back as he pushes into me.

I feel his dick in my stomach and I lose myself to the sensation. He doesn't pause, pulling all the way out and back in. I moan and close my eyes, turning my head to the side.

He moves his hands to my hips and when he pulls out of me again, he flips me over in a rapid motion.

As soon as my knees hit the mattress, he jerks my hips up and thrusts into me from behind so hard that I lose my breath.

This time, he remains deep inside, slowing his movements to a pulse.

"I can see your ring from here," he breathes. I'm on all fours, my cheeks flushed with heat. "You're mine now."

His.

"I want you to say it, babe," he growls, increasing the tempo. I move my right hand to my clit, rubbing with my index finger.

Between my own finger and his deep thrusts, I feel myself getting to that place of pure bliss. I'd do anything to get there. "I'm yours," I whisper.

"Louder," he demands.

"I'm. Yours." I forced the words out between pants.

His fingernails dig into my hips, holding me in place as he pulls in and out violently. I match his pace with my finger and the orgasm rolls over me, heating my core and bursting outwards.

I barely hear my own moans as my head gets lighter and I collapse on the bed. Zander doesn't miss a beat, continuing his thrusts and following me into oblivion.

He collapses on top of me and I feel his heart racing in his chest, matching my own.

I peek my eyes open and see the ring on my hand.

See? We do love each other.

Chapter Nineteen

Marlie

"I'm so glad you'll be in class today, chica, it wasn't the same without you," Eli says brightly, rolling down the passenger window in my car. I'm giving him a ride today because his sister borrowed his car. We left together from work and just finished grabbing dinner since we had time to kill before class.

"Aww, I love you too, Eli." I smile at him and roll my own window down, deciding to relish in his infectious energy and the free flowing air coursing through the car.

"And you come back as an engaged woman!" he exclaims, pumping his fist in the air.

I spent most of my return to work on Monday scouring the internet for anything I could find on engagement fears and anxiety. I read countless articles and blogs, most of them saying the same thing: engagement anxiety is normal.

A few discussion forums had women who said they followed through with the marriage and ended up divorced years later, but they were far and few between. The consensus seemed to be that the fear came from the long-term commitment, and they married their partners and lived happily ever after.

The readings lulled my anxieties, sending them to the recesses of my mind. But whenever the engagement was brought up again, the first feeling to register was panic.

Being so new, I was receiving a lot of attention over the whole ordeal. Each time, I was able to settle the panic down a little easier.

I laugh into the wind, my hair blowing behind me as we get close to the theater. "I'm still the same person."

"Yeah, but soon you'll be Mrs. Hayes." My heart falters for a moment, but I recover just as quickly.

"Who says I'm changing my last name?" I retort, pulling into the theater parking lot. Finding all the spaces full, I exit and drive down the street in search of a parallel spot. I locate an area with free spaces and pull into one. I roll both of the windows up and cut the engine, grabbing my yellow cardigan and exiting the car.

I wait for Eli to circle around and meet me when I hear an engine accelerating. I turn and find a large truck racing up the road, the white paint shining with a fresh clean. I take a few steps back, plastering myself to my car to keep safe from the truck.

The engine cuts and the driver's door opens. I see a pair of brown oxfords followed by navy slacks. My eyes roam up to a white fitted shirt, the chest muscles beneath flexing as the man holds the door open so he can step down from the vehicle. My breath hitches in my throat when I reach his face.

He puts his keys in his pocket distractedly, then shuts his door and checks his reflection in the mirror. Stubble covers his strong jaw, and his brilliant green eyes are analyzing. I see my own reflection behind him and find that my mouth is ajar. I quickly snap it shut when Chain's eyes meet mine in the mirror.

There's a pause; a moment with no time. It feels like an eternity, but it couldn't be more than half a second. Chain smirks at me and I look away, the embarrassment of the photo I sent flooding back.

He turns towards us and Eli says, "'Sup, Chain?"

"Eli, Marlie," he gives us each a nod, walking past us. Eli and I step in line with him and we head towards the theater.

I pull my cardigan across my chest and cross my arms, holding it in place. Keeping a deliberate step behind Chain and Eli, I sneak a look at Chain.

His dark hair is begging me to reach out and grab it, the small wave visible from the back. His broad shoulders are confident, swaying slightly with his assured steps. My eyes travel lower and land on his ass, perfectly rounded and evidently muscular.

The small voice shouting at me from the back of my mind snaps me out of my daze. I force my eyes up and stare straight ahead to the space where Chain is *not*. I pick up my pace, falling into line next to Eli so he's between us.

You're allowed to find people attractive.

Attractive is an understatement. Chain was exactly my type, with his tall stature, light eyes, and dark hair.

Zander doesn't have light eyes.

So, what? I love Zander. He's my boyfriend. Crap, I mean fiancé.

We arrive at the door to the building and I reach out my left hand as Chain reaches out his right. My hand lands first, causing his hand to cover mine. His palm is rough and his hand is so big, it completely covers mine.

Before I can study the feel of it any longer, he folds his fingers and sweeps them off my hand, muttering an apology as I glance at him. His eyes are bulging from his head and he's openly staring at my hand. Alerted, I whip my head back to my hand, thinking there must be a bug on me.

But there's no bug. No, there is only the lone diamond sitting atop my lone hand on the lone door. It's blaringly obvious in this position.

My stomach sinks, a pit growing in my stomach. As if burned by a scorching fire, I yank my hand off the door and tuck it into the pocket of my cardigan, attempting to hide what's already been seen. I feel my cheeks flush and I can't look up.

Why am I embarrassed right now?

I made my peace with this decision. I confirmed on the internet that I suffered from engagement anxiety, nothing more. I hardly flinch when people congratulate me or ask me questions about the wedding.

So what is going on right now??

I finally raise my head, the silence overwhelming me. I look to Eli, who is watching Chain and I like a tennis match. He diverts his attention to the door and opens it, catching my eye when he holds it open for us.

I'm a deer frozen in headlights, waiting for Chain to move. Because I am incapable.

"Okay, then... see you inside," Eli says, scrambling up the stairs. I try to speak, but I can't form a single word. The door closes slowly behind him with a final, resolute snap.

"Congratulations are in order, I see," Chain says evenly. I look up to his eyes, and they are no longer the bright green I'm accustomed to seeing. There's a darkness to them, a shadow looming over.

"Thanks," I mumble. I dig my hand further into my pocket but there's no more room, so my fingers crumple into the cotton.

"Let's see it," he says, holding his hand out expectantly. I hesitate, not wanting to free my hand from its dark hiding place, safe from the light.

Sensing my hesitation, he continues, "Come on, you must be excited." But his words don't match his eyes.

You're being crazy, you're seeing things.

Deciding to stop being so ridiculous, I pull my hand out. It's only when I place my four fingers on Chain's hand that I notice I'm shaking.

"Mmmm, .5 carat diamond. Lovely," he comments, his tone casual; neutral. I'm hyper aware of all the millimeters of skin touching each other, each zing shooting through me like a livewire.

"Yeah," I say. "Wait. How do you know the size?"

"My, er, father is a jeweler."

"Oh, was that your first job or something?"

There's a pause before he responds. "You could say that."

I ponder on his strange reply before brushing it off. It's better if I don't learn more about him. I glance back down at my hand.

"Well, I love it," I say louder than I intend, as if being heard makes it more believable. His eyes snap up to mine, searching. I feel an inexplicable need to give him what he seeks, but I don't know what that is.

In truth, I don't love the ring. I haven't gotten used to the weight of it on my hand, and it catches on all my clothes when I get dressed. It's also very plain. But many women would love it, and Zander picked it out himself.

Zander.

His name grounds me back to reality. I pull my hand out of Chain's and reach for the door. "We should get inside."

He answers by grabbing hold of the door. His presence behind me as I trek up the stairs unnerves me, causing me to miss a step and twist my ankle, falling towards the enclosing wall of the narrow steps. His strong arm catches me before I can make it all the way down, and my upper back falls into his warm, hard chest.

Acting of its own accord, my body naturally leans into him and my eyes flutter closed with the instant tranquility

I'm gifted. His arm loosens, allowing me to fall deeper into the embrace.

God, Chain's—

His name forces my eyes open and I stand up in one fluid motion. I wheel around and find Chain looking at me, his arm still in midair. The shadows in his eyes are gone, replaced by an emotion I can't put my finger on. Before I can analyze it further, he clears his throat and the emotion goes with it.

"Good thing I was behind you. That would have been a nasty fall."

"Yeah, um, thanks." I stare at him, wishing for the look to return. It doesn't.

"Anytime, Mar." He moves past me and I'm left standing alone, looking down the flight of stairs. His last words left me with the same warmth I felt when I'd fallen into him.

In college, I had the nickname MarsBar, which died out after my ex and I broke up. But no one's called me Mar before.

I pick at the loose thread on my cardigan, watching as Chain performs a scene with Liv. They're speaking but the words don't register. I've been unfocused throughout the entire class. The anxiety I've been keeping at bay returns tenfold. Something is there. Something I can't name—can't quite put my finger on—exists when I'm around Chain.

But what does it mean? Why does it feel like I come alive with just a look from him? Why did his light touch make me tremble in weak submission?

And then the deep-rooted fear strikes.

Does this mean I don't love Zander?

I glance at the ring resting on my finger, which twinkles under the stage lights. I leave the poor cardigan's thread alone in favor of twirling the ring with my thumb. The movement calms my nerves and gives me something besides the tension in my stomach to focus on.

It's just his attractiveness. The guy is gorgeous, any woman probably feels like this around him.

I tear my gaze from the ring but allow my thumb to continue its pattern. When I look back on the stage, my thumb halts midspin. Chain has Liv in what seems to be a very loving embrace. I sit straighter in my chair and watch the scene with rapt attention.

"...maybe we've been holding this off for too long." I catch the end of Liv's sentence.

Chain starts to rub his hand up and down one of Liv's arms while holding her head against his chest. I feel a silent rumble in my chest and my jaw clenches unexpectedly.

Suddenly, I'm imagining him rubbing *my* arm that way. I'm imagining placing my head on his chest, allowing him to hold me.

Chain's words rip the rug my imagination stands on right from under its feet. "I know I love you, but we can't go back down that road."

"Cut! Excellent job," Jon shouts from the back of the room. Chain immediately releases Liv and my jaw unlocks. "We'll wrap up with that, folks. I hope you've enjoyed week 6."

Chain and Liv make their way off stage as Jon continues, "Please don't forget, week 10 is our final class, which will be our student performance. Start telling your dear friends and family, they won't want to miss it!"

I bolt out of my seat and out of the class, succeeding in being the first one out. I race down the stairs, eager to get the hell out of here and into my own bed, away from all these feelings. When the night air hits my face, I stop dead in my tracks.

Eli.

My head falls back and I let out a groan, remembering I gave him a ride today. Of all days, why today?

"Woah, I didn't know you hated class that much." The gravelly voice behind me has me snap my head in its direction, finding none other than Chain leaning his shoulder against the building wall with a lazy grin on his luscious lips.

I wonder what they'd taste like on mine. Would he like it if I sucked the bottom lip before tracing it with my tongue? The tip of my tongue trails along my own bottom lip when I realize I'm openly staring at him. I pull my scandalous tongue back into the confine of my mouth and straighten before responding.

"I've just had a long day," I say, turning away and taking a step towards the parking lot.

Bullshit, you're running.

"I'll walk with you," he says. I feel him walking towards me, the sparks in my back going off from the energy buzzing between us.

"No need," I brush him off, quickening my pace.

"We parked next to each other, remember?" *Damn it.* "Don't you have to wait for Eli, anyway?"

I don't respond, and I know I must seem extremely rude. There's no reason for my hostility, and quite honestly, I can't pin down why I'm acting this way.

You have feelings for him.

The pang I feel in my chest confirms the assertion. I ignore it, further hurrying my steps so that I'm nearly sprinting. Chain catches up easily, his long legs able to cover more ground than my own. I don't acknowledge his presence, keeping my head focused ahead.

I don't have feelings for Chain. He's hot as fuck, but that's where it ends.

Then why do you refuse to talk to him?

I will talk to him!

The ring on my finger catches on my jeans. Annoyed, I curl my hand into a fist to prevent it from occurring again. I take a deep breath as we turn down the street where our cars are parked.

With the need to prove to myself that nothing is happening, I speak. "So, you like trucks?"

Chain turns his face toward me, but I can see his mocking grin from my periphery. I dig my keys out of my pocket as he responds.

"Yeah, I like trucks. They get the job done."

"Job? I thought you were an attorney."

"I am. It's a manner of speaking."

"Oh, right." I feel stupid for the way I'm acting, but for the love of god, I can't help myself.

"I like the accessibility it provides me."

We reach my car and I unlock the door. I pause with my *right* hand on the handle and look up, finding Chain giving me a quizzical look.

Before I can question him on it, I hear Eli shout behind me, "Don't forget about me, chica!"

I watch as Eli runs up the street and reaches my car. I laugh as he bends over, exaggeratedly placing his hands on his thighs in mock exhaustion.

"Shut up." I give him a playful shove on the shoulder, and he stands up grinning. From my periphery, I notice Chain tense. I open my door and Eli circles the car, opening his own door. He waves to Chain and gets in. Getting into my own seat, I place my hand on the door in preparation to close it. There's no hiding the ring this time, seeing as my left hand is closest to the door.

"See ya," I say. I glance up at Chain, and his eyes peel from my hand to meet my eyes. There's a decent amount of space and a whole car door in between us, but the energy explodes and makes me feel like I can't breathe from the proximity.

His eyes are alight with a fire, though I can't place why. I don't get the chance to figure it out, either. He gives me a slight nod and walks towards his truck.

I watch him for a moment before shutting my door and putting the key into the ignition. I feel Eli's eyes on me, so I turn and find him giving me an arrogant smirk.

"What?" I say, turning the key.

"You are so—"

He halts and whips his head to the steering wheel when the engine sputters and doesn't start. I try again and again, but my Blueberry doesn't turn on.

"Damn, girly, I think your car is conched out," Eli says.

"Yeah, you think?" Frustrated, I yank my car door open and hop out, slamming the door behind me and rushing to the hood. I reach beneath it, pulling the lever that releases the latch so I can lift it.

Eli's door opens and shuts, and he joins me behind the hood. I'm not exactly sure why I opened it, because I have no idea what I'm supposed to be looking for.

"FUCK!" I shout into the night sky, slamming the hood closed. Eli places a hand on my shoulder in a comforting grip.

"Can Zander pick us up?" he asks. That's when I hear Chain's truck engine roar to life behind me. We both whip our heads around, watching as he pulls out of his spot and U-turns to drive out of the neighborhood.

"What a fucking asshole, he's not even going to check on us?" I say indignantly to Eli. I use the fuel of his behavior to convince myself that he's a waste of my time.

Those feelings are purely physical. Why would you want someone like that?

I throw my hands over my face in frustration. Between the engagement and Chain, I've had enough! Then my car shits the bed, and Chain pulling away is the straw that breaks the camel's back.

"It's going to be alright," Eli says soothingly, rubbing my shoulder.

"Get in."

My head snaps in the direction of Chain's voice. He's leaning out of the open window of his truck, eyeing Eli with tight lips.

"Thanks, man." Eli releases me and walks towards his truck.

"No! You don't have to do that, I'll call—"

"Just get in the damn car, Marlie." Chain's gaze roams over me before landing on my eyes. I'm not sure what he sees, but his soften before he stares out of the windshield. Eli's already made himself comfortable in the backseat.

Great, so I have to sit in the passenger seat.

In opposition to my thought, my stomach does a summersault. I huff and lock my car, then rush over to the passenger door, the lights turning on when I open it.

Chain steps on the gas as soon as I've closed the door and the light in the car begins to dim. We pull up to the stop sign as the light extinguishes.

"You can drop me off first, man, I live closer than Marlie," Eli says, then rambles off his address so Chain can put it into his GPS. His phone map is mirrored on the screen in the dash, showing Eli's place as 7 minutes away. They take up a comfortable conversation and I stare out the window, trying to get a grip.

Do I have feelings for Chain? That's impossible. Right? Yeah, impossible. I hardly know him. I love my boyfriend. I mean, my fiancé. AH! Zander. I love Zander.

Time is moving much too fast, and we're pulling up to Eli's house before I'm ready.

You're freaking out over nothing, he's just a friend.

Yeah, a friend. Eli gets out and says goodbye, then Chain pulls back onto the road and hands me his phone. I take it and enter my address into the GPS. ETA: 14 minutes.

"So, what are you going to do about your car?" he asks when I hand him his phone back.

Shit, I hadn't even thought about that. "I'm not sure, I guess I'll call a towing company in the morning."

Realizing I should let Zander know about the situation, I pull my phone out of my pocket. The screen lights up and I see a message from my mom.

> Mother: Let's get dinner to celebrate that new ring!

"Ugh," I grunt out.

"Something wrong?" Chain peers at me for a moment before keeping his focus on the road, but I melt at the note of concern I hear laced in his tone.

"Just my mom," I say, swiping and opening my messages. Ignoring hers, I click on my chat with Zander.

I start to type out a text when Chain's words make me pause.

"Parents, huh?" He has one hand on top of the steering wheel, gripping confidently as his eyes take in his surroundings. He looks in utter control, his free arm propped on the center console. He's relaxed and focused. His hair looks absolutely scrumptious, and I find myself wanting to run my hands through it before—

Stop.

I revert my attention back to my phone and type out my message to Zander.

> Me: My car wouldn't start :(I got a ride from Chain. Be there soon.

I read it over before hitting send. Should I write 'a student' instead of Chain? Deciding to keep Chain, I hit send before I can change my mind. He's just a friend, what's the big deal? I'm sure Zander won't care.

I glance back and see the delivered notification, which quickly changes to read. The three dots populate as Zander begins typing.

> Zander: Damn babe. We'll figure it out in the morning. Tell Chain I say hey.

See? No big deal.

"I'm really starting to enjoy improv," Chain says conversationally. We fall into an easy discussion of the things we've been learning, the funnier scenes we've watched, and our thoughts on the student show.

It's so easy to laugh with him. When we pull up to my neighborhood, I feel the sadness creep over me that we won't be able to keep talking.

"Thank you so much for the ride," I say as he puts the truck into park in front of my building. His hand brushes the handle, almost as if he's going to open the door, before he drops it and looks out the window. As he takes in the surroundings, I suddenly feel shy.

"Anytime," he replies, turning to look at me. His green eyes are nearly glowing in the darkness of the car, the shadows of before gone as if they never existed.

Breaking the contact, I open the door and hop down from the truck. When I turn back to shut the door, his blazing eyes shoot up from my lower half, causing my breathing to hitch.

"Thanks again," I say breathlessly. I shut the door before he can respond and walk around the front of the truck, the headlights beaming on me as I pass.

I'm immersed in the dark night as I take the path up to my door before my breathing returns to normal. I hear his engine roar as he drives away.

Chapter Twenty

Marlie

"Excellent work today! I can feel you opening up your hearts to the moment," Jon says emphatically as Lorraine and Toni return to their seats. "I think in the next class, you will really start to feel the growth."

I feel the truth in his words, knowing I've already changed from these last 7 weeks. I'm much more aware of my emotions and the patterns in my actions. Acting on the stage requires such focus and meaning, that it's starting to transfer to my personal life.

I'm not sure that I like it. I'm not sure that I was ever aware I even had a chasm of churning emotions closed off to me for so long.

"Before you go, I want to present you with an opportunity." Jon pauses for effect, eyes roaming to each of us before continuing. "We have a workshop being held by some of Chicago's well versed improvisers. There are a few spots open and we are offering them to our students."

He looks around expectantly, waiting for our reaction. He certainly has our attention, but when no one jumps out of their seats, clapping exuberantly, he sighs dramatically. "This doesn't happen often. If you enjoy what we're doing, this workshop will sharpen your skills in unimaginable ways."

I look at Eli next to me and he gives me a slight shake of his head. Damn, he probably has plans. I look around to gauge everyone else's interest. Chain is staring at Jon with narrowed eyes, his hand on his chin and his thumb rubbing pensively.

What would it feel like if he caressed me that way? Down my neck to my breasts, rubbing slow circles around my nipples...

"Well, that is all. I hope to see some of you tomorrow. You can sign up on our website." Jon dismisses us and I blink my eyes a few times, shaking the thoughts of Chain. Who knew a thumb could be sexy?

Anything could be sexy on that man.

I chuckle internally and stand up. This past week, I came to terms with my attraction to Chain. I'm allowed to find other men attractive without it meaning anything. It's been a while since I laid eyes on someone so appealing and my body just didn't know how to react.

"You can't do the workshop?" I say to Eli as we leave the room. Our classmates are chattering freely around us.

"Nah, I've got a family thing. Sounds cool though, you should do it."

I don't have anything better going on tomorrow. I'll have to cancel our usual plans with Stella and Jace, but I am enjoying improv and maybe Jon is right about honing my skills.

"Yeah, I will." I pull out my phone to type in Sparkle Comedy's website and check the workshop information. I follow Eli's feet to guide me out as I scroll the site.

Suddenly, my feet hit the air instead of the ground. I fling my arms out, dropping my phone in the process. It crashes down the flight of stairs and my body follows. My knees slam into the steps and I curl like a ball, rolling haphazardly.

I throw my hands out and finally skid to a stop about mid-flight, crumpling helplessly. I lift my arm up to find the railing and *fuck*, that hurts. I swat around blindly, my eyes closed shut with the pain and shock of the fall.

My hand meets a strong, calloused grip and I feel fingers close around mine, pulling me up. Another hand reaches under my armpit, steadying me so I can stand up straight. I look up and find Chain holding me, his eyes seeking mine with worry. I can see the emotion painted all over his features, his eyes roaming over me and his eyebrows knitted together. His lips are in a taught frown.

I catch my breath and remove my hand from his, patting my hair and fixing the hem of my shirt that has risen up, revealing my midriff above my low rise jeans.

Chain watches my movements as I fix my shirt, and I lift my gaze to find his eyes on the exact spot where my stomach was showing a moment ago. Eli comes up behind Chain, eyes assessing me for injury.

"I'm going to have to start escorting you up and down these stairs," Chain says, having the nerve to sound irritated. Does he not realize I'm the one who fell here?

"I'm fine," I huff. Running my fingers through my hair one last time, I turn and take the final steps to the flat, steady ground below. Eli is two steps behind me. Chain remains standing in the same place where he'd helped me up. The rest of the class is behind him, watching us.

Damn it, everyone saw.

I give a small smile and wave, saying, "I'm okay, guys."

Everyone looks relieved and, as if orchestrated, resumes their conversations and walks down the stairs. I open the door and allow the fresh air to wash over me, the sudden draft blowing my hair back. I hold the door wide as I walk out so Eli can follow.

"I can't believe you're abandoning me in the workshop," I joke, attempting to distract Eli—and myself—from what just happened.

"I really wish I could go." He really looks downhearted, which is not a look I see on him often.

"Aw, I'll make sure to fill you in on the whole thing Monday."

"You have to! Hey—" He stops short, forcing me to turn back.

I give him a quizzical look. "What's up?"

"Nevermind." He closes the space between us and waits for me to continue walking.

"No, no, no, you're not getting off that easy!" I shove his shoulder playfully with my own.

"I just, well I kind of have a thing for Lorraine," he says shyly. I've never seen him so out of his element.

"A crush?!" I am actually shocked because Eli is the epitome of a playboy. Work all week, drink and fuck all weekend.

"I don't know what's happening to me," he says, shaking his head. He looks as though he tasted milk that went sour a week ago.

"Well, lucky Lorraine," I say. I want to joke with him, but something tells me this is not the time. His nose is still wrinkled; he's obviously having trouble with this.

"Why is Lorraine lucky?" I feel a nudge at my left shoulder before Chain steps in between Eli and I. The surprise causes me to inhale sharply, catching a scent of mint.

I try not to focus on the tingling from his too brief touch. I try not to take a bigger breath so I can study his aroma. I try not to turn my face towards his so I can drink in his features.

But I'm a really unfocused student with an unquenched thirst. All at once, I turn towards him, take a deep breath, and bring my right fingers to lightly brush my shoulder before letting my hand drop.

My eyes shut of their own accord and I have to force them back open. Thank god Chain's looking at Eli, who seems to be saying something that I cannot for the life of me interpret.

"How about you, Marlie?" Chain turns toward me and I swear it's in slow motion. It's as if I'm watching a pre-recorded moment in time.

His eyes find mine and the video goes from slow motion to pause. You would think that this wouldn't keep happening, the way time freezes. This moment is a lake and I'm caught below the surface of thin ice. But I don't drown in the water; it's quiet and I can breathe.

His green eyes echo the enchantment I feel. He doesn't break the contact, and though something deep in my chest tells me not to, I force my eyes away when I hear Eli speaking.

"She'll be there," he says.

Be where? Oh, the workshop!

"See you then. Oh, and here," Chain says, handing me my phone. When I take it, he picks up his pace before I can thank him.

"You really are a klutz," Eli chides. I reply with a punch to his arm.

Maybe being a klutz has its perks, though.

Zander was half asleep in bed when I got home. I laid by him while I signed up for the workshop, then crept to the bathroom after he fell asleep.

As I brush my teeth, the bristles rubbing rapidly over my gums, I listen to my thoughts.

It's interesting how you can grow so accustomed to the sound of your own mind. When the words become cyclical, it becomes easier and easier to tune them out.

That's why the relentless siege of the past weeks has worn me down. I'm forced to listen to these new thoughts that I never thought I'd think. I'm forced to feel feelings I have absolutely no control over.

What is wrong with you? There can't be anything with anyone else. You're engaged.

I love Zander. There's absolutely nothing wrong between us.

Do you really believe that? You guys have absolutely nothing in common.

So? We love each other and get along.

Getting along and not arguing are two different things.

I bet Chain and I have more in common.

Guilt floods me and my knees feel weak. I drop the toothbrush into the sink under the running water, the clatter of the porcelain ringing in my ears. I look at the water splattered on the mirror as I grip the counter, willing myself to regain control.

How can you be feeling something for someone else? You've been cheated on, you know what it feels like to be emotionally beaten. You can't do that to Zander.

It's these words that force my eyes to stare at themselves in the reflection of the mirror. I look directly into my pupils, ignoring the shades of brown and honey.

Caramel.

I clamp my eyelids shut and shake my head, trying to rid myself of *his* voice. Not only do I fail, his eyes dance in the darkness of my closed lids, the sparkle in them daring me to indulge.

Just this once, I do.

Tying my shoelaces, I glance at the time on my phone. I've got an hour and a half before I need to be at the workshop, and I'm going for a run. I don't run as often as I used to, but it helps clear my head. Zander is still sleeping, so I got ready downstairs.

I grab my phone and pop the headphones into my ears. I blast a hip hop station on Spotify, feeding off the energy the music provides. A half-hour later, I return drenched in sweat with a clear mind. Zander is in the kitchen, slumped by the coffee machine.

"Morning, babe!" I pop a kiss on his lips and reach for the cupboard above him, grabbing a cup for myself. I select a white ceramic mug that says 'I'm cute' in a thick, cursive script. Zander gifted it to me for my birthday last year. I have the best boyfriend. *Damn it*—fiancé!

"I still can't believe we're getting married," I tell him. He reaches for his mug as the final drips of his coffee fall from the Keurig machine.

"You're so chipper this morning," he says, stifling a yawn. He takes a large sip from his steaming mug, spitting it back into the cup when it burns him. "Fuck!"

I stifle a laugh. "Why wouldn't I be? I love you." I put a new pod into the Keurig and place my cup, pressing the button on the machine.

"I love you too, babe," Zander replies, giving me my favorite half smile. The left side of his lips and face turn up, and his eyes twinkle mischievously. Although, the twinkle is a bit delayed this morning.

"I'm going to a workshop for improv today. Jon told us about it last minute."

"Jon? Oh, the teacher?"

"Yep. I'll text Stella to let her know."

"Jace and I can play online, if anything."

I nod and grab my freshly poured mug, then carefully trek upstairs. I place my mug on the dresser in our room and pull out my phone to text Stella.

I see a notification from our improv class WhatsApp group. I slide my phone open and start reading the messages.

> Damon: who else signed up for the workshop??

> Liv: Me!

> Lorraine: I'll be there

> Gaby: same

> Chain: How could I not?

My stomach somersaults at the sight of his name. Ignoring it, I keep reading.

> Toni: I won't be able to make it, I had a shift at work

> Eli: sorry dudes, wish I could. Don't miss me too much.

I chuckle at Eli's words, send my reply to the group that I'm in, then toss my phone on the bed. I hurriedly undress and shower, then throw on my favorite flared, faded jeans and a dark green, V-neck shirt.

I chug my lukewarm coffee and race down the steps with the empty mug. I place it in the sink and grab a banana before reaching the door to leave.

"I'm out of here!" I shout to Zander. He rises from his gaming chair, removing the headset and walking over to me. I open the door impatiently. I'm pushing it time-wise, and I don't want to be the last one there.

Zander presses a tender kiss to my lips. "Break a leg, rockstar," he whispers over my lips. I smile and break it off, then bolt out of the door. I don't even bother to shut it, knowing Zander will close it behind me.

Once I'm on the road and feel confident that I'm on time, I turn up the music and settle into the drive. I wonder what the workshop will be about and muse over different topics. It strikes me how much I've grown to love improv over the last few weeks. I need to remember to thank Eli for making sure we didn't end up in one of those other classes.

Improv is so fun, and I've learned so much about human emotion and motivation. It's hard to even imagine how I lived life before having these classes. I feel more alive when I'm performing than I have in a long time.

The last time I had this much fun was with my ex, before he cheated on me and shattered my heart. The start of our relationship was basically a fairytale. He was thoughtful, he treated me well, he showered me with gifts. I never would have thought that he could do what he did to me. That's why I no longer take stock in niceties and romantic gestures. He did it all and more, yet he still destroyed me.

I'll never trust someone as fully as I did him. But Zander comes close. He's so easygoing and nice, it's hard to imagine him ever hurting me. I feel safe with him. He's my rock in an unsteady world.

I'm not sure why I was so worried about the engagement. It had to be what all those articles and bloggers said, just the nerves from a big life decision and commitment. Zander and I fit together like two peas in a pod.

I'm allowed to find Chain, or any other man, attractive. That doesn't dismiss what Zander and I have. Our sweet, tender kiss today proved that.

I'll have fun at this workshop and see my improv friends, then go home to hang out with my future husband.

So why is my heart floating to the thought of seeing Chain soon?

Chapter Twenty-One

Marlie

Stella: Hey, we'll head over soon!

Stella's message comes through as I pull into the nearly empty parking lot at the theater building. Damn it, I forgot to tell her. I park and quickly reply to her.

Me: I forgot to let you know I signed up for an improv workshop. Sorry :/

She reads it instantly and starts replying.

Stella: I know, Zander told Jason. I wanted to give you a hard time ;) have fun I'm so happy for you!!!

I roll my eyes with a smirk on my face, sending her back one word: jerk.

I stuff my phone into my pocket and pull down the visor to check myself in the mirror. My chocolate brown orbs stare back at me, the bright sun highlighting the lighter notes. My lips are bright and hydrated, and my hair is brushed neatly for once.

I give myself a small smile, then slap the visor back into its place. The reflection of my necklace flashes in the mirror, and I bring my hand up to it. I hold it gingerly, glancing down. My chin digs into my throat from the effort to look at the dazzling Z hanging from the thin strand.

I lock the doors after exiting the car and head into the building, making sure to securely grip the railing so as not to fall again. I enter the theater and find it full of people, many of whom I don't know. I locate a few of my classmates in the third and fourth rows, chatting animatedly.

I take a seat next to Damon and jump right into the small talk, feeling comfortable. We've all grown closer as the weeks have gone by, and I'm starting to feel like they're actual friends.

I feel him before I see him. I feel a buzz through my limbs and a sudden alertness. I turn my head from Liv, who's sharing a story about a trip to the Maldives, to confirm what I've grown accustomed to knowing.

Chain takes the seat next to me, his casual, white T-shirt pairing well with his loose jeans. Both hug his frame in a way that make him look appetizing. His hair has that perfect wave to it and his jaw loosens when he gives me a small smile.

I tap my foot repetitively to remind me that time is still moving. I give him a short wave and allow my eyes to meet his briefly; I refuse to get sucked into their depths. Returning my attention to Liv, I swap my foot tapping for toying with the pendant on my necklace. I picture my kiss with Zander this morning and a small smile plays on my lips.

"I'm excited to see what we'll learn," Chain comments. I turn back to face him and find him watching the stage. I follow his gaze where a man of about 35 years old is moving the chairs around with a tablet tucked into his armpit.

"Yeah, me too." I assume the man on the stage is Gabriel Turner, the name listed on the website as the host of the workshop.

Turning my attention away from him, I look at Chain. Now that the initial reaction has passed, I'm finding it rather easy to be around him today.

Obviously, the engagement anxiety and the freshness of his attraction had me out of sorts. Now that I'm sure of my choice with Zander and I've seen Chain a few times, he's losing his effect on me. He turns to me and I realize I've probably been staring at him far too long, lost in thought. I give him an awkward smile that he returns confidently.

"I didn't expect to like this as much as I do," he says.

"Tell me about it. I was forced into this through work, but I'm finding it very entertaining."

"Must be a cool job. Where do you work?"

"It's absolutely not. I work in the mailing center at Symbiosis."

"Not a lot of companies offer someone an improv class."

"True. But I'm no lawyer or anything."

He smirks at that. I hate how aware I am of his arm lying so close to mine on the armrest of his chair, the narrow space thrumming with energy. "I'm sure you balance the scales of justice, anyway. Those stacks of paper must be perfectly equal at all times if you're handling them."

His joke reminds me that he never replied to my photo. I frown, feeling stupid and embarrassed for ever sending it to begin with.

It's nearly imperceptible, but Chain's eyes narrow. I get the strange feeling that he knows where my mind went. His mouth opens with the intent to speak but before he can, the guy on stage calls our attention.

"Let's get this party started!"

The 4 hour workshop passes in a blur. Jon was not being dramatic when he said that this would really help hone our skills. I feel like I've learned so much in such a short amount of time. Gabriel was amazing, and I met other improvisers that are in higher levels or part of the theater's cast.

Since I sat next to Chain for the entirety of the workshop, I couldn't help but notice that we tend to laugh at the same exact parts in scenes. When I would hear his deep chuckles, I felt so content, and in the most comfortable way. There was also a sense of longing, as if I could only listen to the sounds of our shared laughter and never need music again.

The theater fills with the sounds of excited voices as Gabriel officially dismisses us. I turn to Chain, who wears a grin as big as my own.

"That was amazing!" I say, standing up from my chair.

"It really was," he breathes in awe. It's hard to describe the exhilaration you feel after sharing a scene on stage and feeding off the energy of the room.

Chain exits the row and we walk out of the theater, closely followed by Damon, Liv, Toni, and Gaby. When we make it to the sidewalk outside of Sparkle Comedy, we huddle into a group to share our thoughts on the workshop as other attendees exit the building.

I feel a tap on my shoulder and turn to find Gabriel smiling at me. "Hey, great job today!"

I smile in return, feeding off his infectious energy. "Thanks! You were fantastic. Thank you so much for everything."

"I'm always happy to share. Hey, are you busy after this?" He looks around at my group then back to me.

"Um—"

"I'm doing a show here with some of my troupe who traveled with me. It starts in half an hour."

"Oh! Yeah, I'd love to watch." I turn to the rest of the group to gauge their reactions. But the only person paying attention is Chain.

He's looking—no, leering—at Gabriel. His eyes are a dark, venomous shade. Before I can process further, Gabriel responds to me, oblivious to Chain's glare.

"Great! Tell your friends. Catch ya in there." He walks towards the parking lot, pulling a pack of cigarettes from his pocket and smacking it into his palm.

I turn back to Chain, but he's listening intently to Damon about a scene that we all watched. Chain's expression is impassive, but his eyes are still not back to their usual, cool emerald.

Did I imagine that?

I shake the thought, deciding it doesn't matter. Chain seems to get ticked off pretty easily, and I'm not going to give it another thought.

"Guys, Gabriel just told me there's a show here in 30. Anyone in?" I announce loudly.

They shout their agreements and we keep talking. I shoot furtive looks at Chain but he doesn't break from his conversation with Damon. 10 minutes before the show, Jessica suggests we go buy our tickets and get seats. I break from the group as they go into the theater so I can use the bathroom. When I return to the booth, they're nowhere to be found.

Did they all go in without me? I shuffle past the booth and peek into the open theater, where I find them sitting and laughing together. I feel left out for some reason. Then guilt starts to settle in at the happiness and joy I was feeling for wanting to spend more time here rather than with Zander. It doesn't even seem like any of them cares if I'm here, anyway. It doesn't seem like *Chain* cares if I'm here.

I turn from the theater, rushing out of the building and into my car. I don't bother to send a message to the group. When I arrive home 25 minutes later, no one has texted me to see where I've gone.

Chapter Twenty-Two

Marlie

Zander and I are cuddled in bed, The Office playing in the background. It's the episode with the dundies awards at Chilis. Pam just told Roy that she wants to stay and watch; that if he had asked her, he would know that.

We tend to watch our favorite episodes over and over again. There's comfort in the known.

Zander strokes my arm lightly as I nuzzle my head into his chest. I love the way the little hairs feel against my cheek.

I hear my phone buzz from the nightstand and I reach my arm around to grab it without moving from Zander, my palm slapping the surface a few times before finding the phone. Unplugging it from the charger, I bring it to my face and see a message to the WhatsApp group.

> Damon: So we're meeting at Vigs after you guys grab dinner?

> Lorraine: Yeah, we should be there in about an hour.

Eli: I might be able to make it for drinks!

Gaby: Fuck yeah bro see u there

I stare at the chat to see if anyone else texts. I glance up at Zander, pondering today's events. After getting home and talking to him, I realized I was overreacting to the show thing. I didn't let them know that I was leaving, and really it was such a casual thing it wasn't out of place for me not to stay. The rejection I felt over not being texted, not even by Chain, proved that I was right where I was supposed to be with Zander.

But the prospect of going out for drinks with my friends excites me. I chew the inside of my cheek as I prepare to ask Zander, knowing he won't want to go. I decide to ask anyway.

"Wanna go out for drinks with some of my improv friends tonight?" I ask him.

He watches the scene play out on the screen before turning to me, stopping his rubbing of my arm. "Not really, babe. To do what?"

"I don't know, hang out I guess. I think there's dancing and karaoke sometimes."

"Oh, my favorite things to do." He says it with his half-smile, my smile. But this time, I don't find the humor in it.

"Sorry I don't like the only thing you like—gaming." I can't stop myself from sounding bitter.

"Hey, I was just playin' around, babe." He removes his hand from around my body and sits up a little straighter, forcing me to move my head from his chest. I lift myself and sit cross-legged, facing him.

"I want to go with my friends. I really like them, they're a lot of fun."

"Okay, then go! I don't have a problem with that. I'm pretty tired, anyway."

"But I want you to come with me." *I want you to want to come with me.*

"Maybe next time, babe, but I really am tired. Plus, I thought we were just going to hang out together tonight. I mean, it's no big deal, but I probably would have planned to game if I knew you wanted to go out."

I stare at him. He goes through phases of staying up late and pushing himself with little to no sleep, only to catch up on it for a few days by going to bed early, sleeping in, or both.

"So your options are to hang out with me and sleep early or stay up late and game?"

Now it's Zander's turn to stare. "What are you talking about?"

"Why can't you stay up late with me? Why can't we ever make plans to, I don't know, do *something* we like together?" I'm just as surprised at the words coming out of my mouth as he is, their truth causing my skin to heat.

"Where is this coming from?"

I roll my eyes, the irritation and anger heightening. The chasm in my chest starts to rumble. "What does it matter where it's coming from? It's true, isn't it? We don't have anything in common."

"That's just not true. We love each other, for starters." Zander's reply does nothing to ease my steadily rising temper.

He reaches for my hand and I snatch it away. I see the hurt flash in his eyes, which causes me to pause. We've never fought about this in the entirety of our relationship.

Yeah, but it has bothered you.

I think about that for a moment, and countless events flash through my mind in bits and pieces. Times I've asked him to go to the park, the movies, the beach, or to see a show, and all the times Zander has told me no.

It seems unrealistic, but somehow I can't understand how I'm only just fully realizing how much this bothers me. Why have I just been riding along in this relationship like nothing matters?

"But we're getting married soon, Zander," I tell him. That has to be what it is, the marriage. The reality that this is what I'll have, forever.

"I know. And I'm so excited."

"But we're just never going to do fun things together?"

"Of course we will. I just don't want to go to a bar tonight. And honestly, I didn't think you cared all that much about this kind of thing. I mean, this is the first time you're bringing something like this up."

He's not wrong, not in the slightest. But his accurate assessment digs at something deeper.

How have I let myself get into this mundane routine? Do I even have any interests?

Well, you like improv. And sex.

Improv is a new discovery. And who the hell doesn't like sex? I think back, trying to remember the last time I really did things for fun. Stella and I used to go to the beach all the time, but it's been so long. Why did we stop going?

"We haven't had sex in a few days, is that what's got you feeling off?" Zander asks, preventing me from delving further into my thoughts.

I feel the anger rise again, mixed in with the confusion and surprise. But I can't blame him for asking. Unhealthy as it may be, it's as much a coping mechanism for me as it is a tool for connection.

I latch onto that excuse, rather than fight about this. "Yeah, you're probably right." I laugh lightly, selling the point that I'm just sexually frustrated.

"Go out with your friends, and we can bang one out early tomorrow. I'm probably going to knock out soon, anyway."

"You don't care that I'm not going to stay with you, even though we had plans?" *Shit plans, apparently, but plans all the same.*

"Nah, I want you to have fun," he says, laying back down and settling his head into his stack of pillows.

I don't move, still shocked by the turn of events. How did we end up here? Me leaving to hang out with friends I made doing something I've come to love, and Zander not caring to come with me or be part of that life.

To be fair, it's not like I've ever made any effort to like video games. But it never bothered Zander. We didn't do anything together because there was really nothing I wanted to do.

But it hasn't always been that way. When I was with Jack, we did so many things together. I loved to go dancing and get way too drunk, singing the songs off key and feeling like the luckiest girl in the world in his arms.

But I wasn't the luckiest girl. I was the dumbest.

I'm suddenly seeing my breakup with Jack through new lenses. I knew that it shattered my trust and crushed my heart. But it never occurred to me that it wrecked my spirit, causing me to lose interest in so many things I loved.

I used to socialize a lot. I thought I stopped because I had finished college, keeping only Stella around as my best friend. But that's not what really happened. The truth is undeniable to me now. I had to pick myself up off the ground that Jack let me collapse on. I had to seal the fissure in the chasm that he created.

I just hadn't realized that I shut off all the light along with the dark.

Me: hey guys, I just parked

I'm waiting in my car in Sparkle Comedy's parking lot. I sent my message two minutes ago and no one has answered, although I can see that Damon, Jessica, and Chain have read it. I feel uneasy at their lack of response. What if they don't want me here?

I hear a honk and look up to find Chain's truck turning into the parking lot. Relief floods my system and I hurry out of the car, locking it and walking over as he parks. Damon, Lorraine, and Jessica are in the car with him.

An older, beige Toyota Corolla pulls into the lot with Gaby driving. I wave at him and he waves back, parking next to Chain. I reach the tail end of the truck as Lorraine and Jessica hop out from the back and Damon leaves from the passenger side.

Lorraine and Jessica take turns giving me a hug as Damon shouts to Gaby. I fall into easy conversation with them about how the show and dinner went. I try to ignore the driver of the truck and the reason he's still sitting in there. It's not my business and shouldn't matter to me.

"Where did you disappear to?" Damon asks as he approaches, leaning his shoulder against the passenger side tail light.

"Oh, I—" The sound of the driver's side door opening causes a temporary lapse in my ability to speak. "I, um, I had plans with my boyf—fiancé."

Damn it, I need to stop doing that. I keep my eyes trained on Damon as Chain locks the doors with a resounding beep. Damon's hazel orbs are light-hearted and humorous, the crinkles by his eyes revealing years of laughter and joy. His curly chestnut hair rests just below his eyebrows.

"Well, we missed you. Chain looked for you around the theater before the show started but when he saw your car was gone from the lot we figured something came up."

He looked for me.

I shouldn't feel the immense relief I feel from this information, but I can't help myself.

Isn't it odd how you can be so wrong about a situation solely based on your own limited perception?

Without permission, my eyes search for Chain. He's standing by the tail light, his toned arms crossed and his posture relaxed while he leans on the side of his truck. His gaze is on Damon, his face unreadable.

I can feel my eyes betraying my emotions, so I school my expression and clear my throat before speaking. "Yeah, I should have texted. Sorry."

I leave out the explanation of *why* I didn't text—that it was a sort of test to Chain's feelings for me. It didn't dawn on me until now. I wanted to know if he felt this undeniable pull to me, the way I feel to him.

Because that's what this is—an undeniable pull. If he had disappeared without a trace, there's no doubt I would have looked for him, just like he looked for me.

Does he feel this gravitation, too, then?

"Girl, don't worry about it! It was last minute anyway," Lorraine says to me, grabbing my hand and pulling me towards the sidewalk that leads to Vigs. We wave goodbye to Jessica, who has to get home.

Chain, Damon, and Gaby follow close behind as we all joke around while walking the short distance to the bar. I'm hyper aware of Chain's presence behind me. I can feel it pulling me towards him like a magnet, but I form a new plan of resistance.

I slow my steps so I can walk next to him. When I reach him, he also slows down. Like a well oiled machine, we match pace and fall behind the group.

Unphased, Marlie. Be his friend.

"So you missed me, huh?" I nudge him with my elbow and ignore the electric pulses shooting through me from the point of contact.

He gives me a briefly bemused look before smirking, a twinkle sparking in his emerald eyes. "It's not the same without the whole gang."

See, we're friends. "Well I'm here now, and I am ready to partaaaaay."

"What's your fiancé doing tonight?" Chain asks. His tone is nonchalant, but when I catch his eye, I find that smoke again.

Interesting.

"He was tired, didn't feel like coming."

We turn to the entrance of the bar and get ID'd by the security guard. It's far more crowded than when we come on Friday nights, the front patio filled with people.

"All right, I'll catch you guys later," Gaby says.

"What? Where are you going?" I say incredulously. "We just got here."

"We're going to see if we can find some hot ass," Damon says.

"We might actually get lucky with the amount of women here tonight," Gaby says, looking around appreciatively. He and Damon have been friends since middle school and signed up for the improv class together. It's no wonder they're in agreement here.

"Well, you can at least hang with us for a bit," Lorraine scoffs. "We came here to be *together.*"

The guard has finished checking our ID's and we're walking inside. I see a group of rowdy guys around the pool table, all dressed in similar attire. The guy lining up the pool stick has black slacks and a white dress shirt that's unbuttoned at the top, a red tie loosened around the collar.

Something about him looks familiar. He swiftly shoots the cue ball at the shiny, red 3 ball, then stands up, straightening the pool stick and holding it next to him. The hairs at the back of my neck stand erect from the recognition.

Fuck, fuck, oh my fucking god.

I halt so suddenly that Lorraine bumps into me, falling back a few steps with a mumbled curse. My eyes are popping out of their sockets. He hasn't noticed me and I need to move before he does. I'm screaming at my legs but they're stuck.

"Jack, how are you doin' buddy?"

A pit grows in my stomach, the realization hitting me like a ton of bricks.

Chain knows my traitorous ex.

Chapter Twenty-Three

Chain

Jack looks over, breaking into a wide grin when he sees me. "Chain! The fuck are you doing here, man?"

"I could ask you the same thing," I say, sauntering over to him and shaking his hand with a head nod. We started at the firm around the same time and have worked numerous cases together.

"I'm celebrating my younger brother's bachelor party, we're heading out of here soon. Starting the night off with some pool." He nods towards the table. I glance around and find a guy who looks similar to Jack.

"Congrats," I tell him when I catch his eye. "I'm Chain."

Jack laughs and claps his hand on my back while his brother throws his hand in my direction.

"Thanks, I'm Joe. Nice to meet you," he says as I shake his hand.

"What brings you here, Chain?" Jack asks me as Joe turns back to his friends.

"I'm out with some of my, uh, improv friends." I glance behind me and do a double take when I see Marlie's expression. She looks like she's seen a ghost, her face pale and her body rigid. Lorraine stands by her, taking in the people around the patio and glancing up at the TV screens, completely oblivious. Gaby and Damon are nowhere to be found.

"Improv?" Jack laughs and I whip my head back to him. He coughs when he meets my icy stare. "I didn't realize you'd signed up for classes."

Jack told me about it and I decided to go for it.

The lie I told Ashley echoes in my mind. Jack glances behind me and then drops the pool stick. It clatters noisily, bouncing on the ground before rolling under the pool table.

"Marlie?!"

I look at Marlie, her eyes unblinking and so wide I can't see her eyelids. I look back at Jack, who's lit up like a kid at Christmas. Almost as if...

My chest rumbles with the realization of how they must know each other. My reaction is uncalled for, but I can't help the jealousy that places a scowl on my face before I can hide it. Marlie and Jack don't notice a thing, having a face off that neither of them seems to want to break.

But Marlie does *not* seem excited the way Jack does. Maybe they aren't exes... maybe there's another story here. The rumble in my chest eases with that possibility.

"How have you been, sweetheart?" Jack says, walking towards her. The bar is still buzzing, pop music playing from the speakers.

Sweetheart???

I'm standing awkwardly to the side as Jack closes the ten foot gap between them. I have a perfect view of the back of his head and her beautiful face, which looks haunted at the sight of him.

What the fuck happened here?

I feel like a peeping tom. I should move, I should find Gaby and Damon, or take Lorraine and give them some privacy. But I can't will myself to leave. I'm compelled to watch this play out, to understand how they know each other.

Marlie blinks a few times and gathers herself, crossing her arms in front of her chest. The color is coming back into her cheeks, and indignation takes over the look of panic she wore moments ago.

"Talk to me, sweetie," he repeats, reaching his hand out to stroke her cheek. My arm twitches with the unexplained need to protect her. Does she want him touching her? It sure doesn't fucking seem like it. I take a step forward, fists clenched, when she speaks.

"I'm, uh, good." I take another step, neither of them noticing.

"I've missed you." His voice is all silk. I've heard it a thousand times with countless women when we're out at a bar. But the way he's talking to Marlie, it's as if she was more than that. Who misses a one-night stand? Maybe she was a recurring fuck.

The swirls in Marlie's eyes turn to a burnt caramel. Her chin lifts a centimeter, an air of confidence replacing the shock and hesitation.

"Well, you laid that bed for yourself, didn't you?" Her tone sends chills down my spine.

"Aww, come on, sweetheart," Jack oozes. He reaches his arm out to her but this time, Marlie takes a step back. That's my cue to step in. "I was an asshole and a dumbass, that doesn't mean I didn't love you."

LOVE?!

I reach Marlie's side but don't look at her, refusing to acknowledge what I'm doing.

"It seems like she doesn't want to speak with you, Jack." My tone is cool as I stare daggers at him. Jack stares at me, his jaw slack in shock. He looks to Marlie then back to me.

Then he laughs. The motherfucker *laughs.*

"Dude, Marlie and I have history. Don't cockblock."

My blood boils. I go from 0 to 60 faster than a Lamborghini and I have no time to think through what I utter.

"She's taken."

That wipes the cocky smirk right off his face. The satisfaction I feel at that slightly dulls the anger, allowing me to think clearly for a moment.

This is Jack, your friend. And that's Marlie, your other friend.

"You're runnin' around on Ashley?" Jack asks, astonished. "That's not your style."

"You have the *audacity* to—" Marlie's shouts are drowned out by Jack's rowdy brother and friends walking up behind him, telling him it's time to go. His brother hands him a shot and he takes it, eyes me and Marlie, then places the glass on a nearby table before allowing his brother and friends to drag him to the exit.

I watch him go, unable to move. My chest rises and falls rapidly with my furious breathing. I can't bring myself to face Marlie, to face what I just did. I know she's still next to me because of the buzzing energy I feel, but she hasn't moved either.

"What the hell was *that* about?" I jump as Lorraine's voice breaks the silence. I was so engrossed in what happened I forgot she was even there. Marlie doesn't respond and neither do I. The anger is slowly simmering, and shame and confusion take over.

I'm not the type of guy whose feelings run his mouth, and yet this isn't the first time this happens. I keep losing control when I'm around her.

I take Marlie in from my periphery, who's staring at the empty space Jack occupied moments ago. This girl is going to be the death of me. I have no business caring about her past. But I've known Jack a long time, and I know how he is with women. How could he have gotten involved with Marlie?

"How do you know Jack?" I can't stop the words from being spoken. Don't ask me why I'm holding my breath. I just need to hear what she says. I need confirmation from her.

My voice breaks the spell his presence had on her and she looks over to me. Her chocolate eyes have no trace of the caramel swirls I've grown attached to.

I watch her expectantly, albeit impatiently. She opens her lips, then smashes them together. I'm about to repeat myself when Lorraine speaks again. I jump in surprise for the second time because it's hard for me to focus on anything but Marlie's answer.

"Do you guys wanna grab a drink before we dive into this mess?" She walks inside without waiting for our answer.

Marlie breaks our eye contact, achieving what I seem unable to do. As she walks away, I'm momentarily freed from the building tension her lack of response has left. My eyes drift towards her perfectly round ass that slightly bounces as her hips sway. Her movements are brisk, the need for her to get away obvious.

A woman's involvement with Jack can only lead to a few places and I don't like any of them for Marlie. The best case scenario is that he fucked her and never called her again. But the stare off, the I miss you, the sweethearts...

The tension returns with the anger boiling in my blood. I've never been more mad at myself for skipping a workout, knowing if I had blown off steam today this wouldn't be so hard. I clench my fist as I follow Marlie through the door she threw open without looking back. The inside is as packed as the patio was, and I have to search to find Lorraine in the center of the crowd around the bar. The air in here is cramped and tense, mirroring and heightening my own emotions.

I look around to see if there are any open tables or areas, finding none. I turn back and return to the patio, needing open space to think clearly. Plus, I want to be able to listen to Marlie's answers without having to fight to be heard.

I watch as a group of women stands up from the back corner table that has a wooden bench and chairs surrounding it. The glasses on their table are empty.

I move quickly, intent on claiming the table for us. I arrive as they make to leave, and one of the women places her hand on my forearm. The muscle flexes from the irritation her action causes.

"Ooooo, strong muscle man over here," she slurs, giggling and wagging her eyebrows while she looks at her friends for appreciation.

"Remove your hand from me, please," I snap. As if burned, she removes her hand. Her eyes widen and she raises her arms in mock surrender before laughing. One of her friends pulls her away and she stumbles before righting herself and leaving.

I take a seat on the bench and pull out my phone to text Marlie and Lorraine. I send them a group message:

> Me: I grabbed the back table on the patio, facing the pool table. Please order me a Macallan, neat. I'll pay in cash.

I toss my phone on the table and lean back, closing my eyes. I spread my arms across the back of the bench, hoping this posture relaxes me. When I open my eyes, I focus on the wall, taking in the wooden planks that crisscross with intertwining vines. As my inhales become deeper, the exhales calm my mind. The reaction I had starts to seem exaggerated.

What kind of hold does this woman have over me? Why do I keep finding myself in these situations where I feel completely out of control? I don't like to feel powerless. And yet, the way I feel around her... it's addictive and intoxicating.

The admission is like an antidote, breaking the illusion spell I've cast over myself. My refusal to lose control, to feel anything other than in power, has had me resisting the magnetic pull I feel towards her. The truth floods in and my body tingles from the release.

God, that feels fucking good. I let out a sigh only I can hear. The feeling is familiar, but the cause is foreign.

As a young kid, I was a victim—to my dad's bullying, my own insecurities, and my mother's denial. When I hit puberty and grew a bit of facial hair, girls at school started showing me attention. The growing confidence I gained from that and wrestling was what gave me the courage to fight back one day.

My father swung at me after I struck out of the baseball game, leading us to lose the game before the playoffs. For the first time in my whole life, I threw my hand out in defense and caught his wrist. I was 14 years old.

While it stopped him momentarily, the look of shock that assaulted his beady eyes is etched into my memory. And though he proceeded to pound his fist into me, I doubled over with blood dripping from my mouth and one single thought—I will fight back.

It was that look of shock that drove me to workout everyday, hours at a time. Each push up was a reminder of what I would not allow him to do to me anymore. Each suspended pull up was the determination to become stronger. Each mile I ran was me outrunning the fear I lived behind.

The fear that I wasn't good enough, that I wasn't strong enough. At 14 years old, I told that fear to fuck off and I made it my life's mission to never cower again.

I need my control. I need my power. I can't go back to the coward I was under my fathers fist.

I'm torn from my remembrance when a glass of whiskey is placed down in front of me. My eyes shoot up and I see Lorraine settling into the bench next to me. I look around, but she's alone.

"She's coming," Lorraine says, a knowing look in her eye.

I don't reply, instead lifting my glass and downing half of it in one go. I know I'm coming off as an asshole, and I really don't give a fuck.

Chain Matthews didn't become the man he is today by giving a shit what others think.

But he didn't loose his cool over a fucking woman, either.

Chapter Twenty-Four

Marlie

Where are your feet? Take deep breaths.

I give myself the pep talk I save for special occasions such as these. The ones that have my heart beating out of my chest. The ones that have the waters in the chasm roaring, refusing to be quieted.

I stare at my reflection in the mirror, seeing the tears in my eyes from holding them wide open for so long. If I didn't force myself to blink, I swear they would stay open permanently. I run my hands through my auburn hair as I take deep breaths, calming my nerves. I feel like my reaction to some guy's presence is ridiculous and dramatic.

The problem is, he's not some guy. He's a guy who ripped my heart out of my chest, crushed it, and left the pulverized dust on the floor.

I know the saying—shattered my heart into a million pieces. See, if my heart were shattered into pieces, you could pick them up and at least *try* to glue them back together. But with one gust of wind, the dust flew off and scattered in the wind, making it impossible to repair.

So to see the man who caused that anguish, was it really such an overreaction?

Of course, I've played innumerable scenarios in my mind as to what it would be like if I ever saw him again. What he would say, what I would say, how we would react. It was pretty much all I could think about in the beginning of our end. As the days, then weeks, went by, the frequency of the thoughts simmered along with my anger. Once years passed and I'd moved on, the fear of it happening went dormant.

I blink heavily, wetting my eyes and popping my lips before releasing the firm grip I have on the bathroom sink.

I'm at the bar with Chain and Lorraine. I'm going to have a good night.

Feeling resolved in my affirmations, I pull open the dingy door to the small and dirty bathroom. I walk out of the hallway and grab my drink from where I left it on the corner of the bar before walking to the patio.

I spot them in the corner Chain said he'd be at. I find him staring directly in front of him, his jaw tense and hard. Lorraine takes a sip of her drink and her eyes roam to me as I walk in their direction. She gives me a wave and excited smile, patting the spot between her and Chain. The short walk in the fresh air with somewhat calmed nerves clears my mind, allowing another thought to take hold.

How could Chain be friends with a guy like Jack?

Before I can get upset, the look Chain wore when he was asking how I knew Jack flashes in my mind. That look screamed fury. Why would he be angry that I know his *friend?*

Deciding to put these thoughts to the back of my mind, I get to the table and Lorraine moves to stand up. I give her a smile with a shake of my head and pull out the empty chair next to her, facing Chain.

I move my drink to my lips, the perspiration on the cold glass mixing with the sweat on my hand, effectively ending thoughts about Jack. The cold liquid on my lips refreshes me, and I'm determined to forget the entire situation.

"So, how *do* you know that guy? What was his name?" Lorraine asks, crossing her legs and putting her glass down.

Well, there goes that plan.

Determined to have my way, I reply curtly, “He’s an ex.”

I take another swig of my drink and place the glass down, then meet Chain’s impervious stare. His emerald eyes are dark and fiery. I again wonder why he looks so pissy about the fact that I know Jack. Why should he care?

“I think the better question is, how does Chain know Jack?” I say to Lorraine without breaking eye contact with Chain. His jaw ticks, his eyes turning steely.

I can’t understand his reaction. *Unless...*

“He’s a coworker. We started together at the firm.” His response is laced with venom, as though he despises that fact.

“I don’t think he realizes you don’t like him,” Lorraine says, her eyes widening and eyebrows raising, looking him up and down as though she’s got Jack all figured out. Chain gives her a once over before returning his gaze to mine.

“We—” he cuts his response short and sits up straighter, one arm falling from the back of the bench to his side as he picks up his glass and swirls the iceless amber liquid with the other.

“It’s fine, really. I just want to have a fun night and forget about him,” I say, willing this entire topic to disappear like the last chug of my drink, which I down in one go. Chain gives me a hard stare before draining his own glass, standing up, and leaving without a word.

What is with him?

“Yeessss! Let’s have fun,” Lorraine cheers, pumping her fist with excitement. She doesn’t seem the least bit fazed by his behavior, and neither should I. “It’s nights like these I wish I didn’t have a girlfriend.”

Well, there goes Eli’s chances for her. “What’s her name?”

"Rebecca. We've been together for a couple of months, nothing serious. If it wasn't for that, I'd be looking for my own piece of ass. I'm missing a good fuck with a guy."

She takes in my look of confusion and rolls her eyes. "I'm bi. Come on, Marlie, keep up."

I giggle and lean back in my chair, the drink finally making its way through my stiff body. I ease into the calming effects and Lorraine's infectious energy. I guess Eli's still got a chance, after all.

"Poor Rebecca," I say, feeling a bit sorry for her. It's never fun to be the one holding a person back.

"Ah," Lorraine says dismissively with a wave of her hand. "We're having fun. I'll have my chance once we're over."

"You don't see a future with her?"

"Pffft. I don't see a future with anyone. I'm all about the moment." She sits back and looks around the patio, her green eyes twinkling from the reflection of the lights strung along the space. Her bleach blonde hair is loud, but not in an obnoxious way. It says, "I'm here, world, take it or leave it."

I like Lorraine.

Her words have me twirling my engagement ring, the solitaire diamond feeling bulky with each spin as it clashes into the fingers beside it. During scenes, I have to turn it upside down so the rock is by my palm. Otherwise, I find that the weight is distracting, or it catches on my clothes.

What would it be like to be all about the moment? I don't ask myself that question enough. Maybe I'm afraid of what I'll find if I do. But Lorraine's words led me to ask it, so I answered.

Confused. Vulnerable. Alive.

I'm confused by what's going on with Chain and these inexplicable interactions we have. It's like when our eyes meet, I'm lifted from the world and transported to a place where only we exist. It's so raw, and real, and unfamiliar, I don't know how to handle it.

I'm vulnerable because I just saw Jack for the first time in years and my emotions were on display for not only him, but anyone who saw. I couldn't do anything besides openly gape at him. The hold he still has over me is now blaringly obvious, and I can't ignore it.

But god, do I feel *alive.* I'm out on a Saturday night for the first time in a long time, without Stella. I'm feeling real feelings, and allowing it. The fact that I feel alive makes me realize just how numb I've truly been.

I blink back tears from my eyes as I pick up my glass absentmindedly, remembering it's empty only when the melted ice touches my lips. The coldness shocks my senses and I look over to Lorraine, who is staring off at the patio, the corners of her lips turned up slightly.

She looks like someone who is sure of herself and her feelings. She's not bogged down by the actions of others. She's alive.

I want to be alive, too.

Chain returned with a round of drinks and we all talked as we enjoyed the ambiance. On my third drink, Gaby and Damon arrived with a round of shots before disappearing again. By my fifth drink, we laughed as we saw them exiting the bar with a woman slung on each of their sides.

I was entranced by Damon's hold on his girl's waist. His touch was so sensual, her smile was so playful, and both their eyes were lust filled.

When was the last time I felt wanted like that?

Drawing a blank, my gaze involuntarily roams to Chain. He's laughing at whatever Lorraine is saying, his white teeth shining through the dim lighting. His eyes are no longer dark, contrasting against his nearly-black hair that has the same soft wave I love.

I want him to want me like that.

The thought flows freely through my mind, the alcohol preventing me from stifling it. And tonight, I find that I quite like it. I'm not sure if it's the alcohol or the newfound desire to be alive, but I want to revel in it. I'm tired of fighting the open fissure in this chasm.

"Well, lovelies, this birdies gotta fly," Lorraine says, gathering her keys and phone off the table. "It's after midnight and"—she hiccups before continuing—"Rebecca is waiting for me."

I stand up and sway just a bit before steadying myself. *Fuck, I cannot drive like this.*

"We'll walk you," Chain says, standing up himself. I know he's kept up with Lorraine and I in drinks, but he doesn't seem inebriated the way we do. It's not fair that guys have a higher tolerance.

"I didn't drive, Chainy boy." Lorraine shoves his shoulder playfully and starts walking towards the exit.

We follow her out to the curb as she types on her phone. "I'm just ordering an Uber," she says.

"We'll wait with you," Chain states.

Aww, that's so nice.

Chain smirks and replies, "I'm sure any man would make sure a woman gets to her car safely."

Fuck, did I say that out loud??

"How drunk are you?" Lorraine laughs as she finishes typing on her phone and then locks the screen.

"I wanna dance," I declare. *Where did that come from?*

"Maybe next time. My ride is pulling up," Lorraine says, watching the road for her driver.

A shiny, black Honda Civic peels up and halts hastily in front of where Lorraine stands. She gives us a short wave with a smirk. The moment her feet leave the concrete sidewalk, the car tires peel off the asphalt and into the night road once more.

"Well, you probably shouldn't drive like this," Chain says.

"Definitely not!" I say loudly. I pull out my phone, thinking I'll call Zander to come pick me up. I find it odd when the only notification on my screen is a text from Eli to the group chat.

Eli: couldn't make it guys

Zander usually would have checked in by now. *He's probably sleeping.*

"I can drive you home," Chain offers. I look back up at him, a second delayed.

"Um," I say. Then what, leave my car here? "I think I'll be okay in a bit. I have some water in my car."

"I really don't mind," he says, taking a step closer to me. My feet move of their own accord, taking a step towards him.

This is wrong. You have a boyfriend. Gah, I mean a fiancé!

I need to destroy these feelings. I am in a committed relationship with a man I love. I have been cheated on. I know what it feels like. This is so, so wrong.

But you're not even choosing to feel these things.

That's the worst part of it all, isn't it? I feel completely helpless to this pull. It's as if my soul has found its home.

"It's fine. I'll wait it out and once the fog clears, I'll head home," I tell him decisively. He opens his mouth as if to argue, but instead closes it with a tick of his jaw and nods in the direction of our cars. His hands are in his pockets, the belt on his jeans visible from the corner where his shirt is wrinkled into his arm.

Goddamn, he looks gorgeous. My own jaw goes slack, and I feel a heat burn through my core, traveling down and settling on my pussy. I start to imagine what it would be like to run my tongue along the skin above his belt and loosen the clip securing his cock. I wonder how big—

Chain clears his throat and my eyes shoot from his groin to his face. He's watching me intently, a smolder in his gaze that matches my own.

Fuck, he saw me checking him out. FUCK! Why was I checking him out? This is WRONG, Marlie.

"Sorry, got lost in thought for a minute there." I avert my gaze and take off towards our cars. I feel him walking close behind me, and I quicken my pace. The sooner we get there, the better. I need some water to clear my head.

When we get to the lot, I unlock my doors, pull the half empty water bottle from the cup holder, and twist the cap off. I chug the remaining water, the heat of the liquid burning down my throat but still quenching my thirst.

I toss the bottle back into the car. It bounces off the passenger seat to the floor below, rolling around before settling by the door. I step back and shut the door roughly, hearing the sharp slam of the metals meeting.

When I turn around, I come face to face with Chain. My nose is mere inches from his chest, my head resting just below his chin. I'm so close I can see the rise and fall of his rapid breaths.

I take a step back, my heel catching on the ground and my ankle twisting. Before I can take the fall, Chain's broad hands shoot out and catch me at the hips, steadying me with his powerful grip. His fingers dig into my tender skin, sending shocks of pleasure shooting through me.

I grip his forearm, leaning on him so I can right my foot and stand up normally. Alcohol does not bode well with my klutz tendencies.

I force my eyes to stay on his chest. I know if our eyes meet, we'll be caught in the wave. I've been fighting to rise to the surface, but I can feel the softening within to flow with the current.

I release my grip on him and I feel his hands loosen on my hips, his fingers grazing softly as he pulls away. I feel their absence like my lungs feel the need for oxygen.

"Sorry I'm such a klutz."

"No need to apologize. I just worry about what happens to you when you're alone."

It's easier when I'm alone because I don't have you distracting me.

He steps back and holds his hand out, indicating for me to walk past. I open the hatchback door of my car so I can sit and sober up. Then, I'll go home and wake Zander up to satisfy the pulsing need in my clit. The tightness of my jean shorts presses on it, teasing me further. I squeeze my thighs and squirm, giving a small release to the pressure I feel building.

Chain comes to stand over me, his large body creating a shadow from the light he's blocking behind him. Feeling like I've stifled these urges, I look up at him.

Nope, I haven't stifled shit. The need resurfaces, this time in my chest cavity. It's an ache that I want soothed. The alcohol still floating through my system makes it really hard to ignore. The darkness makes it difficult for me to read Chain's expression but he must feel this energy. It's crackling.

I absentmindedly reach for my necklace and when my fingers find the Z, I freeze. I tear my eyes from his direction. Guilt replaces the ache I felt from needing to touch him, feel him. I'm consumed by the guilt, swallowing down the lump in my throat.

The only good news about this is it's sobering me up. The vitality I feel from these interactions replaces the booze.

Chain is just a friend. A very, very sexy friend. You love Zander. You belong with Zander.

As my thoughts try to convince me, I tug on the Z with my thumb and index finger. But rather than feeling the pressure on the back of my neck, I feel it in my heart.

Chapter Twenty-Five

Chain

"Why do you still wear that necklace if you're engaged?" Shit. I meant to ask a casual, friendly question, like if she plans on taking the next improv class. But she started playing with that damned necklace and I had to know. It's becoming clear that I cannot control the filter on my mouth when I'm around her. I have no choice but to be honest.

At least I was able to keep the bitterness out of my tone.

"Oh, um—" she drops the pendant and looks up at me. She's just as breathtaking in the dark as she is in the light. Her eyes still shine and the light freckles peppered across her nose shift when she raises her brows. "It wasn't like a promise necklace or something."

I snort.

"What?"

"Let me clue you in. If a man gives you a piece of jewelry, he's claiming you."

Marlie's eyes narrow before she rolls them. "That's a machismo way of thinking."

I laugh heartily this time. "Maybe so, but take it from a *friend*—" the word burns on my tongue, requiring me to swallow before finishing. "He was trying to claim you."

She looks at me thoughtfully, as though she's really taking in what I've said.

"That's fine though, right? You guys are engaged," I add after a stretch of silence.

We need to get away from this conversation. The feelings surfacing are not safe, and I will not entertain any thoughts about a relationship while she's in one. Fuck, while *I'm* in one.

"Yeah," she says slowly. Her eyes have glazed over, as if she's lost in thought. I move to sit next to her in her trunk but it's a tight space.

"Why don't we hang on my truck bed? There's more room." I don't wait for her reply as I start to walk to my Chevy. I cannot risk having our bodies touching. It's clear that it causes some strange chemical reaction, and I'm not sure how much of that I can take. It's the same reason I didn't offer to dance with her—I can't risk these intimate moments becoming anything more. I hear the slam of her trunk and my lips tug into a smile, which turns into a frown in the next second.

What is it about this girl that feels so good? So right? I can't shake it and I can't stop it. And for the first time, I'm feeling like I want more.

I've never felt this way, and it scares me. But I can't deny it anymore.

I pull the tailgate down and step up, taking a seat and letting my legs dangle off. I make sure to sit as close to the edge as possible so Marlie has plenty of room. If I'm forced to touch her again I don't think I will be able to control myself.

She follows me onto the truck and when she's comfortably seated, I turn my head towards her and cross my arms.

"Are you going to join the next level?" I ask her. My senses are tingling, the hairs on my arms standing up. I've got my mind trained to focus, but my body is acting of its own accord.

"You know, I really want to," she says, looking out across the parking lot. "I really thought this was just going to be another chore. A stupid course to finish so I could toss the completion certificate at HR and call it a day."

"But you've fallen in love with it?" *I know I have.*

She turns to me and licks her bottom lip, biting down on it before replying, "That's one way of phrasing it."

Fuck, I can't do this. Her tongue swiping across her lip has my dick throbbing. I move my hips and rearrange my sitting position so the jeans I'm wearing form a crease over the area, hiding my growing cock. I don't need my lust on display.

"I know what you mean. I wanted to take a stand-up comedy class, but I couldn't find any. This was the next best thing."

She looks surprised at my admission. "Standup comedy, huh?"

"What, you don't find me funny?" I laugh.

"It's not that, necessarily," she says. "You're not *not* funny. You just seem so... serious?"

I throw my hand on my chest in mock indignance. "Got it, not funny."

"No! Oh my god, you are funny, Chain. I just meant that I wouldn't expect a lawyer to have a secret dream of being a comedian."

"You seem to have a lot of preconceived notions about lawyers. Why—" and then it clicks.

My eyes dart to hers, searching for confirmation. I find it instantly when she averts her gaze and looks down at her swinging converse. Left, right, left, right.

Deciding it wouldn't be the friendly thing to do to press the issue, I don't. "Well, I dreamed of being a comedian as a child. I love making people feel joy, even if just for a moment."

"That's..." She trails off, her feet stilling. "That's great."

I dig my hand into my pocket, pulling out a tin.

"Mint?" I offer. She reaches her hand out and I put one in her hand before tossing one into my mouth. We sit in comfortable silence, the only sound being that of the wind lightly blowing the trees around us.

"Do you ever feel like you're wearing a mask?" I blurt out. I'm not fully sure where the confession came from. I guess her doubt of my desire to be something other than a man in a suit, emanating power. Can't she see that it's a need, not a want?

Of course she can't, Chain. You've perfected this facade to ensure that you're never the weak one.

"What do you mean?"

"Like you put on a show for the world. Like you make sure to be who you have to be."

She stays quiet for an uncomfortable amount of time, gazing at the sky above. The need to fill the silence itches at my tongue, but I resist the urge to scratch it. Instead, I watch as she pensively stares at the stars, or maybe the constellations. Or maybe she's looking but not seeing, mulling over what I've said.

Because I've basically admitted, on some level, that I wear a mask. A truth I've entrusted to no one until tonight.

"No," she says. "I mean, I get it. I've acted certain ways when I needed to. But I wouldn't call it a mask."

She finally turns to me. Our eyes lock and I'm forever fucked. Keeping something like this in the dark, even to myself most times, has created a fear of it coming to light. I expected to feel judged, or told I was crazy.

Her eyes reflect the moonlight above and all I see is understanding.

This truth brings me to another, and then another, and then another. A chest that has been locked up tight has been opened and tossed on the ground, scattering all the things I've kept buried within.

I'm living a half life. I keep relationships at surface level and focus on my career because it feeds my feelings of inferiority. I'm with a woman I knew wasn't for me from the instant we met, yet I'm still with her 3 years later.

Ashley. Her name sends a wave of nausea over me. Not only for the fact that I can no longer deny just how unhappy I am with her, but because I know what that truth means.

And it requires action.

Marlie's words snap me out of the bombardment of truths zooming through my mind. "I hope you're not wearing a mask now."

I really feel like I'm not. I look at her again and her penetrating gaze sends a ripple of pleasure through me. A moment passes where we hang in tandem, focusing on each other and nothing more.

I want to tell her I'm not. I want to dive into the sincere depths of her irises and explore all of her other hopes.

But she's engaged to be married, and I have a girlfriend. So instead, I smirk.

"There'd be no way for you to know, would there?"

She smirks back, a playful gleam in her eye. "I like to think of myself as a decent judge of character."

"Oh, yeah? I don't think so, Mar. The lawyer you have me pegged as seems a bit off. I suppose..." I trail off, remembering about Jack and not wanting to force her to discuss something she doesn't want to.

And it's none of your business.

The tightening in my chest begs to differ, but I choose to ignore it.

"Why do you call me Mar?"

"I don't know. Marlie, Mar—it just made sense. What, no one calls you Mar?"

"Oddly enough, no." She's frowning, as if the thought makes her question her circle of friends.

"Well, unless you oppose, I plan to."

"No opposition here, your honor." She holds up three fingers like she's in a damn courtroom. I roll my eyes.

"You're thinking of a judge."

"Oh, whatever." We laugh and settle into another stretch of companionable silence. The air between us is alive with that familiar energy, the one that makes me want to do all the things I shouldn't.

"Well, as long as you know whether you're wearing the mask or not is all that really matters, right? The worst is when you don't even know who you are anymore." Her return to our earlier conversation surprises me but the truth in her words have me staring in admiration.

"Well I've made you laugh, so the comedian thing shouldn't seem too far of a stretch anymore."

"I didn't laugh! It was half smiles, at *best.*"

"Then why are you holding back a laugh now?"

We both start giggling, losing ourselves to the moment. I can't remember the last time I felt this loose, this free.

Too fucking long ago.

Our conversation evolves into our interests and personal lives. What work is like, our favorite things, and fun stories. It excites me to know we have the same taste in shows and music. The way she looks up to the left when remembering details about her escapades with her friends makes my heart glow with warmth.

When my eyelids start to feel heavy and the absence of the sound of cars on the roads reminds me it must be late, I ask her, "How are you feeling? You think you're ready to go?" She looks significantly calmer and clear-eyed.

She pulls out her phone, the time 3:42 am flashing across the screen before answering, "Yeah. Damn, it got late fast."

"Time flies when you're having fun, right?" I joke, keeping my tone light. But my stomach does a flip, making me acutely aware that it was anything but.

She laughs, sliding forward on the truck door before hopping down and landing on both feet steadily. "That's right."

I hop down from the tailgate and shut the door in one swift motion, then wipe my hands before motioning towards her car.

"Thanks again for waiting with me," she says when we reach the trunk of her car. She's looking up at me, her long eyelashes batting a few times.

"I'm not sure you thanked me yet, but you're welcome just the same." I'm not sure what leads me to do it, but I give her a playful punch on the shoulder. She looks surprised—rightfully so. It's certainly out of character for me. I guess that's how desperately I need to feel close to her. I'm punching her like a dad playing with his 6 year old.

Or like she plays with Eli.

An awkward silence hangs over us, the exact kind that you see in a sappy rom-com when a couple is about to have their first fucking kiss. Those scenes always cause me to cringe a bit inside, seeming so vulnerable. But in this instance, I wish we were one of those couples.

End this, now.

"Okay, well, get home safe."

"Thanks, again."

"You're welcome, again, again."

She grins and her eyes shine so bright. It's like watching a shooting star, and my heart knows what it's wishing for.

I take that thought as my cue and pivot on my heel, crushing any chance my heart thinks it has.

She's engaged. You are in a relationship.

The racing of my heart tells me that it doesn't care. I head back to my truck, trying to control the palpitations. I get into the driver's seat of my Chevy Silverado, comforting myself with the control I'll feel with the wheel in my reign.

As I back out of the lot and pull onto the road to head home, the realization hits me square in the face: for once, I was not wearing a mask.

Chapter Twenty-Six

Chain

"CHAIN!" Ashley's shout startles me out of my dreamless sleep. I bat my eyes open; the first thing I see is the alarm clock on my nightstand. I'm groggy, so I know I couldn't have slept much.

That, and you were out late.

The clock reads 10:13 am, the bright red numbers flashing at me. I groan, realizing I've slept in later than I normally do.

"I'm up," I mumble, hoping to god this is the last I'll hear of this.

"We had plans for brunch!" she shouts, her hands on her hips. She looks pissed, and I honestly can't even blame her. I did give her my word.

"Sorry, I'm gettin' up." I roll out of bed, landing heavily on my feet. I make my way to the bathroom, throwing cold water on my face before taking a piss and brushing my teeth.

When I walk back out of the bathroom, I find Ashley sitting at the edge of the couch, waiting for me.

"Get dressed, we're running late," she says. I go into the room and throw on a light teal and white striped polo with fitted jeans, checking my appearance briefly in the long mirror before meeting her back in the living room.

"Let's do this," I say, more to myself than to her. Ashley had a big brunch planned with her friends and I committed to it, somehow completely forgetting it until she woke me up this morning.

I normally wouldn't attend something like this, but she left town Monday so we haven't seen each other all week. I figured it was the least I could do. I took care of work when I got back from the theater Friday night to free up this Sunday morning. I hadn't anticipated being out so late last night.

The thought brings Marlie's face into my vision and my stomach does a weird swooping thing.

Ashley doesn't answer but leads the way to the front door and yanks it open. I walk up behind her and hold it open, waiting for her to walk through before I follow and lock the door behind us.

We take the ride down on the elevator and reach Ashley's Audi A7. She saunters to the passenger side and I hold her door open obligingly, playing into the charade. We're pulling onto the road at 10:27 am.

The silence on the ride over to the restaurant is deafening. I know I've fucked up, and I'm searching for the typical guilt I'd feel that isn't there.

This isn't right.

The words provide me a different culpability. When I'd normally just feel sorry and chalk the shitty behavior up to our song and dance, today I feel wrong. Like I'm wearing someone else's shoes that are my size; they fit but they're not accustomed to my foot. Today, I don't want to sing or dance to this tune.

When have you ever, really?

The pang in my chest hurts. The realization comes crashing down on me, like a giant bucket of ice cold water.

I take my eyes off the road for a moment and glance at Ashley, who has her head turned to the window. The scowl she wears is not surprising. But for the first time, I see something else, too.

I see how my behaviors have caused her anger. I also see... a woman I am not in love with, and truthfully never have been. And while I've always known it deep inside, it's never bothered me the way it does now.

I tear my gaze from her and focus on the road. I grimace, refusing to let this spiral out of control right now. I'll figure it out later. What does it matter that I don't have deep feelings for her? That's not something I want, anyway. Is it?

Caramel swirls in chocolate eyes blink at me. I shake my head and pop open the tin of mints I keep in the car, tossing one into my mouth. "How was your trip?"

I don't need to look at her face to know that she's rolling her eyes. But she answers me anyway. Maybe she's aware of this dance, too. "It was fine enough. Grace wanted to go out for drinks and I swear the only reason..."

I half-listen to her talk about her sister and the time they spent together. I actually quite like Ashley's sister, but Ashley always feels attacked by her one way or another. We're close to the restaurant and my thoughts threaten to drift back into doubt.

Is this really what you want to deal with forever?

I pull up to the valet and exit the car, handing the keys over silently to the gentleman who immediately walked to the driver's side. I circle the car and hold Ashley's door open, providing her my hand as support for her to walk out in her *very* high-heeled shoes.

She gives me a small smile that I actually see reflected in her eyes. How is she so accepting of my crappy behavior? How can this not bother her?

It didn't seem to bother you much before, either.

Fuck. What the fuck is going on? Ashley places her arm in the crook of my elbow as I walk us into the restaurant. I can't stop listening to the thoughts that berate me.

She doesn't care because she wants to be seen with a man on her arm, that's the extent of this.

We've been at this pretense for a few years. The reality of the situation is not what's new. It's the thoughts that are coming from it, the feelings I'm getting. Where I used to be okay with this, now I'm not.

I continue to try and snap myself out of this rabbit hole I've jumped down as Ashley checks in with the host. They lead us to a table in the center of the restaurant where I see her friend, Lauren, seated next to a surfer looking blonde dude. The guy stands up and greets us, giving me a handshake with a smile and placing a light kiss on Ashley's cheek.

We take the open seats in front of them, leaving the two seats to our right and their left empty. I don't even know who's coming to this brunch. The waiter takes our drink orders and I sip on the water that was already waiting for us.

"The others are coming soon, then we'll order our food!" Lauren says excitedly to Ashley. They pick up a conversation quickly and I make small talk with surfer dude, whose name is Jake.

Once the others arrive, we place our orders and receive our drinks. We get our plates and Ashley notes promptly that she got scrambled eggs rather than the ordered over-easy. Since it wasn't the waiter who brought our food to the table, she scans the restaurant, locating him with another group. When he walks away she raises her hand, catching his attention.

He walks over quickly and opens his mouth to speak when Ashley cuts him off. "This isn't what I ordered."

She pushes the plate forward an inch, then crosses her arms in front of her chest. I place my hand on her knee, giving her a light squeeze.

"Oh, I'm so sorry about that," the waiter says. His tone, however, doesn't match the sincerity of his words. I can't even say I blame the guy; the attitude in Ashley's voice was evident.

The waiter reaches for her plate but she waves him off before he can get to it. "I don't want to be the only one not eating. Just forget about it."

It hurts to keep my face neutral. It's just like her to act like this.

"Would you like us to have the right eggs brought over while you start eating?" the waiter says. This time, he doesn't bother to pretend that he cares.

"I eat my eggs *first*. I'll just have these, it's fine. In the future, do your job right."

The waiter looks at me, then back at Ashley. She uncrosses her arms and picks up her fork. I squeeze her knee again, trying to keep her from causing more of a scene. All her friends are staring at their plates or pretending not to notice, except for Lauren. Of course Lauren is staring daggers at the waiter, as if he's completely ruined our brunch.

Following Ashley's suit, I grab my fork when the waiter surprises me by speaking again. "With all due respect, why did you call me over to inform me of the problem with your eggs if you didn't intend to have it corrected?"

Ashley's jaw drops before she whips her head in my direction. She's giving me a look that reads, "Are you going to do something about this?"

The guy is definitely being a dick now. I can't even blame him, and I honestly don't care to defend Ashley. I don't make a conscious decision to do what I do next. I pick up my knife and cut into my omelet before leaning my head forward towards my fork. I see from my peripheral that the waiter stalks off and Ashley is still staring at me.

Maybe on some subconscious level, I want to piss her off. This is not a part of our dance. I'm the man, I'm supposed to protect and defend her. Even if she is acting like a cunt. But I can't summon the desire to do it, even if it makes me look like a dick to her friends.

So, instead, I take a bite of my food and start chewing.

The tension lasted about 30 seconds before the guy to the right of Lauren made a joke about shitty waitstaff. I didn't bother to remember the names of the other people there, staying quiet while they laughed and ate. Ashley and I didn't interact for the rest of the brunch, and we drove the ride home in silence.

I didn't open her door when the valet pulled up and I didn't open it for her when we got back to the apartment. She said nothing.

The moment the apartment door snapped shut, she rounded on me. "What the fuck was that?"

I place the keys on the kitchen counter and watch her coolly. "You were being a bitch."

Her jaw drops and she scoffs. "That waiter—"

"That waiter was doing his job. There were a lot of other ways you could have spoken to him."

"Since when does it matter if someone was doing their job? My order was fucked up. It was his job to ensure it was done properly."

"We don't have to eat there again."

"We definitely won't! And after the way you acted, I don't know how I'll ever look at my friends the same way."

I look into her eyes and search them, looking for... something. Anything to give me an inclination to care.

"You can't expect me to defend your shitty behavior."

"You didn't have a problem doing it before!" She's shouting, her finger pointed at me accusingly.

"Maybe I don't want to keep partaking in this charade." I try to keep my tone even; I can feel the emotion bubbling up from that chest I've worked so hard to keep shut tight.

"What's that supposed to mean?" Her voice conveys extreme offense. Suddenly, I'm watching this scene play out as if I'm a fly on the wall. It's like we're in a shitty movie that's overdramatizing everything.

But I'm here, and there's no turning back now.

"I'm tired of acting like we're happy. I'm tired of acting like something we're not!" My tone rises and I take a deep breath to stay in check.

"Acting? I'm not acting, Chain."

Her words shatter the mental barrier I didn't know existed. This is who she is. For so long, it's who I tried to be. But it's not. And if she's not acting...

"Well, I am."

The gravity in my tone sets something off in her. I see the fear and denial in her eyes. She slowly takes a few steps towards me. I don't move, holding her stare. She reaches me and places her manicured fingers on my chest, moving them down towards my abdomen. One hand parts with the other, reaching towards my dick.

It hardens of its own volition, reacting to the human touch. The emotions swirling in my chest make their way to my dick instead, and I get an overwhelming urge to fuck the shit out of her.

She's using sex to manipulate you.

I hear the voice but I don't really give a fuck. The blood rushing to my throbbing cock is all I can focus on. I place my hand on the back of her head and grab her hair, giving it a rough pull before forcing her lips to meet mine. They clash violently before my tongue swipes across them, granting me access. Her tongue meets mine as she rubs circles on my dick over my pants with her thumb.

I need more, now. I pull her hair and hold her to me while simultaneously taking steps forward, stopping only when the back of her knees meet the couch. I rip my lips off of her, grabbing her hips and twisting her around forcefully.

I pop the button on my jeans and yank the zipper down, pulling them off with my boxers in one swift motion. They fall to the ground as I jerk her dress up. As I hook my finger around her lace underwear, she tries to turn around.

I grip her hip with my other hand and hold her in place, pulling her underwear down to join my clothes on the floor. *I'm staying in control of this.*

Ashley waits motionless as I yank my wallet out of my jeans pocket and pull a condom out, ripping the foil with my teeth. I roll on the condom and return one hand to her hip while my free hand pushes on her lower back. Her arms fly forward to catch her on the couch and I thrust my hips forward, my cock entering her swiftly.

She's not super wet yet, seeing as this happened in the spur of the moment and she's using it to hold onto me. I know she is, but the need to cum has overtaken any logical sense to think through this situation.

I pull out and thrust back in as she whimpers. I don't stop, trusting that she'll let me know if this is too much. I could be more caring, but my actions are fueled by the stuffed anger and discontentment I've held in for so long.

I pick up my pace, thrusting harder and faster. Her whimpers turn into moans as she slickens my cock with her growing wetness, and my head falls back with the pleasure of it. I grip her hips harder, forcing her to take all of me.

I want to talk to her, to tell her she's being a good girl for taking me like this. But I don't free the words from my lips. Because the part of me that isn't being driven with feral need knows that this is over and she's only doing this to tether me to her.

I feel her clenching on my dick, the walls getting tighter as she gets closer to orgasm. Who knew she was capable of that? Maybe she would have liked me dominating her, after all. If only she'd allowed it. I take my hand off her low back and move it around to her clit, keeping my dick deep in her while pulsing and rubbing.

She shouts my name as she comes, which brings me close to the edge but I hold off until she finishes. When I feel her body loosen, I remove my hand and put it back on her hip, then fuck her mercilessly. Her body pulls forward, resisting me, but I maintain my grip on her hips and push her onto my dick while thrusting in and out.

When I come, I do so silently.

I collapse over her body, forcing her under me on the couch. Our chests rise and fall heavily with the sharp breaths of air we take. My heart shifts from a thunder to its normal beat.

Once I start coming down from the high, I feel a sinking in my stomach.

I shouldn't have fucked her. Not when I'm about to break up with her. And definitely not when I was wishing I was inside of somebody else.

Chapter Twenty-Seven

Marlie

I roll over, the sleep in my eyes heavy. I keep them closed, intent on drifting back to sleep. My stupid bladder is screaming at me to relieve it. I choose to ignore it in favor of more shut eye.

I'm half asleep when I remember Chain telling me to get home safe. The memory forces my eyes wide open and I shoot up in bed. I look over to find Zander sleeping soundly, his mouth ajar and a light snore escaping him. His breaths are steady and they calm me, but only for a moment.

Guilt creeps in and takes over. My breath hitches and I quietly get out of bed, escaping to the bathroom to relieve my bladder and gather my thoughts. Then, I brush my teeth and try to scrub away the reminders of last night.

Jack. Chain. Lorraine. Chain. Drunkenness. Chain.

The thought of him brings heat to my cheeks. I blink hard and spit into the sink, rinsing my toothbrush, then my mouth. I go back into the room and tuck myself back into bed quietly, careful not to wake Zander. I look at the clock near the bed—10:27 am. I let myself get lost in my thoughts, trying to sort through them.

Why was Chain acting like that with Jack? He probably just wanted to make sure I was safe. Why does it feel like every time he touches me, my skin lights on fire? Why did I feel guilty when I looked over at Zander? I'm happy with him, right? I wouldn't be with him if I wasn't. The Chain thing is just an attraction. So why does it feel deeper, more real?

I go in circles, searching for answers and coming up empty. By the time Zander stirs in his sleep half an hour later, I've spiraled into a guilt ridden mess. I prod at his side, hoping it will wake him up.

I have to talk to him. I need to make sure we're okay.

"Hey, babe," he murmurs, peeking one eye at me while the other stays closed. He rolls onto his side to face me and forces the other eye open. "How was your night?"

"I need to talk to you," I blurt out. The anxiety is rolling through my body and I want it to go away. I *need* it to go away.

Zander becomes more attentive to my words, leaning up on an elbow and rubbing the sleep out of his eye. "Are you okay?"

"I don't feel right," I confess.

"What's wrong?" he says soothingly. His voice calms my nerves a bit, but I force the rest of the words out.

"I think I have a crush on someone."

He laughs lightly. "A crush?"

"Why are you laughing?"

"Babe, it's normal to find other people attractive."

"No, I know that," I say adamantly. Can't he see how serious this feels?

"Do you not want to be with me?" he asks.

"Of course I do," I respond automatically.

"Then it can't be anything serious. I'm not mad if you have a crush on someone."

I'm stunned into silence. His dismissal of my confession feels very... wrong. Like he's not getting it. Maybe I'm not explaining it right.

"I think it might actually be more than that," I say. He eyes me warily.

"Did something happen last night?" he asks.

"What? No. I mean, I saw Jack at the bar, but that's besides the point."

"Jack, your ex?"

"What other Jack would I be talking about?"

"I just wanted to be sure. Is that the crush you're talking about?"

I snap. "No, of course not! He's an asshole."

"I'm confused right now."

I explain the run in with Jack, including his assumption that Chain was my boyfriend.

"Chain was probably just looking out for you. He's got a girlfriend, doesn't he?"

"Yeah, Ashley. But that's not the point." I continue on, explaining how I needed to wait for the alcohol to subside so I could drive home. He interrupts to ask, "Why didn't you call me? I could have picked you up."

His question jolts me. Why didn't I call him? I search through the hazy memory.

"Oh, because I checked my phone and saw that you hadn't messaged me. So I figured you were sleeping."

"I mean, I was. But I would have picked you up if you'd called."

"Chain offered to wait with me, so I just... did," I finish lamely. Saying *his* name sent a shiver down my spine. I tense, apprehensive at how Zander will react.

But he responds normally. Why wouldn't he? He has no idea what's been going on in my head for weeks on end. "Oh, that was nice of him."

Before I can respond, my phone vibrates on the nightstand.

Mother iMessage

"Oh, crap!" I jump out of bed and rush to my closet, pulling out a pair of jeans from the dresser, and a floral shirt that's hanging.

"Oh, you have lunch with your mom, right?" Zander says, watching me from his place in bed. He readjusts so that his back leans on the pillows against the headboard.

"Yeah, I'm supposed to meet her at 11:30! I'm definitely going to be late." I scramble to get my clothes on and grab a pair of flats, shoving my feet into them. I swipe on the message she sent me and send a reply.

Me: Running a few mins late, be there shortly.

"So who's the guy you think you have a crush on??"

I pocket my phone and sit at the edge of the bed. I look at Zander but my mind is still on last night, replaying the conversation I had with Chain. Remembering how he smiled at me with eyes clearer than I've ever seen them lets the butterflies loose in my belly.

This is so wrong. I know what it feels like to be cheated on, to be left for someone else. How could I do this? I need to tell him.

"Chain." Another shiver shoots down my spine, goosebumps pricking my skin.

Zander eyes me carefully and I watch as the pieces of my story click for him. He doesn't speak for what feels like forever.

"Do you want to be with him?" His direct question cuts straight through the guilt to my core.

Do I?

I hadn't even thought that far ahead; the guilt and confusion and everything in between didn't let me. The longer I think his question through, the more guilt I feel. My silence cannot sound good to him.

"I want to be with you," I reply, ending the quiet tension.

He lets out a breath he must have been holding. "So what are we talking about here? If you think the guy is hot, I honestly don't blame you."

I laugh nervously and stare down at my hands folded in my lap. He leans over and lifts my chin with his finger, searching my eyes.

"Are you sure nothing happened?" he asks again.

"Nothing happened! We talked for a while and"—I pause, looking for the right words—"I don't know. He's really cool and it feels like there's some connection there."

Zander drops his finger, continuing to watch me. "If we're meant to be, we will be. I think we are."

I give him a small smile. His response is so Zander, and for once, I don't like it. Is he really okay with me just wanting someone else?

"So you don't care that I have feelings for someone else?"

"Feelings? I thought you said you had a crush."

"What's the difference?!"

"I don't know, a crush seems like a fleeting thing. But feelings, those are like... developed over time."

Fuck. He's exactly right.

"Marlie?" he says softly. I look up at him, the realization written all over my face. I don't know what to say, so I say nothing.

"Go to your mom. We can talk more later. I'm going over to my parents house soon."

I hop off the bed and pop a kiss on his lips. "I love you."

"Seriously, babe, next time—call me. I'm always here for you. And, I love you, too."

"I will, promise."

I grab my keys and leave the townhouse. Once I'm in my car with the ignition turned on, I pause with my hands on the steering wheel before reversing. I take a deep breath, settling the concoction of fear, anxiety, and guilt. I pull out and get lost in my thoughts once again as I drive to meet my mother.

The more I think about my conversation with Zander, and the more distance I get from last night, the stupider I start to feel. There's no way I could be with anyone else. I love Zander, he's my safety net. *And* we're engaged. Our lives are so intertwined, with our best friends and plans for the future. Plus, we rarely fight.

The memory of Chain's touch infiltrates my reasoning, sending a jolt of electricity through my heart that pumps into my veins. It both excites me and riddles me with fear.

My heart aches, confirming two things: I want Chain and I don't want to lose Zander.

I got to the restaurant a few minutes late, meeting Mother at the front bench of Laroom's. Yep, we're at her favorite restaurant—again.

We were seated promptly and we placed our orders. Now, she's rambling on about ideas for the wedding. *I am not in the headspace for this.*

"We could do the rehearsal dinner here, they serve a delicious steak," she says.

"I'm vegetarian," I mumble, but either she doesn't hear me, or pretends not to, as she continues.

"We'll have to go dress shopping. It can take *weeks* for some of these stores to get the shipments in."

"Well, there's plenty of time. I'm in no rush."

She laughs and waves her hand in the air. "Don't be ridiculous, sweetie, there's no time like the present! What is there to wait for?"

To figure out what the hell is going on with this weird crush thing.

I didn't expect that thought to cross my mind, but I know it's true. How am I supposed to marry Zander when I keep thinking about Chain? Feeling a desperate need to understand what's going on with me, I decide to open up to her.

"Did you ever have doubts about marrying Dad?" I ask her tentatively.

"Of course, honey. Everyone has doubts," she replies patronizingly. "As long as they're a decent person with an income, what more could you ask for?"

I don't know what else I expected from her. Maybe to be empathetic or compassionate. But who was I kidding? My mother is neither of those things on a good day. Not to mention, I don't think I ever once saw her and Dad kissing or being affectionate with each other growing up. They certainly love each other on some level, but I wouldn't award them couple of the year.

That's just one of the many ways she and I are different. I crave true love and meaning; she is fine living above the surface with a business-like relationship. To a degree, I get it. Her mother, my grandmother, grew up on the much poorer side and it was always a big deal to them. We certainly weren't rich growing up, but I'm an only child and I never wanted for anything. Whether it's that, my personality, or a mixture of both, that led to me not seeking that out in a relationship, I don't know.

And Zander is certainly a decent man with an income. He's more than decent. He's supportive, understanding, if not a bit boring and simple. But we've never had any real issues.

So why does it feel like deep down, in the pits of the chasm, something is terribly off? Like I'm hanging onto a hope that somehow this will just go away once we're married? Like the happily ever after will come into existence the moment we say "I do"?

I'm so lost in my thoughts, I'm not even aware I didn't respond until my mother speaks up again. "Zander is a great man. Better than I would have thought you'd end up with."

She says it offhandedly, but her insinuation digs deep. Resentment rebuilds the wall I tried to put down. It's always a mistake to try with her; I should know better.

"You're right, he's great."

"Is he treating you poorly?" she asks, arching an eyebrow knowingly.

"No, mom. Everything is fine."

As we eat our lunch, I repeat those words to myself until I believe they're true. *Mostly.*

"She's home, I'll hop back on later."

I wipe my feet off on the welcome mat before locking the door and looking towards Zander. He removes his headphones and places them next to his gaming console before walking over to me. I lean in to give him a light kiss, and while he lets me place it on his lips, he doesn't return the sentiment.

"Were you waiting for me?" I ask, pulling back and looking into his cooled eyes. He averts his gaze and nods towards the staircase.

"Let's talk upstairs."

Extremely confused, I take off my shoes and leave them at the foot of the stairs before following him up. The soft, albeit old, carpet tickles my bare feet. I get to the landing as he enters our room, and I get an ominous feeling.

Zander sits on his side of the bed so I climb onto my side, sitting cross-legged and facing him. I watch him in silence, waiting for him to say something. He lays back and stares up at the ceiling.

As I open my mouth to speak, he says, “I talked to Jace.”

I wait again. Nothing. “Okay…”

“I had more time to think about this crush.”

My heart sinks and the guilt that’s been intermittently bubbling at the surface splashes out. Panic overtakes me so suddenly that I speak without thinking. “I don’t even know why I brought it up. It’s nothing.”

He looks over at me, and his eyebrows pinch together ever so slightly. “I really didn’t think so before. But when you left…”

I say nothing, waiting with bated breath. All I can think to myself is *please, no*. I don’t want to fuck this up. We’re so set up. We’re comfortable. We love each other. I don’t want things to change.

“When I got back from my parents', I started gaming with Jace and it was nagging at me. When I talked to Jace about it, I realized why.”

When he doesn’t continue, I ask, “Why?”

“You didn’t call me.”

I'm confused at first, thinking he meant when I left for lunch with my mom. But then I realize he’s referring to last night. I didn’t call him for a ride.

“You always reach out to me to be there for you. And you definitely would have texted me to tell me Jack was at the bar.” He’s absolutely correct. “Why didn’t you, Marlie?”

He looks straight at me now. His eyes penetrate mine, shaking me to my core. I’ve never seen him look so solemn.

“Because… I felt bad waking you up,” I say weakly. It's bullshit and we both know it. That hadn’t stopped me in the past.

“Did you want to be with him?”

I think back. "That's not what I thought in the moment. I just... I wasn't thinking clearly."

"Maybe you were thinking more clearly than you realize."

"Zander, I—" I hear the plea in my voice. "I swear, I don't mean it."

You sure about that?

I stomp on that voice and return Zander's deep stare. He's looking into my soul for the truth. I'm not sure what he finds, but I force that voice down with everything in me.

"I'll take your word for it. You have no reason to lie to me," he says decisively. "We'll see how this all plays out, one way or another."

His declaration, the truth in it, sends chills up my spine. They creep up my neck and it feels like each strand of hair is standing.

"Nothing is going to play out. I want to be with you."

"I believe you." It seems like he means it, too.

"I'll stop going to improv."

"What? No," he shakes his head. "You don't have to do that. I don't *want* you to do that. I want you to have fun. Plus, you need it for work, right?"

I had forgotten that along the way, somehow. Probably because I'm truly enjoying it. "Right. But nothing is worth losing you."

"You can't lose what's meant for you, Marlie."

He leans forward and pops a kiss on my lips, then pulls me toward him. I lay my head on his chest and he grabs the television remote from the nightstand, powering on The Office.

"Wait." I shoot up, his arm falling off of my shoulders and onto the bed with a loud thud. "After Lorraine left, I checked my phone to call you. But *you*"—I point an accusing finger at him—"hadn't written to *me*."

His eyebrows raise in surprise. "I was asleep."

My finger falls pathetically onto my thigh and I gape at him. "Oh," I finally let out weakly.

"I fell asleep pretty quickly after you left."

"Well, never mind, then."

He gives me my favorite lopsided grin and I lay back onto his chest, snuggling in as he wraps his arm around me. I try to distract myself with the show playing when a thought crosses my mind.

"Why haven't you ever called me Mar?"

He laughs. "That's random. Um, I don't know. I guess because Marlie already feels like a nickname, ya know?"

"Yeah..."

"Do you want me to?" He turns his head to me and the traces of humor are gone.

"No, no. Just a random thought."

He places a light kiss on my head and turns his attention back to the show. I try to follow suit but I keep hearing Chain's voice calling me Mar.

I can't stop thinking about how much I liked it.

Chapter Twenty-Eight

Chain

"I don't know what else you want me to say," I say exasperatedly.

"I want you to tell me what the hell happened," Valerie says, dumbfounded.

"I'll tell you more when I get there." I hang up using the hands free button on my steering wheel, then hyper-extend my arms with the force I put into holding the wheel.

I didn't plan this out, contrary to my typical behavior, so I'm forced to stay with my mom while I decide where to go. I can't stay with Ashley since I broke up with her.

I knew I had to do it after that brunch.

You mean, after that night...

I hate that I don't know what the fuck has gotten into me. I can't stop thinking about her. It's driving me mad. Now that I'm free of Ashley and driving to my parents' house, it's all I can think about.

My hand on her hip, steadying her so she wouldn't fall. The gleam in her eyes as I told her what I really wanted out of life.

The fact that she's happily engaged. The word feels like acid on my tongue, burning the pleasure I felt just a moment before.

I have to accept that it's out of my control—my least favorite statement. I curl and flex my fingers around the wheel to contain the displeasure the powerlessness sends through me.

I hate being out of control. But I refuse to impede on a relationship, on another man's territory. It makes me sound like a caveman and I don't give a damn. She's taken, by choice. That's all I need to know.

But I couldn't stay in that relationship with Ashley any longer. Once the mask came off for me, and I felt who I really was that night with Marlie, I couldn't keep pretending. I couldn't just accept that I was doomed to a loveless life with couples counseling.

How was I ever able to accept that before? Sure, I didn't know she'd go as far as to say we needed work. It's not that we needed work, it's that we didn't work. And for a long time, I was o-fucking-kay with that.

Not anymore. Not since I started this improv class and met these new friends and Marlie...

Her name sends a wave of giddiness through me, which I stomp out just as quickly.

She has a fiancé. There's no chance for you.

My breakup with Ashley had nothing to do with Marlie. It's what she did to me, what she awakened in me. It made me realize that's what I want. Not some half-assed, sorry excuse for a relationship. I want love and I deserve to feel the way I do around Marlie with the person that's meant for me.

And Ashley is not that. Never was that. Never will be that.

My phone pings, bringing me out of my reverie. I glance over to where it's encased snugly in its holder on my dash.

Ashley iMessage

The eye roll comes naturally. What in the world could she possibly want so soon?

I'm entering the gate at my parents' complex, and I decide to wait until I've pulled into the driveway before checking the messages. Yes, plural. She sent three more messages as I gave the guard my ID.

I take back my ID and toss the paper security notice on my dash, then drive past the lifted gate and down the few streets to their house. When the truck is in park, I remove my phone from its place and slide the screen to read her messages.

> Ashley: Chain, don't do this. We can work on this.

> Ashley: Please.

> Ashley: When you come to get your stuff, will you make sure to leave the makeup I have in your car?

> Ashley: Let's just talk this through.

A knot builds in the pit of my stomach. I feel sorry for her. It's my fault she's going through this. I shouldn't have let this drag on so long. I should have known better than to think this could be it for me.

> Me: I think it's better if we don't speak anymore. I'll leave the makeup when I pick up my stuff.

The message stays on delivered but she starts typing immediately. I hit the lock button on my phone and toss it into the passenger seat, leaning back and reaching my arm to grab the bag I packed for the night that's tossed on the floor.

I don't even make it halfway up the path when Valerie bursts through the door, feet landing heavily with each rushed step she takes towards me.

"Oh, honey!" She throws her arms around me and the weight of her body on mine forces me to take a steading step back.

"Valerie, I'm fine." When she doesn't let up, I add, "Really."

"Oh, thank god. I hated that woman." She laughs and releases me, giving me a once over before keeping her stare on my face. "What happened?"

"Can I make it through the door first?" I don't wait for her permission as I brush past her and enter the house.

The freezing temperature she always keeps the AC at hits my skin, giving me instant goosebumps. My eyes roam across the open plan, finding dear, old Dad staring at the large TV screen mounted on the wall. Valerie's poodle is sleeping deeply at his feet, not even noticing I've arrived.

I hear Valerie walk in behind me and shut the door. She takes my bag off my shoulder before saying, "Go say hi."

How is it my job to say hello to him, when he hasn't even glanced my way?

Deciding I'd rather not fight this out after the day I've had, I walk towards my father. I know he hears me. I know he knows I'm approaching.

"Frank." It's the most I'm willing to give. He finally removes his gaze from the television and over to me. He gives me a watchful eye before shifting in his seat, readying himself to stand up. He makes a show of it, ensuring I know just how disruptive I'm being.

Unfortunately for him, I stopped giving a damn whether I bothered him or not. He resents me for the simple fact that I don't desire his affection anymore.

"How are you, Chain?" he asks. Before I can reply, he continues, "Everything at the firm going well?"

"Excellent," I say smoothly. It's such a typical, cold-hearted fatherly act, what he does. I wish I could say that the outcome is different. But it's a tale as old as time, I suppose.

A power hungry father breeds a power hungry son. They're at odds and have no true connection, save for business matters. The end.

I'm long past giving a fuck, so I turn without another word and head towards the room that used to be mine down the hall off the living room. I hear his ass land on the couch with a soft plop.

When I get to my—*the*—room, Valerie is sitting at the foot of the bed, waiting for me.

"It means a lot to him, you know," she says quietly. She always tries to make excuses for him.

"Save it," I tell her, my tone leaving no room for argument. She looks down in defeat. I step up next to her and open the bag she placed on the bed, rummaging for my toiletries so I can shower and go to sleep.

"Are you going to tell me what happened?" she presses.

"I told you. It wasn't working out and I was done."

I look at her with a stare of finality. She opens and shuts her mouth, then says, "Well, I can't say I'm sorry. She was awfully bitchy, so good riddance."

I give her a small grin and pull her head into my chest. She wraps her arms around my waist and we hug for a moment before I pull back, her arms loosening before dropping.

Taking the cue, she stands up. "Welcome home, Chain."

I don't comment, because this is not my home. I'll be out of here as quickly as possible.

I follow her out of the room and turn left to the bathroom. It looks the same as it always did, with minimal wall art and a neatly organized stand stocked with toilet paper and other bathroom essentials. I place my toiletry bag on the sink and unzip it, then decide against removing my items. The less I settle in, the better.

I peel off my shirt first, then my shorts and boxers. There's a small stain from the pre-cum before fucking Ashley. I shudder before catching my own reflection in the mirror.

My piercing green eyes take in my broad shoulders, not as fit as they once were. I'd become complacent in that meaningless relationship. How had I let myself go so easily? My abdomen was flat, but not muscular. I decided right then that I would get back to my gym regimen.

It was time to start being me.

I turn the shower knob to hot and wait until steam begins to rise. I immerse myself under the water, soaking it into my hair with a few strokes of my hands, front to back. I pour the soap from the bottle of 3-in-1 into my hands and rub it into my scalp. The aggressiveness with which I scrub reminds me of the irritation of today's events.

I meant what I said to Valerie. There wasn't much more to say really. The part I kept hidden was how I knew this all along. I knew that we were never a match. The only question left was how I was once okay with it when I no longer am.

Marlie.

I feel a throb in my cock as her name crosses my mind. The image of her stunning brown eyes and auburn hair sends another pulse. I can't get the look of her smiling with a twinkle in her eye out of my head after Saturday night.

She's engaged.

I know I can't have her. It's not why I broke up with Ashley, anyway. But alone with my thoughts in this steaming shower after mediocre sex and a breakup have me wanting for more. Today's fuck held off the carnal need, but the real desire for Marlie wasn't yet curbed.

My palm makes its way to my now rock hard penis and I grasp at the head, sliding down to the base. The bit of soap left in my hand makes for a pleasant lubricant, and I feel my vein pulse with satisfaction.

What better way to rid yourself of her?

The image of Marlie's smile returns and I start to slide my hand up and down my cock slowly. The smile morphs into a sensual lip bite, her eyes filled with lust—for me.

I get lost in my thoughts of her. She's in the shower with me, beads of water dripping down her perfect face, before she drops to her knees and takes my bulging dick into her mouth.

It's no longer my hand stroking me, but her luscious tongue. The soap becomes her spit and I can't stop a quiet growl from erupting in my chest.

That's it, baby. You're such a good girl for taking it.

The words I would say to her swim across my mind and I get hazy with the building orgasm. My eyes are completely shut now, blocking out reality. I just need to come to her this one time and let this silly crush go along with my release.

I imagine her moaning as her tongue laps at my cock, taking all of me in. I feel myself getting closer to the edge and I cup my balls with my free hand, increasing the pace of my fist. My hips thrust in time with the pace of my hand and I grip harder, feeling the head of my dick swell with the rush of blood.

I'm so close. Don't stop, baby.

I imagine my hand is pulling her hair rather than my balls, and her dreamt up words are my undoing.

I love your fat cock in my mouth.

Cum shoots from me and I double over with the pleasure coursing through my veins, starting in my center and extending to the very ends of me. More comes out of me from this vision than my fuck from earlier.

Goddamn.

My hand slows in contradiction to my racing heart, my head pleasantly light and clear.

Now you won't be bothered with thoughts of her.

I wake to the sound of the alarm I set on my phone the night before. I turn it off, confirming the time is right: 7:00 am.

I roll out of bed in an instant and walk to the bathroom. I knocked out as soon as I finished showering, sleepy with the high of my orgasm. I start to think about the work day ahead and all the things I pushed off that should have been done yesterday.

I'd freed my time to attend that awful brunch and then had the unexpected breakup, so I didn't get to any of it. Today was going to be a busy day. And I had to figure out when I was going back to the apartment to get my things.

I feel relieved knowing I won't have to see Ashley again after this. I'll have to ask someone for help so I can get this done efficiently. Valerie definitely doesn't have the strength to carry all that stuff and I'd buy all new things before asking Frank.

I'll give Jack a call—

The thought of his name sends immediate rage through me. My fingers clench into fists and a ball forms in the pit of my stomach.

Fucking Jack.

I still never found out why Marlie was so worked up over the guy, but it wasn't hard to guess. I've known Jack for years and we've grown close. The sole fact that he dated her was enough to have my blood boiling the way it is.

So much for jerking her out, asshole.

I push that thought aside, deciding if she wouldn't give me answers, then he would. I get back to my temporary room and dress for the day, then shoot a text to Jack, telling him to meet me at the bakery downstairs from our office in 30.

I'm sitting in my parked truck, listening to the noise of the air conditioning blowing from the vents. Staring straight ahead, I take collected breaths and focus on the task ahead. Glancing at the time, I grab a mint out of the tin in the console and pop it in my mouth before opening the truck door.

I step down, shutting the door and locking it before taking even steps towards the bakery. Lizzie's Bakery is the hub for the local offices to get their caffeine fix, a snack, or a quick lunch. While I do love their espresso, I won't be ordering one this morning.

I look into the open shop through the large windows. It's not as packed as it usually is on a Monday morning. I spot Jack towards the back corner by the food display, typing away on his laptop. The tables near him are empty.

Perfect.

I pull the door open and the bells on the door hinge tinkle, alerting any listening customers of my presence. Jack doesn't raise his head, distracted with whatever he's working on.

I walk over, shoulders pressed back and chest rising and falling with my controlled breathing. I leer at Jack, willing him to look up at me. But he doesn't until I slowly pull out the chair in front of him, exaggerating the movement so the scrape on the floor carries.

His face lights up when he sees me, oblivious to my icy stare and clenched jaw. It's not like he should be wise to my purpose to meet with him today. Until Saturday, I considered him a close friend and ally.

"Chain! Wait 'til I fill you in on what happened Saturday," he says, promptly shutting his laptop closed and leaning forward in his seat expectantly.

"I don't give a fuck what happened Saturday." I don't take my eyes off him as he finally meets my stare. The comprehension that turns his lips down and has him sit back fills me with a sick satisfaction.

"Tell me what happened with Marlie." I cut straight to the point. I don't have time for games and I want fucking answers. His eyes widen and he gives a slight shake of his head, taken aback by the seemingly random inquiry.

"Uh, she um, we—"

"Spit it the fuck out." His nervousness is only serving to piss me off, loosening the control I have on whatever emotions these are. Rage, I suppose, but the reason for them is what I don't want to decipher. I just know I need to understand what happened—what caused her to react that way to him.

"She's my ex from college, man," he rushes out. "How do you even know her?"

"Why did you break up?" I pointedly ignore his question. I'm the one asking questions here.

"She broke up with me," he says shortly, crossing his arms in front of his chest. "Why didn't you just ask her? What's the big fucking deal here, Chain?"

What is the big fucking deal?

I've hardly admitted to *myself* the way she makes me feel, let alone to anyone else. I'm sure as fuck not going to give any information to him. But I can't shake the look Marlie had on her face that night, and I need to understand why.

"What did you do?" I try a different angle. I'm not a trained attorney for nothing, and if there's anything I've learned, it's that the phrasing of your questions makes the difference between a denial and a confession.

But Jack is an attorney too, and it comes with the territory to evade answers. "It's not really that simple. I've missed her for a long time and have tried to make amends, but she won't hear it."

His unclear answers are doing nothing for me, lifting the lid on the pot of my rage a bit more. I clench my jaw and my nostrils flare. I lean forward and place my elbows on the table, clasping my hands and unclenching my jaw with an inhalation.

"What did you do?"

"I fucked up one night, man. I slept with another chick at a party." The words could sound remorseful, but his tone reveals his true feelings. He thinks it's no big deal, that he didn't do anything wrong.

I don't move, staring him down until he's forced to hold my eye. He doesn't waver, looking a bit confused but nonetheless powerful.

What a mistake.

"Here's what's going to happen." I unclench my hands to lightly dust off my jacket at the chest, then reunite them. "You have until the end of today to get your shit out of the office and never show your face around me again."

Jack gapes at me. I don't blame him. I allow him a moment to let my words sink in.

"Chain, what the fuck—"

"If I do see you again after 5 pm today, there will be consequences."

I don't give him a chance to respond, standing up affirmatively and fixing my tie before turning and strolling between the tables to leave. I turn back when I'm halfway to the exit and add, "The same goes if I find out you've had any contact with her."

He's gone pale white and keeps opening and closing his mouth like a fish out of water.

As the bakery door snaps shut behind me, I don't doubt he will take me seriously. Why wouldn't he? He's not stupid enough to risk me revealing his secret.

Chapter Twenty-Nine

Marlie

I walk out of the mailroom for my break and pull my phone out of my pocket. My heart drops when I see nine missed calls on my screen. I quickly unlock my phone, finding they're from an unknown number. I don't hesitate to tap on it and call back. Has someone been hurt? What if Mother had a car accident? My mind spins a mile a minute while the steady ring of the line blares in my ear.

"Marlie?" a deep, familiar male voice says. My immediate thought is that it's Chain. I quickly brush that hopeful thought off, knowing it's not his voice and that there's no reason for him to call me.

"Who is this? Is something wrong?" I ask, my pitch squeaky and my speech hurried with the adrenaline swimming through my veins.

"It's Jack," the voice replies.

I halt in my tracks and my stomach falls out of my ass. Jack? Why is he calling me?

"Marlie?" he says into the deafening silence.

"I don't want anything to do with you." I disconnect the line before he can respond. How did he even get my number? I changed it after our breakup, when he wouldn't stop calling me.

I resume walking down the hall and step to the flat outside. The sun is in the middle of the sky and I welcome the warmth it gives to my ice cold office skin. I close my eyes for a brief moment and take a deep breath when I feel my phone vibrate in my hand.

I expect it to continue vibrating with Jack's call, but it doesn't. Feeling safe, I glance at the screen to see an incoming text from him instead.

Just delete it. Don't get sucked into his bullshit.

It's a good thing I'm not a cat, because my curiosity gets the better of me. I need to know what he wants.

I'll just see what he has to say and delete it after.

Jack: So you're with Chain now?

My stomach does a summersault. What in the world? Not what I was expecting from him. His question out of left field has me typing back a reply before I can think better of it.

Me: I'm sorry, what?

He reads my message and starts typing. When 30 seconds pass, the three dots disappear from the screen. I look up and around, finding no one around me. I walk out to the small area with benches where employees can break.

I glance back down at our chat as I feel the slight vibration of his message coming in. It fills the screen and I have to scroll up to start from the beginning.

Jack: I never wanted things to end with us. I fucked up once. I tried to reach out to you for months, thinking you were just ignoring me. It wasn't until I finally heard the recording and realized you'd changed your number that I stopped trying. I thought about you all the time. When I saw you the other night, look-

> ing so stunning, it reminded me of all the great times we had together. Chain approached me this morning and told me to back off. I shouldn't have, I'm not supposed to, but I used one of my work databases to find your number. I have to know if you're with him. It seems ridiculous, I know, but seeing you the other night made me realize just how much I need you.

One time?! He's the same piece of shit he always was. Not to mention, why did he only just look up my new number? He's had years. He couldn't have missed me enough.

When the hurt and anger simmer, I reread his message twice. Chain approached him? Why in the world would he do that? He doesn't even know what happened between Jack and I.

Unless... Jack told him. He must have. But why would Chain tell him to back off?

I open a new message tab and type in Chain's name. I begin typing a message when I see the photo of the scales I sent weeks ago.

He never even answered your last text.

But why would a friend care enough to talk to Jack? He clearly stated Chain approached him.

My brain feels heavy with the whirlwind of thoughts at Jack's message. Locking my phone, I tuck it into my pocket and head back to my desk. I'm not going to text Chain anything. If he's snooping around my business, let him.

I have a fiancé. I'm happy. And I don't owe Jack any answers.

On our drive home, Zander and I sit in companionable silence as my mind reels with this morning's event. As much as I tried to ignore it, it was all I could think about today. I talked to Eli about it, but he was just as shocked about all the recent events as I was. I had to restrain myself from prying information out of Jack. As much as I felt it shouldn't matter, I needed to know why Chain approached him.

He was probably just curious after Saturday. They work together.

But to tell him to back off? Back off from what, even? I have nothing with Jack.

"How was work?" Zander's question tears me from my thoughts.

"Oh, it was just work. Got a lot done."

"I had to deal with a huge problem, this guy..." I let him tell me about his day, providing oh's, ah's, and that's crazy's at the appropriate times. I tried to focus but I just couldn't.

Maybe I should call Stella when I get home and ask her about this. She'd know just what to say and do. But clueing in Stella to all this would require me to give her a lot of details, and she knows me too well. She's going to see right through my motives.

We haven't talked about my confession to Zander. I know Jace told her about it; there's no way he didn't. I'd normally be bothered by the fact that she didn't reach out to me, but frankly, I like pretending the whole thing never even happened.

And Stella talking to me would just force me to release all these hidden thoughts and feelings that I just couldn't share with her. We're all best friends. There's no way she would understand. It's wrong for me to even have *thought* I felt something for Chain.

When Zander finishes venting, I decide to tell him about this morning's event. "You won't believe who called me today."

"Who?" he asks curiously.

"Jack."

"Seriously? How? Didn't you change your number after the breakup?"

"Yeah, I did. I have no idea how he got my number." The lie comes out smoothly, and it wasn't a conscious decision. But after I've said it, I know I don't want to tell him about the texts. That would force him to wonder the same thing I wonder—why did Chain give two shits about my relationship with Jack?

"That's crazy! What did you say?"

"I hung up on him and blocked him." Another lie. I wanted to block him. My thumb hovered over the button when I returned to my desk. But I couldn't press it. What if he sent more messages that provided more answers?

"How do you feel? Why didn't you mention it earlier?"

"I had a lot going on at work." *I didn't even plan on telling you.* "But it just reaffirms how I feel about him. He's a piece of trash and I want nothing to do with him. I can't believe he still even tries."

"Yeah... I mean you are a catch," Zander says with a lopsided grin. He takes his hand off the gear shift and places it on my lower thigh, giving a light squeeze. I place my hand over his and link our fingers together.

"Thanks, babe," I say with a big smile.

"I'm sorry you had to go through that," he says. I face him and allow his warmth to course through me; he's always so understanding. When we pull up to our street and he puts the truck in park, I release our hands and get out. I fight the one recurring thought that won't leave me be: What did Chain say to Jack?

Chapter Thirty

Marlie

The week passed in a blur and I'm grateful it's finally Friday. I'm walking up the stairs to class 8 of improv, a bundle of nerves.

Excited nerves at the idea of getting back up on the stage and playing. I would have never guessed how much I'd like this acting stuff, but it's become the best part of my week.

Anxious nerves at the thought of seeing Chain again. This is our first encounter after the night at the bar Saturday. So much has happened since then. I'm not sure if I should bring up Jack's text. I don't know if the dynamic between us will feel different after our conversation. I'm afraid of how I'll act around him after my admission to Zander.

I enter the theater and find most of the class already there. I scan the people sitting, feeling disappointed when I don't see Chain. Maybe he won't be here today and I won't have to deal with all the apprehension I've faced leading to tonight. But the let down I feel at the fact that he's not here tells me I'd rather deal with the apprehension than not see him at all.

Eli is in the seat closest to the aisle in the second row on the left. I make my way over to him and slide in front of him to take the seat next to him.

"Hey, chica," he says distractedly while scrolling through his phone.

"I deserve all your attention, Eli." My joke earns me a smirk as he double taps the screen, liking a post of a woman in a revealing bikini before locking the phone and sliding it into his pocket.

"I thought you have a thing for Lorraine," I say, giving him a nudge in his ribs with my elbow.

"Shhhhh!"

I laugh. "Well, you should know she has a girlfriend. Although," I pause, recollecting the conversation from Saturday. "She doesn't seem serious about it."

"Damn," he says. He actually looks crestfallen.

"Aww, you really like her, huh?"

"It's whatever," he says, brushing it off. But the look in his eyes tells a different story.

The hair on my skin rises and I feel a coolness on my nape. I look up from Eli to the corner where the door is. My stomach drops.

Chain.

He saunters in decisively, an air of confidence exuding from him—more so than usual. It heats my core and I feel my cheeks redden.

Stop it! I yell at my uninhibited body, willing it to subdue.

He's dressed in a dark green polo and khaki cargos. As he makes his way up the aisle, his eyes roam across the stage and chairs, landing on me.

His emerald eyes brighten when they meet my brown ones, and he falters. It's nearly imperceptible, but I saw his shoulder shudder with the near pause in his gait. I wonder if he notices the racing of my pulse likely reflected in the depths of my now wide eyes, or the yearning in my heart. He keeps walking though, forcing his eyes away from mine and onto the empty seat he takes across the aisle from Eli.

He settles into the seat, his ass not touching the back so he's leaning against it. He puts his right elbow on the arm rest near the aisle and places his head in his index finger and thumb, then starts talking to Damon, who's seated next to him.

"I don't need to be tied down, anyway," Eli says. I move my focus from Chain to Eli. His lips are tilted up ever so slightly, the twinkle in his eye confirming he saw what I was doing.

But did he know how I was feeling? I feel my cheeks redden even more with the rising heat of embarrassment at being caught. I'm saved from responding to him by Jon's booming voice from the back of the room, "Hello, improvisers, and welcome to class 8!"

I stare ahead at the empty stage, refusing to meet Eli's expectant eye. Jon hops, literally hops, onto the stage and turns to face us with a beaming smile. The lingering conversations taper off as he gains the classes full attention.

"Today, we are going to explore physicality. We touched on this during our first class, but physicality plays a major role in our job as actors. Even more so as improvisers. Communication does not—" he cuts himself off abruptly and claps his hands together. "Liv! Nice of you to join us tonight. Take a seat quickly, now. We are discussing today's focus on physicality."

He waits as she takes a seat in the front left row before continuing. "Communication does not require words. In fact, action says much more than words, especially on the stage. Today, we will be exploring how to communicate feelings effectively, sans words."

He looks around with a toothy grin. Since we've learned how Jon is about reaction, we all do our best to look intrigued and excited. His grin falters before he steps off the stage and takes his usual seat a few rows removed from us.

"Any volunteers to go first?"

The anticipatory nerves I entered class with today are what drives me to rise from my seat. In my periphery, I see a blur of dark green movement. I try to sit back down but Jon shouts, "Excellent! Marlie and Chain!"

Fuck, fuck, fuck, fuck, fuck.

So much for avoiding him. The irony that my apprehension of seeing him caused me to volunteer is not lost on me. I glance over to Chain, who drops a tin of mints onto his seat before walking to the stage with his chin up.

He doesn't look at me.

The sting of that is what pushes me to move past Eli and raise my own chin, leaping on the stage in a similar fashion to Jon. I take up the spot near the front of the stage, a few feet away from Chain.

He takes the initiative to ask for a suggestion. "Can someone please give me a place?"

"Let's try starting it out as if we're an actual audience, Chain," Jon says in a clipped tone.

My body tenses, expecting Chain to react to Jon's typical snarky comments. I give him a sideways look, and while I notice a tick in his jaw, he doesn't retort. Instead, he rushes behind the stage's side curtain, then bursts out with a jump and his hands in the air.

He runs up to the front of the stage and shouts, "Welcome to Sparkle Comedy!"

The class laughs and I stifle a giggle as he remains planted with his hands in the air, wiggling his fingers for added effect.

"Can one of you *lovely* people give me the name of a place, any place?" He almost sounds like an auctioneer, and I don't even try to wipe the shit eating grin off my face.

So he does have a playful side.

Various classmates start shouting, but Toni's voice is the loudest.

"Car!"

I'm instantly zapped back to Saturday night, when we sat on his tailgate. Without a conscious thought, I turn to look at Chain. It's something I've realized we do often in improv. You check in with your partner before starting a scene. Almost like a silent, "Hey, we've got this; I trust you."

But the look we exchange is the farthest thing from that. I can tell that his thoughts have drifted to the same place mine have.

He looks away quickly, and turns his back to me. He grabs the two chairs at the back of the stage, lifts them a few inches, and walks them to the center of the stage. He places them with a half-foot space in between, as if they're the front seats of a car.

He takes a seat in what would be the driver's side and places his hands on an imaginary wheel. As I take my first step towards the make-believe passenger seat, Jon speaks.

"Let's try not going for the obvious. Think, what would be an odd use of the car?"

I stop and look at Chain. I act on the first thought that takes hold after Jon's suggestion. I walk over to Chain's side of the car, act as if I'm opening the door, and plop right down on his lap. I didn't process the thought of doing it, I just went with my gut.

I am now regretting my decision. The warmth from the feel of his body on the back of my legs and butt sent a jolt of excitement through me.

"Yes!" Jon shouts jubilantly, obviously pleased with my choice.

I'm sitting perpendicular to him, as if my legs were hanging out of the open car door. But really, it's just the two of us on a simple black stage chair, and an audience of classmates watching us.

I refuse to look at him, staring at the wall in front of me instead. You could cut the silence with a knife, it's that tangible. A quiet patience, waiting to see our scene play out.

"I have to go," Chain says, his voice husky. It's a few decibels deeper than his already deep voice, and the sound of it sends a tingle up my spine. My entire body is on alert. I wonder if I would feel this way if I had sat on any other classmate.

My heart skips a beat, affirming the answer.

It's hard to focus when all I want to think about is his body touching mine; the way it makes me want to turn my head ninety degrees and stare into his brilliant emerald eyes. Maybe he would brush the loose strand of hair on my face and tuck it behind my ear. His fingers could graze my cheek slowly, trailing down to my lips before leaning forward—

"Daddy will be back from work soon," Chain says, and the class bursts into laughter.

My cheeks redden at the polarity of my thoughts and the reality he just set for us. He made me his kid.

Say something!

"I don't want you to leave!" I say in a high pitched, whiny voice, doing my best impression of a little girl who loves her dada. I fold my arms across my chest in a pout. When my shoulders hunch, it causes my ass to rub on his lap. It takes everything in me not to audibly react.

The swooping feeling between my legs is the furthest reaction from a kid to her dad, and it reddens my cheeks even more. I feel my heartbeat pulsing in my ears. I refuse to look at Chain.

"We'll play when I get back. If I don't work, we won't have a house to live in."

My mind is so focused on the feel of his hands moving to my hips and trying to move me off of him that I can't process any response. How is he able to focus on this when all I can think about is the desire coursing through my body?

I let his hands guide me off and I step down from the car. I feel the loss of contact immediately, and my brain thinks of a reply.

"Is that why you and momma fight so much?"

"Excellent! That is a great statement to add!" Jon exclaims, interrupting our scene. "Do we all see how Marlie was able to create an inference from his words?"

Jon's voice fades into the background and my mind reels.

I shouldn't have liked that. Why was I having those thoughts? Why does this keep happening?!

Panic and guilt flood me and it's all I can think about. When Chain stands up from the chair and moves off the stage, I follow suit.

"Next two!" Jon shouts. When I'm back in my seat, I chance a glance at Chain, who's resumed the exact position he was in before, staring pointedly at the stage and stuffing the mints into this pocket.

I feel embarrassed. I'm having all these heated reactions and he was completely focused on the acting; on what we were supposed to be doing. These feelings are ridiculous, and obviously one sided.

But why did he talk to Jack, then?

The rest of class passed by quickly, and I made the decision to ask Chain about the Jack situation. It's driven me crazy all week, and try as I might, I couldn't shake the need to understand.

Liv, Lorraine, and Eli are talking right outside of the theater. I rush down the stairs to make sure I catch Chain before he leaves. I exit and keep a brisk pace down the sidewalk and to the parking lot. But when I get there, I don't see anyone.

The light from the amber glow reflecting off the cars doesn't light up the entire lot, so I walk between cars to make sure he's not here. When I reach the end, I start to turn back when I remember that he usually parks down the road. I look out and see that his truck is parallel parked in front of a quaint home.

I pivot to return to the sidewalk and my eyes land on Chain walking down the lot towards me. Seeing him in the dim lighting with no one around and the distant sounds of cars on the road melts my insides. Alone like this, I can't deny what seeing him does to me.

His hair is a bit more ruffled than it normally is, and it strikes me that he's not in his usual attire. He's dressed more casually today, and there's an air of change about him. He gives me a head nod and my heart does a happy dance.

I'm really fucked.

It's hard for me to deny it at this moment. His chiseled jaw, his confident gait, his dark hair and structured eyebrows; they are my undoing.

And those lips? I want to feel them on mine. I want to feel them all over me.

I subconsciously start twirling the ring on my left hand and that rips me from my fantasizing.

You. Have. A. Fiancé.

"You okay, Mar?" Chain asks me. The use of the nickname sends a zing down my spine.

"Yeah," I reply, realizing I must look quite odd just standing here in the dim lighting, staring at him. Could he tell I was fantasizing about him? That he stirs feelings in me that haven't been stirred before? That I'm a horrible person for feeling this way about him when I have a man who I love at home, who loves me in return?

Chain halts in front of me at the invisible line of my personal space. The line that separates us as friends instead of lovers.

"Did you get home okay on Saturday?" he asks. I stop playing with my ring and snap my eyes up to meet his.

"I did, yeah. Thanks for waiting with me," I say quietly.

"Of course," he says. There's a stillness in the air. I can feel the pressure of the unspoken words between us on my chest and shoulders, weighing down on me. His eyes are full of a heat that must be mirrored in my own. Which means...

"Why did you tell Jack we're together?" I blurt the words out so I don't finish those risky thoughts.

His eyes quickly turn from flaming hot to ice. I didn't even know someone could look so different in such a short amount of time. If I wasn't watching him so intently, I likely would have missed the change.

"That's not what I told him," he replies smoothly, his tone laced with venom.

My eyes narrow. "What *did* you tell him?"

Chain readjusts his stance, lightly picking up one foot, then the other. He crosses his arms and tucks his fists into his armpits, watching me closely. His eyes never leave mine, but I can tell he's calculating.

I wait, but all I get is silence.

"Chain?"

"To back off."

Huh? "Back off *what*?"

"You."

You. Three little letters, making up one little word—you.

Me.

It's my turn to be silent. I look away with wide eyes and furrowed brows, the realization of what he's saying setting in.

"Did he contact you?" Chain asks, his voice so quiet it's almost a whisper. But in his tone is a threat; I feel it in the way the hairs on my arms stand up.

"He called and texted," I admit, matching his nearly-whispered tone.

"I'm sorry."

His voice is so sincere that I don't know how to respond. What is he sorry for? And why was he talking to Jack about me in the first place?

"Why did you tell him to back off?" I'm louder now, demanding an answer. I look back into his eyes and see a swirl of emotion in his irises before he lifts his chin and blocks them out.

"I wanted an explanation for Saturday night."

"An explanation?" I'm surprised by his answer.

"You looked like you saw a ghost. It hu—confused me."

"I told you I didn't want to talk about it," I say with indignation. "You had no right."

He doesn't answer immediately. "I know, I just—"

"Yoooo!" Eli's voice shocks me into reality, remembering my surroundings. He claps Chain on the shoulder before standing beside us.

"Hey, Eli," Chain says, breaking our stare and looking over to him. He holds his hand out for a shake and then drops his arms to his side, resuming a neutral position.

"Class was fun today, huh?" Eli says conversationally.

The memory of being on Chain's lap flashes in my mind and I feel the heat rise to my cheeks. My clit pulses with arousal, leading me to wonder what it would be like to sit on his lap for *other* reasons.

"Yeah, I'm really enjoying it," Chain replies. You'd have no idea from the tone of his voice that we were having a pretty serious conversation just before.

"Alright, I gotta ask. What's with the change in clothes, man?" Leave it to Eli to ask whatever comes to mind.

"Oh, um"—Chain glances my way before looking back at Eli—"I didn't go to work today because I was moving the rest of my stuff."

Moving?

"Sweet, you got a new place?" Eli asks.

"Actually, I broke up with Ashley. I moved in with my mom, for now."

My eyes just about pop out of my skull. I'm stunned; absolutely floored. Thank god I haven't spoken yet, because I won't be able to now.

Him and Ashley broke up. He talked to Jack about me. His earlier words echo in my mind.

You.

My heart pounds at the dots I'm connecting. I can feel each forceful beat in my chest.

He likes me. He has to have a thing for me. He must feel what I feel.

The realization excites me the first second, then sends dread through me in the next. I can't deny this any longer and I feel crazy. How can I have feelings for someone I barely even know? While I'm engaged to the supposed love of my life? I can't do that to Zander. I love Zander!

The guilt and exhilaration billow, sending a wave of nausea over me.

No, no, no. This cannot be happening. I'm not this person! I love my boyfri—gahhh, my fiancé!

How can I be feeling these things when I'm with someone else? What does this mean for Zander and I?

"Damn, you okay?" Eli asks, his eyebrows creasing with concern.

"I'm fi—"

"Yeah, def—"

Chain and I start to answer at the same time when I realize my mistake. Eli gives me an inquisitive look and I refuse to look at Chain, who's staring right at me.

"Definitely. Sometimes it's just not the one, you know?" Chain finally replies, facing Eli.

My eyes shoot to him at his words. I stare into his emerald depths as I contemplate his words. Not the one...

Zander's my one, right?

Chapter Thirty-One

Marlie

"Shoot him! SHOOT HIM, YOU IDIOT!!!" Zander's yells pierce my ears the moment I walk through the door.

I toss my purse onto the couch that sits against the wall next to the door and walk over to him at his gaming chair in front of the giant TV screen. There's a lot of commotion on the screen involving characters running around in army gear.

I walk right in front of him and lift my leg over his thighs, straddling his lap while facing him. I watch his pupils zero in on me. He drops his controller so it falls into the space where our groins meet. He uses both hands to pull down his headphones, letting them fall around his neck.

His hands grab my breasts, then travel down and out to grip my waist. I rock my hips on his thighs, approving of his touch. I can still hear repetitive gunshots and weird clicking sounds boom out of the forgotten headphones.

"Mmm, well hello," he murmurs, nuzzling his head into my neck. His nose runs along my ear and he peppers my neck with kisses.

"I'm really excited for our trip," I say while leaning my head to the side to allow him more access. About six months ago, Zander suggested we plan a trip to a cabin in Georgia, like we used to do when we first started dating. I thought he was just being spontaneous; now I know he was planning to propose to me.

We'll stay in a cozy cabin, make lots of love, and take long naps. I'll get to catch up on reading while he listens to music. Our prior trips were some of the best times of our relationship, and I want to get back to that.

"Where are we going?" I hear a distant voice ask from the microphone. I smile sheepishly and look at Zander, who uses a hand to toss the headphones off his head before returning it to my waist.

"Me, too, babe." He continues trailing kisses along my neck and towards my breast.

I need to feel connected to you, to make sure we're meant to be. "I'm tired of the mundane. It's been so long since we did a trip just the two of us."

"Too long. Luckily, everything's already set up." His hands slide up my stomach, lifting my shirt. He frees my left breast from the confines of my bra, then takes my nipple into his mouth. His tongue seductively swirls around my nipple before he gives it a playful nip.

"Maybe we should put this on hold until we get there tomorrow," I tease.

"I don't think so." He cups my breast, warming my now wet, cold, and exposed nipple. This is exactly what we need. A getaway, just the two of us.

Everything is going to be fine. This trip will rid me of those stupid feelings for Chain.

We made the 6 hour drive to the cabin with no hiccups. We took off from work on Monday, so that gives us two days to lean into our trip. I'm currently sprawled in a chair on the patio that faces the woods with a book in hand. The problem is, I can't concentrate. I've lost count of how many times I've had to reread the same page. The words aren't processing because I can't get *him* out of my brain.

I've decided to at least stop thinking his name. It seems to be the only control I can exercise. Every song we listened to on the drive over today somehow reminded me of Ch—*him*—no matter how unromantic the song would be.

I would start to fantasize about his lips on mine. Or I would think about a funny scene he played in during class. Or I'd think about our conversation on his truck bed.

But mostly, I remembered his word—*you.*

The incessant, intrusive thoughts created a flood of guilt in my system. I couldn't stop thinking about him, but I also couldn't deny what I felt any longer.

I thought this trip with Zander would remind me of all the reasons I love him. So far, all it's done is make me realize a lot of things that annoy me about him.

Like how he never seems to care about anything. It's not like I never realized he can be aloof. It's just that it used to be something I adored. He was carefree, willing to go with any flow, and always wanting to make me happy.

Or the fact that he doesn't even *like* the beach. The beach is my favorite place in the whole world! But instead, we're at a cabin. Don't get me wrong, it's a beautiful cabin with wood planks, the smell of greenery, and fires at night. But it's not the beach.

Again, I knew this. It's not new information. Something has shifted in me over these last few weeks. I don't want to be someone who just goes with the flow. I don't want to live a mediocre life, working and hanging around aimlessly.

I've found a new passion—improv. It awoke the person inside me who I didn't even know was trapped. When the chasm broke open in me that day, weeks ago now, she decided to crawl out and make herself known.

The fissure that has allowed the waters to first roar in defiance, then evaporate in acceptance, refuses to be resealed or ignored.

The craziest part is that this newfound chasm speaks to me. When I'm around Zander, I feel unsettled by its rumbling. When I'm at the theater and all my new friends, especially *him,* a calmness settles in. I'm sure that the chasm was always there, I just wasn't attuned to it.

Stella was right. Jack screwed me up more than I ever cared to admit. But what was I supposed to do now that I knew the truth of it? Am I really happy with Zander? I have to be. There's nothing really *wrong.* We have great sex. We get along. We share similar dreams for the future.

At least, you did.

What do I even dream anymore? Will I really be satisfied with a mediocre job and the routine of mundane living?

Suddenly, I want to *really* live. I want to travel to far off places. I want to explore more improv. I want to do home projects! I've somehow convinced myself that I'm happy spending an entire Sunday at home, sleeping and watching TV.

But I'm not.

In agreement, the rumbling in the chasm settles and the anxiety lessens. I want to start being true to myself. In fact, I need to. This open hole inside doesn't leave me a choice.

Can I do those things with Zander?

I ended up reading a total of ten pages. Ten measly pages out of a 300 page book was all I could focus on. Zander had fallen asleep with his music playing quietly in the background, and his absence allowed me to feel a bit more comfortable.

Not that we were talking a lot before he napped, anyway. The silences that used to feel companionable just feel empty now. We really don't have a whole lot to talk about, and the conversations we do have feel superficial or necessary.

Not like when you and Chain talked that night.

I silently seethe at the fact that his name even crossed my mind.

But that was the other thing, too. Zander being awake was a constant reminder that I'm basically cheating on him. Right? I'm in a committed relationship, one that's preparing for marriage, and I'm fantasizing about another man.

The guilt of it was chipping away at my sanity.

And honestly? I'm getting tired of fighting it. I'm tired of trying to control my feelings and thoughts so that I can feel okay around Zander.

But what will happen if I let go?

The truth. The truth will happen.

What is the truth?

"Babe?" Zander's faint voice forces me back to reality.

I look over at him, wide-eyed from being spaced out. I focus on him sitting next to me on his own chair and give him a small smile. But it doesn't reach my eyes, I know it.

"You okay?" The look of concern sends another pang of guilt. My stomach hurts. *I can't do this.*

"Yeah, I'm good!" I give him a bigger smile, forcing my eyes to crinkle. "Just dazed out from all this relaxation."

Zander lets out a small chuckle, the relief evident in his warm, brown eyes. "Yeah, that nap really helped me out."

The fact that he bought my lie makes me feel even worse; guiltier that I lied, and sadder that he can't even tell when I'm actually happy. We've both settled into this complacency. How can it not bother him??

It didn't bother you before, either.

The truth of that stirs emotions in me. I can't even name them, I'm feeling so many at once.

God, how did I get to this place?

"I'm gonna shower," I say.

"Okay," Zander says, standing up and stretching.

The bathroom door snaps shut behind me and I pull my mini shampoo and conditioner bottles out of our toiletry bag, placing them on the small soap dish in the shower.

I take off my clothes slowly, then stand in front of the mirror. My eyes rake over the reflection of my body, then my face. I meet my own eyes and I can see the turmoil brewing.

I turn on the shower and get in without testing the temperature. I welcome the frigid water that soothes the heat on my skin. Maybe it will evaporate the feelings within.

What is the truth?

My brain asks the question again. In the solitude of the bathroom, I allow myself to explore as the water soaks into my hair and drips down my body.

I know I love Zander. That isn't a question. But something these past few months has shifted within me, forcing me to look at our relationship from a different angle.

Is it possible to love someone and they're still not right for you? What if I got with him at a point in my life where this was what I needed? And what if those needs have changed? What if I lost myself as a protection to not get hurt again? I feel the thoughts resonate in my heart and the chasm settles, confirming they're true.

I chose a man who would never do anything to hurt me. He's simple and safe. There's no question about that.

But safety has a consequence. In sacrificing pain, you also sacrifice pleasure. I've lost out on doing so many fun things while we spend our Sundays watching TV and just hanging out.

There's nothing wrong with doing that, but deep down I know it's not me. How I'm only realizing this now is beyond me, but I know that it's true. I don't want to live a menial existence, passing time in complacency.

I want to live.

A tear rolls down my cheek. I don't think I can truly live with Zander. He's so calm and easy and I love that about him. A part of me wants to latch onto that and never let go. The thought alone sets off the roaring waters in the chasm.

Fear sets in and I ignore the ripples of tension within me. If I don't latch onto him, to the part of me that needs this stability, what will happen to us? To me?

My hand trembles as I squirt soap into my palm and rub my hands together. I lather my scalp but my arms are shaky.

I'll lose him. I'll lose Zander and I can't lose him. I need him. We've gone through so much together. We're engaged! He's my future.

I need to gain control of these *bullshit* feelings. I've probably been feeling so intensely about Chain because it's my fearful brain trying to escape from the good thing I have going with Zander. And let's face it—the guy *is* hot as fuck.

We're going to be just fine. I'll be just fine. I'm not going to let these doubts and fears rule my life. I finish my shower and grab a towel from the rack, exiting and drying myself off. I wrap the towel around my body, tucking it into itself under my armpit.

I open the bathroom door, the sudden chill raising the hairs on my arms. I find Zander laid back on the navy blue couch with his feet propped on the oak coffee table, the TV remote loose in his hand. From the sounds of it, he's watching the sports channel.

I break left and go into the room so I can change. I take my towel and wipe down my body, then wrap it around my hair and twist so it stays in place. When I turn towards the closet to get to my suitcase, Zander's body in the doorway causes me to jump.

"Ahhh! Oh my god, you scared the *crap* out of me," I tell him in one breath with my hand over my heart.

He leans against the doorframe and smirks, his eyes twinkling with amusement as he crosses his arms over his chest.

"What are you doing with that sexy body?" he asks playfully. He's still in the khaki shorts and navy blue V-neck he tossed on. A few of his chest hairs peek out, which I've always loved.

Pushing my thoughts from the shower to the back of my mind, I twirl my hips in a silly dance. Zander pushes his shoulder off the frame and walks up to me slowly, placing his hands on my hips.

I allow the warmth from his grip to draw me in and soothe me. There's safety in the known, and I revel in it at this moment. His eyes search mine, and I let myself get wrapped up in his depths.

I take my hands and run them down my chest and over my exposed breasts, cupping them and giving him a seductive smile. He gives me my favorite lopsided grin before crushing his lips to mine. Our tongues meet and do their dance.

His hands cover my own and squeeze, my nipples pebbling under our combined touch. It feels so good and distracting, and I want more. I need more.

I move my hands down my stomach, forcing him to follow. I pause and he removes one hand to cup my sex, rubbing his palm lightly over it. My clit reacts on command, pulsing with the need for pleasure; for the reminder that I love him and he makes me feel amazing.

He continues to rub as he takes steps forward, my butt eventually knocking into the mattress. I sit on it and he uses one knee to spread my legs. Our tongues haven't stopped their samba, and I'm caught up in this whirlwind of pleasure.

I instantly feel the removal of his palm from my pussy but his finger rubbing on my clit has me forgetting just as quickly. I rub my hands over his chest and shoulders, appreciating the stocky stature of him.

His finger teases ever so slowly over my clit and he slows his tongue down to match the pace. Our kiss feels more sensual now. I spread my legs wider so I press into his finger, telling him I want more. He quickens his pace, and I moan into his mouth with a gasp.

I bundle his shirt into my fists and force him on top of me as my back hits the soft mattress. I prefer our home bed, which is firm enough to support our sexual endeavors. But for tonight, the plush of this one will do.

He doesn't stop circling my clit as he pulls his shorts off each hip, then shimmies to let it drop around his knees. He lifts out one leg, then the other, and my clit throbs with need.

"Fuck me," I breathe.

"How do you want it?" he asks between heated kisses.

After a second of thought, I break our kiss and turn around, raising my hips in the air and digging my face into the mattress. The softness allows my face to sink in and I find that I like the restriction of air from it.

My ass is lifted high, allowing entrance to my now soaked opening. He doesn't waste any time in guiding his dick and slowly, so slowly, pushing in. I let out a huge moan as his thick cock forces my walls wider. He responds with a groan and pulls out, quickly thrusting back in.

We find our rhythm, my finger taking over his job on my clit. I meet his thrusts with my own and within minutes we're both panting. I can feel him hardening within me and he grabs my hips.

My body is loving this, but my mind has begun to wander. Forcing myself to focus, I concentrate on the electric pulses the rubbing on my clit jolts through my body. I focus on the feel of his dick entering and exiting, picking up speed.

"Harder," I grunt out. He obliges with his next thrust, sending my hips forward with the intensity.

Suddenly, I'm accosted with a flash of electric green eyes. My finger pauses with the shock, but my clit throbs harder than it has in ages. I blink my eyes hard and try to take a deep breath, but my mouth stuffed into the mattress restricts the air from fully reaching my lungs.

I'm feeling too damn good to resist the thoughts and I let go. I return my fingers to assault my clit, and it pulses in appreciation. My head gets dizzy with the pleasure coursing through me, and I think of him.

It's not Zander's hand rubbing along my ass, it's *his.* When Zander groans again, *his* face flashes across my mind. *His* broad shoulders and chiseled chest are trickling with sweat, and his dilated eyes are nearly black with lust.

I want to be with you, only you.

My imagination whispers his voice to me, and the words heighten my pleasure, getting me really close.

"I'm so close, babe," Zander grunts at the same time that my imagination whispers: *I left Ashley for you.*

I let out a high pitched moan as my orgasm rips through my body and my head feels like it's floating. This feeling of pure bliss is all I want. I feel Zander pull out and hear the noise of his fist over his dick, slick with my wetness.

He collapses in the bed next to me and my hips fall to the mattress, both of us panting.

My body feels amazing and light, but my head instantly clouds over with the realization of what just happened.

I came to the thought of a man, and it wasn't the one inside me. Not just any man, either.

Chain.

Chapter Thirty-Two

Chain

Nine. Ten. Eleeeven. Twelvvvve.

The weights clang on the machine after I let the curling bars go. The adrenaline coursing through my veins from the intensity of my workout gives me the release I've been seeking. I let myself go a bit when I was with Ashley. I've missed the burn in my muscles and the rigor of gaining strength.

I wipe the sweat off my brow and stand up to wait out the time before my second set. I pace the few feet next to the machine, unable to stand still with the buzz of energy.

After about 60 seconds, I return to the machine and move the weight up another 5 lbs, then grip the handles and curl my arms in preparation. My muscles flex in response. I complete my second and third sets, then head to the sauna in the men's locker room.

Luckily I'm the only one inside. I don't need to see an old, naked man, or be forced to make small talk with another gym-goer. I want to sit on the wooden planks in peace. As I feel the heat seep in through my pores, I glance around the small space.

This would be a fun place to fuck someone.

My newfound freedom has me hornier than ever. I feel like a teenager again, ready to screw any girl who glances my way. Maybe I should sign up for a dating site and put myself back out there.

I'm hesitant, though. I want to focus on myself. I've decided I'm going to rededicate myself to a fitness regimen and look into buying a house. I was stuck in that stuffed up apartment that Ashley loved long enough. The only redeeming factor was that I could save up some money, since she and I split the rent.

This has been my best week in a long time. The weight that's been lifted off my chest has me flying freer than a bird. I get a little lonely in bed at night, sure, but it's better than her body next to me.

There's only been one thing that's bugged me.

Jack.

I'm still contemplating how to handle that situation. His office had been emptied out by the time I got into the office Tuesday morning and I thought this problem had been eradicated. News spread quickly of his leaving because he felt 'burnt out'. I internally relished the fact that he succumbed to my demands.

Well, partially, at least. After finding out he did reach out to Marlie, I've tossed around ideas as to how to handle this dilemma. He should have known better than to fuck with me; to disobey me. My fists clench with the rising anger in my chest.

I really didn't think he would call her. Why would he? She acted like he was the plague and wanted nothing to do with him.

But he did. And I can't let it slide. When I made the threat, I figured if he didn't quit I would tell our boss that Jack had slept with his wife at one of the networking parties they hosted months ago.

I walked in on them in the bathroom. Seriously—how is anyone dumb enough to forget to lock the damned door? They were certainly drunk enough to make that mistake. Jack called me the next day and swore up and down that she came onto him and that he was too drunk to make the right decision.

It's not that I didn't believe him; James' wife certainly wasn't an angel. I've seen her hanging off an assortment of men over the years at these parties. James is typically too wrapped up in discussions to notice. But I know Jack, and well... he's not going to pass up an opportunity to fuck a beautiful woman like that.

I promised him not to say anything because really, I could care less about involving myself in the drama. If she was giving it up to Jack in the bathroom of her own home, it was obvious this was an ongoing habit of hers. Let James figure it out in his own time.

The real thing to think about was how I ever got along with Jack in the first place. I should have known that his transgressions would be our undoing. Especially because I don't condone cheating in the slightest.

But Jack *did* quit. His shit was gone, and I considered this matter settled. Then I find out that he *fucking* called her. How the fuck did he get her number anyway? Maybe she never changed it...

Somehow, telling James about Jack's *indiscretion* doesn't seem like the right move anymore. Not to mention, it implicates me in the fact that I never confessed it to him; that I kept Jack's secret.

No, this has become a matter of retribution. A fuck you to the fact that he not only screwed over Marlie, but he didn't heed my warning. I can't let that shit go.

It's not in my nature.

My entire body is alive and dripping with sweat. I look at the time and realize I've been in here for about twenty minutes, lost in thought. I exit and grab my gym bag from the lockers. I resume my musing as I drive back to Valerie's. I know what I want to do to him—I want to tear him limb from limb. I want to fuck him up so bad, he doesn't remember his own name.

But that's a part of me I shut down over a decade ago. It got me into enough trouble in high school, but it was also what got me through living with my dad. Once I learned to defend myself, he couldn't put his hands on me anymore. Not if he wanted to get out scratch free.

Since he knew I could level with him physically, he upped the ante on the verbal abuse. My mom continued to enable it, and I needed an outlet. I joined the high school wrestling team, and spent my free time practicing or fighting people I didn't like. I never backed down and I always won.

By junior year, no one fucked with me. I decided to turn a new leaf in college, leaving the fighting life behind me. It felt too close to my dad, and while I would never hit a woman, it didn't feel like enough justification to hit men I had problems with, either. I continued exercising, using it as a form of physical release. But I didn't want to exude my power with punches. Once I decided to study law, I replaced fists with a suit.

I pull into the driveway at Valerie's house and put the truck into park. I blast the rock radio and let myself get carried away with the thumping of the bass that feeds the adrenaline and anger thrumming through my veins.

What other option do I have? It's fuck him up or let him get away with it. Telling the boss about Jack's lay with his wife will only screw me over at this point. Marlie made it clear she wants nothing to do with him.

I have to follow through on my word, and there's no better way to do that than with a fist to the face.

I'm pacing the sidewalk in front of the prestigious Bayford condominium building with my fists clenched. I'm wearing a black hat low on my forehead so I'm not easily distinguished. It's a busy street, and I'm hoping that will work for me rather than against me.

I plan to make this quick. I know where Jack lives because I've been here countless times after nights out at the bar, or to discuss a case we worked on. The nearly full moon shines bright, illuminating the area.

They say full moons bring out the crazies. I'm not sure if I believe that, but I'll let it take the blame for the half-cocked decision I'm making tonight.

This is a risk for me. If I'm seen by anyone I know, or worse, arrested, I'll be fired from the firm in a heartbeat. Likely even disbarred. They can't have that image tattering their name, and I wouldn't blame them.

But I can't let this slide. The motherfucker needs to pay for what he did to Marlie, and for not listening to me.

The problem is, I don't know when he'll be home. It's already 10:30 and I've been here twenty minutes. I didn't see his car parked on the street where he usually leaves it. Maybe he parked in the garage for once. I can't gain access to check, so I've resorted to waiting outside, albeit impatiently.

I tried to stand off to the side with a perfect view of the entrance, but the building nerves wouldn't let me stand still. I can't fully explain what's gotten into me. I should have let this go. I *need* to let this go.

I stop mid-step and stare up at the high rise, trying to convince myself that I should leave. Let this motherfucker walk away unscathed, and I'll get back to business.

Marlie's not even my girl.

The thought causes my insides to clench with possession. Possession that's unwarranted. She's not mine, and she never will be. She's marrying *Zander*. His name tastes sour on my tongue, and my jaw clenches.

I resume my pacing. This is a fool's run. I'm a fool, fighting a fight that doesn't belong to me.

Except it does. He did what you told him not to.

I shouldn't have meddled to begin with, but I had to know what went on between them. Being friends with Jack for years wouldn't let me leave curiosity alone. Maybe if he'd been just another piece of shit I had no connection to, I wouldn't have felt moved to confront him.

But if she was mine...

I wouldn't have let anyone get away with cheating on her. Or doing her any other wrong, for that matter. Jack was a friend, and while I've always known about his indiscretions, they finally became personal.

I hear a car door slam closely followed by the *beep beep* of the doors locking. I snap my head in the direction of the sound and my eyes land on him.

My heart races, pounding in my chest. The adrenaline I crave so dearly thrums through my blood and I feel the tingle in my fingertips. I stalk over to him in calculated, measured steps.

Jack's head turns and finds mine, his eyes widening in fear.

That's right motherfucker.

"Chain—"

I cock my fist and take the final step between us, throwing my whole body into the punch. It lands square in his face and I hear the resounding crack as he's thrown back onto the pavement.

My knuckles throb in the most satisfying way. I tower over him and see blood gushing from his nose. I grab his shirt and yank him up, tossing him in front of me.

"Ch—"

His voice is cut off by the second punch I hurl, this time a jab across his cheek. His entire head turns and he covers his face with his hands. It takes every ounce of control I can muster to stop before I seriously injure him. As much as I want to, that leads to too many questions.

I put my mouth to his ear and my own steely voice sounds foreign to me.

"Don't. Ever. Disobey me again."

I grab his shoulders and shove him to the ground with a lazy push. He collapses, weakened by my hits. Not that he was that strong to begin with.

I cross the street and turn down a road that leads to a set of restaurants. I keep my pace quick and focused, searching for my car in a dark and dirty alleyway. The lack of light helps with not being identified, but so does the lack of camera footage.

I risk a look back to see Jack being lifted by an unfamiliar person, likely a neighbor or passerby. He's waving his hands as if in dismissal. I return my attention forward and smirk. I'm taken back to the way I felt all those years ago, proving dominance over those weaker than I.

Even if cameras did see me tonight, Jack should know better than to say shit about this *now*.

Chapter Thirty-Three

Marlie

The trip with Zander this past weekend did the exact *opposite* of what I needed it to do. I feel more shaky about our relationship, and I'm consumed with guilt.

It's made it hard to focus at work. It's made it hard to enjoy our time together. Yet here I am, on Thursday night, with my head lying on his chest. While I'm here physically, my mind is elsewhere.

We have The Office playing, and the scene it switches to calls my attention. I've seen it a thousand times; it's one of my favorites—Casino Night, the finale of season two.

Pam says good night to her fiancé, who goes home while she stays to continue enjoying the company's casino night. Jim finally gathers the courage to tell Pam his feelings—that he's in love with her. He approaches her, she cracks a joke, and he laughs. But then he tells her he needs to talk to her about something.

And he just says it—"I'm in love with you."

This scene always made me scoff at Pam. How could she not see that Jim was in love with her?! It was as obvious as expecting rain after seeing dark clouds. Everyone else can see it, why can't she see?

But tonight, my heart clenches for her. It's not that she was ignorant of his feelings for her; she was completely unaware of her own feelings for *him*. Because facing them would mean making a choice—a choice she didn't want to have to make.

That's why she says she can't. It's not that she can't be with Jim because she's engaged. It's that she can't face what she feels for him. It's evident in the next scene, where she willingly returns his passionate kiss.

The guilt I've grown accustomed to feeling creeps into my thoughts again. It's with me while I work, when I shower, while we fuck. It's even snuck into my dreams, causing restless nights.

I need to talk to someone about this. I haven't said a word to anyone because it feels so wrong. And my best friend is married to Zander's best friend. I know she's there for me, but I'm afraid of what it will mean for our friendship.

Plus, I'm not even sure of what's going on. I just know that I don't know. It's so exhausting and it's been driving me insane.

After Pam tells Jim she really is going to marry Roy, they part and I feel my heart shatter for him *and* her. She's just letting the love of her life walk away because of her commitment to a man that's not right for her.

Is that what I'm doing? Am I holding onto the relationship with Zander out of loyalty? Out of fear of the unknown?

I can't keep cycling through the same questions that have invaded my mental space. With the heartache and guilt fueling my decision, I look up at Zander without lifting my head off his comforting chest.

"I think I'm going to see if Stella can go to the beach this weekend," I tell him.

"It's been a while since you guys have gone," he replies, slowly peeling his eyes from the screen to look at me. "Go for it, babe."

I reach for my phone on the nightstand and unplug it from the charger, returning to the crook of Zander's shoulder. I pull up my iMessages with Stella and read the last one she sent.

> Stella: I miss you!!! We need to do something soon.

I hadn't responded because I got sidetracked at work. I type out my message and quickly hit send so I don't lose the nerve.

> Me: I miss you too! How about the beach Saturday? I could use some sand and sun.

She reads the message immediately and I smile, watching the screen as she types.

> Stella: Yes!! I'll be at your place around 8.

I double-tap to heart the message, then lock the phone and put it back on my nightstand with the charger.

Zander's phone vibrates not a minute later. He grabs it and reads the message. "Jace and I are going to game while you guys are gone. Fuck yes!"

He texts something back, his movements causing my head to shake a bit. He puts his phone back on his nightstand before turning out the lamp and popping a kiss on my head.

"Night, babe," he says.

"Night," I reply, snuggling deeper into him. I draw in a long breath through my nose, inhaling his light citrusy smell. And while it comforts me, I find myself dreaming of mint as I drift off to sleep.

"You comin' out with us tonight, Marlie?" Eli asks me.

We're standing outside of Sparkle Comedy after class along with the rest of our friends. I peel my eyes away from Chain, who's raptly listening to Damon speak about something. My own thoughts have been so loud that I don't know what he's saying.

"I don't think so," I say slowly. "I'm going to the beach with Stella tomorrow and I've got to be up early." *Plus, I want to stay the hell away from Chain so I can think properly.*

"Aw, come on," he pouts. "It's the weekend, so what if you lose a little sleep?"

Easy for him to say. I've been losing sleep all week. Instead, I reply with a forced chuckle. "Next time, promise."

"How is Stella? Still with Jace?"

I can't help the sincere belly laugh I belt out. I feel Chain's eyes on me, but I force my eyes to stay on Eli. "Yes, they're still married."

"Yeah, yeah." He waves his hand in the air flippantly. "She's such a baddie, it's too bad she's taken."

I give him a calculated look. "Stella would rip you to *pieces*. And didn't you have a thing for another *baddie*?"

I give him a pointed look but don't say more. Lorraine is amongst our circle, talking with Liv.

"I'm only joking. I would never come between them," he deflects. I smirk and he gives me a light nudge in the ribs with his elbow.

Of their own volition, my eyes roam to where Chain stands and I catch his slightly narrowed eyes watching the place where Eli had just nudged me. Once my eyes land on him, his own flick up and like magnets, we're locked in each other's gaze. I don't think I could ever get over those emerald eyes. They're astounding. They draw me in like a moth to a flame: the light I so desperately need.

But, I'm afraid to get burned.

I watch as the green turns a shade darker and his pupils dilate. I can't help the sharp intake of breath and the clenching of my core, immediately dampening at his heated gaze. Unconsciously, I start to fiddle with my engagement ring, and it roots me back to reality. I tear my eyes away from him and look back to Eli.

"I'm gonna get going," I tell him. He looks up from his phone and gives me puppy eyes.

"One drink," he pleads.

I can't. I can't be around him, it's too much. The intensity of his stares, the constant awareness of the electric current that zaps between us, it's too distracting. I need to focus on Zander and I.

"I can't," I say firmly. I start heading towards my car and Eli falls into step beside me.

"You don't have to walk with me!"

"It's fine, the lot's right there. Stop being so prideful."

I roll my eyes and smile at him. He's the best.

"I'm so glad you took this class with me."

"With you? I saved you from IT nerds and snobby writers," he scoffs jokingly.

"IT nerds? Zander—"

I cut myself off when I feel a presence step on my left, accompanied by a faint scent of mint. I don't have to look to know who it is.

"Zander, what?" his velvety voice asks, turning my insides to liquid. I look behind me to see the rest of the class still grouped up. I refuse to meet his gaze so I focus on the path in front of me.

"He's in IT," I say tersely.

"Is he now? That's a great career choice," Chain replies conversationally. "That's the way of the world these days."

"I was just messing around, Marlie," Eli says apologetically.

"It's fine," I tell him before looking at Chain. I force a wall around my feelings, refusing to allow myself the enjoyment of his company. "I was just leaving. I can't go out tonight."

"I heard," he says curtly. He's the one keeping his eyes focused in front of him now, and that irritates me.

"So, I'll see you later," I say, ignoring the ache I feel at the thought of not seeing him for another week.

Stop it.

I pick up my pace, walking ahead. Eli quickens his own pace to keep up, and a moment later, Chain also falls in line.

"I had to grab something from my car. Have a good night, then," he says before he takes long strides ahead.

When we reach my car, I unlock it and wave to Eli. "Have fun tonight. Don't get into trouble."

"Impossible," he says with a mischievous grin.

"*Too* much trouble, then," I amend, returning his grin. It's hard not to be infected with his energy.

I get into the car and turn the engine on, putting the car into reverse. I look up and involuntarily search for Chain, finding him shutting the door to his truck and walking back towards the theater.

I can't help but notice that he's empty handed.

Chapter Thirty-Four

Chain

I take a sip of my drink and scope out the crowd at Vigs, which is busier than a typical Friday night. I've tried to get into the conversation with Eli, Liv, Lorraine, Damon, and Toni, but I'm feeling restless tonight. Work ran late and because of class, I couldn't make it to the gym like I wanted to.

It doesn't help that my dick has been aching to cum. It's strange, really. I was with Ashley for years and never felt the sexual drive I've felt in the last couple weeks since our breakup. It only proves to me further that I made the right decision.

I'm more than ready to move on. It's shitty, but I really don't miss her at all. I want to find someone who's right for me and will satisfy all my needs, including the physical. I finally ended the conversations, telling her we need space in order to get past the breakup. I blocked her, so I'm not sure if she's continued messaging me or not.

My eyes roam over a group of attractive women by the bar. I could easily approach them, buy a few drinks, and likely take one home by the end of the night. Or rather, to my truck. I don't have a home right now. Not for lack of trying. I'm hunting the market for the right place so I can get the hell out of my parents' house.

I toy with the idea of starting up a conversation with the brunette that's laughing, but when the bar light hits her eyes, all I can think is they don't shine the way Marlie's do. I grit my teeth in frustration. This is a new theme lately. Little things somehow lead back to thoughts of her. A waft of perfume at the office, or her car on the road.

She's engaged, you can't have her.

I repeat the mantra I've told myself each time, trying to force myself out of this. But I've been failing. I mentally kicked myself for trying to walk with her and Eli when she was leaving.

But I didn't want to say goodbye. I wanted to savor any moment I could in her presence. I know it's wrong. Just because I'm free now doesn't mean she is.

I return my focus to the group around me, trying to get caught up in the conversation. Eli catches my eye and glances down at my drink before holding up his own and saying, "Want to get another round?"

Not waiting for an answer, he downs what's left of his rum and coke. I follow suit and finish off my Macallan, standing up decidedly and letting the back of my legs push the chair away. I follow Eli up to the crowded bar. We wait behind another set of guys so we can order.

"So what's your plan now that you're flying solo?" he shouts. Between the upbeat music and the mass of people, it's hard to be heard.

"I'm looking into buying a house," I respond, leaning my head closer to him so I don't have to speak too loudly.

"Awesome, man," he says approvingly, nodding his head. "How about dating?"

"I'm not really looking for anything serious," I tell him. "I want to focus on getting my shit together first."

He gives me a sly grin. "That doesn't mean you can't date."

"I don't want to mislead someone."

"As long as you're honest, you can't be held responsible for that. I always tell women I meet that I'm just looking for fun, nothing more."

He has a point. I glance towards that group of women, looking for the brunette. Eli follows my line of sight.

"Now you're thinking," he says.

My lips tilt up and I side eye him. "I like you."

He gives me a light punch on the arm. "I like you, too, Chain."

The guys in front of us squeeze between us, donning a drink in each hand. Eli starts to move up when the guy next to him boulders past, causing Eli to stumble into me.

Not tonight.

I move past Eli and tap the guy on the shoulder. He looks at me, arching his eyebrow that has a scar gashed through it. He gives me a once over before turning back.

Wrong move.

"AY!" I call to him. Noting my tone, he looks at me again. I plaster on a pleasant smile. "You must not have seen us. We were next."

He scoffs and turns away from me again. My jaw ticks with the rising aggravation from this guy. I clench my fists and my knuckles ache, reminding me they're still busted up from my altercation with Jack.

I decide to use it to my advantage so I don't have to physically touch this man tonight.

I squeeze my arm between his and the person next to us, placing my fist onto the bar, palm down. The swelling and redness are evident, even in the dimmer lighting. The man looks down and I see his eyes widen before jerking up to meet mine.

I don't say anything, only giving him a hard stare. Lucky for him, he understands what I'm trying to tell him.

“Sorry, I didn’t see you guys,” he glances back at Eli and then moves. I step into his spot, then place my hand on Eli’s back to guide him next to me. Eli is watching me with wide eyes too, though not from fear.

“Well, damn,” he comments appreciatively. “The lawyers got some heat.”

I smirk in response, then look around for the bartender. I flag her with a wave of my hand, and she mouths, "One second,” as she places a drink in front of the customer she’s serving.

“The fuck happened to your knuckles?” Eli asks.

“Long story,” I reply curtly.

He eyes me a moment longer. I watch him debate whether to push it further. I help him decide by returning my gaze towards the bartender, who is hurriedly making her way to us.

“What can I get you guys?”

“Two Woodfords, neat,” Eli quips before I’m able to.

“Great choice,” I comment, eyeing him approvingly as the bartender turns her back to us. We watch in admiration as she stands on her tiptoes to grab the bottle from the shelves of liquor lining the wall, accentuating the curve of her ass. *It’s a nice ass*. She grabs two glasses, pulls off the cap, and begins to pour.

“Here you are.” She places them in front of us under two napkins.

“Add it to my tab, Eli Rosario.” He grabs the drinks, handing me one.

“Cheers.” I raise my glass to his and we clink them before each taking a sip.

“To a damn hot night,” Eli says declaratively, leading us back to the group.

I fumble with my keys, searching for the one to the front door. It's dark and Valerie forgot to leave the front porch light on. She's not used to me being around.

Locating it, I bring it to the lock and wiggle it. The moment I open the door, I hear shouting.

"... goddamn it, Valerie, you never listen!" The loud thump that follows has me running towards my father's slurred speech.

I find them in the kitchen near the island. Valerie's holding the side of her scrunched face and the rage ignites in me, my father's actions the gasoline to the fire always burning from his abuse.

"BACK OFF!" I shout. I stalk over to him and force him away from her by shoving him right in the shoulders.

"This doesn't concern you, son," he says with a menacing tone.

"I'm no son of yours," I spit, moving between him and Valerie as he takes an unstable step towards her.

"I tried to give you everything, Chain. You could have had a jewelry store."

"I don't want *shit* from you."

He continues as if he didn't hear me. He's so drunk, he probably didn't. "Instead, you wasted precious time in law scho—"

"Go to bed." I shove him again for good measure. Unlike Jack, Dad's been on the receiving end of my fists countless times. He actually *does* know better.

"We're talking it out," he slurs. "Your mother just doesn't know how to stop spending all my money."

"I'm not going to tell you again."

He just stands there, his hazy eyes taking in my erect posture and clenched jaw. I crack my knuckles in front of him for effect. I really don't want to revert back to my old ways twice in a month, but I will if I have to.

"Sleep it off." The plea that escapes into my words sickens me. I feel pathetic, back in a predicament I resent with every fiber of my being. I feel the immediate relief when he takes a couple of staggered steps back, then turns towards his bedroom. *Their* bedroom. Once he's gone, I turn back to my mom.

"Valerie, what the fuck." I rush over to her and pull her arm away, taking in the gash in her eyebrow and the swelling in her eye.

"He's getting sloppy," she says with a small smile.

"IT'S NOT A FUCKING JOKE!" I roar. I throw her hand back at her, disgusted. "Why do you allow him to do this to you?!"

"Shhh, let's go outside," she says in a loud whisper, her eyes dashing to the direction of their bedroom.

I stomp past her and open the french doors, turning on the light. I take a seat in one of the four chairs surrounding a patio table and tap my foot incessantly, willing the pulsing energy to leave me. As soon as her ass hits the chair, I round on her.

"I thought you said this stopped." I force my voice to sound calm.

"It did, for a while," she says. "I just forgot to tell you it picked back up again."

"*Stop* joking about this!" My voice rises and the small smirk she wore falls from her face.

"I didn't want to worry you. He's my problem, not yours."

I whip my head away from hers and stare out at the pool. There's hardly any light from the crescent moon, but the water is eerily still. There's no wind tonight, which is odd for early March.

"Why didn't you tell me?" I ask quietly. She doesn't answer right away, looking out at the water with me.

"I didn't want you to feel an obligation to return home, or to do anything at all," she says. "He's done enough damage. And I'm the one who chose to stay, not you."

"Why? Why stay?"

She doesn't answer, and I don't press it. I'm not sure there's anything she could say that would help me fucking understand. I relish the comfortable silence we've always shared, even in the darkest of times. Possibly even because of them.

I work to bring my heart rate down and even my breathing.

"Distract me. Tell me something going on with you," she says, just as she always did.

I sift through the recent weeks. The familiar anger forces Jack to the forefront of my mind, followed by the reason for my fist to his face.

Marlie.

"I've got a thing for a girl who's engaged," I tell her, certain she'll eat this up like candy. It's funny how quickly you can fall right back into old patterns. This was one of ours.

"Ooooh," she says, the glimmer in her eyes dimmed by her wince when she smiles widely. The swelling around her eye is worsening; she won't be able to leave home for a few days.

I feel the whiskey from earlier swirling in my stomach, sickened by the whole thing. Once you escape something for a while, coming back to it makes it seem worse. I always hated it, but it's no longer normal for me.

Yet I'm still here, trying to distract her with something I know she'll love to hear. If nothing else, my son of a bitch father's actions did force us to become close in a way. I've always felt very comfortable telling her things, almost like a best friend.

"It's not a big deal," I tell her. *But it is.*

Shut up.

"How did you meet? What do you mean, a thing? What's her name? How—"

"Woah, chill." I cut off her interrogation. "We met at improv, and her name's not important."

I can't say her name out loud. This was a mistake. I need to forget about her, not confess my feelings to my mom.

"But what thing? That must be really hard," she sympathizes.

"It's fine, really," I say, more to myself than to her.

The truth is, it's been a real mind fuck to constantly be thinking about her. It's not something I want to be doing, and it's out of my control. *Particularly* because I can't have her.

"Please tell me she's nothing like Ashley," Valerie pleads. I can't help but chortle.

"Nothing," I reassure her.

"Well, that's too bad she's engaged," she says thoughtfully.

I roll my eyes. "He seems like a nice guy, I'm sure she'll be very happy."

"Do you think she likes you?"

Her question stumps me. I hadn't ever considered it. Any thoughts of her never went towards a future because I was with Ashley and she was with Zander.

Losing Ashley allowed me to slip into some *improper* thoughts of Mar, but I'd worked to rid myself of those. The night in the shower springs to mind and just as before, the idea of her luscious lips wrapped around my cock has blood rushing to its head.

I readjust my seat in the chair. "Of course not, she's *engaged.*"

Valerie smirks at me, then gazes back over the pool.

"Engaged ain't married."

Chapter Thirty-Five

Marlie

My nerves have my throat feeling tight and constricted, like I have to fight for every deep breath I take. As I walk to Stella's car, I try and get it together so she doesn't pick up on it right away.

I want to wait until we're at the beach, butts on the sand, before divulging all of my feelings and fears from these past few months. They've been slowly building, and they're ready to erupt.

Just hold on a bit longer, I tell them, as if you can just talk to your feelings. My own humor puts a small smile on my face, and I open her door with it plastered on.

"I'm so exciiiiited!" she screams at me while I toss my bag over the seat into the back.

Her energy seeps into my pores, lending me enough to push those feelings back down. I feel them resist, the waters crashing into the walls, but I meet her gaze and they recede when I see the gleam in her eyes.

"I know! It's been way too long," I say.

"Not my fault," she scoffs as she looks over her shoulder before pulling onto the road. "You're so busy these days."

"Not *that* busy."

"Friday nights were a big deal for us! Now you waste them at that *improv* place," she says in mock disgust. If she were anyone else, I'd worry that she actually meant it.

"You should have joined me!" I say. Internally, I'm so grateful she didn't, or there's no way I could have hidden all of this from her.

We've been friends for so long that we know each other too well. Even when we first met, there was a natural, intuitive understanding. That, along with the time we've known each other, has made it so we can't hide anything for long, if at all.

"Not my thing, babe," she says. "But I *so* love it for you."

I smile and I know she sees it from her periphery while her eyes are trained on the road. She's always been a focused driver; hands on 10 and 2, and eyes on the road, "Where they belong," as she'd always say.

"So, how's married life?" I ask her. I lean back in my seat, my head hitting the headrest with a light thud.

"It's exactly the same. We're on the hunt for a house now, though!"

"Ohhh, that's exciting!"

She updates me on the process and their plans for the rest of the ride, and I use it as the perfect distraction I so desperately need. I don't want to overthink about what I'm going to say to her. I want it to come out like word vomit because, well, it is.

Once we've parked, unloaded, and found our beach spot, we lather on sunscreen and lay back on our towels as we feel the sun bake our skin. We're wearing similar floral two-piece suits, but where mine is black with pink, hers is white with teal.

This is the best place to be in the entire world. I listen to the waves crashing gently on the sand and the distant sounds of laughter with the light breeze blowing through my hair, calming me in a way nothing else can. I'm not sure I could have this conversation with her anywhere else.

"I need to talk to you," I force out, ignoring the lump in my throat, courtesy of the fear and guilt I've kept inside.

Her head snaps to me immediately, and in the next moment she's sitting up with her legs crossed, facing me.

"Oh, shit," she says seriously.

Can't hide anything.

I rush the words out, hoping that will make this easier. "I've been doubting my engagement to Zander."

She doesn't flinch and her eyes don't widen; she's not surprised.

"You knew?" I say, shock lacing my tone, although I'm not sure why. We really haven't hung out much, both busy with our own lives. We've had our regular Saturdays with the guys but nothing like this has come up.

"There were a lot of small things, but then I saw the look in your eyes the night of the engagement. I could just tell..." She trails off, looking down at her clasped hands between her thighs.

"And you didn't say anything because...?" I elongated the last word.

"I could ask you the same thing." Her eyes meet mine with a challenge but I can tell she's not upset, just curious. I let out a harsh breath. Tears well in my eyes and I break our stare, looking out at the water.

"I've been too scared," I finally say, forcing myself to look at her. *It's now or never.* "We're all best friends, I didn't know how you'd react."

"I'm *your* best friend, Marlie. Before Jason, before Zander, we were friends. Nothing will ever come between us."

Her words instantly remove the fear of her judgment or any other reaction. At this point, I've thought of it all.

A small smile plays on my lips. "I don't know what I was thinking."

"Well, why don't you tell me now? Start from the beginning."

I sit up and face the ocean, Stella mimicking my stance. I spend the next 20 minutes telling her everything from the moment of the engagement: the Google searches, the internal battles, my fears and anxieties, and the trip to the cabin.

"... and I didn't want you to tell Jace and him to feel some responsibility to tell Zander, or for you guys to be in a weird position. But I couldn't hold it in anymore. I've been going crazy," I conclude with a short laugh.

"You haven't talked to anyone about this?" she says with a gasp. When I shake my head, her eyes reflect such compassion and sympathy that the tears return to my eyes. "That had to be so hard. But I get it."

"I don't know what to do."

"What brought all of this on? Just the engagement?" she pries with a knowing look in her eye.

She can't know.

"I mean, there's this guy in our improv class I think is hot," I say nonchalantly. I won't meet her eyes.

"The one we saw at the bar?" she offers.

I whip my head to her at that question.

"I thought you forgot about that," I say.

"He's hot as fuck," she says with a bite of her lower lip. "Plus, you can't forget a name like *Chain*."

"I know," I comment, unable to help myself. "But there's been this, like, weird feeling connection thing and I... I can't make any sense of it."

Stella doesn't reply, a pensive look overcoming her. I let her absorb it all, because it really is a lot. I stare out at the ocean, watching as the white foam from the crashing waves slowly recedes back into the water.

A continual drift, at the mercy of wherever the current takes it.

"It's really not about that though," I continue when she doesn't speak. "It's really been since the engagement. Things got so real for me, and I haven't been able to shake it since. I was just saying I wasn't even sure if I *wanted* to get married, and then he proposed?! I probably brought it onto myself. When we danced at your wedding, I said I wanted to get married. You guys made it look so easy. I didn't know I was giving him the green light to propose to me!"

"But you told Zander you had a crush on him," Stella says inquisitively. When she sees my confused look, she adds, "Chain."

"Okay, what the *hell*, Stella!" I gently toss the bottle of sunscreen laying next to me at her. "What's with all the secrecy?!"

She tosses the bottle back at me. "I could ask you the same thing!!!"

Touché.

"Were you mad at me?" I ask weakly.

"Not mad, but... hurt. We're best friends. Why wouldn't you come to me with this?"

I open my mouth to reply but she continues. "I get it. Deep down, I already knew. And it really has nothing to do with why I never brought any of it up."

We're silent for a moment, and when she doesn't go on, I ask, "Okay, then why?"

"I felt like it was something you had to figure out on your own."

The moment the words leave her mouth, I feel it resonate in the deepest part of me.

"I thought maybe Jace didn't tell you," I say, but really I knew he would probably tell her.

“Please, we tell each other everything,” she says with a roll of her eyes.

“Well it was a moment of weakness,” I tell her. “I felt so shitty and guilty and wrong... I mean, I’ve been cheated on. I know what that feels like.”

“Okay, but Marlie,” she says matter of factly. “You’re not cheating on Zander.”

“I shouldn’t be feeling these things!” The confession forces tears to spill from my eyes, hot and rushed. They’ve needed this release, the one I’ve forced back. Now that they’re finally free, they don’t stop.

“You can’t help how you feel,” she says sympathetically. I swipe at my eyes angrily.

“He hasn’t done anything wrong. Zander is *amazing*. Why am I doubting us so much?”

She pulls out a small packet of tissues from her bag, opening it and handing me one. I take it with a look that says, “Seriously? You packed tissues?”

After stowing the pack back in her bag, she looks deep into my eyes and takes hold of my left hand.

“Just because someone is amazing doesn’t mean they’re amazing for *you*.”

The tears continue to fall, chilling with the wind as they roll down my cheeks, chin, then chest. I don’t bother to hold back the sob that overtakes me and I throw my hands over my face, letting the emotions take over.

My sobs are lost to the crashes of the waves.

A light sunburn, empty heart, and few hours later, we’re on our way back to the condo. We’d planned to meet the guys there and hang out the rest of the night, like we usually do on a Saturday.

My heart may be empty, but I also feel more at peace than I have in weeks. I've finally gotten all of these warring emotions off my chest, and I don't have to carry them alone anymore.

We spent the rest of the trip relaxing, taking in the sun, and swimming in the ocean. Each time a wave rolled over us, I felt it strip away the judgments and emotions I'd been holding onto. The salt wiped the remaining tears and I was free.

But now that we're in the confines of metal and on our way back to reality, I realize that although I dumped my feelings, I didn't make any decisions.

"So what am I supposed to do now?" I ask Stella, my chest tightening.

"I think you know what you have to do," she says quietly. The pang is like a knife to the gut.

"I don't even know if I want to end things with him," I tell her, my eyes watering again. I close them tightly, willing them to stay in.

She doesn't respond right away, flipping on her blinker to merge into the next lane so we can get on the expressway.

"What if you just tell him how you've been feeling? Maybe call off the engagement," she offers, quickly glancing at me before keeping her focus on the road. But that glance was enough for her to add, "That doesn't have to mean it's over. Just that you're thinking things through."

"He's such a good guy. Am I crazy??"

"You're not crazy. And you can always resume the engagement if you change your mind. But you can't keep making plans when your heart's not in it."

Ugh. I know she's right. My heart knows she's right. The calm waters in the chasm of my soul know she's right.

"What do I even *say?*"

She brings the car to a slow as we approach the red light before the entrance ramp. Once we're at a stop, she turns her whole head to me.

"The truth."

Chapter Thirty-Six

Marlie

We pull up to the complex and Stella parks the car in a vacant parallel spot on the road. Once she puts the car in park, she grabs her bag from the back and opens her door. I don't move. The nerves have been slowly rising and I'm not sure they have a peak. Just when I think it can't feel worse, it does.

"I can't do this."

"Yes, you can." She reaches for my hand and grips it hard. "Zander loves you. He will understand."

I let out the breath I *knew* I was holding. "That's true."

It's the mantra I chant silently as we walk into the condo.

"You're back!" Jace shouts when he hears the door open.

"The beach felt so nice," Stella replies, tossing her bag on the couch and walking to the chair where he sits. She plops a kiss on his lips while he keeps his focus on the screen.

"I missed you, babe," Zander says, keeping his own eyes locked on the screen while tapping a button repeatedly on his controller. I walk over to him but I can't bring myself to place my guilty lips on his.

"We're finishing this last round and then we'll log off," he says.

I look at Stella and she meets my gaze. She must sense the desperation, announcing, "We'll wait upstairs."

We take the trip to the bedroom and I collapse face first onto the mattress. I hear the door close gently behind me, then her weight by my head as she sits on the bed.

"It's going to be okay." She rubs my back soothingly.

"It doesn't feel like that right now," I moan, my voice muffled.

"I know. But the truth hurts sometimes."

Time to get it together. You can do this.

"I just feel like the biggest bitch in the whole world," I whine. *Okay, one more minute.*

"You haven't done anything wrong! You can't help how you feel," she says exasperatedly. I snap my head up to hers.

"How would you feel if Jace told you he wasn't sure about marrying you?"

She can't hide the hurt I see reflected in her eyes, even if she tries to cover it up defiantly.

"I would understand," she says, but her tone lacks the proper conviction.

"Yeah, right. You'd be hurt. Who the *fuck* wouldn't be?!"

"Fine, yes! It would hurt! But it's also not your fault. You can't—"

The distant pounding of footsteps on the stairs cuts her off. She looks towards the door, then back to me. I sit up and hold her eyes, willing her blue-gray orbs to help me through this. She gives me a tight smile as I hear the door open.

Zander plops down next to me as I sit up. He slings his arm around my shoulders and gives me a wet kiss on my face. The exchange is reminiscent of a dog welcoming you home.

"Hi," I say, trying to put on a sugary tone with my forced smile. From my periphery, I see Jace give Stella a passionate kiss, then lay down on his side, propping his head on his arm.

"You okay?" Zander asks.

"Yeah, fine." My pitch sounds too high, even to my own ears. "I'm just tired."

"You guys were out there a while," he affirms.

"It was like 5 hours," Stella says with an eye roll. "You guys don't know what you're missing."

"The only thing I think I missed is that ass in your bikini," Jace says, smacking her butt with a resounding pop. She laughs and for a moment, I forget what I'm feeling and what I have to do. I admire their natural flow, the way they just make sense.

And then it hurts, everywhere. I want that, and I know I don't have it with Zander. I shrug his arm off and stand in one motion, stretching my arms over my head. He doesn't seem to notice that I was subtly blowing him off as he leans back on the bed and turns towards Stella and Jace.

"So what's the plan for tonight?" he asks casually.

"Let's—"

"Actually"—Stella slaps her hand onto Jace's thigh—"I'm really worn out from the beach. I think I wanna call it for today."

"Aww." Jace's disappointment is evident. I say nothing. Zander looks at me and says, "We can have our own night, then."

He has no fucking clue.

Jace and Stella stand up. She gives me a huge hug, each of us holding on a moment longer than we normally would. As she lets go, her hands sliding down my arms, I feel her support stick to my skin, providing me the strength I need and can't seem to find within.

"I love you," I tell her, my eyes searching hers. I can see my own pain reflected in hers.

"Love you." She gives my hands a final squeeze before letting go. I feel the loss immediately. I've never felt so alone.

"Next weekend!" Jace proclaims, oblivious to what's about to happen.

There won't be a next weekend.

My lower lip starts to tremble and I'm doubting if I can do this. Panic sets in. My heart races and my eyes well with tears.

Hold it in just a little longer.

They exit the room and Zander follows to let them out. I sit at the edge of the middle of the bed, throwing my hands over my face.

I need to get it together. It's going to be okay. I can do this. Zander will understand.

The truth is, I don't need Zander's understanding; I need my own. But this moment, although not a breakup, is a breaking.

My fingers are shaking over my eyelids, and time passes much too quickly. I hear Zander's footsteps returning upstairs and I lower my hands, willing the trembling to stop.

It doesn't.

"Hey, babe," he says as he walks back in. When he sees me, he rushes to stand in front of me.

"Are you okay??"

"Sit down."

I pat the bed next to me, unable to look at him; unable to face what I'm about to do.

As if in slow motion, he sits next to me on the bed. I scoot back and cross my legs, turning to face him.

Look at him.

I force my eyes to inch up. I open my mouth but no words come out. My mind is blank. I can't think beyond the flood of emotion and panic coursing through me.

"You're scaring me," he says. He grabs my shoulders and gives me a small shake. My eyes shoot to his and I force myself to hold his penetrating stare. "Marlie?"

"I—I—"

"You can tell me anything." He gives my shoulders a reassuring squeeze before dropping his hands to mine, holding them.

I pull them away gently.

"I don't know if I want to get married."

It's so quiet, I can hear a dish clank from the neighboring unit and the steady click from the ceiling fan.

His smile fades slowly, his normally bright eyes widening with surprise. There's a knife in my gut, I'm certain of it, twisting and digging deeper.

"You don't know?" he asks with quiet control, keeping his tone even.

Fuck. "I'm having doubts about us."

He sits up straighter. I can no longer see his eyelids.

He breaks eye contact, looking to the bed frame, as if it holds the answers to the questions he must be asking himself. He runs his hands through his hair, then snaps his head back to me.

"Why?" he breathes.

I look down and toy with the ring on my finger, sliding it between my knuckles.

"I've just... I can't shake the feeling of doubt," I tell him, my voice trembling. The tears are welling, begging to fall.

I let them. I feel them as they fall onto my hands in my lap.

"So you want to break up?"

Always so direct.

"No!" I snap my eyes to his, willing him to see that I love him, that I want to be with him.

But do I?

The tears keep falling.

"I need you to explain, Marlie."

There's no humor in his tone. I'm not used to hearing him so solemn; it stings.

"Ever since our engagement, I've been battling this, like, anxiety," I start, the words rushing out in an attempt to make him understand. To make *me* understand. "I kept telling myself that it was just normal fears. I even Googled it and that's what so many people said. But it hasn't gone away. It's kept getting worse. I finally talked to Stella about it."

I stare into the depths of his eyes, a burnt shade making them seem almost black. But he won't meet my eyes; he won't look at me.

And I don't blame him. How could he? I'm breaking his heart. I'm breaking my own.

When he doesn't reply, I continue. "I just... I don't want to move forward with a wedding when I'm feeling like this."

His eyes snap to mine, finally looking at me. Mine widen as his narrow.

"Feeling what, exactly, Marlie?"

"I—I—I don't know!"

"Yes, you do!" he shouts. More tears rush to my eyes, falling quickly like rain patters from the roof. I feel them wet my hands and legs, but I don't move to wipe them. "You wouldn't be telling me this if you didn't know how you feel!"

The knife pulls out and strikes me again, hurting more with the already oozing wound.

"God, just be *honest*!"

I shake my head, my face contorted with the free flowing tears and the truth that I don't want to say. Once I do, there's no going back.

"Say it," he says through clenched teeth. There's no shouting now. He demands it with a calculated calm.

"I don't know if I want to be with you," I whisper through a quiet sob, my head hanging.

I'm not sure how long we sit there. I feel him stand up at some point and hear his footsteps as he starts pacing in front of the bed.

I look up at the wall that replaced his absence. From my periphery, I can see him taking a few steps, pivoting, taking a few steps, pivoting; over and over again.

Time has ceased to exist. I'm not sure how much of it has passed when he suddenly halts, turning towards me.

"You don't want to be with me."

His words force the knife deeper into my gut, and the pain signals my brain to retract my words, to take it all back.

"No, no!" I'm shouting now, begging him to hear me. "I do! I'm just, I'm so confused, and I'm tired of feeling all of this doubt!"

He doesn't show any evidence of compassion or empathy. He stares at me coldly, and I know I deserve it.

"You're just afraid of losing me."

His words push me and I feel myself falling through the wide open space in the chasm, because I know he's right.

"Because! I love you!" I say through the choked tears. They haven't stopped falling all this time and my eyes burn.

"That's not enough," he says.

How is he so calm?

I cry harder, though it feels impossible. The ragged breaths I draw in, then exhale, hurt my chest and I just want this feeling to go away.

"So, what do we do from here?" he asks.

I turn my head to look at him, my body following to face him.

"What?" I breathe.

"Who's going to stay in the condo? And we'll have to figure out the savings..."

His voice becomes muffled by the pain shooting through me.

"I don't want to break up!" I shout, cutting him off. "I need time to figure this out."

"You—"

"You told me when we got engaged that we didn't have to do this. That if it was too soon, you would understand!"

"But you said yes, Marlie!" I hear the anger in his tone now. "You said yes, and now you want to take it back because you're too scared to do what you need to do."

I sob so hard, my head throbs from the pressure.

"Hey," he says gently, tugging my chin up with a finger, forcing me to look at him. The sobs don't stop, my chest heaving with the struggle of breathing.

"I—love—you," I say between choked sobs.

"I know you do," he says. The anger is gone, replaced by pity.

"Please, please, I don't want to break up," I beg him.

He searches my eyes, and he must find whatever he's looking for.

"Okay. Okay."

"I love you," I say again, willing it to be enough to fix this.

"I love you, too. I *want* to be with you, Marlie. But there's only so much I can take before I have to step away."

I nod my head, thankful for the turn this has taken.

I'm okay, we're okay.

"How do you always look so beautiful, even when you cry?" he says with pure adoration. It melts my heart and breaks it all at once. "They're sparkling."

I throw my hands around his neck and my face into his chest, soaking his shirt with the old and fresh tears. He wraps his arms around me, holding me snug.

His light, citrusy scent comforts me, and I let it.

At some point, we moved to lay on the bed and cuddled, falling asleep with my head on his heart and his arm around my shoulder. The tears dried, but the gaping hole in my gut and the broken pieces of my heart remained.

We have the TV on now, The Office playing in the background as Zander plays a game on his phone. In the show, Jim moved to a different office to get away from Pam, and Pam broke off her engagement with Roy.

It's making me feel so much worse, honestly. But I refuse to change the episode or say something to Zander. I don't want to tip him off to the continuing doubt running through my head.

How are we supposed to stay together if we're not going to get married? Can he just go back? Is that what I want?

So many questions with absolutely no answers. My brain isn't capable of providing them.

Instead of searching for the answers I need, I dig my head deeper into Zander's chest.

“I'm sorry,” I say. He does a few more taps on his phone screen, then looks over at me. He sighs.

“You don't ever need to apologize for the truth, Marlie,” he says.

"Okay."

The truth.

Chapter Thirty-Seven

Marlie

I didn't notice I expected things to go back to normal until I realized that they didn't. Sunday passed by in a blur as we binge-watched TV all day and cuddled.

On our way to work Monday, Zander was abnormally quiet. We had gone to bed after our usual routine, nothing feeling out of the ordinary.

A night of sleep has a way of making a person process things, even on the unconscious level.

He only replied to the messages I sent him during the workday, not initiating any conversation. And when I asked if he was ready for lunch, he declined, stating that he had to work through lunch.

But I can count the amount of times that's happened in the entirety of our relationship on one hand.

He'd already made plans to game with Jace that night, so I hung out in bed alone, scrolling on my phone and texting with Stella.

I caught her up on the events of Saturday, telling her how we left things. When I told her that I loved Zander and still wanted to be with him, she only had one reply: I know you do. I couldn't shake the feeling that she was holding back her true thoughts. But I didn't push for them and she didn't press it.

After I brushed my teeth and laid in bed to fall asleep, I was certain we were okay and this would become water under the bridge. Even if the relentless doubt kept trying to rear its head.

But on our drive home after work Tuesday, I couldn't deny it anymore. We'd met up for lunch this time, but Zander gave me short replies to any questions I asked and only picked at his food. We spent the last half-hour of the break scrolling through our phones in silence.

When he put the car into park at the condo complex, he turned to me.

"You need to take off the ring."

The way he said it so bluntly, with shadows over his normally expressive brown eyes, confirmed that he'd been ruminating over this for days.

I opened and closed my mouth in shock, trying to formulate words.

"You don't want to get married, so let's make it real," he added. The wound in my gut throbbed with his words.

"But...why? Why does it matter if I keep wearing it?"

"Why do you want to wear it if we're not engaged?" he countered.

I didn't have an answer, and the look on his face said he knew that. I slowly moved the ring past my knuckles and off my finger. *The* finger.

I held it in my fingertips and offered it to him, but he didn't place his palm out or make any move to take it from me.

"I don't want it back. But you can't keep wearing it if this is where we are."

Tears welled in my eyes, my hand suspended with the ring in front of him.

"Why are you doing this?" I whispered, a tear falling from my right eye, then my left. I glanced around to see if anyone was bearing witness to what was happening between us.

The skies were blue with splashes of white clouds. The sun was shining and the trees were rustling with the wind. I watched a bird hop off a tree branch before taking flight.

The outside world moved on, but ours had stopped. Because I knew with the removal of the ring was the removal of whatever was left of what we were trying to salvage.

"I'm not doing anything, Marlie. We're not engaged, so there's no need to wear an *engagement* ring."

He enunciated the word in such a condescending tone, one I was not familiar with. Heartbreak can shatter a person and make them do things they wouldn't normally do.

I did this to him; to us.

I nodded my head in defeat and acceptance, feeling my heart shatter into a million pieces. They sunk to the bottom of the chasm—that *fucking* chasm—that is forever open.

And now I lay here after 2 am, tears falling silently on my pillow while he sleeps on his side, replaying that moment over and over. Haunted partially by his words, partially by the lighter feeling of my hand now that the ring is no longer on it.

I'm losing him. I feel it in my soul, in the way the waters in that godforsaken chasm have finally calmed. And I'd love to say that's what hurts the most, but it's not.

It's that when I removed the ring, I finally felt free.

I called out of work Wednesday after a sleepless night. Zander only nodded his head in understanding before he left to work, and I didn't leave bed all day.

I'm honestly not sure what happened after that, but suddenly it was Friday and I was driving home from work, alone. Zander didn't want to ride together yesterday or today.

Eli's out of town, and the timing couldn't have been more perfect. I *know* he would have noticed my miserable existence and the missing ring, and I *know* I wouldn't have lied to him about why. I was already dreading tonight.

I didn't want to have to plaster on a fake smile. I didn't want to chance someone noticing the lone finger, or the sadness behind my eyes. I wasn't ready to talk about this yet.

Although, I'm not really sure what *this* is. Zander and I have barely spoken since he told me to remove the ring. He's been busying himself with video games, and I've been avoiding asking why.

When I got home from work, I quickly changed, hardly paying any attention to the clothes I was choosing. I grabbed a bag of chips from the cupboard and left the condo, hoping to avoid Zander.

I drove to the improv theater, arriving much too early. I put the car in park and leaned back in my seat, blasting music from the speakers. I open my phone and decide to dig into the messages I've ignored all week.

I open Stella's chat first:

> Wednesday 07:42 am: I'm peeling a little on my shoulders! We need more beach days so I can tan this pale skin.

> Wednesday 12:31 pm: Do you prefer teal or brown for bathroom walls?

> Wednesday 4:58 pm: Are you okay??

> Wednesday 10:29 pm: Heard about the ring. I'm here if you need me < 3

> Friday 2:31 pm: I miss you.

Guilt floods me as I realize just how much I've missed the last few days. I type out a quick response to her:

> Me: Hey, I'm alive. Trying to process everything. I'll call you this weekend.

I open Mother's message next:

> Thursday 1:01 pm: Honey, I found a wonderful location for your reception! Call me when you get a chance to discuss.

I can't find it in me to reply to that one. I open the group chat for improv, reading the messages from earlier today:

> Jessica: GUYS the sign up for level 2 is open! Who's signing up?

> Eli: I'm in! I won't be there tonight, out of town. Don't miss me too much ;)

Liv: I am

Damon: Me too

Lorraine: I want to! If you think I'm going to miss out on you guys making fools of yourselves, you're crazy

Eli: the only fool is you

Damon: I'm a fool, I'll admit it

Gaby: LOL just signed up

I try to continue scrolling a few times, searching for more messages, before accepting that I've reached the end.

The person's response I care about the most isn't there.

I've refused to even *think* his name since all this happened. But in opening the chat, I couldn't prevent it from happening. Chain didn't reply and I couldn't imagine improv without him.

The thought of his name sent a shiver up my spine. I've been so consumed with the heartache and depression of the engagement breakup with Zander that I haven't had to try very hard to ignore thoughts of *him*.

Now that I'm away from our condo and parked in front of the theater I've been traveling to weekly, my guard against thoughts of him is down.

The familiar guilt appears with the thought of him, but there's something else, too. Something... sweet. Anticipation?

I'm so fucked up. How can I be thinking of Chain while I'm trying to figure things out with Zander?

I glance at the clock, confirming that it's about time to walk into class. I'll probably be the first one there. I prepare my text for the class and hit send before walking in.

Me: I'm definitely signing up!

Chapter Thirty-Eight

Chain

Ping.

The sound from my phone alerts me of an incoming message. I ignore it, focusing on the bumper to bumper traffic I've found myself in. Luckily, I can see the accident that happened just ahead, so I won't be stuck in it for long.

My phone goes off again, this time chiming for an incoming call. Trey's face lights up the screen and I press the answer button on my steering wheel.

"Trey, my man," I say distractedly. My eyes are trained on the car in front of me, riding as close to the bumper as I can without crashing into it. I *refuse* to get caught at this red light.

"Matthews! You comin' out with us tomorrow night?" Trey asks as the light turns yellow. I pull through the road, the tail-end of my truck stuck under the light.

This guy needs to move!

"Chain?" Trey asks.

"Yeah, yeah, I'm here," I say in a clipped tone.

"You good?" he asks. The car finally moves and I turn into the next lane, passing the accident and speeding up. The clock confirms I only have a few minutes before I'm late.

"I'm on my way to this class," I tell him, settling into my seat now that I'm actually moving faster than 5 mph. "What's happening tomorrow?"

"We're going out to celebrate Don's birthday."

Fuck, I forgot about that. "Yeah, I'll be there. Where at?" I pull into the theater parking lot, having seen an empty space.

"Fuck yeah! The Meeting Place. 8 pm."

I chuckle at his zeal. "I'll see you there."

"Later," he says, and the line clicks off.

I park the truck and head inside, taking the steps two at a time to make sure I'm on time. After the small race and the bulk I've put on from the nightly gym sessions, I yank the door open with more force than I intended, causing a few heads to glance my way before returning their attention to Jon.

"—so we'll be rehearsing for that," he informs the class as I quickly scan the seats for an empty one. I catch an empty seat in the third row on the right next to—

Marlie.

Just the sight of her profile and the long strands of auburn hair send a jolt of excitement through me. My feet move before my mind catches up to the decision. She doesn't look over until I'm seated and facing Jon, forcing myself to focus on him.

She's in a relationship.

"The call sheet will be sent to you by Wednesday of next week. It will outline the beats of the show and what partner will be in each scene with you."

Maybe Marlie and I will be paired in a scene together.

"In this level, only two person scenes are performed, just like we've learned in class. Should you continue your improvisational acting journey, you will learn multiple person scenes in level 3."

Is she going to continue taking classes?

"Level 2 is where you will learn games, similar to those you see on TV."

She's engaged, stop thinking about her.

"I know some of you have already signed up for the next level, and for that I applaud you. It looks like I will be teaching that class."

Valerie's voice echoes in my mind: *Engaged ain't married.*

I glance at Marlie, finding her with a fixed stare on Jon and a clenched jaw. She looks different... sadder? There are dark circles under her eyes and her mouth is pressed in a tight, thin line. Has she lost weight, too?

Her head moves and before I can turn my attention back to Jon, her eyes trap mine, stopping all logical thought.

Fuck, her eyes are mesmerizing, though they're darker tonight. I feel like I can see into the depths of her soul. Why is the light gone? I—

She quirks an eyebrow at me and I snap back to reality. Schooling my expression, I give her a slight nod before turning back to Jon. She moves her hand from the chair arm to her lap, and I catch the motion in my periphery. The absence of shimmering light is apparent to me instantly.

The ring is gone.

My heart accelerates of its own volition, and I try to talk it down like calming an overexcited child.

It means nothing. It could be at the shop for resizing, or she just didn't want to wear it today, or fuck, any other reason.

I feel a strange, light feeling in my chest, and it takes a moment to process it.

Hope. Fucking hope.

I brace for the usual disgust I'd feel, but it doesn't come. Confused, I tune back into Jon rather than dig into what that might mean.

"Although you will not know *who* you're performing with, we are going to rehearse the format of the show tonight," he says, peering at us with expectation.

We used to feign excitement to appease him, but now, I could feel my sincere excitement reflected among my peers. Turns out, improv is actually pretty great.

I haven't shaken that small blossom of hope that sprouted in my chest at the sight of her naked finger. I confirmed when she went up for her first scene that her finger was indeed stripped of that metal. Frank could check if she left the ring at his shop, but I refuse to ask him for any favors. Not to mention, I have no business looking into her life. *She's not mine.*

I shouldn't feel this hope. But it's not the hope that bothers me. Hope makes sense. It's the *damn* absence of my usual distaste for the feeling of hope that bothers me.

Hope is dangerous. Hope has only ever served to disappoint me.

Because of that fact, I have no tolerance for it. So the fact that I seem to be allowing it, albeit uncontrollably, irritates me.

She has to still be engaged. How often do you hear of a broken engagement?

All the logic in the world couldn't stop the part of my brain, *the hopeful part,* that whispers: *but what if she isn't?*

So, what if she isn't? The question I didn't want to think about answering. A dangerous question. So *what* if the engagement is broken? That wouldn't equate to anything happening between us.

I've tried for weeks and I can't seem to smash the idea of her. Lying in bed, wearing nothing but boxers, I've replayed the image of her more times than I can count. I don't know what the *fuck* it is about her, but I can't get her out of my system.

Maybe I really do just need a good fuck. Tomorrow, I'm going out with the guys, which would be the perfect place for an opportunity like that to arise.

I'll fuck a girl that looks like Marlie, get her out of my system, and be done with this once and for good.

Feeling assured with that decision, I swipe open my tablet to look at the house I'd placed an offer on. I need it to be accepted so I can get the fuck out of this house.

It's time to live my life the way I want to.

Checking my own reflection in Valerie's full length mirror, I can't help but feel satisfied with my appearance. I trimmed my beard, something I normally save for Sundays, giving my jaw a sharp, sleek look. My hair is freshly washed but tossed casually, the typical gel I wear to work foregone.

I went with a pair of navy slacks and a white, V-neck shirt, displaying the evidence of my recent muscle growth. Grabbing the watch I placed on the dresser, I strap the leather band on my wrist and clasp it at the appropriate tightness. My forearm flexes as I open and close my fist, checking the fit before letting my arm drop.

One last glance in the mirror and I head to the front door, grabbing my keys and wallet from the small table and shoving them into the pocket that doesn't have my cell phone.

"I'm leaving!" I shout to the household, then exit and slam the door behind me before I can be bothered with a response. I pull the keys from my pocket and unlock the truck, giving a small smirk as I stare at it.

Damn, I love that truck.

When I open my phone and swipe to open the maps application, I see the notification from our improv group chat.

I read the messages I missed and my stomach does a flip at the sight of Marlie's name, confirming her attendance for the next level.

Fuck. It. Out.

I clamp my mouth shut and grind my teeth together. I open maps and enter The Meeting Place, then place my phone into the holder. I stare out at the sky, the setting sun painting it a deep orange.

Tonight, I'm letting loose.

"All right, all right!" Trey shouts over the noise of the bar. The thumping of the pop song's beat and the laughter of the crowd have an infectious energy that I've become one with.

"It's Don's *fucking* birthday," he says drunkenly, slapping Donald on the back before raising his shot glass. "A toast is in order."

The group of us grab one of the many shot glasses from the table, brought over by Trey himself a few minutes ago. It took a moment to round us all up. In attendance were the guys from the firm, some of Don's friends, and any plus ones.

I raise my glass, my arm light from the many drinks I've consumed. I'm not sure what this shot is, but it's clear. It's definitely *not* my usual whiskey.

"May the best of your past be the worst of your future," Trey toasts with warmth in his voice. I can't help but find solace in his words. "AND DRINK UP, ASSHOLES!!!"

At once, we lift our shot glasses and try to clink them together. After a few hours and more than a few drinks, our glasses land in different places and clink haphazardly.

I shoot the warm liquid into my mouth, throwing my head back so it goes straight down my throat.

Blech, vodka.

I slam the glass down on the table harder than I intended to, and it shatters. It's either too loud or I'm too drunk to hear the glass breaking, and I start to laugh.

"The gym's treatin' you well, Matthews," Greg comments.

I let out another chuckle. "Yeah, I guess so. Or I've had one too many tonight."

"Nothin' wrong with either," Greg says with a smile and a nudge to my ribs. "How's life been, man?"

"I can't complain," I say, taking a sip of my old-fashioned.

Ahh, now that's a drink.

"What do you think of that case we're handling? You think the guy is really innocent?" he asks. I only half pay attention as we discuss our current case. My eyes scan the room, searching for reddish hair and caramel tinged eyes.

I've been doing this all night. I've watched the place fill up and I've seen people come and go. At first, there was no woman who fit the bill. With each drink I had, the pursuit changed from finding someone who looks like her to stop *looking* for her.

The most fucked up part is I don't know why I can't shake her; why I can't get her out of my head.

"Scoot over," a soft, female voice says over Greg's incessant talking. I tear my gaze away from the crowd to the seat occupied by him, seeing a woman scooching into the booth next to him.

She's got red hair.

Strawberry blonde, but still. Her eyes are bright blue, nothing like Marlie's.

Whoever said blue eyes are the brightest was so wrong.

"Who are you?" I ask her, staring into those icy depths. The alcohol in my system has me even more forward than I normally am, and I am not modest by any means.

"Stacy," she replies.

"Chain," I reply, holding the eye contact she hasn't broken.

"She's my cousin, in town for a few days," Greg remarks. I break eye contact with her at this, because they couldn't look less alike. Greg has dark features, thick eyebrows, and a softer look.

Stacy is pale skinned with thin eyebrows and a hard edge about her. I find myself oddly drawn to her tonight. Maybe it's the alcohol, or the raging need for a sexual distraction, but I want her.

Maybe it's just the damn reddish hair.

"Greg, can I talk to you for a moment?" I ask him, nodding towards the bar, away from our table and Stacy.

He stands up in answer, and I turn to Stacy as I stand.

"Need a drink?"

"I'll have whatever you're having," she says without looking at me, her eyes scanning the bar. The same way I was moments ago.

I quirk my eyebrow at her but say nothing. I follow Greg to the bar and order two old-fashioneds after he orders his whiskey, neat.

"Is she off limits?" I ask him point blank. The alcohol has removed whatever little beating around the bush I might normally attempt.

"I don't make claims on women," he replies. "She can make her own choices."

I eye him appreciatively. "I agree, but I never know how someone else will feel."

The bartender places our drinks on the bar top.

"Add it to my tab. Matthews," I tell him. He gives a curt nod as he turns towards the next group of customers. Greg and I return to the table, him breaking off to talk with the other guys, me replacing his empty seat next to Stacy.

"Enjoy," I say, sliding the drink over to her. She catches it as it slides to her along the table, picking it up in a swift motion and taking a large sip. I notice the shattered glass still littered on the table and realize I need to have that taken care of.

"Mmm, old-fashioned," she says appreciatively without so much as a wince. She places the drink on the table and turns to me, giving me a slow roam with her eyes. I recognize that look; she's assessing me, and I let her.

"A woman who knows her drink, I see," I tell her, following the statement with a sip from my own glass.

"A cocky man who thinks a woman *can't* know her drink," she comments with a perfectly arched brow.

My eyes drop to her lips for the briefest of seconds before meeting her blue orbs again. They may not be the brightest... but they are beautiful.

"Not *can't*," I counter. "Just usually *don't*."

"Hmm," she hums, unimpressed. She tears her eyes away from me to return to her watch of the crowd.

"For the record, I have been drinking these all night," I say.

She slowly brings her gaze back to mine. Her crystal blue eyes display the curiosity I feel.

"Why are you here?" she asks.

"For Donald's birthday," I reply, knowing that's not what she's asking.

"Donald's over there."

I follow her hot pink, nail-polished finger to the crowd, where a makeshift dance floor has started. Don holds his drink in the hand raised above a petite woman, while his other hand is placed loosely on her hip. Their hips are swaying off beat, likely from the alcohol consumption. His eyes are closed and his drink is sloshing dangerously.

"Why are *you* here?" I counter, yet again. Banter is to an attorney as porn is to a teenager. The excitement has my dick throbbing appreciatively.

"Visiting my cousin," she nods in the direction of Greg.

"Greg's over there," I tell her with a smirk, enjoying the game we've created. She gets a mischievous twinkle in her eyes and it sends blood to my cock, causing it to lose its softness.

"But you're here," she says seductively. She knows what she wants and she is prepared to take it.

"And you're here."

"You wanna get out of here?"

I answer by sliding out of the booth and rising from my seat. I grab my glass and finish the contents in one go, placing it back down on the table with more control this time.

Which reminds me, this glass needs cleaning up.

I hold my hand out to her and she places her long, slender fingers on my palm. It takes me a moment to close my hand over hers, the alcohol slowing my senses. Before standing up, she polishes off her own drink and I give her a full, teeth showing smile.

She stands and I turn, intertwining our fingers. I look over and see Donald with the same woman, dancing without a care in the world. He won't even notice I'm gone.

I approach the bartender to pay the tab and let him know about the broken glass. He nods and pulls out a walkie talkie, speaking into it. I assume it's to notify someone, but I can't hear over the noise and the distraction of the soft hand in mine.

I ordered an Uber through the app and 15 minutes later, we're at her hotel. There's a comfortable silence between us. She shares my lack of need for small talk and pleasantries.

When she scans the keycard to unlock the door, I tug on the handle and open it for her. Once she's through the threshold, I grab her waist and twist her to face me, pushing her up against the wall. The door bangs shut behind me as my heated gaze meets hers.

Her eyes don't look so blue in the darkness of her hotel room. There's a looming mystery there, one that I want to explore. I bring my greedy lips to hers, fervently swiping my tongue across her lips before plunging into her mouth.

She meets my energy and rhythm, and within seconds, we're panting with exertion. My hands still gripping her waist possessively, I haul her from the wall and lead her back towards the open room. The back of her legs meet the mattress and she bends her knees to land on the bed.

I bring my knee between her thighs, spreading her legs and hoisting myself above her. She obliges by lying down. I finally release her mouth to trail kisses down her jaw, then neckline, sucking on the soft spot between her neck and shoulder.

She moans in pleasure, and the sound makes my already throbbing cock go rock hard. One hand remains on her waist, the other massaging her full breast. As I start kneading through her shirt, moving the bra cup out of my way impatiently, I feel a vibration against my leg.

"Shit, sorry," she says, leaning up and pulling her phone from her pocket. The pause makes me aware of my quick, deep breaths, and the racing of my heart. The room is so dark that I catch the image of a man smiling from her illuminated phone screen. Right before she swipes to answer, I see the name Hubby with a heart and ring emoji.

"Hello?" she says breathlessly.

The whiskey fog delays the realization, but it sinks in like a foot in quicksand.

She's married?!

"Hey, honey. Yeah, I'm back at the hotel," she says, peering up at me through thin lashes and holding up her finger, indicating to give her a minute. I jump off of her, backing up and hitting the dresser housing the TV. I stagger forward and stare at her. How could I have missed this? I glance down at her left hand.

Empty.

My heart still pounds, but it's in a different race now.

"He had a great time. I'm pretty sure he's screwing the girl he was dancing with by now."

Fuck, fuck, fuck!

Bile burns my throat as I stare at Stacy, wide-eyed. She returns my stare but there's no look of apology or remorse. No... she looks *annoyed* that her goddamn husband is calling!

I shake my head and take a step back before turning on my heels and heading straight for the exit. I don't fuck with taken women.

"I gotta use the bathroom, sweetie, let me call you right back," I hear her say as I tear the door open. I'm down the hallway by the time she makes it out.

"Chain!"

I ignore her, continuing my paced steps to the elevator. I hear the rushed pounding of her footsteps behind me.

"Chain," she says as her hand grabs my arm, tugging. I turn and yank my arm out of her grip. I can feel the disgust worn on my face.

"You're married." It's not a question.

"Engaged," she says, her eyes narrowing slightly, as if the semantics make a difference. She reaches for my arm again, and I step back, shaking my head.

"Find someone else," I tell her before turning back towards the elevator.

I only hear silence as I press the call button. I keep my attention focused on the door slit, waiting for it to open. Once it does, I enter without a backward glance. As the doors shut, I hear the distant steps of her walking away.

I make it to the lobby and out of the building, standing at the street corner so I can order an Uber to take me home. I drank too much to drive, so I'll pick up my car tomorrow. The Uber is 5 minutes away, so I open my emails to sift through work stuff. I open an email from the opposing counsel and find that my eyes are a little blurry.

Damn alcohol.

I pocket my phone and stare out at the passing cars instead. My thoughts stray back to the kisses I shared with Stacy, acutely aware of the betrayal that now lines my lips. Does she intentionally remove her ring? Does she ever wear one at all? Would I have even noticed??

You noticed Marlie's ring was missing.

Frustration builds in my chest. I want her out of my damn head. So much so, that I didn't even bother to *look* at Stacy's hand. Not that it would have done me any good, seeing as there was no ring there. And she was very willing to go to bed with me.

I hate what just happened; that I played any part in someone's betrayal. But the frustration wasn't because of Stacy. It was *her.*

Why wasn't she wearing her ring on Friday? The tired look of her gorgeous face flashes across my mind and I can't shake the feeling that something wasn't right. The glimmer she normally wears wasn't there, shadows tinting her sweet eyes.

It doesn't matter.

I crush the hope that I refuse to feel. I hardly even know her, anyway. I need to let this go. She's probably having the ring resized, or cleaned, or whatever else you do with a ring.

The Uber driver pulls up and I approach the car, gripping the handle as I look back at the scorned chance to fuck her out of my system. Maybe redheads are only trouble. Blue eyes are definitely *not* the brightest. As I settle in my seat and the driver pulls away, I find one piece of consolation.

Engaged *is* married.

Chapter Thirty-Nine

Marlie

This has been one of the hardest weekends of my life. Sundays are usually our day to cuddle and watch TV, hang out in bed, and maybe have sex. Or on the rare occasion, play a board game.

I mean, we are watching TV. And although his arm is around me, I couldn't feel more distant. We've hardly spoken to each other. It's not like we ever had tons to say, but the complete absence of conversation is a stark difference.

I've been trying to give him space to process it all, but the growing coldness has increased my anxiety and guilt. I'm so focused on figuring out how to fix this, I haven't thought of much else. As Netflix loads the new episode of whatever show has been playing, because I haven't been able to pay attention to any of it, I sit up so suddenly that his arm jerks.

"I hate this," I tell him.

"What?" he replies with feigned ignorance, keeping his eyes trained on the television. But his eyes lack their previous warmth.

"*This,*" I say, waving my arm between us. "This distance."

He takes his time peeling his eyes away from the TV to bore into mine. I note a steely resolve in his dark irises.

"What did you expect, Marlie?" he asks, his eyes searching my wide ones.

"I..."

What did I expect?

"I don't know," I finally reply after coming up blank, gulping down the lump in my throat.

He sighs, and breaks our eye contact. I look down, not sure what to say. I really don't know what I expected.

"I want things to go back to normal."

"Normal? You mean go back to where you weren't being honest with yourself?"

The pang I feel from the iciness in his tone pains me, and the fear causes the lump in my throat to reform.

He must see it expressed on my face because his eyes soften a tiny bit.

"You don't get to deny the truth just because you don't want to face the consequences," he says.

I look down again, the guilt plaguing me.

"I don't want to feel this way," I mumble.

"I know, babe- *Marlie*." He shakes his head. "But you do. As much as it hurts me, I don't want you to deny it."

A single tear forms and quickly rolls down my cheek, falling onto the bed. The single dot it forms on the bed sheet quickly spreads, seeping in.

"We'll be okay, though, right?" I look up at him hopefully, my eyes wet.

He gives me a small, toothless smile, his eyebrows raising. "I don't know if I can do this, Marlie."

My heart sinks to the bottom of my chest, lying there helplessly. It *fucking* hurts.

"What does that mean?" The tears free fall.

There's a beat of silence before he speaks. "We break up."

1:21 am. It's been hours since he spoke those words.

We break up.

It's funny he said we.

I'm breaking. He's breaking. But there is no *we*.

Neither of us has slept. We've been lying side by side on our respective sides of the bed. Not touching. Not speaking. I sobbed for thirty minutes after his words, and he comforted me with a lonely pat to the knee.

So many thoughts have crossed my mind. So many things I want to say. Each time I open my mouth to express them, I snap it back shut, changing my mind. But when the clock changes to 1:22, I pluck up the courage to speak.

"Zander?" I ask into the darkness. He's silent for so long that I turn to check if he fell asleep. When I move, he responds.

"Yeah?"

"I hate this."

He exhales a deep belly breath. "Me, too."

"We don't have to break up," I say. I peer at him through my lashes, eyes straining in the dark. I make out his silhouette, lying flat on his back and staring up at the ceiling.

"We do," he says simply. It feels like the words are being carved into my heart, dauntingly slow. "I know you don't want to lose me, but the day you came home from the beach was the day you finally got honest."

Honesty is so fucking overrated. If honesty burns like this, like my skin is searing and my blood is turning to smoke, I don't want honesty.

I feel the tears rise again as acid burns down my throat, the taste of it a mixture of remorse and fear.

This wouldn't be happening if you had been honest with yourself from the start.

Had I always been doubtful of our relationship? Was it ever enough?

I really feel like it was. He was exactly who I needed for a long time. It wasn't that I never loved him. I wasn't fully myself without even realizing it. I want to explore new things and be free. I don't want to live in a dull routine where I constantly know what to expect. Improv opened that door for me. It gave me access to the parts of myself that had been shut down for too long.

If my silence irked Zander, he masked it well. I didn't know what to say because he was right, and it was hard to concede to that.

"I want to say we can work this out," he says pensively. "I do."

When he doesn't continue, I add, "But?"

"But that's not going to change anything. I've thought a lot this past week, and this has all been slowly building. From not being sure about marriage, to the crush on..."

He trails off and the air gets thick with the implication in the silence. The guilt that threatens to overtake me doesn't quite make it. Zander's understanding is more than I deserve.

"It doesn't have to be this horribly sad thing. We can appreciate the time we spent together and the growth we shared. The fact that you *are* being honest with yourself is more than some people can say in their lifetime."

Tears spill over and I cry silently, trying to find the solace those words were meant to offer. How is he so nice and understanding? How is he able to think things like that through this heartache?

"It's like you're not even bothered by this," I say spitefully.

It's at this moment, after having laid in the same position for hours, that he turns to me. I make out his features from the outside lights peeking in through the window.

"Don't think, for one *fucking* second, that this isn't the hardest thing I've ever had to go through."

Chills take over my body at the gravity in his tone. Even though I can't see his eyes in the darkness, I still have to look away. There's such a vulnerability in his statement, confirming what I tried to prevent from happening.

He's breaking.

"Please," I say so softly that he doesn't hear me. I try again, adding, "We can make this work."

"I don't want to *make* it work, ba- Marlie. I deserve to be with someone who fully wants me. Just like you deserve someone you fully want."

Tears stream down my face silently. Every truth he utters feels like a punch to the gut, making it harder and harder to stay put together.

"Right?" he says quietly.

"I love you," I offer in reply.

"I love you, too." His fingertips brush my hand, sending tingles up my arm. His touch feels so good, reminding me that he's still here. It contrasts the ever-growing distance of this week.

I reach my fingers to grab his, then adjust our hands so we're holding onto each other. He doesn't exactly hold my hand back, but he doesn't pull away.

What are you doing?

I know this is wrong. I need to let him go. But my hand tightens around his, and he brushes his thumb across the back of mine.

I move my head toward him to find him still. I can't make out his eyes but I can see that his mouth is slightly open. The air changes between us suddenly, like a heater was turned on and gusted between us.

His thumb stops its tender stroke and he tugs on my hand, urging me closer. I scoot over to him, first with my hips and legs, then my upper body. He lets my hand drop so he can wrap his arm around my waist as we lay on our sides, facing each other.

Our faces are close enough that I feel his breath tickle my nose. I can pick up the scents of his citrusy cologne and I inhale deeply, committing it to memory. I need to find the comfort that it's always brought me.

He suddenly grabs my waist and moves his head to mine, closing the gap between us. The movement is so unexpected that the moment his lips meet mine, I moan in sweet appreciation and yearning.

His lips move urgently over mine, begging for me to grant him access. Our tongues clash in a heady mixture of desire, heartbreak, love, and pain, and *god* it feels so good.

My hands reach out and find his shoulders, grasping desperately. I pull him closer so our bodies fuse together. I can't get any closer, but I try anyway. If I can just force us together and hold onto this moment, then everything will be okay.

He wiggles his other hand free and our mouths move rapidly, absorbing and taking everything we need. I suck his lower lip and he groans as his hands palm my breasts greedily.

I didn't bother to put on a shirt since it's nothing he hasn't seen before. I feel my panties moisten and I move my hands off his shoulders to remove his boxers and caress his throbbing dick.

Once the boxers are shoved past his knees, I move my leg over him, refusing to waste any time. I straddle him, lowering myself in one swift motion. My pussy clenches around him instantly and he breaks our kiss to toss his head back in pleasure.

We've never moved so hastily. He doesn't give me time to even lift my hips once before he starts thrusting, pounding into me. The sound of our bodies clashing reverberates around us, and I get lost in the pleasure and our moans.

I meet his hips with my own, my clit rubbing against him, bringing me closer to release. He knows me well enough to know that I'm nearing my orgasm but he slows down. He returns his mouth to mine, this time with a deep, sensual kiss.

Our breathing is heavy, inhaling and exhaling at the same time. I let him slow us down, my clit making its disappointment known with various pulses. I tease the tip of my tongue around his lips but he doesn't open. His jaw tenses before he bites down on my bottom lip, *hard.*

I yelp in ecstasy and pain; his teeth haven't released me. I feel the need to push him off, but I allow him to hurt me, to release the vengeance I deserve. He finally removes his teeth, scraping them against the marks on my lip, and I pick up the pace of my riding again. This time, he remains still, allowing me to control his pleasure.

"Tell me you hate me," he grits out between pants.

"What?" I breathe out, the T nearly silent.

"Tell me you hate me. Say it like you mean it." He starts to thrust his hips to match my pace, waiting for the words.

What the hell?

Feeling too good to question him further, I place my hands on his chest and hold myself upright while bouncing on his cock.

"I hate you."

"Like you *mean it,*" he commands, thrusting harder.

"I HATE YOU!" I shout forcefully, heating my eyes with the anger he needs. His responding thrusts and lust-filled eyes pull me over the edge, my walls pulsing over his dick and my clit spasming over him where it meets at each thrust.

I slow down as the high sedates me, but he doesn't concede. Gripping my hip with one hand, he thrusts and turns my body in a 180, lying me on my back with him on top. He doesn't miss a beat, slamming his dick into me the moment my ass bounces on the mattress.

I moan so loudly that I'm sure the neighbors hear me in their sleep. He's relentless, pounding into me at a fast, steady rhythm, not allowing me to feel out the high I reached just a moment ago. He tucks his head between my ear and shoulder when he finally pulls out, his cum spurting all over my belly.

The sweat I didn't notice building on my forehead trickles into my eye and I blink hard to try and prevent the burn; it doesn't work.

Zander doesn't look up from his dick when he finishes coming. He didn't moan or express real pleasure, either. He gets up and pulls a dirty shirt from his hamper, tossing it to me without even looking. He grabs a sock and wipes off his dick, then goes to the bathroom.

My stomach sinks as my breathing slows to a normal rate, my heart beat following it. I wipe the cum off with his shirt and toss it into his hamper.

The silence rings in my ears after Zander's absence. I move back to my side of the bed, feeling more awkward than I ever have after sex. The way he rushed out of here and avoided eye contact has me feeling so self-conscious, I'm confused by what even happened.

I hear the bathroom door open and I stare at the hallway, anticipating his return. It's still dark and I can't make out his eyes, but I know he's not looking at me. I can feel the change in the suffocating air between us, filled with the smell of our sex.

"Hey," I say softly. "You know I don't actually—"

"This doesn't change anything." The shards from the ice in his tone hit me in the gut, causing me to inhale sharply.

"Okay," I whisper. I resume staring up at the ceiling. He crawls into bed and turns on his side, facing the wall with his back to me.

The heat at my core sizzles out and the tears resume their path down my cheeks, dripping down my neck. He's made it clear what this was.

His release was not from pleasure, it was from me.

I hit send on the reply email, my pinky finger shaking as it hits enter on the keyboard.

I've been trembling all morning, fighting the tears that threaten to spill over at any moment. My reflection in the mirror revealed the dark circles under my eyes and the puffiness in my eyelids. I tried rinsing my face with water after brushing my teeth, but you can't hide the truth, especially when the evidence is physical. I got no sleep but refused to call out of work again. I'm going to have to get on with my life sooner or later.

I glance at the clock in the lower right hand corner for the tenth time in 5 minutes, frustrated to see it's still only 10:57 am.

"You wanna take a break, chica?" Eli's voice drifts over from my right.

I hesitate in answering. On one hand, I don't want him to notice something is wrong, but on the other, it would be nice to get some fresh air and distract myself for a bit. I told him Monday about me doubting the engagement, but I haven't updated him about removing the ring and now, the breakup.

"Yes, please," I decide, locking my computer and pushing away from my desk. I swirl in the rolling chair and stand up, stretching my hands above my head. Lack of sleep makes my body so tense.

I hear Eli clack on his keys before standing up. When I feel him next to me, we walk in tandem to the exit, making our way out to the lake. Eli walks to one of the picnic tables and sits. I take the opposite side and continue facing the water.

How many lunches and breaks have Zander and I taken here? The absence of him is so strong in a place where I'm used to feeling him everywhere. He hasn't written to me today, but I didn't expect him to. His messages had been so far and few between last week and now with our breakup being permanent, it's only logical that he would stop altogether.

"So, tell me," Eli says, taking a sip from the aluminum reusable water bottle he usually travels with.

"What?" I reply, my voice croaky from the repressed emotions and lack of sleep.

"Cut the crap, Marlie," he scoffs. "You're paler than a ghost on Halloween and your eyes look like you rose from the dead."

"Jeez, asshole."

"In the best way possible. Come on, you know you're gorgeous." I look at him and catch him mid eyeroll. "Now spill it."

"We broke up."

"I thought you were already broken up?"

"I mean, I broke off the engagement, but now—"

"It was a matter of time."

"That doesn't mean it hurts any less now that it's official," I snap, annoyed at his lack of empathy.

"That's true," he concedes. "I just hate seeing you miserable."

"Yeah, well..." I trail off, unsure of what else to say. Sometimes, there's no way out but through.

"We never really got to talk about it, though. Why the sudden change?"

"I don't know," I admit truthfully. "After starting improv and making new friends, something in me shifted. When he proposed, I freaked out, Eli. Like for real. But everything I read online from other people said it was just engagement anxiety and that it would pass. So, I believed it. And it did pass, for a little while."

"But what caused it? What changed?" Eli presses.

"It was a bunch of things, like I said. Improv, the engage ment..."

"Chain?" Eli asks with a smirk.

I whack his arm. "No!"

"Your cheeks are red, liar," he says with a laugh.

"I mean, obviously the guy is good looking, but-"

"Good looking? Pfft," Eli interrupts. "I'm as straight as they come, but he's hot as *fuck*."

I giggle. "Right, but that doesn't have anything to do with it."

Just a little bit to do with it.

"I've seen the way you two interact," Eli says thoughtfully, the playfulness gone. "It's like... watching two magnets fighting to connect."

I stare at him as he takes another sip from his water bottle, rendered speechless. When he puts the cap back on, he meets my gaze and shrugs.

"I call it like I see it. You know this," he says. "Zander's a nice guy, but I've never seen... whatever I see when you and Chain are around each other."

Fuck, was I that obvious? I thought I—

Wait.

"Me *and* Chain?" I ask before I can help myself.

He gives me a pointed look. "Girl, he stares at you like you're his world. And the way he jumps to help you, protect you, all that shit... it's obvious."

"Oh…" I say. My brain goes into overdrive, flashing through all the interactions we've had. I start to see what Eli means. I must have been too busy denying my own feelings to even notice any of his.

"Well, whatever," I push, refusing to go down that path. "That's not the point. The point is, shit changed and I couldn't fight it anymore. But now I'm not sure that I made the right choice. It's really hard."

My voice cracks and a tear spills over. I don't even bother to wipe it off, tired of fighting, even with them.

Eli frowns and gives me a look of sympathy. *Finally.*

"The truth hurts, chica. It will get easier, I promise."

There's that damn word again.

"Thanks," I mumble as another tear rolls down my cheek. This time, I brush it away.

"Chain could be a nice distraction," he jokes. I shove his arm again and he laughs.

"Seriously, that's not what this is about."

"I know," he says, his face turning serious. "Sometimes people are put in our lives to make us face ourselves."

His words resonate deep within me, the chasm waters lapping contentedly. He glances down at his phone and jumps up.

"Vamos, break's over!"

I follow him off the dock and back up to the mailroom. When I log back into my computer, I see a notification blinking on the task bar. I open my messages and find one from Zander, causing my stomach to drop.

> Zander: I can't stop crying. I had to run to the bathroom and hide in there for 20 minutes.

If I thought I ever felt guilty before, it was nothing compared to this. Zander, crying?! I saw him tear up once when he found out the family dog died. The man wasn't one to cry. My fingers are shaking again as I type out my reply.

> Me: I'm so sorry. Want to meet up and talk?

I watch as he types, then stops, then types, then stops. It's not until 2 minutes of anxiously watching the small chat window that his reply comes through.

> Zander: I need space. I'm going to pack up my things and move out tonight. I can't do this anymore, it's too hard.

The sobs wrack my body in a tsunami rush. It feels like the chasm's waters are pouring through my eyes, stinging from the previous dryness of my earlier cry sessions. I rush out of the room unseeing, somehow reaching the bathroom and locking myself into a stall.

I sit on the toilet and pour my heart out, feeling the pain and hurt from the reality of this situation.

We're over. It's really over. And even though I basically asked for it, it's the hardest thing I've ever fucking done.

Chapter Forty

Chain

"How are you feeling?" I hear Eli asking Marlie. I've been acutely aware of her presence the entire time we've been back here. Jon has us in the green room, the area backstage where you wait between sets.

There's a section of chairs across from a small, old-school plasma TV on the wall. It's got the live footage of the camera facing the stage. I sit in the corner chair and stare blankly at the screen, pretending to watch Jon set up the stage but really listening intently to their conversation.

"Better," she replies softly. It's the first time I've heard her speak in the fifteen or so minutes we've been holed up back here. Her voice is louder than all the surrounding chatter of the other classmates.

What is there to be better about? I glance down to where she sits next to Eli in the chairs opposite me. Eli is standing in front of her, blocking her face from view. But I can see her left hand, and I am strangely pleased to find the ring still missing.

Quit it, man.

I return my gaze to the TV screen and try to tune them out, but it's impossible.

"Did he get all his stuff out?" Eli asks.

"Yeah," she replies weakly. *They can't be talking about Zander...*

"It will get easier."

"I know," she says, her voice shaky. I can't stop myself from stealing a look at her. Eli shifts his feet at the same moment I turn my head and I catch a glimpse of her face. Her normally bright, caramel-laced eyes are glazed over and dark.

My stomach sinks at the sight of the sadness she's wearing. I find myself hurting from the fact that she's feeling any pain at all. The feeling is strange; I don't normally take on someone else's emotions.

"Let's go out tonight after the show. We'll invite the others and have fun." Eli takes the seat next to her and nudges her arm on the chair, wiggling his eyebrows encouragingly. I feel a spurt of excitement at the prospect of going out with Marlie tonight. Even in pain, I just want to be around her.

"I don't—"

"10 minutes 'til show time, all!" Jon shouts as he swings the door wide open. "Time to share your brilliance with the world!"

Everyone starts clapping, used to Jon's antics after 10 weeks of him. I clap along half-heartedly. The apprehension in the air is palpable.

"You've all checked the call sheet?" He looks around at us nodding our heads. "Any last minute questions? No? Well, break legs then. I'm going to finish greeting our guests and will be on the stage to introduce you just after 7:30 pm."

He saunters back to the door leading to the lobby. When he reaches for the door knob, he pauses and shouts through the rising chatter.

"Run a few warmups while you wait!"

The chatter stops immediately and he leaves, making a dramatic exit. I roll my eyes.

Fucking Jon.

"Let's do this, guys!" Eli pumps his fist in the air enthusiastically. We circle up and Marlie sidles up next to me. The small space between us feels electrically charged; the hairs on my arms rise as goosebumps coat my skin.

"Are you okay?" The words escaped from my lips before I realized it was happening.

What is it about this woman that causes me to lose control?

Her hand brushes mine as her head whips to me, our eyes locking instantly.

Somehow, the fire I feel heating my core is hotter than ever before. I watch her chocolate eyes blaze with the caramel swirls I love. She doesn't look joyful but... contemplative, alert. And it's fucking *sexy.*

"Why do you ask that?" she whispers, her eyes searching mine. I'm not sure what she finds reflected in them because the feelings I'm having are so foreign. And the truth is, I have no fucking clue why I asked.

It seems like whenever I'm around her, my emotions take over and rule my brain. It's something I actively work against in all parts of my life. But with her, I don't mind it.

"How about Bunny, Bunny?" I hear Jessica ask.

I clear my throat and slowly, regretfully, tear my gaze away from Marlie.

A few classmates mutter their agreement and we set out on warming up, even though I didn't need it.

The look in Marlie's eyes took care of that.

"Cheers to an epic first show!" Damon shouts in the noisy bar, his glass raised up to the rest of ours. We clink and shoot back our lemon drop shots. Not my personal preference, but I'll partake in the festivities of the group.

I place my shot glass down amongst everyone else's and from the corner of my eye, I see a busser scurry towards our table to remove them. We're the largest group at Vigs tonight, but it's surprisingly packed. Most Friday nights are dead after class, only picking up once it's later in the night.

Luckily, we were able to get our usual spot in the back corner. I take a seat in a free chair next to Eli and pick up the glass of whiskey I was nursing before Damon bought the round of shots.

Everyone's been ecstatic after our show, high on the laughs and applause we received from the crowd. It seems like everyone is continuing to the next level and it surprised me how excited I was over it. It feels like we all have a natural compatibility.

"Dude, you were hilarious tonight," Eli tells me with a slap on the back. He holds his own glass of whiskey, on the rocks rather than neat.

"Only because you were setting me up so smoothly," I reply with a grin. Eli and I were paired for one of the scenes and it couldn't have gone better. He really was a great player.

"Well, it's like Jon says—take care of your partner and they'll take care of you."

"Yeah... the guy can be a dick but he's got his points."

I suddenly feel the hair on the back of my neck rise up, an awareness creeping across my skin, and I don't need to investigate further. Marlie plops down in the seat next to Eli.

She looks significantly happier than she did at the start of the night. The sparkle in her eyes has returned and she's smiling broadly. It sends a wave of pleasure rolling through me, and I frown in response.

She's not mine. Her pleasures and sorrows shouldn't affect me the way that they do.

"What a great night! Exactly what I needed," she exclaims, settling back on the couch.

"See? You'll get over it in no time," Eli says encouragingly, rubbing her shoulder.

The action sends a twinge of jealousy through my chest. Jealousy that I shouldn't be feeling.

"Over what?" I ask, painting my voice with innocent curiosity rather than dire need. Marlie's eyes snap to mine and widen by a fraction, as if she didn't realize I was sitting here.

The swirls of caramel are highlighted by the warm brown V-neck shirt she wears with a pair of tight jeans. Even seated, I can see the accentuated curves of her hips and I stare appreciatively before forcing my eyes back to hers.

It took everything in me during the show to keep my focus on her scenes rather than her ass, hugged perfectly by the denim she wore. I swallow air and force the thoughts away, but the small blush of her cheeks tells me she may see the lust filling my eyes.

"Oh, Zander and I, um"—she clears her throat before continuing—"we broke up."

"I had a feeling," I reply before I can filter my mouth, the all consuming joy clouding my judgment. "I noticed you weren't wearing the ring." I nod towards her hand, *the* hand, in response to the quizzical look she gives.

"Oh," she says, glancing down and rubbing the empty finger with her thumb, then moving her hand off her lap so her fingers curl below her thigh and out of sight.

"I'm sorry," I tell her with sincerity, seeing the pain behind her dark irises. I look away, providing her the privacy I feel she needs to deal with it.

"It's fine," she replies.

A thought crosses my mind, and again, before I can think it through, I ask, "Did he do something to you?"

She laughs in a morose sort of way. "Not at all. If anyone did something, it's me."

Relief floods me, assuaging the thought that maybe she was cheated on again. Or worse, that he put his hands on her. "Good. I didn't want to have to—"

I cut myself off from confessing to actions I shouldn't have partaken in to begin with, especially because they concerned a woman that wasn't mine.

"Have to what?" she asks, sounding more confused than ever. I feel Eli shift next to me and look in his direction. I watch as his narrowed eyes analyze me, glancing down at my knuckles, then back up to my eyes. I see the lightbulb go off in his mind, connecting the dots. I shake my head a fraction of an inch, silently begging him to keep his mouth shut.

"I just wanted to make sure he didn't hurt you," I say with a light chuckle.

"Marlie ended things. She wasn't feeling it," Eli supplies.

Wasn't feeling it? What in the fuck does that mean?

Every fiber of my being wants to ask but I refrain, clenching my jaw.

"Well, if there's anything I can do..." I trail off, feeling stupider by the moment. What the hell can I do?

"Thanks," she says, and the penetrating stare she gives me makes me feel like she actually appreciated my sentiment.

"So," I say after taking a sip of my drink. "Why do you think it's so busy tonight?"

"It's karaoke night," Eli replies automatically.

An hour and a couple drinks later, sure enough, the karaoke stand is being set up in the space across from our spot. The chairs and tables are cleared off, leaving a small 'stage' area.

"You gotta sing something, man," Damon says to me.

"Only if Marlie joins me," I reply, giving her a smirk. The alcohol flooding my veins paired with the recent news of her breakup have made me a concoction of flirty and risky. I'm in the mood to fuck around and find out.

"Oh yeah?" she replies with a smirk of her own. She's standing by Damon, a glass of some pink liquid in her hand and a smile glued to her face. I'm not sure I've ever seen her this happy.

"You can pick the song," I offer.

"All right, then."

Her smile turns mischievous and the look in her eyes causes my dick to respond greedily. Then she unknowingly taunts me, turning towards the karaoke stand and walking over. The way her hips sway has me mesmerized, and it's only after I hear my name three times that I tear my eyes from her sexy body and find the person attached to the voice.

Eli.

He's got the cockiest smirk on his face with a knowing look in his eye. The blood rushing to my dick stops and my eyes narrow.

"Oh, Chainy boy," he says with a tsk.

"Fuck off," I mutter, gulping down the rest of my drink and turning towards the bar to get a refill. I take two steps before I feel him on my right, joining me.

"So, tell me I'm wrong," Eli says.

"Wrong about?"

"You gonna make me say it?"

I halt when I reach the bar and turn my face towards him. Making direct eye contact, I do what any established attorney does—deny. "I don't know what you're talking about."

The idiot smirks again, and I can't help but feel a kinship to him. He's not doing it in a malicious way, but a familial one. Like we've been friends for years and he's calling me on my shit.

"Have it your way, pretty boy," he says.

"Pretty boy?!" I burst into laughter. It warms my insides knowing Marlie has such a great friend. She only deserves the best.

"I know that you know that I know," he continues with a serious expression. But I see the twitch of his lips, resisting his own grin.

"Two Glenlivets, neat," I tell Abraham, the bartender we've come to know. He gives a curt nod and turns toward the liquor shelves. Turning back to Eli, I say, "I'm not icing a 'Livet."

"Whatever you say, dude. Just know, I'm in support of it," he says. I turn towards the karaoke stand, where Marlie is bent over what I can only assume is the piece of paper she's writing the song on.

My eyes dart to her ass, unable to resist the thought of me sliding my arms around her waist and feeling her right on my—

Eli's laugh breaks my fantasy and I shoot him what I believe is a murderous look. It has the opposite effect, however, and he only looks more amused.

"I like you, but you really piss me off," I seethe.

"It's part of my charm," he says with a casual shrug. Hating that the asshole sees right through me and I'm only proving him right, I chance one more look over to her. She's laughing as she hands the paper to the woman running the karaoke tonight.

"Are you opening a tab?" Abraham asks. Returning my attention to him, he nudges the two drinks to us and wipes his hand on a rag.

"It's under Matthews," I reply, grabbing the two drinks and thrusting one into Eli's chest. The amber liquid sloshes dangerously but doesn't escape, and the moment he grabs the glass I stalk off.

I return to my chair at our corner, prepared to join the conversation between Jessica, Gaby, and Damon. The moment my ass hits the metal, the karaoke woman's voice belts from the speakers.

“Hello, hello, helloooo, party people!” The bar patrons go wild like they're the crowd at a fucking concert.

“We're starting tonight off strong with a throwback I think we *all* know and love. Please welcome up—Chain and Marlie!”

The crowd continues cheering and Jess, Gaby, and Damon whip their heads to me, laughing and applauding.

“Kill it, man!” Gaby says as I place my untouched drink down on the table. Exaggerating my lack of amusement, I place my hands on my thighs and rise up slowly.

I walk up the short distance and find Marlie waiting for me with two mics in her hand.

“I gave her a tip to let us sing first,” she informs me, handing me a mic. The pure joy reflected in her eyes fills me with such pleasure, the annoyance I might normally feel at going into this blind drops away.

“Why am I afraid this is going to suck?” I ask her as I slide the switch on the mic, the little red indicator light turning on.

“Be very, very afraid, Chain,” she says with a mock solemn look. I laugh and the background music cuts off. I look up at the small monitor and fight the eye roll as I see the name of the song.

“Barbie Girl” by Aqua.

“Seriously?” I turn to her and she laughs with such mirth, I can't help but join her.

I'd sing this song in my sleep if it meant putting that beautiful smile on her face.

Chapter Forty-One

Marlie

I wake up and stretch my legs, feeling stiff after last night. A huge smile breaks out on my face as I remember belting out the lyrics to "Barbie Girl" with Chain. He was so into it by the end, even if there was an undertone of annoyance at first.

I turn my head and my heart sinks as I see the empty spot next to me. I should have known that smile wouldn't last.

It's been really hard since Zander moved out. I didn't think the breakup could hurt any worse, but his moving out proved that wrong. I didn't realize that his physical presence was keeping me afloat.

Luckily, today is Saturday, which means I don't have to avoid him at work or feel aches when I see all the places we frequented together. I don't have to stare at his name on the chat log under favorites. My brain keeps shouting at me to remove him from the list, but I can't bring myself to do it. Once he's off that favorites list, I have to accept that we're through.

I need to brush my teeth and take a shower; my legs are sticky from the show and bar last night. But my body feels like lead and I don't care about my disgusting mouth. Nothing really seems to matter right now. Instead, I grab my phone and check for any missed messages. There aren't any, and that makes me feel worse.

He's done a great job at losing me. I could text him, but it feels wrong. I fucked him over, who am I to bother him and ask for his attention? I made the decision to respect his request for space and distance. I have to fight any thoughts I have of checking in on him or trying to convince him I made a grave mistake.

But deep down, I know I didn't. As much as this hurts, it also feels right. Zander is amazing. He's so sweet and kind; we never had any real issues. But obviously, that's not all that matters. Not to me. I need more. I need a soul-deep connection. I want to relate on more levels than just a potential future. I want to have similar interests, travel the world, do things!

Zander and I didn't have that. We could have forced it, but it wasn't there naturally. I was more broken than I realized when we first got together, still damaged from past hurts. Jack fucked up my ability to trust, so I went for a guy who was safe. I knew Zander would never hurt me.

But that safety prohibited the ability for me to truly live. Hindsight is a fucked up thing. If only I could have realized all these things in the beginning.

I feel physical pain in my gut, that small space between my ribs. I forgot how much a breakup can really hurt, even on a physical level. I should probably get up and scrub the condo clean, maybe rearrange the furniture, to remove Zander from the walls.

Instead, I toss my phone back onto the nightstand and stare at the empty space above me. I'm not sure how long I spend there, feeling like a speck of dirt in the mud, before I finally throw my blanket off me and slouch off to the bathroom.

I unlock the door to the condo after arriving back from work Monday, sluggish from the lack of sleep I got the night before. I lock the door after entering and head straight to our room—*my* room—upstairs, forgoing dinner in favor of sleep.

I flop down on my side of the bed out of habit, then force myself to scoot to the middle.

Maybe I won't feel as sad in the morning if there isn't a spot for him in the bed.

Mother 7:32 pm: Call me when you get a chance

I lock the screen on my phone after seeing the text, unable to bring myself to tell her the truth. I haven't answered any of her past messages and she's still planning a party for an engagement that doesn't exist.

I roll over and stare at the bright red numbers on the alarm clock: 3:52 am.

I need to get some sleep before work but it's like my brain is on crack. I know it's the adrenaline from all the emotions, but that doesn't make it easier.

"Hey, how are you feeling?" Eli asks as he tosses his laptop bag by his chair, landing in his seat and swiveling towards his monitors.

"Same as yesterday," I reply in a dull tone. He clacks away at his keyboard and I stare at the same email I've been needing to send to HR for half an hour now, letting them know I completed the improv course so I can be reimbursed.

"At least we start level 2 today!" he says enthusiastically.

"Yeah."

I don't have the energy to pretend to be someone I'm not.

"Come on, come out with us," Lorraine pouts, pulling on my arm. "Puhleaaaseeee! We missed you last week."

Ugh. Every part of me is dreading going out after class. We just finished the second week of level 2. I've somehow been able to force myself to go through the motions of my routine.

Monday through Friday: work. Friday night: improv class. Saturday: hang out with Stella. Sunday: survive.

I give her the only smile I can muster, which is weak at best, and concede. "Okay."

"Yay!!!" she squeals, linking her arm with mine and pulling us towards Vigs. My sight catches on Chain, who has a hand in his pocket, watching me. He doesn't look away when my eyes land on his. On the contrary, his chin juts up an inch as if he's making sure I *know* he's watching me.

My stomach tightens and my body is alight with the heat of the fire that's sparked within me.

Maybe this won't be so bad.

As we make the short walk to the bar, I try to focus on the chatter around me, but it's hard. It's been nearly impossible to focus on anything other than this desolate chasm inside me.

It seems the water has dried up. The constant churning and crashes, or the still calms before the storm, were more of a comfort than I ever realized.

Because now all I feel is emptiness.

Lost in thought, I suddenly walk into a hard body and stumble back. A strong, calloused hand holds my forearm, steadying me.

When did we make it to Vigs?

"You okay?" A gruff voice pulls me back to the present, grounding me. I look up and find Chain. His green eyes are dark, mostly covered by his pupils. There's a strong look of... concern? I can't be sure.

"Yeah, sorry," I reply slowly. "I was out of it for a minute there."

He drops my arm but not his stare. He gives me a once over, as if assessing me, before giving a short nod and turning.

"Longer than a minute," he mumbles.

What's he talking about?

I want to ask, but I can't muster up the energy to do so. He holds the door open to the bar and I walk through, thanking him before asking, "Where's everyone else?"

"They're inside already."

"Oh."

"I stayed back to make sure you were following."

Wasn't I walking with Lorraine? Where did she go?

"Thanks, you didn't have to do that."

He makes a sharp right to the bar, walking in front of me so I'm forced to come to a halt.

"Drink?" he asks, staring at the shelves of liquor.

"Um, yeah," I say, shaking off the whiplash and standing next to him. There's a comfortable distance between us, like any friends would stand close to each other. But the air between us still crackles with electricity. Even with the constant sadness, like that cliché dark cloud that won't stop following me around, I feel it between us.

That draw. That pull. That immovable energy I swear I could touch if I just reach out and try.

But I don't. I can't. My heart is so heavy and I don't believe there's anything that will ever lighten the load. So I do my best to ignore the current.

"What can I get you?" Abraham says to us, his eyes volleying between Chain and I.

"I'll take a Glenlivet, neat," he says automatically, then turns to me.

"Um." *What do I want?* They watch me expectantly. "Surprise me."

Abraham laughs and I add, "Make it strong."

I'm going to need it to make it through tonight. I can only force so many smiles before quitting the fake act.

Chain continues to watch me, penetrating me with his analytical eyes. I squirm, feeling as though he can see right through me.

"So, how are the scales of justice?" I ask, blurting out the first thing I can think of.

He chuckles. "The scales of justice? I'm not sure they're ever *really* balanced."

My eyebrows furrow in response. "Damn, that's pretty deep."

He shrugs as Abraham slides over his glass of whiskey, which flickers yellow as the overhead bar light shines through it. Catching it, he lifts it to his lips in one swift motion, taking a long swig.

"How do you drink that stuff?" I ask, my nose wrinkling.

He smirks. "You ever had *decent* whiskey before? This isn't Jack Daniels."

I think about it for a moment. "I guess not."

He tilts the glass to me in offerance, and I take it. I bring the glass up to my nose, inhaling lightly.

"It doesn't smell bad," I comment, bringing the glass to my lips and taking a small sip.

That's actually... not bad. The typical burn I've felt from any other whiskey I've tried is absent. There's a lightness to this one, and I finally understand what people mean when they say it's smooth. I feel like there's a hint of flavor, too.

"Is that... vanilla?" I ask, moving my tongue against the roof of my mouth to try and sense it.

"Maybe you're a whiskey drinker, after all," Chain replies approvingly, taking the glass from my hand. His fingertips brush mine, causing immediate tingles.

Between the warmth in my chest from his drink and the livewire in my fingers, this is panning out to be a good night.

"How are you, babe?" Stella asks me. I tear my gaze from the glass bottles sparkling under the single bar light.

"Fine," I reply, meeting her eyes only for a moment before staring out at the water. We're in our usual spot at the patio bar of The Meeting Place, where you get the best view.

"How are you, *really*?" she repeats, her hand resting on mine atop the grainy, walnut wood bar top.

Her touch forces my burning eyes to meet her grayish-blue ones. The concern reflected in them sends a stab of pain to my gut. I hate worrying her.

"I'm... I'm getting there," I try again.

"Are you getting more sleep?"

"A little."

"What about food?"

"I'm forcing myself."

"Well, you look like you're going to disappear through the walls soon. I wish I didn't eat when I was upset or stressed. All I want to do is lose myself in junk food and sweets."

I laugh, but it doesn't reach my eyes. She gives me an empathetic look and squeezes my hand.

"You know it's going to be okay, right?"

"I know." I really do.

I'd been doing a lot of Google searches on the nights my mind wouldn't settle. I found an article that explained a broken heart can actually feel like physical pain. It also said that breakups can hurt so much because there is a sense of withdrawal, like with drugs. Our bodies sync up with people, so when they're gone, you physically miss them. Not to mention, there's a sense of longing and sadness.

I also read articles on how to reconnect with yourself. I've started journaling, which has helped let out all these emotions. Between that and improv, I feel like I'm getting to know myself better. I feel like I'm *actually* healing.

My new reality sank in when I was driving home from week 3 of level two last night. As much as this sucks, and my heart was hurting, and my eyes were burning, I didn't really miss Zander all that much. I miss having someone around. I miss being able to sleep normally. I miss the comfort of the known.

That's ultimately why I haven't reached out to him, or bothered trying to get us back together. As time continues to pass and the pain gets a little easier, I feel strengthened with the truth of the matter.

I made the right decision in being honest.

"Here are your drinks, ladies," Luke says with a grin, breaking through my thoughts.

"Thanks, Lukey," Stella says cheerfully, grabbing our drinks and sliding mine to me.

"Since when do you drink whiskey, anyway?" she asks with an arched brow.

I take a sip, my chest heating in the trail of the traveling liquid. I feel a smile play at my lips when I taste the hints of vanilla on my tongue.

I toy with the ring in my palm, staring out at the water. It's been over 4 weeks since the breakup, and I decided to commemorate that with a depressing walk around the park where he proposed.

I brought the ring with me and I'm really not sure why. I asked him the day after he moved out if he wanted it back, but he said no. I told him I didn't want it and would throw it away, but he said he didn't care what I did with it.

I'm not sure why I didn't throw it away that day. Probably because that's just another thing that makes this change permanent. But before I went for this walk, I found myself unconsciously digging the ring out of his old nightstand drawer I had tossed it in after he moved out. I also found his necklace in there, the one with the M pendant. He must have left it when he got all of his stuff. I really should've taken mine off and left it with his in the drawer, but I didn't. I only grabbed the ring.

As I play with it now, feeling the smooth, cold metal on my soft fingers, I have the sudden urge to throw it in the little pond. Right in front of the spot where he proposed all those months ago, and I was forced to face the realization that I felt doubt about us.

I glance down at the ring. The reflection of the sun in the diamond momentarily blinds me. Without giving it another thought, I throw my arm back and swing it forward, watching as the ring drops into the water with a quiet plop.

Once the ripples clear, I turn back and walk slowly toward the condo.

Fuck, keep your head down, maybe he won't notice you.

"Hey, Marlie," Zander says with his usual lopsided grin and a head nod.

"Oh, hi," I mumble, pulling on the straps of my laptop backpack. Zander steps in line with me as we walk towards our cars after work.

"How have you been?" he asks. He actually sounds okay, too. I find that this bothers me. Not because I want him to be broken up over me or something, but because he doesn't seem to ever have strong feelings about *anything*.

How could I not have noticed this in the entirety of our relationship? I really was under a damn rock.

"I've been okay," I reply, keeping a higher pitch to my voice. "How about you?"

"Pretty good," he says.

"Good."

We walk in silence and I'm thankful the awkwardness I expected to feel isn't there.

"So what's up with Chain? You hittin' that yet?"

My cheeks redden and my head whips to him. His eyes have a twinkle of mirth but there's something beneath them too... resentment? Jealousy?

"What? No, why would you say that?"

"I mean, we're not together anymore and you said you have a thing for him. Why wouldn't you?"

His tone is so casual and his assessment logical, but I can't help feeling that he's really fishing here.

"I didn't break up with you because of Chain."

"Oh, now you broke up with me? Pretty sure I made you pull the trigger on that, babe."

His tone is light, yet it's anything but friendly. And the way he called me babe gives me the ick. I slow my steps and he mimics, not letting me out of this.

"Are you pissed at me?" I ask, stopping in the middle of the paved road. The people rushing to their cars behind us walk around.

"Not at all," he says with a flippant tone. "I'm happy you're following your truth."

I stare at him blankly. "Um, okay."

"So why aren't you with him?"

I give him an incredulous look, my mouth ajar. "I don't even know if he likes me like that! And that wasn't the point of—"

"Why the hell wouldn't he like you? The one time we met him at the mall he definitely checked you out. Not sure if that's his MO but he'd be crazy not to love you."

I choke on my own dignity. "Love?!"

Zander puts his hands up in mock surrender. "Just an expression, chill out."

He returns his gait to the parking lot. I follow.

"We *just* broke up, Zander."

He belts out a hollow laugh. "Please, don't hesitate on my account."

I feel tears burn at the back of my eyes. He's obviously pissed and I don't blame him. But it still hurts like shit.

We reach the first row of cars and he pauses, looking at me. Noting the wetness in my eyes, he sighs and rubs his hand through his hair.

"I'm sorry. I'm feeling all kinds of shit. This has been really hard."

"Yeah," I say, my voice shaky with tears at the brim of my eyelids.

Please don't fall, please don't fall.

"I didn't break up with you because of Chain." *That was just one of the symptoms.*

He eyes me suspiciously, then lets out another sigh.

"I'm gonna go." He points down the lane where he must have parked. "Take care of yourself, Marlie."

"You, too." A single tear falls.

He starts to turn then looks back at me. "I do mean it, though. Be happy."

I watch him walk away as another tear slips out. His blessing feels strange, because now that I have it, I realize I needed it. I didn't notice I'd still been carrying around the guilt.

I only realize it now that I'm free.

Chapter Forty-Two

Chain

"Valerie!" I shout across the house from the room I've been occupying. I finish tousling my hair dry with the towel, then toss it into the hamper.

"I'm coming!" she shouts in response. A moment later, she opens the bedroom door and gives me a once over.

"Let's go," I tell her, grabbing my keys and wallet off the dresser and sliding them into my pocket. My phone occupies the other one.

"I thought you'd be longer at the gym, let me just go grab my stuff."

"Hurry up!" I joke.

"Don't rush me!"

Twenty minutes later, we're pulling into the movie theater parking lot. I find a spot and put the car in park, removing my phone from its holder.

The screen lights up and I see my pending notifications from apps and messages. One in particular catches my eye.

WhatsApp message: Marlie in Improv Class

Unable to resist, I slide open the notification to the group chat. It takes a moment to load, and I tap my foot impatiently.

> Marlie: Hey! You guys down to hang out tonight?

Yes, my brain replies immediately. Does her text mean she's doing better?

These past few weeks, she's looked like the shell of the person I've gotten to know. I know it's part of the process and all that shit they always say, but that doesn't stop me from wanting to take her pain away. It's taken every ounce of willpower I have to stop myself from texting her, or calling her, just to check in and see how she's doing. This is *not* the time for me to get closer to her, no matter how much I want to. And as much as I'd like to make her feel better, it's not my job to do that.

If things are going to happen for us, it won't be under these conditions.

There's a small voice in the back of my mind that fears her pain means she's still in love with Zander, and I feel a tinge of jealousy and desperation. I still don't really know what happened, other than she ended things. She says he didn't cheat on her, but what if she was lying? Why would she suddenly end an engagement if something hadn't gone terribly wrong?

These are the questions that have haunted my waking thoughts when I have moments of free time. I'm not sure when she began to consume my thoughts, but I know that she has. And as much as I want the answers, I made a decision to let her have her space and not ask for anything she's not willing to give.

But this text is a definite offering—and I'm not passing the opportunity up.

> Me: I'm in!

Is the exclamation point too much? I ponder, my thumb hovering over the send button. The phone vibrates with an incoming message.

Damon: Can't, watching my nephew tonight

I hit send before I lose my nerve, exclamation point and all.

"Honey, what are you doing??" Valerie calls from the open passenger door of my truck, her arm slung across it.

"Sorry, I'm coming," I say, locking my phone and tucking it into my jeans before getting out.

"I had to repeat myself three times before you answered! Are you okay?" she asks, slamming her door shut and meeting me at the end of the truck.

"Yeah, sorry," I mumble.

I was just distracted with the idea of seeing this girl I can't stop thinking about. Everything's fine.

I adjust my shirt as I watch my reflection in the mirror, assessing my choice in apparel. I decided to stick with casual, donning a pair of jeans and a forest green polo. My brown boat shoes pair with the outfit nicely, and they happen to be my favorite pair of shoes, though I don't get to wear them often. I meet my own gaze and raise my eyebrows in anticipation. Even though this is a meeting as friends, the nerves rolling around my stomach make it feel like a date.

It's not.

No one else could go tonight, so it's only going to be Marlie and I. A part of me thought she'd bail when she found out it would only be us, but she texted me separately to arrange the plans. I'm picking her up and we're going to eat at La Corte della Pioggia. She asked for suggestions and that's the only place I ever want to go.

We didn't plan anything beyond that. Maybe we'll only have dinner and call it a night. Or we'll figure out somewhere to go. I don't care. I'm honestly just excited to see her, and hear more about what she's going through. I want to learn anything there is to know about her, including what pains her.

You sound like a lovesick sap.

The thought doesn't bother me, though.

15 minutes later, I pull up to the condo complex she resides in. I pull off of the road and put the car in park, pulling out my phone to shoot off a text letting her know I'm here. The message changes to read as soon as it's sent.

30 seconds later, I see her coming down the walkway. The sight of her instantly sends the nerves in my core swarming like bees.

I guess she's the honey.

I smirk briefly at my own stupidity, then my jaw drops an inch as I watch her walk closer. The flowy, light pink top she has on accentuates her curves and reaches to the very top of her thighs. A necklace is tucked into the scoop neck that hides her breasts, and there are little ridges on the sleeves. Her flared, ripped jeans are just as tight, and I find myself dying to know what she looks like without any clothes on.

God, what I could do to those tits...

I clench my jaw and force myself to not go down fantasy road, my dick already hardening at the idea of having her for my own. Fisting her hair with a firm tug and holding her lips to mine, tasting her sweet tongue. I could—

Stop, focus.

I take a deep breath, filling my chest and ignoring the pulse to my cock as the blood rushes to it. Marlie has made it to my truck and I hop out of it in a rush, scurrying past her to open the passenger door.

She laughs, stepping up and into the truck.

"Hi," she says, and I can't help but wonder how I never realized what a beautiful word that really is.

"Hi, Mar," I reply, my voice low. Her eyes find mine and I hold her gaze, admiring the return of the caramel swirls to her beautiful orbs.

She breaks our eye contact by turning away, but I don't miss the red tint on her cheeks. The rush of excitement I feel at the prospect tells me what I already know—I want this woman.

Give her time. She just got out of an engagement.

I circle back to the driver's side and put the car into drive.

"Ready?" I ask.

"Ready."

We spend the twenty minute drive in easy conversation, talking about our recent improv classes and the different scenes we've enjoyed. Marlie tells me that her favorite scenes so far are longform duos, where you just get a word and run with it in an extended scene. I tell her my preferred scenes are games because I enjoy the audience interaction and input.

On my drive to pick her up, I had the typical worries of 'what will we talk about', 'will this be weird', etc. But the moment we drove away from her complex, I wondered how I ever had those fears at all. Talking to her was as natural as breathing.

We got a table out by the water, something she actually requested before I got the chance to. It sent a rumble of appreciation through me to know that we both prefer sitting outside.

"Well, thanks for coming out with me! Too bad no one else could make it," she says as she opens her menu.

"Yeah, no problem," I say casually, but inside I feel a tinge of disappointment.

Is she upset that she only got to hang out with me? Does this mean more to me than it does to her?

"Chain?" Marlie pulls me out of my thoughts, realizing I was staring out at the water.

"Yes?"

"I asked, what do you usually get here?"

I point out a few of my favorite dishes to her, and that's when I learn she's a vegetarian.

"Shit, I didn't realize—"

"It's fine! I can always make something work."

"Well, I think their pastas are all delicious. They have a vegetarian one." I point to the section on her menu, then open my own menu to the drinks list, desperate for something to take the edge off. I'm not used to feeling so...

Damn, what is this feeling called?

"Good evening, folks." The waiter interrupts my thoughts before I can finish. I really need that drink. I can feel the frustration bubbling from getting trapped up in my head. "I'm Anthony, I'll be your server this evening."

"Hi, Anthony," Marlie quips, a smile on her face. She's happier than I've seen her in weeks, and I wonder what's changed.

Maybe it's the waiter.

A tinge of jealousy erupts in my chest, causing it to tighten.

Chill the fuck out dude, and focus.

I just want her to smile at me like that.

"Can I start you off with anything to drink?"

Shooting one more glance at the menu, I close it and say, "I'll take an old-fashioned, please, Anthony. Marlie?"

"I want wine." I smile at the simplicity of her statement.

"What kind do you like?" Anthony asks.

"Bring me your favorite," she says, that bright smile still playing on her lips. She meets my stare and a twinkle appears, causing me to smile without permission.

"I'll be right back," Anthony says, jotting it in his book and walking away.

"That's a bit daring of you, isn't it?"

"Ever since I tried that whiskey of yours, I've decided to branch out," she replies thoughtfully. "I guess I don't even really know what I like."

"Hmm, I like your way of thinking."

She smiles with a small bite of her lip, then returns her focus to the menu. Her cheeks turn slightly pink.

The waiter returns with our drinks and we order our food. Marlie did go with the veggie pasta, and I selected the grilled salmon with potatoes and asparagus. After he takes our menus, we fall into companionable silence as we sip our drinks and look out at the water.

Or rather, she looks at the water, and I look at *her* looking at the water. As I drink her in, I realize that I actually don't know all that much about her. I'm determined to change that tonight.

"So what do you—"

"This wine is actually—"

We start and stop at the same time, chuckling.

"I was going to ask about the wine," I say.

"It's great! I'll have to ask him what it's called."

"Why did you want to go out tonight?" I ask, deciding to cut right to the point. I've never been one for small talk. As much as I want to know everything there is to know about her, her favorite color tells me far less than the reasoning behind her decisions ever will.

"I needed to get out," she replies after a long pull from her glass. Placing it down, she continues, "I haven't really left much since the breakup, but I'm ready now."

"Ready, how?" I ask.

"I don't want to wallow anymore. I feel secure in my decision, so it's time to move on."

"I see," I say. *Should I ask?* Fuck it. "What happened, anyway?"

"With Zander?" she asks, eyeing me. I nod.

"It just didn't feel right. It's hard to explain... remember when you asked me about wearing masks? Well, I think I had been wearing a mask that hid me even to myself. When Zander proposed, I just couldn't shake the gnawing doubt. Trust me, I really tried. Finally, I got honest."

"What do you mean, you tried?" I ask, genuinely curious and wanting to understand.

"I told you, it's hard to explain," she says with a frustrated look. She runs her hand through her hair, and the image of me pulling on it flashes again. "It's like I didn't even know that I was with someone who wasn't right for me. Like, nothing was wrong. Zander was great, and sweet, and loving... but he just wasn't the one, you know? But I had convinced myself he was."

"I see," I comment, nodding my head studiously. "How did he take it?"

She blows out a breath, takes a sip of her drink, and speaks once the glass is returned to the table. "I think I totally fucked him over."

I can see the weight of her decision come over her. Her shoulders slump and the brightness in her eyes dims a bit.

"I mean, if it was your truth..." I trail off as her eyes dart to mine at the word truth. "You can't be held responsible for that."

"That's what everyone keeps saying," she mutters. "Anyway, I saw him yesterday and he seems to be doing okay."

"Saw him yesterday?" I say, tone sharper than I intend. I clear my throat before adding, "Why?"

"We ran into each other leaving work," she says as if this is common knowledge.

"Oh, I forgot you worked together." *Did I know that?* The tension I didn't realize gathered in my body loosened.

"Yeah, I mean we don't work in the same department or anything, so it's really been fine. This is the first time we've run into each other since we broke up."

"Do you think you guys will get back together?" I ask, my casual tone hiding my true feelings. As direct as I am, this is a question I might normally refrain from. But, as is customary when I'm around her, it slips out before I can stop it.

"No," she says assuredly. A lightness takes over me; there's no denying that my feelings are strong for her. When my mind begins to put up its usual protest, I rethink.

What's wrong with having feelings for her? She's single. I'm single. There's nothing wrong with this.

"I won't be getting back with Ashley, either," I declare, unasked. I feel sure in my choice to voice that truth, even if it puts me in a somewhat vulnerable place.

All Marlie has to do is ask herself why I would make that known for the reason to be obvious. I'm pleasantly surprised to find that I don't even care.

We carried on conversation as naturally as we did on the ride over. When the waiter arrived with our food, I was enraptured by a story she was telling me about her and Stella going to a concert.

Marlie enjoyed her pasta. The salmon tasted better than it ever had the many times I'd eaten it before. I couldn't be sure if that was due to the chef or the company.

The waiter returned to us with the refills of our drinks, as requested, and the bill. I didn't give him a chance to place it on the table between us, handing him more than enough cash to cover the bill and tip.

"No, you don't have to pay for me!" Marlie says, throwing her hand into her purse, likely searching for her card.

"I know," I say. The waiter eyes Marlie briefly. When she doesn't say anything and stops frantically digging in her purse, he gives a nod before turning away with the cash and bill.

"I'll get us next time," she says.

"So there *will* be a next time?" I say, raising my replenished old-fashioned to my lips with a smirk. I inhale slowly through my nose, reveling in the orange aromas before taking a sip. The liquor lights my tongue and burns down my throat, fueling the flirtatious energy that's building. I stare at her, admiring the reflection of the setting sun on her light eyes and the way the red in her hair shines. I'm not sure how much time passes before she finally looks at me.

"We hangout after class all the time!"

My stomach dips from her response, but then our eyes lock in that magical way they have so many times these last few months. This time, there's freedom in it. We're not restrained by anything. Her cheeks are already red from the wine, but I see those swirls in her eyes sparkle.

Maybe she does feel this, too.

"Let's do something fun!" she exclaims, standing up abruptly. Her hips bump the table and it shudders, my drink sloshing softly.

"Okay!" I recover quickly and leap up in a more controlled manner, matching her energy. It's one of the masks I've perfected wearing: following the energy of others. Except this time, I actually want to be excited with her.

"I know just the place," she says with a mischievous grin.

I'm tempted to ask her where we're going, but the answer doesn't matter. I'd follow her anywhere.

Chapter Forty-Three

Chain

"You're taking me dancing?" I ask, eyeing the lounge. The music blasting through the walls reverberates in my mind. I've never been here before and I'm always hesitant in new surroundings. It's hard to remain in control when you don't even know where the bathrooms are.

"It'll be fun!" she shouts over the thumping bass. I follow her to the door and grab it, holding it open for her to walk through. She makes an immediate right to a door that leads to the patio.

I follow her, seeing as she's familiar with this place. As if she's reading my mind, she turns her head to shout, "Stella and I used to come here all the time!"

I nod my head although she can't see me. I'm out of my element here, and I slide my mask of aloofness on. But I'm taking in all of my surroundings, analyzing and familiarizing myself.

There are small round cocktail tables scattered throughout the patio with no chairs. Along the metal fence are benches with bright blue cushions. Lights are strung along the enclosure, giving a cozy and alive energy to the area.

I didn't get to look inside, so I have no idea if there are a lot of people in there or not. The patio has a couple in the back left corner, and there's a group of girls directly in front of us.

Marlie leads us to the middle and plops down on one of the benches, patting the spot next to her.

“Should I get us drinks first?” I ask, looking around even though I already know there isn’t a bar out here.

“Someone will walk by,” she replies. Satisfied, I take the seat next to her, adjusting myself so I’m turned toward her at a 45 degree angle, crossing my leg over my knee.

“It’s okay, you know,” she says, eyeing me with understanding. Her words allow the mask to fall off. I’m not sure what it is about this woman that makes me feel so comfortable, but it feels fucking amazing.

"Why don't you and Stella come here anymore?"

She sits back, crosses her arms, and thinks for a moment. "I kind of lost myself there for a bit."

I stare at her, unashamed. Does that mean she's found herself again?

“So, what do you do outside of improv and lawyering? What are Chain’s big plans?” she asks with a wave of her hands in the shape of a rainbow.

I chuckle. “I do ‘lawyer’ a lot. My work is enjoyable for me. But my end goal is to open my own firm.”

“What about stand-up? I thought you said that it was always a dream of yours.”

“I mean, it was...”

“Why don’t you pursue it?”

The curiosity in her eyes coupled with the intrigued furrow of her brow tells me she genuinely cares. She’s not interested in the boxes of life that I check.

“I don’t know... life got in the way, I guess.”

“Promise me you’ll think about it.”

“About what, pursuing stand-up?”

“Yeah!” she says with an eager nod. “Or at least something to do with it.”

My eyes bore into hers, searching for any ulterior motive or something other than the light shining through.

"Yeah, okay," I concede, coming up empty.

"I want to get the hell out of my job."

"What exactly is it that you do?"

She provides a thorough explanation of her day-to-day tasks in the mailing room. When I ask what she'd rather do instead, she replies that she really doesn't know. She needs to do soul-searching.

I never knew that was the perfect answer until I heard it.

A server interrupts our conversation and jots down our drink order. I order my usual whiskey and she asks for the same. As the server walks away, she calls out, "And bring us a round of tequila shots!"

My eyes dart to her, finding a satisfied grin on her face. I copy it, feeling more comfortable and relaxed than I have in years.

What is it about this woman that makes me feel this way?

It's not something I can explain. There's an undeniable, deep connection that I can't control or ignore. The most puzzling part is that it doesn't bother me. On the contrary, it *excites* me. It makes me feel alive.

"It sounds like you're on the start of a wonderful journey," I say. Her eyes twinkle in response.

The server returns with a tray of glasses, placing coasters out before setting down the two glasses of whiskey and the clear shots of tequila, rimmed each with a lime wedge and salt.

Marlie's hands respond immediately, grabbing the shot glasses and handing me one. When I take it, she raises her own and opens her mouth to speak.

"To new beginnings," I say before she gets a chance.

She smiles broadly, knowingly, as if she was prepared to say the same thing. "To new beginnings," she repeats. We clink glasses, lick the salt off, and shoot the shots.

She licks her lips in one swift motion and removes her lime from the glass, capturing it in her mouth and sucking deeply. She didn't wince or rush to subdue the burn that we welcomed from the shot. Blood rushes to my cock at the speed of lightning as I wonder how deeply she could suck *me* down. I eye her thick, luscious lips, wondering how they'd feel wrapped around me.

I'm so entranced, my poor lime stays forgotten on the glass.

She discards the rind in her empty glass and looks up at me through her long lashes. Her eyes smolder when she sees what can only be an intense, lustful look on my face. I would normally try to school it, removing my thoughts from being clear and on display. But I already reasoned that there's no point denying my attraction to her.

And it's obvious now she feels the same.

"Want to dance?" she asks breathlessly.

I stand in response, hesitating only a moment before holding my hand out. She places her long, slender fingers into my palm and I clasp them firmly; the lack of jewelry is most apparent to me.

As we walk towards the door that leads inside, the music changes from a smooth beat to a song I recognize. It takes me a moment to realize it's "Die For You" by The Weeknd.

I hold the door open for her, dropping her hand so she can walk through. The bass pumps louder with the access inside, and I quickly follow her into the crowd.

I'm flabbergasted that I didn't notice the massive amounts of people that are in here. How did I not hear the noise or catch the movement from my periphery when we first arrived?

Marlie. She distracts me in the best and worst ways, but it's a distraction that I want. That I *need.*

We cut through the bodies bobbing and swaying, some of the sweat from their glistening skin rubbing on my bare arms. I'm so close to Marlie that her ass slightly rubs my front as we make our way through the crowd.

When she halts abruptly, I crash into her. Because of the people surrounding us, she doesn't fall, but that doesn't stop me from throwing my arms out and gripping her forearms in preparation.

She laughs in response. "I'm not *always* a klutz," she shouts.

I lower my mouth to her ear, my light stubble brushing her earlobe so delicately that the sensation is featherlight on my skin. "I beg to differ," I rasp out, my voice huskier than I intended. The close proximity of her and the people around me has me feeling sensual. The lighting from the strobe lights dances all around us, making it impossible to see consistently.

She laughs again, the sound music to my ears.

Fuck, I have it bad. I'm thinking in clichés.

"Shut up and dance," she says, swaying her hips in time with the beat and raising her arms to come over her head.

I obey her order, forcing my mind to get out of the gutter and into the moment. I move my waist in time with hers. Without a thought, I reach my hands out, landing on her swaying hips. My hands fuse with her body, keeping rhythm. I can feel her body heat through her top, making me want to feel her skin all over me.

My heart rate picks up and my breathing hitches as my cock fills with blood. My grip on her hips tightens as I have to physically restrain myself from crashing my lips onto hers.

Luckily, Marlie doesn't seem to notice. When the light passes over her face, I see she's got her eyes closed and a giant, closed-lipped smile plastered across her face. My fingers toy with her top as I keep moving along with her to the beat. My stomach keeps getting that swoopy feeling and I grip her so tightly, she might bruise tomorrow. *Oh, how I'd love to see her marked by me...*

Marlie suddenly spins, doing a 180 and returning to her hypnotic rhythm. Except now, her ass rubs greedily on my dick, which hardens more than I thought it could in response.

Fuck, I'm not going to be able to restrain myself.

I wrap my arms around her waist and pull her closer, my dick wishing to give her everything her body is asking for. She doesn't seem to mind me holding her this way, so I tuck my face into her neck. I inhale deeply, smelling light jasmine and fresh rain. Who the fuck knew a scent could be such a fucking turn on? In all my past fucks and relationships, I don't think I even *noticed* their scents.

I glance around the dance floor and find that most people are grinding the way we are.

Maybe this isn't something special to her like it is to me, then. Maybe she just wants a good time for the moment and isn't getting turned on the way I am.

My cock throbs angrily, begging to be touched. The layers of clothing between our skin is tantalizing torture and I'm slowly getting lost to the ache of needing her.

I move my head back, refusing to inhale her scent and risk not being able to take it further. I move my hands to her hips and spin her around so she's facing me, putting a more reasonable distance between us.

The strobe light flashes past us again and I see her eyes are widened but alive. The brown is the lightest I've ever seen it and the swirls stand out in contrast.

She just got out of a relationship. Cool it the fuck off.

We continue swaying to the beats, the air between us statically charged, but I maintain control over the unignorable need for her.

"Why didn't you ever text me back?"

"What?" My breath hitches but I keep my expression neutral.

"I texted you a picture of a scale, and you never responded."

I can feel her penetrating eyes on me, but I keep mine trained on the road ahead.

"I... it didn't feel right, given the circumstances."

"What circumstances?" she asks with a laugh.

Fuck, she's not making this any easier.

"Ashley was the possessive type." I give her a half-truth, but if she presses me anymore I know I won't be able to withhold the rest from her.

"Oh, I see." *And given that I found you sexy as hell, I couldn't respond.*

"I didn't mean to put you in a weird position," she says quietly, a tinge of remorse lacing her words.

"It's fine, really. How could you have known?"

She doesn't respond and I don't add anything to my statement. It's better we don't go down this road.

The road where I confess that her texting me made me feel something, and responding would have only added fuel to the fire. And since we were both in relationships, it would have felt inappropriate.

I follow the GPS instructions and pull down the road to her place. When I throw the gear into park, I exit the car and quickly circle to her door, opening it. I hold out a hand to help her down the steep drop to the ground, and she thanks me with a giggle.

"No, thank you. I had a great time tonight." *Can you sound any more basic?*

"Good, I'm glad."

She beams at me and adjusts her purse.

"Well, thanks for the ride. See ya," she says, her smile fading and her eyes wide. She hesitates for a moment and I'm enraptured by the reflection of the moon in her twinkling eyes.

"Any time," I reply, unmoving. My eyes glance down as she bites her lower lip, wishing I could be the one to bite it. She turns and walks up the sidewalk to her condo.

I shut the door and circle back to the driver's side, opening the door and halting before getting in.

Fuck it.

I don't allow myself to think it through as I run after her, my shoes pounding on the pavement. Marlie starts to look back as I grab her arm, turning her and pulling her into me.

With her face inches from mine, I search her wide eyes.

"I couldn't... I didn't want to wait."

Chapter Forty-Four

Marlie

Chain's lips crash onto mine and my eyes flutter shut with a sigh. Nothing has ever felt so *right*.

His kiss is hurried at first, moving against mine in a rushed need. I know, because I feel it, too. Months of denying myself and my feelings are being forced into this moment. And the way he's kissing me with the same energy, it makes me certain he's felt the same way.

He's a bit out of breath, probably from running to me, but as his breath slows down so does our kiss. His tongue dances over my lower lip, silently asking for permission. I grant it, opening my mouth and bringing my tongue to meet his. I moan in response, embarrassed he has such an effect on me so quickly.

The embarrassment fades when he matches it with a groan of his own, one of his hands circling to my low back and the other gripping the back of my neck. His hold feels possessive, like he has me and never wants to let me go.

Please don't.

Our tongues circle slowly in a provocative tango, taking in everything we've never been able to explore. My pussy clenches as I feel a surge of wetness trickle down. Chain presses into my lower back, pushing me closer to him.

My nipples harden and I push my hips into him, feeling his hardness in my center. The hand he has on my neck loosens, slowly trailing into my hair. He pulls firmly, breaking our kiss. He's so close that our noses brush, our chests rising and falling rapidly with our ragged breaths. His electric eyes search mine, dilated with lust. I imagine mine look similar.

"Do you..." he trails off, his eyes glancing towards the condo building before returning to stare at me with a tilt of his lips.

"Yes," I breathe out, nodding fervently. But neither of us moves. His eyes are filled with the same desire I feel. I move my face towards him and he closes the gap, our lips meeting once more. This kiss isn't rushed like the last one. He takes his time, our lips moving slowly before our tongues meet again.

Feeling brave, I nibble his lower lip and he groans in appreciation. I swipe my tongue over it before sucking it into my mouth, and I groan with him. His hands tentatively grip my hips, as if they're not sure if it's too much too soon.

I think it's far overdue.

I run my hands up his chest, feeling his chest harden under my graze. His pelvis tilts towards mine, pushing his erection into the soft pad over my core.

My pussy heats and slickens with another rush of wetness as I meet his hips with my own, pulsing with the need to be touched.

"Come on," I mumble against his lips. He pushes his tongue back into my mouth and I forget my thoughts, enraptured in the feeling of him on me.

This is actually happening.

I pull back from him and turn, forcing him to follow me. He catches up in a few strides, taking my hand in his with a tension filled squeeze. *Sexual* tension. It's enough that we take our pace to a near run.

I fumble the keys to the door and he catches them before they fall. He hands them to me with a smirk, to which I shove him playfully and open the door. As we cross the threshold, it dawns on me that he's never been here before.

I turn to face him and hold my hands up. "This is my place."

Chain's eyes don't leave me, full of need and wanting. I drop my hands to my sides and he pounces, this time wrapping his arms around my waist. He backs me up against the front door, causing a loud thump when my body hits it.

I let out a giggle and I feel him smirk against my lips. I'm so ecstatic that my head feels as light as a balloon, prepared to fly off into the sky. Our lips haven't stopped moving, coming together and apart in a perfectly synchronized swim.

I moan again, this time without a care in the world. His lips feel so good on mine and I. Need. More. I move my lips against his with such desire that I'm panting. I'd normally be more embarrassed, but I'm too enthralled to care.

His hands slowly explore my back, moving up and forward to my breasts. When he captures them in his hands, he pulls back and I stare up at him, wide-eyed and breathless.

"I love your place," he says with a teasing grin, squeezing my breast firmly.

"It likes you, too."

His eyes lower to my lips but he doesn't move, watching as I swipe my tongue across them. It wasn't intentional, but it feels like a happy accident when I see his pupils dilate.

"I think you've forgotten to show me the most important room, though," Chain says, his gaze still locked on my lips.

"What room?" I ask, completely mesmerized by his lustful gaze and the steady pulse of my second, and more important, heart beat.

"Your bedroom."

Duh.

"Follow me," I say as his hands drop from my breasts and I lead him up the stairs.

"Gladly," he replies as he follows me. I turn my head to watch him and find his eyes glued to my ass. I make sure to take the steps cautiously so I don't fall and ruin the show, putting some extra pep in my step and swaying my hips.

When he reaches the landing, he pulls me into him and burrows his head into my neck.

"I want to remember your smell forever," he says appreciatively, his arms wrapped around me.

"Mmm." His fingers move lightly across my belly, just above the waistband of my jeans. I want his fingers lower, right over the spot where it aches. I walk us to my room while he holds me.

Just a few more minutes.

I walk through the threshold of my room and suddenly feel a bit awkward. This is the room I shared with Zander. This is the bed we fucked on countless times.

Mental note: get new furniture.

I flip on the light switch and stare at the plain, white walls for a moment. I've never hated them more than I do now. "This is my room," I say with a wave of my hand. Chain removes his hands from me and steps to my side, giving it a quick glance, then landing on me.

"It's perfect."

He switches off the light and I'm temporarily blinded. But he wastes no time in bringing his lips to mine and melding our bodies together. He walks me towards the bed and I fall onto it gladly.

He moves his mouth from my lips to my jaw, leaving wet kisses along it. I bend my head over to grant him more access and he takes it, sucking my earlobe into his mouth.

"I want you so fucking bad, Marlie..." he whispers into my ear, then trails more kisses down my neck.

"I know. Me too," I breathe.

"This"—he waves a hand between us before placing it on my inner thigh—"I could die tonight and feel like I lived a full life because I finally had just a *chance* with you."

I throw my lips on his and our breaths mix together in a heady mixture of lust, desire, passion, and care. We tear our clothes off in desperation as our lips continue to find each other. When we finally come up for air, he pulls back and grabs the wallet from his jeans.

Removing a condom, he tears the packet open with his teeth, spitting the piece of foil onto the ground. I prop up on my elbows to watch him roll the latex over his cock and goddamn if that isn't the sexiest thing I've ever seen. He leans back, drops the wrapper on the nightstand, and fumbles with the night lamp, flicking it on.

"I want to see you."

His words melt my insides. He strokes the head a few times with a flutter of his eyes before inching towards me on his knees. I drop down to my back and he wastes no time in crawling over me and placing his throbbing erection at my opening.

"I..." I lose my ability to speak as he pierces me with a soul-deep look.

"I know," he whispers after a long silence passes, my eyes volleying between his. We maintain eye contact as he presses inside me, agonizingly slow.

"Fuuuuck," I moan, my eyes rolling into my head and my back arching.

"Uh-uh," he groans. "I want to watch you come undone as you take me."

He's all the way in now. I can feel his balls touching my asshole and my pussy clenches with the pleasure of his wide girth.

"Marlie."

Fuck.

I force my eyes back open and meet his heated gaze. If looks could kill, his weapon of choice would be gasoline and a match. I feel like I'm burning up and it's the best fucking feeling. I've never felt like this, ever.

He starts to return the way he came, pulling out just as tantalizingly slow. My clit throbs with the lack of warmth from his body meeting my own.

I moan and my eyes flutter, threatening to roll back again.

Chain stops moving and I blink hard.

"That's a good girl. When your eyes close, I stop. Understood?"

I watch him with wide eyes, my pussy surging with wetness all over again. My walls tighten over his dick and I feel him throb in response.

"Answer me."

I nod my head because I am absolutely incapable of words. Chain gives me a sexy as hell, arrogant smirk. If he was like this normally, I'd tell him to fly a kite. But deep inside me, knowing what he's doing to me, and owning that fact—it's my undoing.

He brings a hand to my breast, cupping it gently before bringing his fingers to my nipple and pinching. *Hard.*

I bite down on my lip in reflex, the taste of blood tinting my tongue a moment later. I release my lip with a gasp, glancing down at my nipple.

He released it as quickly as he pinched, the cool air causing a sting while he palms my breast soothingly.

"Let's try again. Do you understand?"

I nod and then gulp. "Yes."

He gives me a wide, proud smile, a pleased glint in his eye. I want to see more of that; be the reason for it.

"You're such a good girl, baby," he drawls out, resuming his slow, torturous removal of his dick inside me. When his tip is at the point of exiting me completely, he thrusts back in so hard, the wind is knocked out of me.

"Fuck!" I gasp, overcome with pleasure. If I ever thought I'd orgasmed before, I have no idea what I'm getting ready to experience.

"You feel so fucking good, Marlie. I could stay buried in your pussy for the rest of my life and die a happy man."

I want to reply, to say something to let him know how much I'm living for this. But words are failing me. My body is overtaken with the pleasure of what he's doing to me.

His half-hooded eyes bore into mine and I focus on not closing them, even though they're begging to. The thrill of pleasing him and following his orders has tingles shooting up my spine.

If this is what our first time feels like, I can't wait to try again. I could live out the rest of my existence in this exact position.

He starts picking up his pace and bites down on his lip, a low growl ripping through his chest. I raise my hands and rub his pecs, then his abdomen. He's firm and strong, but not in an obvious way. I want to memorize his body like I'm studying for the bar exam.

"It's like your pussy was made for me."

I moan in response, because his words are just *doing* it for me. He quickens his pace, sliding in and out smoothly because I'm sopping wet for him. He bends over me so his arms are around me. I cling onto his formed shoulders and bite down when he thrusts in as deep as he can.

"Fuck, Chain," I say through clenched teeth. He pulls all the way out and I urge my hips forward to find him again.

"So greedy for me, baby." I can hear his smirk and it makes me go feral, loving how much he loves doing this to me.

"I need you," I say, my voice returning with the loss of contact. He groans and thrusts into me again. He leaves no room for mercy, pounding into me repeatedly. My clit throbs with each rub of his body on mine and I dig my nails into his shoulders, tensing with the nearing explosion my body is going to have.

"Give it to me, Marlie. Show me how much you like my cock in you."

His words send me over the edge, my clit erupting with pleasure that shoots throughout my entire body. My legs shake around his hips, where I didn't even realize I'd clung on. He continues thrusting, this time in shorter, deeper, strides. My arms and legs go limp and he places a tender kiss on my temple before whispering in my ear.

"We're not done yet."

He wraps an arm around my back and holds me up, returning to his speedy tempo. My clit screams from the sensitivity and I clamp my legs around his waist to resist the sensation.

"Open up for me, Marlie," he says, his voice all sex. I loosen my muscles and moan from the all consuming feeling. "That's it. That's my good girl."

He places a kiss on my head before resuming his deep, penetrating thrusts. I start to whimper and while normally I'd find it pathetic, I can't bring myself to care. The feeling of too much is evolving to just right. Chain pierces me with his eyes. They're so dark, I wouldn't know they were green if this was the first time I saw them. His pupils are completely blown out and they're nearly closed.

"I'm going to cum for you, baby. This is all for you."

I move my hips in time with his and he goes off like a bomb, his eyes rolling into the back of his head and his neck dropping. He moans and holds me so close to him that I lose my breath. When he finally stops moving and softens around me, I search for his eyes.

I find them instantly and watch the green reemerge from the ashes. He gives me a heart melting smile and I place my lips on his. In an instant, our energy goes from passionate need to sugary joy.

Keeping his lips on mine, he slowly pulls his dick out of me and serenades me gently with his tongue. The kiss is so sensual and deep, I lose myself in it. My head is about to float away from my body from the high of my orgasm and the tenderness in this kiss.

He eventually breaks our kiss and lets me go. Totally sated, I roll onto my stomach, my head nestled into the pillow. Chain's voice drifts over to me as I feel his weight shift on the bed.

"I'm going to go clean off real quick."

"Mmm," is all I can get out. I've never been fucked so good.

I realize as I hear his steps on the carpet that he doesn't know where the bathroom is. From the sounds I hear, I think he's figured it out. He returns a moment later. I feel his weight sink into the bed and then a warm, wet towel is wiped on my vagina. Normally, the sudden sensations would shock me, but I'm too relaxed to react.

"Thanks," I say, peeking my eyes open. The only light is the lamp that he hastily turned on, his shadow reflected on the wall. I'm lying on what used to be my side of the bed, before I stopped sharing it.

Chain finishes cleaning me off and tosses the towel into my hamper. I hear the dull thud as it hits the wall and presumably lands on the clothes already in it. I wouldn't actually know, since I can't even seem to lift my head.

He lays down next to me and I watch him through half-closed lids. He rustles around, getting comfortable with the pillows and pulling the blanket over him.

"Are you sleeping here?" I ask, lifting my head a bit with more awareness.

"Yeah, is that okay?"

"Oh, um"—*of course it is*—"sure, I just didn't know what was happening."

"What, did you think I was just gonna fuck you and leave?"

"I guess I didn't really think about it," I say.

Chain turns on his side to face me and wraps his arm around my waist, pulling me in. I'm certain my body has never fit so perfectly into another before. His warmth emanates around me. He adjusts so he's lying on his back and I lay my head on his chest.

It feels so familiar and yet... so contrasting. My eyes flutter closed and I inhale his addicting scent. I could sleep like this forever. I feel his breaths even, his head resting on mine.

I wonder if he can smell me, too.

As the ecstasy of the night settles, my thoughts slowly drift.

Is this too soon? Am I wrong for enjoying this so much? Did I leave Zander just for Chain?

No. I'm not going to do this. I ended things with Zander because he wasn't the one for me. As hard as it's been losing him, I know it was the right decision.

And I'm allowed to do whatever I want with my freedom. I'm going to enjoy this, whatever it is.

Chapter Forty-Five

Marlie

I wake up to the sun beaming through the blinds, confirming it must be mid-morning. I move my leg, which rubs on another leg.

Shit! I'm with Chain. Oh my god, this was real.

I turn my head to look at his face and find his eyes closed. He looks more serene than I've ever seen him. His chest lifts and falls with his deep breathing, my head moving with it.

I want to lay here forever, but my bladder is screaming at me. Moving as quietly as possible, I get out of bed and go to the bathroom. Only when I catch my reflection in the mirror do I remember that I'm completely naked.

I pee and return to the room, finding Chain awake and on his phone.

Unsure of what to say or do, I get back into bed but stay on my side. He looks over at me and gives me a wide smile, his eyes crinkling with nothing but pure joy.

"Come here," he says, lifting the blanket so I can return to my spot next to him.

I scoot closer and whisper, "Good morning."

"Indeed it is, beautiful," he replies into my hair, placing a gentle kiss on it.

"Last night was..." I trail off, unable to find the appropriate word.

"I know," he says breathlessly, and I feel his lips tilt up against my head. We cuddle in silence for a few moments.

As we breathe in the same air, I feel a sense of peace I haven't known in so long.

"I realize this may be too soon," Chain starts, breaking the silence. I hold my breath, unsure of how he'll follow up that sentence. "I didn't mean to... pounce on you like that."

I laugh, relief washing over me. "I thought you were going somewhere else with that."

"What did you think I was going to say?" He angles his face towards me and I move mine back so we're facing each other. I'm momentarily stunned when I look into his emerald green eyes, shining brighter than ever.

"I don't know..." My nerves take over with the sudden vulnerability I feel. How am I supposed to tell him I don't see this as a one time thing?

"Tell me."

His eyes look so earnest and open, I summon the courage to put my feelings on the table.

"I thought maybe you'd say that it was just a one time thing," I mumble, my throat tight with the anxiety of his reaction.

It's his turn to laugh this time. His eyes search mine, although I'm not sure what he's looking for.

"You have no idea, do you?" he says, his eyes penetrating mine with a look of desire and admiration.

"What?" I breathe.

He gives me a bashful smile, one I'm not used to seeing on his normally confident and smooth features. He looks down, and I'm sure he feels as nervous as I do.

"I've wanted you for a long time, Marlie."

His words play on repeat in my mind and I'm unable to answer, temporarily stunned. I'm startled out of it when I hear my phone vibrate on the nightstand. Wide-eyed, I ignore it.

"Really?"

Really? That's all you can say?

He chuckles. "Really. I felt drawn to you from the moment we met. But you were engaged, and I had a girlfriend. I accepted it, figuring the feelings would pass. They never did, though. On the contrary, they got stronger."

"I can't believe this," I say.

"Why?"

"I've felt the same way. Like a pull towards you... like we were destined to crash into each other all along."

Our eyes are locked. This moment feels surreal, like I've only dreamed of it and will wake up at any moment. My mind reels, playing back all the moments since we've met. The inability to look away, the conversations, the touches.

"I know," he says, his voice softer than I've ever heard it. I feel like he knows exactly what I'm thinking.

He's really felt it this whole time, too?

My phone vibrates again, likely the reminder of the message I received. I break our eye contact and he releases his grip on me. I grab my phone and glance at the notification.

> Landlord: Good morning. Will you be renewing your lease? It's up at the end of the month.

My landlord, of all people, is the one pulling me from this moment. Glancing at the time, I see it's 8:13 am. Since Zander and I broke up, I've been getting up a lot earlier and it honestly feels so much better.

I put the phone back and return to Chain's embrace. I feel his dick rub my thigh and it hardens slightly.

"It's just my landlord," I inform him with a dismissive wave of my hand.

"On a Sunday? That's weird."

"My lease is expiring. She's asking if I'm renewing."

"Are you?"

"No, I'm going to move into a smaller place. I need to find one, though."

"Oh, okay," he replies and I think I note a hint of sadness in his tone. "I'm in the process of buying a house, actually."

"Oh, really?" I say excitedly. "That's awesome!"

Zander and I had been saving for a while, although I really had to push us to do it. I think he would have been content to stay in this place forever.

"It's under contract, but if all goes well I should have the keys soon."

"Wow! Well if you need help with anything, let me know."

"I'm planning on painting and getting some new appliances. It's not my dream house by any means, but it will do for now."

"Where is it?"

"It's actually right in front of the theater. You know that quaint, rose-colored house down the street where I often have to park my car?"

"Yes!"

I'm thrusted into a memory of the first time I saw that house, on the night of our first improv class.

"It's close to my office so I figured, why not. When I told the realtor the area I was looking at, it was the first house he showed me. It wasn't even on the market yet. But it's in a great location and will be a perfect investment for the future."

"Doesn't hurt that you'll be close to the theater, either."

"Exactly," he replies with a grin.

"I'm really happy for you," I tell him with a matching grin.

We fall into easy conversation about his plans for the house, his hands on me the whole time. His thumb rubs circles over my hip bone and I snuggle closer to him, our naked bodies joined. He tells me about how he's been working out and wants to start taking a stand-up comedy class.

"It sounds like you've been doing great since..." I trail off, unsure if that's an appropriate topic to broach after last night.

"Yeah, I–" He's cut off by the vibrations of his phone. He grabs it from the place he dropped it on the bed, the name Greg flashing on the screen.

"I gotta take this," he says, swiping to answer the call. "Hey, Greg." A muffled voice comes in on the other end. Giving him his privacy, I free myself from him and stand up, returning to the bathroom to brush my teeth.

This all feels so natural, like we've done this a thousand times. After rinsing, I find a spare toothbrush in the cabinet below the sink. I place it on the counter and exit, nearly walking right into Chain.

"Oh! I put a toothbrush on the counter for you," I tell him, moving to step around him. He grabs my wrist and brings his lips to mine, his tongue swiping my lips open immediately. I meet his slow and passionate kiss eagerly.

Pulling back, he thanks me. I want more, but I feel suddenly hesitant and shy. I don't want to come on too strong. Plus, he put on his pants to walk over here, but I'm completely naked.

"Stay with me?" he asks, ending my ruminations. I nod and back up into the bathroom, standing to the side while he brushes his teeth. I watch him in the mirror, keen on learning all his behaviors, even just the morning routine.

My eyes roam over his shoulders and I blush instantly, spotting the indentations left behind from my fingernails. His eyes meet mine in the mirror. When he sees my expression, and the reason for it, he smirks and takes some water from the faucet. After he spits, he straightens and turns to me.

"Shower?"

I nod again, the shyness causing my brain to forget how to speak. He doesn't hesitate to remove his jeans, freeing his already hard penis. My eyes widen, impressed at the length of him that is even more apparent in the bright bathroom light.

"You're so sexy," he murmurs, bringing his hand to grip his erection. I raise my gaze to his lustful, hooded eyes.

I close the gap between us and he wastes no time in grabbing both of my hips, molding my body to his. I kiss him hungrily, ready for another round of the amazing sex we had last night. His thick cock rests between us and I move my hips to appease the ache I feel from my clit.

He returns my kiss just as hungrily, his hands tightening over my hips before moving up to my waist. This time, I take the lead and guide us towards the shower. His hands don't stop roaming over my body and I take his dick in one hand while reaching the other to find the shower knob. After a few swats in the air, I locate it and turn the knob.

"What temperature?" I ask between wet, sloppy kisses.

"Hot," he replies, squeezing my ass and lifting me. I loop my legs around him and he steps into the tub.

"Perfect," I say with a soft moan. He turns us so I'm under the shower head, my hair quickly soaking with the steaming water. I tilt my head back and he lurches forward, taking my bottom lip between his teeth. His erection pokes at my ass and I moan.

"You are so fucking sexy," he groans, releasing my lip and lightly placing me down in the shower. He reaches both hands out and moves my hair off my neck. He leans towards my neck and then halts suddenly. Pulling back, his eyes lose their lustful look and are replaced by a new fire.

I glance down and realize what warranted his reaction. I've been wearing this *fucking* necklace, so accustomed to it that I haven't taken it off.

"Oh, shit," I say. "I forgot about it."

"You're mine now," he growls, grasping the necklace and ripping it off in one clean sweep. I felt it pull on my neck before it broke, falling to the ceramic tub with a clang.

He wraps the same hand he used to break the necklace off around my throat, pulling me to him. When his lips crash onto mine, I can feel him claiming me. The act feels so possessive, it elicits a strong reaction in me. My pussy floods with warmth and wetness, and I thrust my tongue into his mouth. I moan so much I lose count of how many times.

He keeps one hand around my throat but lets the other roam freely, exploring my shoulders, breast, waist, hips, and ass. He leaves the best place for last. When his hand *finally* reaches the area above my clit, he teases me with featherlight touches from his fingertips.

"Say it," he growls against my lips. I know intuitively what he's asking for.

"I'm yours."

I feel him smirk against my lips. "Good girl." He hums his appreciation and moves a single finger to my clit, pressing lightly and circling slowly. I groan and thrust my hips forward, begging him to ease the ache.

"Patience, baby," he says with a smirk. "I should punish you for wearing that *fucking* thing."

"Ugh, don't be an asshole," I let out in frustration.

"Hmm, is that what you think? I'm an asshole?" He continues circling slowly, pausing to slip his finger into my soaking pussy before resuming. His lips are right over mine, his minty breath tickling my face when we speak. I want to feel that minty freshness right over my clit.

"No," I let out after a beat. If I thought he was an asshole, we wouldn't be doing this. He's being a dominant tease, and it's absolutely doing it for me.

He squeezes my throat and moves his lips to my ear, nibbling as he asks, "Do you trust me?"

I inhale through my nose sharply, taken aback by such an intimate question. But the answer falls from my lips without a second thought. "Yes."

He grips my neck harder, lodging my breath in my throat. My pussy clenches and he runs his finger across it entirely before removing it, leaving me to feel the cold emptiness.

He releases my earlobe and pulls back. "Suck my dick."

I drop to my knees immediately, the shower continuing to pour over my head and back. I run my hands up his thighs, then take his balls in one and the base of his cock in the other.

I glance up at him, water droplets falling over my long lashes. I blink so I can stare at his heated eyes, looking at me with such desire that I want nothing more than to please him anyway I can. The fact that I put that look in his eyes, that unfiltered, raw desire, makes me feel empowered.

I move my lips slowly to his cock, squeezing the base and not breaking eye contact. Just like he wanted to watch me, I want to see the look in his eyes when I take him fully. When my lips reach the head, I swipe my tongue across it before opening wide and taking him in.

"Fuck, baby," he says, his eyes rolling into the back of his head. He throws an arm out to the side to grasp the wall. I suck him all the way in, my lips meeting my hand, then slowly release him while trailing my tongue along. His wide, long dick won't make it to the back of my throat without me gagging.

I move to release him for a gasp of air but he brings his free hand to my head and catches some of my hair while pushing me back onto his dick. I expect to feel the resistance I normally do when a guy tries to control my movements like this.

I didn't expect to feel turned on, my stomach dropping with excitement. He guides me to take all of him again, this time not letting me stop at the base where my hand is. I drop my hand and move forward a little but I start to gag.

"Relax, baby. Breathe," he says. I obey him, letting my jaw go slack. I didn't even realize it was tense. I hollow out my cheeks and take a breath through my nose.

"That's it, baby. Fuck, you suck my dick like a pornstar."

A pornstar??

Again, the expected reaction doesn't come. That should probably feel like an insult but I find myself liking the compliment, feeling like I'm as good as a professional. Like no one else can make him feel this good.

I start to move up and down, taking him all the way in and all the way out. His breathing becomes more labored between groans and the next time I try to take his dick back in my mouth, he holds my head in place by my hair. The scalp stings a little but it only causes my clit to ache more.

"Stand up." I stand up.

"Turn around." I turn around.

His hands glide over my ass, circling a few times before spreading my cheeks. My asshole clenches and my pussy throbs with the ache and need for *something*.

"Have you ever been fucked here, Marlie?"

My eyes widen in response but he can't see them.

"You're awfully forward, you know that?"

"Does that bother you?" He stops moving his hands, his palms staying in place.

Does it? Honestly, it's refreshing. I like knowing where he's at and what he wants. "No."

His hands resume their exploration, pulling my cheeks apart one more time before releasing them. Then he brings a hand down to my ass cheek sharply, the sound heightened from the water droplets.

"Fuck," I grunt, my eyes rolling into the back of my head. I reach my hands out and hold myself against the wall at an angle.

"Answer me," he says as his wet finger trails over my asshole.

I nod my head fervently. "Once."

"Zander?"

Is he really bringing up my ex right now??

I shake my head. His finger stops moving.

"Jack?"

I nod slowly. We tried it one time and I hated it. It was tight, it hurt, and I bled for a week after.

"Did you like it?"

I shake my head. He resumes his trailing, moving over the soft spot between my pussy and ass. His finger hovers at my entrance, feeling around the wetness.

"You're going to like it with me."

The idea of trying it sends a thrill through my core and my pussy blazes with heat. But he inserts his finger into my pussy and then brings it to my mouth, coating my lips with my juices.

I peek the tip of my tongue out so his finger glides over it, and he growls in response.

"You are so perfect for me, Marlie. The way you react to me pleases me very much."

I'm as good a feminist as the next woman. But the shit this man keeps saying is very quickly causing me to doubt that within myself.

"I want to please you," I whisper the words without consciously giving myself permission to speak them. I know they're true, though. I'm ready to let this man do just about anything to me, just so I can keep feeling this good.

"I want to please you, too. Nothing would give me greater joy."

I feel him move behind me, the shower curtain pulling back and a waft of cold air entering. I turn my head and watch him dig a condom out of his pants. He tears it open and lets the foil drop to the ground, then rolls the condom over his dick.

He planned this.

The thought of that excites me. He places his hands on my hips and guides his full, thick cock into me. I'm surprised to feel a hint of disappointment that he's not in the other hole, but that's quickly stamped out by him filling me.

"You feel so *fucking* good, Chain."

"I know, baby, I know. It's like you were made for me."

I moan and we start a steady rhythm, the shower pouring down on us and his hips meeting my ass cheeks with each round. His hands grip me harder as the pleasure builds.

He grabs one of my hands and brings it to his lips, sucking my index finger into his mouth. He releases it and my hand drops. A moment later, he slaps my ass swiftly and I jump from the shock and pain.

"Ow!"

"Rub yourself," he demands, slapping me again in the exact same spot. The hot water pattering relentlessly causes it to sting.

I bring the index finger he sucked to my clit and he brings his hand back to my hips. He holds tightly as he thrusts all the way in and all the way out. I tighten around him as my finger vibrates at high speed over my clit. My legs start to quiver from standing on my tiptoes, but I don't care.

I want to come so fucking badly.

"Good girl, baby. Do you like rubbing yourself while I fuck you?"

"Mmhmm."

"What if I was watching you from outside the shower, rubbing myself to you? Would you like that?"

My pussy surges in response. I moan embarrassingly loud; there's no way the neighbors didn't hear it. *Good thing I'm moving.* He stops suddenly and my stomach plummets. I whine and he tsks.

"You'll learn, baby. But I have to teach you. *Answer me.*"

"I would *love* that," I say automatically, pushing my hips back. I feel the tip of his cock but he pulls back. I whine again.

He slaps my ass harder than before, in the exact same spot, the bastard. I lurch forward and throw my hands out to the wall.

"You'll have your chance to lead, baby. But that's not today."

He rubs the sore spot on my ass soothingly, then slowly pushes his cock into me. I moan in pleasure and he slaps down hard on the exact same spot. I yelp out and squirm but he quickly grabs my hips and holds me in place.

"You're okay. You can take it."

He leans forward and kisses my neck, trailing little nips along the line that leads to my shoulder. The stinging melts away in favor of him all over me and in me.

"Keep rubbing, baby girl," he whispers into my ear. I waste no time in taking my finger to my clit because I don't want him to slap me again and I want to escalate the orgasmic feeling of his dick in me.

He leans back and grips one hip, curling the other hand around my neck and gripping firmly. It doesn't hurt, but I'm locked into place and my airway is constricted.

"You're going to come for me just like this, baby girl."

"Yes, sir," I say a bit sarcastically. Chain growls in response and I take a mental note to say that more often. He maintains the perfect pace and I rub on my clit, bringing myself close to orgasm.

"You do this to me, Marlie. You make my dick throb with the need of you. I want to fuck you just so I can watch and hear what I do to you."

He tightens his grip around my neck and I moan, going off like a rocket. My legs shake and give out, and I can't get enough air into my lungs. Chain holds me up by my neck and hip, causing my orgasm to crescendo. He quickens his own pace and follows me, holding himself deep inside me while gripping my hip so hard that I feel his fingers on my bone.

"Fuck," he groans and I turn to a pile of mush below him.

We stand there for a moment, my body slumped against the shower wall with Chain buried deep inside me. Our breaths slow to a normal rhythm and I listen to the shower pour over us. Chain eventually pulls out of me and I stand, slowly regaining the strength back to my body.

He presses a kiss to the back of my head, right where he was pulling my hair. I turn around and he gives me a sated smile, his eyes crinkling.

"You are my *fucking* favorite," he says, pulling me in for a hug. I wrap my arms around his waist and inhale deeply, smelling the water droplets and mint. I sigh audibly and he holds me closer.

"Come on, let's get you washed up."

He reaches over me and grabs the bottle of shampoo, pouring some into his hand. He washes my head, then his own. He pulls us under the water together, and the soap runs down the drain.

"Ashley was one lucky gal to be getting all that action," I muse aloud, then clamp my jaw shut when the words I uttered register.

But Chain just chuckles. “We didn’t really get into any of that.”

“Oh?” I say, equally relieved that it wasn’t true and that he didn’t seem to care about my comment.

“We weren’t right for each other. We barely had sex as it was, and I didn’t really let loose like I have with you.”

“Oh,” I repeat, smiling internally.

He rubs the conditioner into my hair as he continues. “To be honest, I’m not sure what came over me. It just felt... right, to do those things with you.”

“You didn’t like it?”

He stops with his hands in my hair. “Are you fucking kidding me?” His eyes search mine, showing me his sincerity. “I loved it.”

“Me too,” I smile widely.

“What I meant is that I feel like I want to do the things that make me happy when I’m around you. I don’t feel inhibited." He pauses. "I’m not wearing a mask.”

My heart flutters, recalling the conversation we had on the back of his truck. The fact that he feels so comfortable with me makes my heart soar.

“That makes me really happy.” It’s his turn to smile widely. We finish washing our bodies and step out of the shower. I run to grab him a towel from the hall closet since I only have mine hanging in here.

We dry off and return to my room, Chain with jeans in hand. He puts them on with his shirt from last night but doesn’t put the boxers on.

“Can you wash these for me? I have to get to work but I don’t want to wear these dirty boxers.”

“You’re going commando to work?” I ask with a giggle.

“Yeah, what’s so funny about that?” he asks.

"I feel like you're always so put together. The idea of you not wearing underwear just, I don't know," I say, laughing harder.

"Just, what?" He pulls my towel wrapped body to him. His eyes are full of mirth but as we deepen the gaze, the energy quickly changes to intense and serious.

"I love your eyes so much, Marlie," he whispers as he volleys between them. "You're so beautiful."

I blush and smile, butterflies swarming my belly. "You're beautiful, too."

We kiss lightly and he steps back, handing me the boxers. "I really have to go, but I don't want to."

"Wait, isn't it Sunday? You're working on a Sunday?"

"I work most days of the year. I make my own schedule for the most part, but there's always something to be done."

"Are you meeting Greg? Is that why he called?"

"Yeah, we need to review a report that just came in for one of our cases. It'll just be us in the office. I won't bore you with the details of it, but we're close to trial."

"I'd love to hear about it!" I hear the excitement in my tone and think I might be too forward, but he gives me a genuine smile.

"I'll catch you up on it later, then."

"Okay," I say with a slump.

"Thank you for... everything."

Thank you? "Um, no, thank you!" I say with too much enthusiasm.

Why is he thanking me?? Was this like a one time hookup deal? Like, 'thanks for the good fuck, see ya'??

"I'll walk you out," I say, pointing towards the bedroom door. He grabs his phone from the nightstand and pats his pockets, a look of confusion coming over him. "Where are my keys?"

My eyes meet his and it hits us at once.

"FUCK!" He runs out of the room and I chase after him, bolting out the front door and to his parked, *idling* truck.

As he throws the door open in a panic, I can't help the hysterical laughter that escapes me. He whips his head to me and for a moment, I think he's pissed. But then he steps down from the truck and joins me.

"What are you doing to me, Mar?" he says once our laughter dies down. His eyes search mine, but I'm at a loss for words. When I don't answer, he says, "I *really* have to go."

I nod and he starts to turn before adding, "Oh, and sorry about your necklace."

"Oh, I really don't care about that. I honestly didn't even notice I was still wearing the damn thing."

He gives me a skeptical look but nods his head, accepting my answer.

"Have a nice day," I say as he shuts his door. He waves and I watch his truck roll down the road, the euphoria of last night leaving with it.

Why didn't he kiss me goodbye?

I spent the rest of the day doing the typical Sunday shit. Well, my new typical Sunday shit. I ran a load of laundry, including Chain's boxers, and cleaned up around the condo. Oh, and I took the Z necklace from the tub with the M necklace in Zander's old nightstand and threw them in the big trash can outside.

I really need to start looking for a new place soon. This condo is too big for just me to stay in, and I want a fresh start. I don't want to be trapped in the memories of Zander and I. Especially now that Chain and I may be a thing.

Right?

The way he left today, without even a kiss, has had me a little worried. I've tried not to think too far into it, but I'd be lying if I said it wasn't gnawing at me. And thanking me after sex? What in the hell is that?

Maybe this was just a fun time for him. It certainly was for me, too, but I want more. I find myself craving him. Now that I've had a taste of that minty goodness, I don't want to stop.

But what if it's only one-sided, and he doesn't feel the same way about me?

He told you he's felt like this for a long time.

Yeah, but he didn't say what this is. Maybe he's just wanted to screw me!

I slam the door on the dryer and lug my laundry basket upstairs. I turn on the television and play How I Met Your Mother in the background as a distraction while I fold the laundry. Once everything is put away, I glance at the clock and find it's 8:13 pm.

That's late enough to get into bed. I'll go to sleep soon and go back to the work grind this week. I strip off my clothes and settle into the center of the bed, then reach for my phone on the nightstand. I plug it in and the screen illuminates, showing three notifications from Chain 15 minutes ago.

My heart skips a beat and I swipe across the screen in such a rush that the phone drops, clattering onto the nightstand.

"Fuck!" I lift up and recollect it, bringing it to me on the bed. I settle back in before swiping again in a calm, collected manner.

Chain loved your photo.

Chain: I can't stop thinking about last night

Chain: and this morning ;)

I smile widely, feeling silly for having worried at all. I laugh at the fact that he actually hearted the photo from months ago. But hey, better late than never, right?

Me: Me neither. I want to do more of that.

It only takes a second for his chat bubble to appear, but the message stays on delivered. He keeps his read receipts off– noted. We start texting back and forth.

Chain: Good, because more is coming.

Me: Does that mean I don't have a choice?

Chain: You always have a choice.

Chain: But no.

Me: Lol. Well in that case...

Chain: Do you like teasing me?

Me: Maybe

Chain: Tease me, then.

I pause, unsure of how to respond. It's honestly unbelievable that he and Ashley didn't have much sex because he seems so confident and I feel a little out of place. What if I can't keep up?

Wait.

I jump out of bed and dig in my bottom drawer, locating a lingerie set I hadn't used in years. It's a black lace, babydoll cut piece that accentuates my breasts and flows over my abdomen with a slit. The thong is more like a scrap of fabric, just covering my vagina and digging all the way into my ass.

I throw it on and jump back in bed, opening my camera. I purse my lips and arch my brow, giving my best seductive look while pressing my breasts together. I snap a few, then send the best one off to him.

I wait with bated breath as the bubbles pop up. After two minutes, my nerves are sky high. I scoot off the bed to remove the outfit, feeling discouraged, when I hear my phone vibrate and lunge at it.

Chapter Forty-Six

Chain

Me: I'm coming over.

Me: Don't change.

Marlie: What if I don't want you to come over?

Oh, baby girl.

I have to work early in the morning, but seeing her in that sexy lingerie left me with no other choice.

Me: Unlock the door for me and wait upstairs.

Marlie: Yes sir

I've never necessarily gotten off on the word 'sir' but her desire to please and obey me on a sexual level changes my feelings on it. My rock hard dick throbs in my fist and I pump a few times before forcing myself to stop.

Wait for Marlie.

I rip the sheets off and make quick work of getting dressed, having to put my shirt on twice because the first time it was backwards. I swipe my keys off the entry table and quietly exit the house. It's a quarter after 9, which means Valerie is probably close to sleep and Frank is passed out drunk.

I speed the entire drive over to her, my cock pulsing with the need to feel her. I had to rub myself through my jeans a few times just to ease the ache. My mind keeps imagining different ways that I'll find her and each excites me more than the next.

But this time, I want to take it slow and easy. I want to make love to her. The need to make her mine took over so thoroughly, that I wanted to make sure she knew it. But now, I just want her to know how I feel about her.

I throw the car into park after finding a free parallel spot. I take out my phone to text her that I'm here before remembering that I told her to unlock the door. I flex my muscles in anticipation of how I'll find her waiting for me.

Damn, I should have picked up flowers.

I make sure to turn the engine off this time, then hop out of my truck and search the area for flowers. Locating a patch of wildflowers near a neighboring complex, I jog over and grab a single yellow flower, picking it near the surrounding grass so there's a long stem.

I open her door and the moment I shut it behind me, I feel nervous. I have a flower in hand and I'm prepared to make love to this woman...

Who the hell have I become?!

I laugh internally, because I know damn well this is exactly where I want to be. I don't care if I'm becoming a lovesick puppy, she's well worth it. I pad up the stairs, making sure I can be heard so I don't scare her. When I get to the landing, I find that her door is shut but there's a flickering light visible from the crack underneath.

As I walk closer with a vise grip on the flower, I smell *her* smell—jasmine and rain. I place my free hand on the door knob and take a deep, steadying breath. I open the door to find three candles on one of the nightstands, casting a sensual light over Marlie's body.

She's sprawled out in the center of the bed, her legs open to display the tiny piece of black fabric covering her sweet center. I lick my lips hungrily, my eyes raking over the rest of her. She did keep the outfit on, but she freed her breasts. One of her hands cups her breast, playing with the nipple in a teasing motion, and the other hand is tossed above her head.

I leave the best for last. Her eyes are hooded and filled with the same heat I feel. She nips at her lower lip, giving me the slightest head nod when my eyes meet hers. I leap onto the bed, forgetting myself, the flower, and any other motive I had.

I need to taste her on my tongue, *now*. I place the flower on her stomach, which is exposed from the split in the lingerie she wears. Leaving the panties on in my haste, I move the scrap of fabric over with my index finger, then lick from her opening to her clit.

She moans instantly, and I'm happy to find that she's already wet. I scoot up and take in her lust filled eyes.

"Were you playing with yourself before I got here?"

"I couldn't help myself," she whispers. My cock throbs and I hump the bed, unable to resist needing *some* sort of touch.

"These lips belong to an angel." I place a tender kiss on her lips.

"But these"—I palm her pussy—"these belong to the damn devil, and I'm ready to burn in hell." My tongue dives into her, soaking up the new surge of wetness and eliciting another moan from her. I move the tip of my tongue to her clit, keeping a slow, torturous pace while I push two fingers inside of her.

I curl them on her G-spot, pulsing and thrumming them against her. She opens her legs further, allowing me to get deeper. I pick up the speed of my tongue and she tightens her legs.

"*Fuck,* Chain."

I smile against her, refusing to stop to speak. I want to make her feel as good as she always makes *me* feel, and this is the surest way to do it. I press my body up and use my shoulders to keep her legs spread for me.

She moans and tells me how close she is. I coax her orgasm out, adding a finger and flicking my tongue on her clit at lightning speed. When she comes, she does so with infinite moans.

"That's it, baby." I kiss her thigh when she's finished, but I leave my fingers inside.

"Mmmm."

I smirk and continue toying with her, feeling all the creaminess from her orgasm.

"Do you have another one for me?"

"Oh, I don't ever really come back to back," she says.

I can't help the cocky grin that washes over me. "That's about to change."

Removing my fingers, I crawl over her and take the flower into my mouth. She laughs when I bring my lips to hers, then takes the flower with her own teeth.

"I needed you so badly I didn't think of stopping for flowers until I got here. I picked this outside."

She takes the flower out of her mouth and places it on the nightstand with no candles. “Honestly? I like this more.”

I kiss her slowly, easing my tongue on hers and exploring all of her. I run my hands across her breasts, her waist and her hips, then slide a single finger down her slit. She’s so wet that I moan.

“That’s all because of you,” she says against my lips. She moves quickly, biting into my neck and sucking.

"Only me?" I extend my neck to provide her more access.

"Only you." *Damn right.*

I run the pad of my finger over her clit lightly and she squirms from the sensitivity. I alternate between fingering her and teasing her clit. She hasn't stopped for air once since relatching onto my neck, and I know damn well she'll leave a mark.

I should care, but I don't.

"Let me—" *let me make love to you.* "Let me show you how much you mean to me."

That makes her release me, and her eyes shoot to mine. We search each other, entering that hypnotic place where our eyes allow our souls to meet.

"Answer me." I use the same words, but they're softer. I don't mean them with the same demand. I mean them with the need to know she wants me to show her; that she feels the same way.

She only nods her head, but that's more than enough. I pull back from her and peel my shirt off, watching as her eyes skim over my bare chest. I unbutton my pants while holding her stare, then dig in the pocket to find a condom.

"Shit."

"What?"

I stare at her as the disappointment washes over me. "I don't have a condom."

She chews the inside of her cheek. "I'm fine not using one if you are."

I keep my eyes trained on her. It's reckless, I know it is. We should get tested first. But then again, we were both in committed relationships.

"I've already told you, I'm *yours*."

Her words make the decision for me. I crawl over her and hold her head as I place a tender kiss on her lips. She swipes her tongue over my bottom lip and I meet it with my own, sighing. I line my dick up with her entrance and we moan at the same time when I push in.

All I can think is how I never want to stop doing this.

Chapter Forty-Seven

Marlie

"A part of me thought maybe you didn't want to keep doing this," I say, nuzzling into his chest.

"If that's what you thought I haven't done a proper job of letting you know just how much you mean to me," he replies with a frown. He moves, jostling me off of him as he stands from the bed.

"Well, abandoning the cuddles doesn't make it any clearer," I say sarcastically. I watch him put his jeans on, sans boxers, zipping and buttoning them. They sit low on his hips and I lick my bottom lip with the memory of all the things he just did to me.

"I'll be right back."

He rushes out of the room and I watch his back as he leaves down the hall to the stairs. I hear the front door slam shut and stare off into the silence as I wonder what the hell he could be doing. He returns a few moments later, the door slamming shut again and his footsteps ascending on the stairs.

"I planned on giving you this on a romantic date," he says with a sheepish grin as he enters the room. "Luckily, I picked this up today so it was still in my car."

I sit up and he takes the spot next to me on the bed, his legs dangling off the side. "You did turn off the ignition this time, right?"

"Yes. *You* weren't there to distract me." He reaches into his pocket and pulls out a small, blue silk bag. He dangles it by the tied strings in front of me and I take it.

"I hope you like it."

I gape at him and he smiles shyly, a look I haven't seen on him before.

What in the world?

I open the bag slowly and reach in, pulling out a necklace. The icy-blue, heart shaped crystal falls, entwined in an infinity symbol with diamonds along one of the ridges. It's strung on a thin chain and it twinkles in the candlelight.

"Wow, this is..."

Beautiful. Surprising. Meaningful. Amazing.

The words sift through my brain but I say none of them, because this is just too much, too soon.

Isn't it?

"I felt bad about breaking your necklace and I wanted to give you a gift. I hope it helps you remember what you mean to me."

"Didn't you tell me once that a man giving you jewelry means they're claiming you?" I ask him with a quirked brow. He only smiles in response.

"Isn't this too soon?" I whisper. I wasn't plan on jumping into something so quickly and somehow, we've had sex a few times and he's basically asking me to be his.

"Too soon according to who? I by no means want to push you. If you don't want to wear it, don't. But I know how I feel and I wanted you to know it, too."

I gape at him again, feeling like a fish out of water. My wide eyes stare at him and he only returns my look with an honest one.

"When did you start to like me?" I blurt out. If he wants me to know how he feels, I want to know all of it.

"A while ago," he says, nudging my leg with his knee. I scoot over and he settles back into the bed, his back resting against the pillows propped on the wall. I remain cross-legged, listening.

"When we first met, it was wild. Nothing I had ever experienced before, that's for sure. It was like... the world stopped for a moment. Like I couldn't hear anything else around me, but I could see so clearly for the first time. You know?"

I nod my head fervently.

"Obviously, I was with Ashley. I soon learned that you were with Zander. So, I just didn't give it much thought. Or I tried not to, anyway. But every time I saw you, every time I thought about you, I couldn't shake this feeling that I needed to be closer to you. To protect you. To know everything there is to know about you."

I stare at him, unblinking. "I felt it, too."

He smiles. "Let me show you something."

"What, did you get me matching earrings?"

He laughs and grabs his phone from the night stand, scrolling through it for a minute.

"You asked me about that photo of the scales, and why I didn't reply. But look at this."

He hands me his phone and it's open to his photo gallery, on a picture of scales. But it's not the photo I sent him. It's a different set of scales in a different place. I tap on the screen and the date and time pop up. I think back to Stella and Jace's wedding, calculating...

Holy shit.

My eyes shoot to his.

"It was the night before I sent my photo."

He nods, a sad and knowing smile painted across his cheeks.

"I thought better of sending it to you after thinking through my intentions. I knew what you were to me, even then. You were never *just* a friend."

His words hover around us, like a magic spell that was cast from a wand. We stare at each other, the same way we always have, and allow the truth of that to settle into our bones.

"Didn't you ever feel guilty?" I ask quietly.

"Guilty? Why would I feel guilty?"

"I felt so wrong. Like, how could I do that to Zander, after I knew the pain of being cheated on?" I tear my eyes away from him.

"We didn't cheat!"

"No, I know. But it just felt wrong. Like I was hurting him, whether he knew it or not."

"You can't help how you feel."

"That's what everyone keeps saying," I mutter.

"Hey," he says softly. I look at him and he gives me a sympathetic look. "What happened with Jack?"

I sigh, but decide it's best if I just fill him in. "We met in college. He was studying pre-law, and I didn't know what the hell I wanted." I give him a tight lipped smile. "I still don't. But we dated for about a year when I found out he was cheating on me. It shattered me and I dumped him."

I watch his eyes turn to fire. "How did you find out?"

"That's actually kind of an interesting story. Probably one Stella could tell you better than I can. But basically, we were all in the car together on our way to a frat party. I opened the center console to get the aux cable and I saw a bracelet in there, which wasn't mine."

"What, and he just admitted that he cheated on you?"

I laugh. "No. I pulled it out and asked him whose it was. He was quick, and said it had to be mine. Obviously, I would know if it was mine or not. Then he said one of his friends must have left it in there or something, that he had no idea whose it was."

"So how did you confirm?"

"I was prepared to let it go. We got to the party and at some point, he took off to say hi to some friends. Stella yanked me into the bathroom and pulled the damn bracelet out of her pocket."

I smile in reminiscence; leave it to Stella to pull some sneaky shit like that.

"She said there was no way one of his friends just left it in the car. We inspected the bracelet for any indication of who it might belong to, but that was a dead end. Her disbelief had me questioning things, though. He had been acting strangely the past few months and I kind of just ignored it."

"Please tell me you went PI on him."

I laugh again. "That's exactly what I did. Well, what Stella and I did. She deserves the credit, really. She took a photo of the bracelet and posted it in the Facebook group for our campus, saying she found it at the party."

"That couldn't have worked."

"Oh, yes it did. We knew it was a long shot. But within the hour, a girl named Sydney Gresher sent her a private message. I didn't know her. They arranged to meet up, and I showed up with Stella. I flat out asked her if she'd hooked up with Jack, and she said yes."

"Wow," Chain says to me with wide eyes.

"It was pretty crazy. I told her he was my boyfriend and she looked so remorseful. She told us the entire story of how they'd been hooking up for a few weeks at parties. She didn't even realize she left the bracelet in his car, but she said it made sense. I guess she would be pretty drunk when it happened. She had no idea he had a girlfriend."

"Well, I hope she also ended things with him," Chain says.

"From the sounds of it, there wasn't a thing to end. It seemed like if the opportunity struck, they fucked and didn't speak again. But that was it. I confronted Jack and he denied it. Eventually, he admitted to one time but I *know* it was more than that. I was already suspicious when we found the bracelet."

"Wait. You said this happened multiple times?"

"Yeah."

"Motherfucker..."

"What?" I ask.

"He lied to me about that, too. He said it happened once."

"Yeah, well, he's a liar. How were you even friends with him, anyway?"

"A lack of proper judgment, obviously. I always knew he fucked around and didn't care who was with who. But we worked together and I just didn't think much of it. I should have, though."

"He's charismatic, that's for sure. It's hard not to like him."

"Yeah... Well, we're not friends anymore. I fucked him up good after he called you."

"You what?!" I exclaim.

"You think I was just going to let him walk away after he tried to talk to you again? Hell no. If I'd known you in college and found out about any of this, I would have beat his ass to a pulp."

"I had no idea you could be so... violent."

"I wrestled for years in high school and college. I was in my prime back then. No way would he have gotten away with that shit."

He looks like he ate a rotten egg, his eyes tinged with disgust and his upper lip curled.

"But you could have been arrested!"

He shrugs. "Worth it."

I smile widely at that. "Thank you for this. Seriously."

"I try to leave my fighting days in the past. It's not a good look for an attorney. But I'd fuck anyone up for you."

I wiggle the necklace, the dangling pendant shining in the reflection of the light. "I meant this."

"Oh," he says. "Can I put it on you?"

I nod my head and hand him the necklace, turning so he can clasp it around my neck. He fixes my hair over it and I turn to face him.

"It's only beautiful *because* of you," he says, affection oozing from his lips. I smile and bite my lower lip, my cheeks reddening with the sincerity I hear in his tone and the sweetness of his compliment.

"I love it," I say. He plants a light, sweet kiss on my lips and then hops out of bed, removing his jeans.

"I need to be up early for work. I wasn't anticipating a late night," he says with a wink.

"You're sleeping over again?"

"Unless you want me to leave." I shake my head and he settles us under the covers.

I never want you to leave.

"Two nights in a row?"

I nod my head at Eli, unable to hide the satisfaction in my grin. He raises his eyebrows.

"And a necklace? Damn, chica, he's in love with you."

"Stop!" The grin is wiped off my face immediately and I stop dead in my tracks. We're on our way back to the mailing room after our break at the lake. I caught him up on everything that happened between Chain and I. Well, *almost* everything. I didn't tell him any details about the sex, or the way he turned me on with just a few authoritative words.

I didn't tell him about how comfortable I felt with him, more comfortable than I've felt with anyone else. I didn't tell him how he easily coaxed orgasms from me like a bee collects pollen. I certainly didn't tell him how I haven't stopped thinking about his dick in my mouth, and how I want it in my ass.

"What?" he scoffs, continuing his brisk walk which forces me to trail behind him. "He's already sleeping over and he gave you *jewelry,* Marlie." He pins me with a pointed look. "And he's knocking out other men because of you."

"You know about that?!" I stop dead in my tracks for the second time. This time, Eli stops with me.

"So he did?"

"You just said he did!"

"I was pretty sure he did. I saw his knuckles, I heard his words. I put two and two together."

"Why do you always seem to know things?"

"Don't hate the player, girlie."

I roll my eyes and stalk off, annoyed with his coy games. He jogs to catch up. "So it's true, then?"

I don't answer him, staring straight ahead.

In love with me?

Goddamn it, I think Eli might be right.

Chapter Forty-Eight

Chain

Me: I'm here

Marlie walks down the path thirty seconds later, her auburn hair blowing wildly behind her. The incoming storm has the winds stronger than usual, and it makes her look stunning. The casual navy and white striped tee fits snugly with her regular, blue jeans.

A common outfit transformed to look like it came straight out of a modeling page. She's so gorgeous and I can't get enough. As she approaches the car I circle to her side to open her door.

"Hi, beautiful," I say.

"You really don't have to open my door every time."

"I want to."

She rolls her eyes but also smiles. Something tells me that while she doesn't expect me to do chivalrous acts, she absolutely loves them.

"You look as gorgeous as always, baby girl."

"Thank you," she says with a blush. "You don't look so bad yourself."

I've gotten accustomed to the improv attire, wearing my own pair of jeans and a dark blue polo. I offered for us to ride together tonight because she's on my way, anyway. Why waste the gas?

And I couldn't wait to see her. What is it about her that makes me want to be around her all the time?

I also want to take her to my new house tonight. I signed and got the keys yesterday, and I'm so excited to show her my new place. But I haven't told her yet.

It feels... vulnerable, somehow. Like showing her where I'll be living and opening up this new side of our relationship will deepen things. I'm acutely aware that we're essentially in the beginning phase of whatever this is.

It's exciting. It's new. It's passionate and fun.

But I can feel something deeper below all of that. There's a feeling of rawness that I want to explore. Something I've never experienced before.

Showing her my new house is potentially showing her where we might live one day. It's crazy to think about a future with Marlie but I can't not think about it. I want to be around her all the time, tell her about my days; you know, that typical corny shit.

Oh, fuck.

"So you guys rode together?"

"Yeah, so? I'm on his way."

"Mhm, sure. That's what it is."

Marlie lands a playful punch on Eli's shoulder and while there's a shallow rumble of envy, I know they're just close friends. I'd never want to control her, but I'd be lying if I didn't want all her touches reserved for me.

I approach them in the parking lot, wiping my hands dry on my jeans since there were no paper towels in the bathroom. I take the mints out of my pocket and pop one into my mouth, holding the tin out when I reach them.

"Thanks, man," Eli says as they each grab one. Pocketing the container, my hand twitches instinctively to reach out and pull Marlie into me. But my brain is resistant.

We haven't outright had the talk, or whatever, regarding whatever *this* is. It all feels so surreal. Only a few weeks ago, she was engaged to another man and I was leaving my excuse of a relationship.

Isn't it too soon for all of this? Shouldn't we take it slow? Should we have given more time to even fuck?

These are the kinds of thoughts that have tormented me all week. But my heart, that organ I've never paid attention to before, has had a lot to say in response.

"Everyone's going over to Vigs, do you want to go?" Marlie asks. Her body faces Eli but I can feel that magnetic pull to her; the same one that had my hand twitching moments ago.

"Sure. But I'd like to show you something first, if that's okay."

"Oh. Um, yeah," she replies, glancing at Eli before taking a step towards me.

"I'll catch you guys there," he says with a knowing smirk. *Asshole probably thinks we're going to fuck.*

Honestly, not a bad idea.

When he runs to catch up with the others across the walkway, I take a step closer to Marlie. Our bodies are so close but neither of us reaches out. The energy hums, and my palms itch with the desire to touch her. Our eyes meet in that magical way they always do.

"What are you showing me?"

"Come on."

I reach out and take her hand, her fingers clasping with mine. I feel an immediate ease in the tension I didn't realize

I was holding. I walk her past the cars and cross the street, pausing in front of the little house that's now mine.

"You closed on the house?" she asks breathlessly.

"Yep." I dig the keys out of my pocket and dangle them in front of her, the jingle ringing in my ears. I don't expect her to reach out and snatch them, then run up the short walkway that leads to the entry.

I laugh as she fumbles with the keys to figure out which one goes to the door. I come up behind her and wind my arms around her waist, planting a kiss on her neck before pulling the right key for her.

"Thanks," she whispers, putting it into the lock. She opens the door but we don't move, staring into the house. It's an open layout with sliding glass doors at the end, looking straight into the yard full of luscious trees.

"There's no power yet, so we'll have to use our phones for light," I explain, stepping away from her. We turn on our phone flashlights and step inside, taking in the white tile floors and the light pink walls.

"It needs a little work, but it'll do for now," I say. "There are 2 bedrooms and 2 bathrooms."

"It's perfect."

I take her down the hallway to the right, which leads to the primary bedroom straight ahead and a spare bedroom to the left. The hallway bathroom is on the right.

"When did you get the keys?" she asks.

"Yesterday."

She stops her perusal of the spare room to stare at me. "This is your first time here?"

"Yes."

"Oh."

"Is that a problem?"

"No, I just..." I patiently wait for her to explain. "I'm part of the first experience here."

I laugh. "Well, I toured it before making an offer. But yes, you are the first guest I've had in ownership."

"That feels like a lot of pressure."

I pull her into me without thinking about it. It feels so natural to hold her, touch her, kiss her. *Fuck her.* How had we ever resisted this?

"I want you here. It's that simple." I plant a tender kiss on her head and hold her, her head resting on my chest.

"Come on, let me show you my bedroom."

I lead her to the primary, watching as she takes the room in.

"When do we get to christen it?"

"Don't tempt me, Marlie. I'll take you right on this cold, hard floor if you ask me to."

Even with just the light of the phones, I can see the heat smolder in her eyes. My dick hardens.

"Take me," she breathes. I'm on her in an instant, pulling her face within a mere inch from mine. My fingers curl around her belt loop, yanking her to me. I inhale deeply, taking in her jasmine scent. I'm pleased to find that she also smells like a hint of mint; like a hint of *me*.

"I should," I draw out slowly. Our breaths mingle in the infinitesimal space between our lips. "I should fuck you bare, right now. Make you scream my name."

She inhales sharply.

"But—we told our friends we'd meet them, and I don't want to rush the first time I fuck you in my house."

I press my erection into her so there's no mistaking how much I want her. She pushes her hips to rub on me in the most erotic way. I pull on her hair from the base, craning her neck so it's exposed to me. I scrape my teeth along her carotid artery, feeling the thrum of her heightened pulse.

I pull back suddenly. "Let's go."

I can hear her panting and my dick jumps in eagerness. *Patience, little friend.*

"Your parents are going to be there?!"

I grip the steering wheel to restrain my laughter at her nervous expression.

"Not parents, just Valerie. My mom," I say.

"It's a little soon for that, don't you think?"

"You seem to have a lot of nerves about the pacing of our relationship."

"So now we're in a relationship?"

"What else would you call this, Mar?"

She chews her bottom lip and stares out the window. I bring my hand to her knee and give it a squeeze.

"We don't have to do anything you don't want to."

"It's not that... I want to. I *want* to, Chain. But I thought..." I give her knee another encouraging squeeze. "I thought I was going to stay single for some time after Zander. You know, get a new place, do my own thing for a while."

"Okay, so do that."

"But I'm meeting your mom!"

"You're helping me paint my house! It doesn't have to be a big deal. Maybe it feels like one to you because this feels more real than you want to admit."

I came to terms with my feelings for Marlie. I thought about them as I would hold her to sleep. In the last week since I'd shown her my house, I spent every night at hers. We fucked, we talked, we cuddled. We did it all. And I decided to stop fighting what she means to me.

"This wasn't how it was supposed to go." I can hear the struggle in her voice, the same struggle I've experienced these past few months.

"Fuck the plan! Fuck. The. Plan. Life is happening while you're *making* plans, Marlie."

I receive nothing but silence. At first I think she needs to let that sink in. But when her silence goes on for minutes, I feel uncertain. Maybe I was too harsh.

"I'm sorry, I don't mean to be pushy."

"You're not being pushy. You're not wrong, Chain. I'm just struggling with it. *You* were never part of the plan."

It's my turn to be silent. I know what she means, but that doesn't stop the sting in my chest.

"I guess it just proves that the best things in life are the ones we can't plan for."

My cheeks hurt from the smile her words plaster on my face.

We spent the weekend painting the walls from pink to white. Each stroke of the paint brush felt like a new color to my life. A new beginning.

She met Valerie and although I had insisted it wasn't a big deal, I could feel that it was. Especially after Valerie called me that night to tell me how much she liked Marlie.

Marlie was going through her own beginning, too. Next weekend we were moving her stuff to her new studio apartment. She would be within a ten minute driving distance but it still felt too far. A crazy part of me wishes we could live together already, but I know that's too ridiculous.

I'd taken the following week off from work to move all my stuff into the house. I kept sleeping at Marlie's, though. She needed help packing after work and I was happy to oblige.

This all feels so different with her. I don't need to know the details of where we'll end up. I just know I need to end up there with her.

Chapter Forty-Nine

Marlie

"I think that's everything!"

We loaded all of my belongings into Chain's truck and the U-Haul I rented. I'm so ready to move forward with the life I didn't plan.

"Can you give me a few minutes to do a last check?" I say to Chain. He's wearing a black hat, black gym shorts, and white tank top. He looks scrumptious and perfect and *mine*.

"Do you want me to come with you?"

"No." He gives me a nod, silently understanding. *I love him for that.*

I go back into the condo and do a tour of the bottom floor first, then the top, leaving the bedroom for last. I say a silent goodbye as all the memories whiz past. I think about all the times Zander and I shared here.

A tear rolls down my cheek and I let the sadness take over. This is it. Out with the old and in with the new. Once I walk out of here, I'm locking the door on this life for the final time.

I start to sob, mourning the life I thought was meant for me. I say a silent thank you to Zander for everything we shared and let him go with a goodbye. I turn out the light and shut the bedroom door, knowing that this is the start of something new.

Chain waits for me at the end of his truck with his arms crossed in front of his chest. When he sees me, he opens them and I run to him, sobbing again.

He pets my hair soothingly, remaining silent because words are not what I need. And somehow, he seems to understand that. When the tears subside, he pulls me away and searches my eyes.

"Ready?"

I nod. "Ready."

He wipes the tear streaks from my cheeks and gives me a sympathetic smile.

"I love you."

Woah.

He responds to my widened eyes. "I know. I know it's too soon. I know you're still grappling with all of this. But I love you, Marlie, and I just needed you to know that."

"I love you, too," I say easily. When the words leave my mouth I don't regret them in the slightest. I feel a rumbling in my chest, and it takes me a moment to realize it's the chasm's fissure shifting to a close.

Our lips meet for the most passionate kiss we've ever shared, backing everything those words mean. And even though I'm moving to a new place, I know that he's my home.

"What do you *mean* the place isn't ready?!"

"I'm so sorry, ma'am—"

"Sorry isn't going to fix my situation! Why didn't you call me?"

"We went to change the keys this morning and he was back in there. It was our fault, we should have changed them right away."

"So kick him out!"

"He's refusing to leave. We're going to have to evict him."

"THIS IS—"

"Marlie." Chain's steady voice breaks my focus, providing a pause in my rage. My head whips to him and his emerald eyes give me the calm I need. "You can keep your things at my place while they sort this out."

I blink a few times, taking a deep breath and willing myself to calm the fuck down. How in the fuck can my place not be ready?!

"That's very kind of you, baby, but that's not the point. What if I had no one?"

"We're so sorry, Ms. Greenwood. We can offer you a full refund of your deposit if you'd prefer not to wait."

I stare at the office manager, the rage bubbling back up again. Chain shifts beside me and his energy grounds me. I breathe in and force myself to respond.

"I need to get out of here. I'll think about it and let you know," I say, grabbing my keys off the counter and stalking out of the office. The door jingles and Chain follows a step behind.

"Hey." He grabs my hand and stops me. I round on him but when I see the kindness in his orbs, I pause.

"I'm sorry, it's just... what in the actual fuck!"

"I know. They're idiots," he says supportively. "Let's just go to my place and we can figure out what to do next."

I huff. "Fine."

I get into the U-Haul and he gets in his truck. I follow him to his house, fuming the whole way there. Here's the thing—if these last few months have taught me *anything,* it's that the universe sends you signs. It waves a damn flag in front of your face, but it's up to you to decipher the meaning.

If I unload these trucks at Chain's house, I know what's going to happen.

I'll never leave.

And it will just be another plan ruined. This was supposed to be *my* time. Live on my own, figure out what I want, and get to know myself.

Ugh, why the fuck are you doing this to me?!

This is one of those times where you can't help but wonder what the fuck is out there pulling the strings.

Maybe it's time to just let them.

"You know, I'm kind of sad that your bed is in here now."

"Why's that?" Chain strokes my arm as I'm cuddled into him.

"I was really hoping you would take me on the floor." He gives me a heated look and I reach to his cock, finding it rock hard already. I stroke it lightly, brushing the head with my fingertips.

"I'm going to do just that. But first, I want to tell you something."

I continue stroking his cock lazily. It responds with short pulses, but Chain's focus is on me.

"I don't want you to feel any pressure. But I don't care if you never leave."

I only smile, because I knew this was coming. I'd already called the apartment complex for my refund.

Chain misreads my silence. "Let me amend that. I *want* you to stay."

"Okay," I say.

"Okay?"

I take his cock in my fist, squeezing and grinding myself into his leg. He growls and jumps over me in an instant, scooping my ass into his hands. My legs wrap around him instinctively and his dick is lined up with my entrance.

"I love that you're mine."

"Willingly," I purr.

He lifts off me, my pussy aching immediately from the loss of heat. He leaps off the bed and points to the floor.

"Come."

I waste no time in moving off the bed and standing in front of him. He assesses me first, his eyes crawling over me from head to toe. He turns hungry, licking his lips with his cock standing at full erection.

"Get on your hands and knees."

I drop to the floor, turning so my ass is to his front. He stands over me, stroking my ass gingerly. I feel as my pussy floods with wetness, my clit throbbing with the need to be touched.

"Don't move," he orders. I hear him shuffle through his dresser drawer and return to my back, then a low pop and a squirt from a bottle.

"Can you take all of me, baby girl?" I nod and he uses two fingers to cover my asshole with the substance. "Say it."

"I can take all of you."

I hear him stroke himself, covering his huge dick with lube, preparing to tear right into me. I'm surprisingly turned on, my pussy and ass clenching in anticipation.

"Once I'm all the way in, you can start playing with yourself. I want you to enjoy this as much as I do. It should go without saying, but if at any point you want me to stop, you say so."

I nod again, then gulp. "Okay."

He drops to his knees and brings a finger to my asshole. It clenches in immediate response.

"You're going to need to relax, baby."

I breathe, begging my muscles to relax. He circles the rim before pushing the pad of his finger in. *Mmm.*

"You like that, don't you, baby girl?"

I moan and nod my head, nearly embarrassed with how wet I am. I push my ass an inch back so his finger goes a little deeper.

"Greedy girl," he growls. "I'm going to give you what you want, don't worry."

He pushes in a second finger, both only a knuckle deep. He pulls them apart, scissoring to stretch me out. I moan and push back a little more, my pussy heating and tightening.

He removes his fingers and I lose my breath as he grips my hips and flips me over. I land on the cold tile floor, my cheek bones smacking into the hardness. Goosebumps cover my skin and my nipples harden.

"I want to watch you take me." He crawls towards me on his knees, lifting my legs and spreading them. He holds my legs with the crook of his elbows as he brings his dick to me.

"Lay down and arch your back, baby."

I do as he instructs, the position opening up my ass to him. His head sits at my tight hole, and I start to pant, my heart racing.

I don't know if I can do this.

"Are you scared?"

He remains in position, motionless. His eyes are hooded and smoldering, giving me confidence to proceed.

"A little."

"You can take it, baby. Lean into the pain."

I nod, unsure of what else I can say. He pushes forward a bit, the pressure building.

"Relax."

I didn't even realize I was clenching again. I focus on deep breaths, feeling myself loosen.

"Good girl." He pushes his tip in slowly. I immediately clench, wanting to reject this pressure. It burns a little, but the amount of lube he has on makes it so it doesn't sting.

"Relax," he says, a bite to his tone. I obey and he pushes forward an inch more. I keep my focus solely on keeping my muscles loose, finding that it helps with the pressure. He bores into my eyes, and when I don't say anything, he pushes all the way forward in one clean motion.

The pain I feel isn't as extreme as I thought it would be, but it's there. I can't grab onto him because I'm lying completely on the floor. I grab my thighs and grip hard, my nails digging into my skin.

"Rub your clit."

I do as he says, and the impact is instantaneous. I dip into my pussy to moisten my finger and then rub my clit at high speed. I moan and both holes tighten in pleasure.

"I'm going to move now."

He slowly pulls out, the pain growing exponentially. But the part I didn't expect is that the pleasure does, too. I lose control, my eyes rolling into the back of my head and my moans turning into animalistic whimpers.

"I knew you would fucking like this. You're such a good girl for me."

I moan more, not caring what I sound like.

"But I need you to look at me."

I'm not sure that I can. I'm high on ecstasy and pleasure, unable to control anything in my body other than the finger rubbing my clit to completion. His head is at the edge and he shoves back into me with alarming power. I scream and my eyes open in shock.

"That's a good girl. Remember, when you close your eyes, I will force you to look at me."

I nod my head like a crazy person, equally afraid and excited. I keep my eyes on him, watching him stare at the place where our bodies are joined. He watches himself move in and out of me in short thrusts.

I'm already so close, my clit throbbing and shooting tingles throughout my entire body. I've never felt this good in my entire life, I'm certain of it. I haven't stopped whimpering and moaning, shouting his name along with gods and fucks.

"I'm taking it easy on you for the first time. The next time I take your tight little asshole, I'm going to make you *bleed."*

I'm not sure if he's serious and at this point, I don't care. The idea of it is what brings me to my climax, literally screaming as I moan his name. My pussy seeps moisture down to my asshole and I feel it coat his dick as it moves in me at a faster pace.

As I peak he shoves into me and joins me in ecstasy, moaning my name as he pumps his cum into me. We come down together and he pulls out of me, dropping my legs and landing on top of me.

"Holy fuck," he pants.

"Goddamn," I say, my eyes shutting. We lay there for a few moments, my breaths short with the comfortable weight of him laying over me.

"I fucking love you," he says over my lips, landing a wet kiss on them. "And I love fucking you."

"Mmmm." That's all I'm capable of saying. He chuckles and lifts off me. I hear the bathroom door open and the sink turn on. He washes his hands and dick, then returns with a warm towel, wiping me clean while I lay with my eyes closed in a pleasant high.

"I love seeing you like this, knowing I did that to you."

"I love that you *can* do this to me," I reply, the high subsiding enough for my voice to return. He tosses the towel to the bathroom floor and scoops me up into his arms, bringing me to the bed. He puts the covers over me and gives me a look of pure adoration.

"I love you."

"I love you, too. And you were right. I *did* like it."

"Everyone's coming at 7, we have to go if we want to get everything ready," Chain says as he packs up the umbrella and his towel. I lift up to my elbows and stare out at the ocean, the sunshine glimmering on the small ripples.

"One last dip in the ocean," I barter. He smiles and obliges, holding his hand out to help me up. We walk quickly across the hot sand, the water lapping around our ankles. I fall into the water and Chain joins me, pulling me to him and holding my back to his front. The pendant hanging from my neck glistens in the sunlight.

"I'm so happy we met, Mar," he whispers into my neck.

"Me, too," I reply, turning my head up to him, squinting against the sun. He kisses me deeply, his love for me pouring from his lips.

"Next time, I'm going to fuck you right in this water," he murmurs against my lips. I bite his lower lip and he turns me around at the waist, gripping my ass and grinding his hard cock into the thin layer between him and my pussy.

We soak in the water for a few more minutes, then pack up the rest of our stuff. We're having a housewarming party for Chain's purchase and my moving in. Of course we invited the improv class, as well as Chain's friends. I was hesitant about inviting Stella and Jace, but Chain was insistent that I should. She'd responded with gusto, saying she couldn't wait to see us together.

I was pretty nervous when we told people we were dating *and* that we were living together. Mother was the scariest, but after she called me stupid and said I was crazy, she came by and complimented Chain on his house. After facing her, she lost the power she had over me. I don't care what she thinks anymore—my happiness is the only one that matters.

Our improv friends were happy for us, most claiming they saw this coming a mile away. Eli was especially obnoxious, rubbing it good and well into our faces that he knew it before we did. I was going to meet Chain's friends as his girlfriend tonight, but he was certain there would be no judgment.

And honestly, I don't even care if there is. It's my life, and I know first hand the events that transpired these past few months to bring us here. I was meant to fall in love with Chain all along.

For the first time in my life, I feel like I'm no longer drifting. I'm finally settling into where I'm meant to be.

Also By Amanda Bentley

Festive Fun Series

The Festive Fun Series is a romantic suspense series with darker themes than your average contemporary romance. If you are looking for light and fluffy holiday reads, this isn't it. The series features mature themes and content that may not be suitable for all audiences. For content warnings, please check the author's profile links @amandabentley-books.

The Holiday Hookup (Festive Fun #1)
Struck by Stupid (Festive Fun # 2)
Sh*t Out of Luck (Festive Fun # 3)
Light Me Up (Festive Fun # 4)

Author's Note

Thank you so much for reading my debut novel! I have so many books planned and hope you'll love them as much as I do. Now, if only I could write them as fast as I dream them...

One of the biggest ways you can show an indie author support is by leaving a review for the book! You can find Drift on Goodreads and Amazon. I'd also love to connect with you on social media! Find me on TikTok and Instagram @amandabentleybooks and join Amanda's Crotch-Splotchers group on Facebook! (To understand the group name, you need to read The Holiday Hookup.)

Epilogues aren't my thing, but I maaay write one. To stay up to date on bonus reads and new releases, follow me on social media and follow the link to sign up for my newsletter! I promise, I don't send out a bunch of spam (I'm not sure how anyone has the time for that, honestly).

Happy reading and stay spicy ;)

Acknowledgments

First and foremost, I need to thank my alpha readers (and best friends), Madeleine and Arley: the AMA chat is where the magic happens, and this book wouldn't be where it is today without you. I love you guys and I hope you know how grateful I am for all the rereads, feedback, hand-holding, and everything in between.

To my beta readers, ReaderEm and K. Clark: Your feedback helped me fine tune Drift into the book that it is. Thanks for being my early supporters!

To the BookTok community: I tear up just thinking about how much support and love there is on a damn app. Without it, I wouldn't be where I am today. The love for books brought us together and I sincerely love so many people I've never even met, all because of the videos we share online. Thank you, thank you, thank you.

And lastly, to YOU: the reader! I say it all the time, but writers can't write if readers don't read. I am so happy your journey brought you to this book and I hope you enjoyed it. I really would love to hear from you, whether through reviews or social media.

Amanda Bentley loves escaping into fictional worlds through reading and writing. A typical Pisces, she's as much a mood writer as she is a mood reader. She likes her book boyfriends morally grey, but she'll read any book with romance (preferably drenched in spice and angst).

When she's not writing, you might find her chasing her wild toddler, or on stage, performing improv with her husband. She's a creative, free spirit, and while she loves a fun adventure, there's no place like her bed with a book.

Amanda can be found on TikTok and Instagram under @amandabentleybooks. Her DM's are always open!

www.ingramcontent.com/pod-product-compliance
Lightning Source LLC
Chambersburg PA
CBHW060019060826
49398CB00032B/218

* 9 7 9 8 9 8 6 8 9 2 3 2 0 *